THE TRESTLE

The Trestle
Copyright © 2025 by James A Engen

ISBN (paperback): 979-8-218-84671-8

THE TRESTLE

A STORY FROM THE EAST SIDE OF SAINT PAUL

JAMES A ENGEN

CONTENTS

CHAPTER 1

THE TRESTLE

The Trestle was the place where kids smoked their first cigarette, drank their first beer, or found somebody to fight. It was all there, and what you found depended on what you were looking for—even life and death decisions.

If a teenage girl frequented the Trestle, it would be considered a scandal, and they would question her virtue. They said girls who hung out at the Trestle had a speech impediment: "They just couldn't say no."

The Trestle—a bridge relic left behind from the old streetcar line that ran through the East Side neighborhood—was about 120 feet long and just shy of twelve feet wide. Back in the fifties while in operation, it ran north and south, whereas the tracks underneath ran east and west.

This line came up 7th Street from downtown Saint Paul to the east and then went north on Hazel Street, over the Trestle for four or five blocks, ran parallel to Curve Street—which is now known as Furness Parkway—then through the old Witches' Woods into North Saint Paul, Mahtomedi, Stillwater, and finally Bayport. If you rode the streetcar the other direction toward Minneapolis, it would go out as far as Lake Minnetonka.

Mitch Dawson's family lived in the farthest northeast corner of the city of Saint Paul, next to the Hillcrest Country Club, which bordered Maplewood. This corner of Saint Paul was affectionately referred to as the upper East Side, but it was tucked away well enough that some people in the city of Saint Paul didn't know where it was.

Mr. Dawson knew all about the Trestle. It was his job to know, actually, because he worked for the state of Minnesota as a bridge and road inspector. He had all kinds of info on the history of the Trestle. For example, he once shared that if you'd have ridden this particular streetcar line before the 1930s, it would have been common to see a cop standing guard over several men handcuffed to their seats: prisoners being shuttled from the jail in Saint Paul out to Stillwater State Prison.

There were several dozen streetcar lines that ran through Saint Paul and Minneapolis; they were the lifeline of the metro area. Over two million people rode the street cars over the Trestle every year. The urban legend was that the automakers and tire manufacturers went across the country and bought up streetcar lines only to close them down to boost bus use (and, naturally, increase their sales). Such a plot has never been confirmed, but it does make one wonder. By the early 1950s, they'd stopped running the street cars.

The Trestle was not designed to double as a footbridge, but that did not stop people from trying to use it as such after they'd eliminated the streetcars. It had no decking, so when people crossed, they had to navigate the entire span on just railroad ties. It was dangerous.

It was clear that people would not stop using it as a footbridge, so the city added decking. They also installed two vertical steel beams on each side of the bridge, about four feet apart, to prevent car crossings. But pedestrians, bikes, motorcycles, and anything else were free to cross.

The bridge was not an obvious feature in the East Side neighborhoods. You couldn't see it from Maryland Avenue because the path to it turned and twisted, about 300 yards from the street. On the other side, the path to the bridge was only about 130 yards but was very hard to see because of tree overgrowth. The bridge was veiled from the casual passersby, which is what made it so fascinating to those seeking adventure, risk, or outright lawbreaking. It was right there—but not.

People knew to park a block or two away from the paths leading to the Trestle, on whichever side was the opposite of where they gathered in the event the cops showed up to break up the party. The cops couldn't cross the Trestle in their cars, so partygoers could cross the Trestle to their cars and flee the scene unidentified.

Despite its reputation, kids used it every day to go to school. Parents forbid their teens from visiting at night because it was so dark and secluded, but still they went. The Trestle was where people from all over the area partied, surrounded by woods and wetland, the creepy 3M warehouses looming to the southeast.

Every morning, dozens of kids crossed the Trestle to go to Hazel Park Junior High, up to the northwest, or the Blessed Sacrament Catholic school to the south. Despite regular use, the paths that led up to the bridge were never maintained, so if the snow was too deep, you'd have to find another way.

The Trestle was the dividing line between the East Side's two public high schools: Johnson High School to the north and Harding High School to the south. They were arch rivals in every regard. Half the kids at Hazel Park Junior High ended up at Harding, whereas the other half went to Johnson, with a few strays straggling over to Hill High School, the all-boys private Catholic school.

The areas south of the Trestle and across from the 3M warehouses were swamps, ponds, and woods—a kid's paradise. There was a vacant area below the Trestle that became more or less a dump, populated by everything from old furniture and busted refrigerators to rusty cars and building materials and scrap. Everyone used it as a dump, and nobody seemed to mind. A kid could get in a lot of trouble in this area, but a smart kid could have a lot of fun.

Situated right next to the Trestle was a business. Given the location, one might think "greasy little car repair shop" or maybe "welding shop," but they'd be wrong. A florist, of all things, with a flower shop and two greenhouses stood watch at the end of the dead-end road next to the Trestle. The lady who owned the floral shop was a neighborhood favorite. Imagine a kid on his first visit to the greenhouse. His mission: to pick out something for his mother's birthday. It could be ten degrees below zero outside, but the flowers inside were in full bloom and the greenhouse was nice and warm. You wouldn't believe all the flowers—how could so many colors and patterns exist?

It was common to see bums riding the slow freight trains on the tracks below the Trestle. Every year around April, they'd come up from their winter digs in Swede Hollow on their way out to their summer spots in the Witches' Woods.

Some kids hopped the slow freight cars and rode them for a mile or so just to say they did it, but a couple of the really stupid or daring types would dangle and drop from the Trestle onto the trains. The Trestle was about thirty-five feet from the tracks below, and the height of a slow freight was about eighteen feet, which left seventeen feet between the Trestle and the top of the boxcar. If you dangled from the Trestle, you would only be about seven or eight feet from the train.

Aaron Tiller was a regular at the Trestle and was there the night that Hal Comers was so hammered that he accepted a dare to dangle and drop onto an oncoming slow freight. Hal dangled right above the tracks and, right on cue, as soon as the slow freight came through, he let go, aiming for the boxcar below. But he bounced off the top of the boxcar, down to the ground, stood up, dusted himself off, and came back up to the

Trestle to have another beer. Everyone present had a good scare watching him bounce from the train.

Dennis Pinder wasn't quite as lucky as Hal. Dennis wasn't very bright but was a nice guy. He was goaded into dangling one night, so he crawled underneath the bridge to the middle and got ready to drop. When a slow freight came by, Dennis lowered himself down and hung from the bottom beam like everyone else did.

Then, the reality of the situation he was in dawned. He got scared—really scared. He couldn't pull himself back up, and he screamed for someone to help him, but nobody could reach for him without putting themselves in the same pickle. Dennis hung there for a few more seconds while the onlookers watched. The caboose was only about a dozen cars away and, unable to hang any longer, Dennis let go. He fell onto one of the last boxcars and flipped to the ground, hitting his head on a railroad tie. Everybody freaked out and split, but Aaron Tiller and a couple of other guys ran down to the tracks to tend to Dennis. The cops and ambulance came.

Aaron said that it felt like the whole thing had happened in slow motion, like a scene from a western—but this was no movie; it was a real-life tragedy.

The ambulance took Dennis away, and the cops asked a lot of questions. The fall had fractured his skull, crushed his orbital socket, and cost him his left eye. Dennis was never the same after that. That incident should have served as a cautionary tale for all the other idiots wanting to do daredevil shit at the Trestle, but of course, after a while, the guys were right back at the Trestle to drink beer and do the same old stupid stunts. Even Dennis went back up there like nothing had ever happened.

Only a year after Dennis's train misadventure, he and some of his buddies were down the tracks at Beaver Lake setting off fireworks. Dennis grabbed a cherry bomb he thought was a dud, and it exploded and blew off his hand and part of his right forearm. Because of that short-sighted grab, Dennis had a glass eye and a hook hand for the rest of his short life. Dennis didn't make it to 30.

There was only one standing order when it came to the Trestle: Make sure you're back over the Trestle before dark. You could spend the whole day at the Trestle playing ditch because there were a million places to hide around there—which was part of the problem parents and the authorities had with the area. If anyone got in trouble or got hurt, they may not find you, especially if you got under the fence at the 3M warehouses. Hardly anyone spent time around these warehouses; they were effectively abandoned. There was all kinds of crap to have fun with over there. In one corner of the expansive yard, rusted machinery and scrap iron were piled up, and all the kids joked about how it was kind of like a 3M machine graveyard. The warehouses had huge smokestacks that rose about 60 feet. Those warehouses used to house munitions during World War II.

One day, one of the older guys got drunk and decided to climb to the top of a smokestack and shoo away all the pigeons. Sure of himself, he guzzled one more beer, put one in his pocket, and started his climb. It only took him a few minutes to reach the top, surprisingly. He stood on the top of that smokestack, waving his hands, scaring pigeons, and drinking the beer he'd pocketed—and somehow, he didn't kill himself doing it.

Another time, a group of neighborhood boys was throwing the football around on the field along Curve Street. It was just about dark, and a motorcycle was screaming up and down the streets through the neighborhood. A black Plymouth Valiant was chasing him. This went on for a couple of minutes before the motorcycle turned south and headed down along Curve Street to where it ended at Ivy Avenue.

"Hey, he's heading for the Trestle!" one boy exclaimed.

The guy on the motorcycle continued south on the dirt path. So did the Valiant. This motorcyclist must've done something really bad for the other guy to be so pissed. Luckily, it seemed the motorcycle rider knew the neighborhood, unlike the guy in the car. The motorcycle cruised smoothly up the path to the Trestle while the car hit every old railroad tie, spike, nail, and tree branch along the way trying to follow. Once the pair hit the last stretch of trail that winds its way up to the Trestle from Maryland Avenue, it was over.

The motorcycle and its rider passed over the Trestle with no problem, but the guy in the car barely saw the two vertical steel beams that stood guard over the Trestle like the bridge trolls of mythology in time. He panicked and swerved hard, swinging the ass end of his car right into one of the beams. The car rolled off the path, down the embankment of the Trestle while the motorcycle cruised south down Hazel Street. The car was totaled. That driver managed to escape but got really banged up in the process, tumbling even further down the embankment into the brush and thistles when he finally got out of his car.

The haunting allure of the Trestle probably began with the legend of Hack Helvik. Henry Helvik, also known as Hack, was a neighborhood kid who lived on Ruth Street and Sherwood Avenue with his mom. Shortly after they stopped running the streetcars over the Trestle, Hack started using the bridge to get to Hazel Park Playground. But one day, Hack never got to the playground, and he never came home. Whatever happened must have happened at the Trestle. They searched high and low for months, but not one trace of him was ever found. No witnesses, no clues, nothing. They thought he might have ended up in a boxcar somewhere in a rail yard hundreds of miles away, but nobody could ever be sure. Lots of stories and different theories of old Hack came and went over the years—maybe a bunch of bums got him, maybe he ran away from home, or perhaps a creepy old guy lured him into his car on the other side of the Trestle. Parents used Hack's story as a cautionary tale: "Don't go up to the Trestle at night; you don't want to end up like Hack Helvik." There were also the ghost stories about old Hack that claim he still walks the Trestle at night.

The creepiest thing about the Hack Helvik story is that he didn't disappear at night; Hack disappeared in broad daylight. Because they never found any trace of him, his poor mother never knew what happened to her son. She had no closure, and they said it drove her insane.

CHAPTER 2

HILLCREST COUNTRY CLUB

Hillcrest Country Club was a hidden gem on the farthest northeast corner of Saint Paul, its front entrance situated on Larpenteur Avenue and McKnight Road. It was an exclusive country club with every refinement of the day. This club had only two requirements for membership: deep pockets and Jewish bloodlines. Ironically, Larpenteur Avenue also hosted two all-Catholic high schools: Hill High School for boys and Archbishop Murray Memorial High School for girls. These two Catholic high schools were only about three-quarters of a mile apart, and this all-Jewish country club was smack dab in the middle.

The property had tennis courts, an Olympic-sized swimming pool, an 18-hole golf course, and a clubhouse with dining and meeting facilities for its members and their guests. The bar and restaurant were first class, and the clubhouse was said to be the best in the Twin Cities

The original Hillcrest Country Club first opened in 1921, but in the 1940s, a group of Jewish businessmen acquired the property and converted it to a Jewish-only operation. That group of businessmen was made up of the three Getz brothers: Sidney, John, and Murray. The Getz brothers bought the Hillcrest Country Club in response to the high level of antisemitism of the time. There were very few Jewish country clubs in the United States, the next closest being in Chicago.

The Getz brothers were a song and dance comedy trio that worked vaudeville, night clubs, and even some movies back in the thirties and forties. They performed all over the country—a pretty big deal in the entertainment world back then. The Getz brothers bought the country club, moved from New York, and fell in love with Saint Paul. Yet not all of Saint Paul fell in love with the Getz brothers. Early on, they struggled with local antisemitism. Jew haters would paint swastikas and profanities all over the buildings of Hillcrest Country Club. The worst of these events occurred Labor Day weekend in 1962, when someone used gasoline to burn a giant swastika on the ninth green, right on the corner of Larpenteur Avenue and McKnight Road, for everyone to see. That green was dug up and replaced the same day it was discovered. This event made national headlines, but they never caught the person who committed this shocking crime. The locals have suspicions of who did it, believing it was somebody in town. After all, there were plenty of people who could have fit the bill.

Despite this and other acts of hate, the Getz brothers succeeded in a very big way. They patterned Hillcrest after the Los Angeles County Club in Los Angeles and the Palm Beach Country Club in Florida, both of which were considered the best in the country. Hillcrest was not close to the scale of those clubs, but it was every bit as refined and professional.

The most exclusive golf tournament in the country every year was held at the Hillcrest Country Club—not in New York, Florida, or California as one might expect. Every August, professional caddies flew in for this event, and the brothers would hire a 20-piece orchestra for the grand ball and a fleet of limousines to shuttle people around.

Every big-time company in the Upper Midwest sponsored this tournament, including Mercedes-Benz. The coolest sponsor, however, was Learjet. Every year, Learjet flew in some new private jets and kept them on display at the Saint Paul airport about five miles away. They sold one or two jets every year. Despite it being one of the most exclusive golf tournaments in the country, there weren't many good golfers. One or two under par usually won it. This tournament was much less about golf than it was about money and influence. There was some heavy betting in this tournament; Murry Getz saw to that.

There weren't many Jews in Saint Paul and virtually none on the east side of town. In addition to the country club, the Getz brothers also owned two liquor stores; a separate Jewish family was in the hardware business, and there were five Jewish cemeteries on the East Side. That's it. The East Side was populated primarily by Scandinavians, Irish, Pollocks, Germans, and Italians. If you were to walk up Wyoming Avenue, you would see all the ethnicities on full display. There were even first-generation immigrants, like Manfred "Manny" Klaus's parents from Germany and Reno and Isabella Petri's parents from Italy.

When Jewish celebrities of note came to the Twin Cities to perform music gigs, comedy, acting, sports, or just to check out of the world for a while, they would make their way to Hillcrest Country Club. It was a safe haven where they could relax in private. It was even rumored that Sandy Koufax stayed at Hillcrest during the '65 All-Star baseball game.

The centerpiece of the ballroom at Hillcrest was a Steinway grand piano. Many great entertainers performed to private audiences on that piano. The story goes that the Getz brothers would sit around the Steinway and sing bawdy songs and tell even bawdier jokes.

Tennis was a big deal at Hillcrest too. It wasn't uncommon to walk past the tennis courts and see celebs playing a few rounds on a Saturday morning.

They had two beautiful bungalows on the golf course, behind the maintenance building. They were all decked out with air conditioning, two bedrooms, television sets, fully stocked wet bars, and private patios. One even had a porch.

The greatest feature of these bungalows was privacy. They were more or less off the radar if somebody wanted to get away from the public eye. It was impossible to confirm, but local stories say that some politicians and those on the other side of the law, known on the national news, stayed in those bungalows. Other special guests would also stay there from time to time.

Sid Getz always said that they built the bungalows "just in case," punctuating the line with a wink. The caddies who worked on the golf course didn't know what to make of Sid's comment the first few summers they worked, but as they got older, they started to hear more stories of John Getz bedding down "stray floozies," as he called them, once in a while. John was known as a world-class ladies' man and was constantly on the make for some old mop squeezer. The caddies always joked about how he looked a little like Don Knotts.

Despite any indiscretions they may have got into, the Getz brothers treated their employees well. One of their favorites at the country club was Margaret Munger. Mrs. Munger ran the kitchen and did all the banquet scheduling. The brothers weren't alone in their favoritism either—everybody loved Mrs. Munger. This was in stark contrast to the sentiment toward her son, Ray. Ray "the Rat" Munger had hair so red you'd want to punch him right in the mouth. He was a big, hulking prick that never missed a chance to be an asshole. Ray caddied at the golf course and made a point of terrorizing all of the younger, smaller caddies, especially those new to the course. You'd always know when Mrs. Munger was at work because you'd see the homeliest little car you ever saw parked in the lot: a yellow, rusty, beat-up 1960 Rambler station wagon that used to be blue. It looked like whoever had painted the car yellow had used a broom.

Gambling of all kinds was a big deal at Hillcrest Country Club, both on the course and in the banquet room, where they would routinely set up small casinos for poker, blackjack, craps—you name it. The amount of money that would change hands during an epic casino night or round of golf with heavy hitters was mind-boggling: It was said to be in the tens of thousands, sometimes even more.

Sid and John Getz ran the day-to-day business of Hillcrest Country Club. The locals didn't see Murray Getz very often because he traveled a lot. Murray was one of the biggest bookmakers in the country. He never missed the action on every football game, boxing match, horse race, and anything else you could possibly bet on. Murray Getz took big action only.

There isn't a better way to illustrate Murray Getz's big action than that time he took up made out with an entire golf course. How, you ask? A big shot attorney in Florida had a controlling interest in a private golf course near Fort Lauderdale. This guy bet heavily with Murray Getz and got in so deep that Murray ended up acquiring the attorney's controlling interest in the course. Ironically, this was a restricted golf course neither Murray Getz nor any other Jew could join. So, old Murray did the only logical thing he could: force out the minority owners, close the course, plow it under, and turn it into a citrus grove. Problem solved.

People often wondered why the Getz brothers didn't stay in show business. Everyone assumed the brothers were well off, but what they didn't know was that they had amassed a king's fortune dealing in real estate—not just in Saint Paul or Minnesota but all over the United States and Canada.

In addition to Hillcrest Country Club, they owned several buildings in downtown Minneapolis, plus miles of property near the airport and Metropolitan Stadium where the Twins and Vikings play. All this is a drop in the bucket compared with their holdings in Las Vegas, Florida, California, and the provinces of Manitoba and Ontario. In truth, they ran their real estate empire out of Hillcrest.

For example, when a new highway was built seemingly in the middle of nowhere, the Getz brothers bought the property around all the projected exits for future truck stops and other buildings. Mr. Dawson started to get to know the brothers about ten years ago, and that was only the start of their relationship. They soon found out that Mr. Dawson worked for the state as a bridge and roadway inspector, which gave him particular insight into construction and where advantaged real estate might exist. There wasn't anything illegal about their conduct, but it's safe to say that when construction started on a new bridge or roadway anywhere in Minnesota, Mr. Dawson's first call was to the Getz brothers.

Mitch always thought they were friends with Mr. Dawson because they lived so close to the golf course and Mr. Dawson drank a lot of Buckhorn beer. But little did Mitch know, his dad had real estate investments, thanks to the Getz brothers, in the way of a duplex property near Grand Avenue in Saint Paul. The brothers had season tickets to the Vikings, and as a nice perk, they'd let the Dawsons use their tickets at least once every season.

In fact, the reason the Dawsons live where they do is because of the Getz brothers. There were dozens of vacant lots available back in the forties and fifties near the golf course—from Larpenteur Avenue to Ivy Avenue. The Getz brothers bought them all.

Mr. and Mrs. Dawson were among the first ones to buy a lot from the brothers. It was Mr. Dawson's goal to move as far from the lower East Side of Saint Paul as possible while still staying on the East Side. Mitch was convinced they lived on the best lot in the area. It was huge.

When Mr. Dawson calls, the Getz brothers always pick up. If he ever needed a favor, the Getz brothers would drop everything to help him out. Thanks to the brothers' presence in his family's life, Mitch gained a sense of what it was like to have important friends early on, and he saw good examples of how relationships were cultivated. It's good to know people.

Years later, the town finally figured out that the reason so many celebrities came to the country club was because the brothers were in the business of financing Hollywood movies and investing in other entertainment ventures. The movies were mostly low budget, but there were some exceptions and some hits. They financed Broadway shows too.

Still, the Getz brothers were some of the nicest and unassuming, generous guys you'd ever meet. They were often dismissed as "those rich Jews up at their country club," but they were a whole lot more than that.

Now, Sid's wife, Sylvia, was a different story. She was very assuming, but she'd probably earned that privilege. Sylvia was a tanned, buxom platinum blond who could've been a Gabor sister. Always dressed to kill, this woman turned heads, flashing diamonds on every finger and playing every bit the part of the younger, well-kept rich wife. Sylvia was built like a brick synagogue. To hear Sid tell it, she could spend it as fast as he could make it—that was the price he had to pay for keeping her in Minnesota and not Manhattan or Bel Air. He said it was all worth it because she looked good, kept the dogs fed, and could suck a cue ball through a keyhole.

When Sylvia entered the room, she wanted all eyes on Sylvia. She craved attention, craved compliments, and was undeniably the belle of every ball. Wherever she went, it would inevitably end up being about her. She expected the royal treatment, and if she didn't get it, her whining sounded like a dentist's drill on a bad tooth. Once or twice a year, she treated an audience to an epic tantrum, usually over some tragedy like her car needing a wash or the cherries in her Manhattan not being round enough. Old Sylvia loved her Manhattans.

When Mitch and his buddies were in ninth grade, they worked at the country club as caddies and helped in the clubhouse or wherever else they were needed. The fact that this crew wasn't old enough to be officially employed wasn't a problem for the Getz brothers; they knew how to get around a few employment rules, like paying them in "tips." So, they'd tend the bungalows, haul luggage and golf bags, water plants, and help with grounds keeping and the driving range—sometimes even driving the tractors. The brothers loved funny people and hated smart asses.

They loved Manny at the golf course because he was as big and strong as a horse. He wasn't so unlike Hoss from *Bonanza*. Manny Klaus could outwork all of us, a trait he learned from his dad, Ferdinand (though everybody just called him Ferdy). Ferdy was Bavarian and had come to the city in the twenties with his family when he was pretty young. He worked hard at a foundry down off Forest Street by 3M. Working hard was something you did with pride, and to not do so was to dishonor your family.

The Getz brothers liked Mitch Dawson, too. He lived about forty yards away from the Country Club, across the street. It wasn't uncommon to find him casually in charge of keeping the guys in line whenever something called for a group effort. He didn't take it upon himself to order the guys around, but if the assigned task didn't get done, Mitch was the one who'd have to answer for it.

"If some of these guys can't follow simple directions," John used to say to him. "I mean, I'll keep them around as caddies, but we need people we can depend on."

"A world champion ladies' man like me can't afford to look bad," he'd add before bursting with laughter. He looked more like Don Knotts every day.

There was some advice that Mr. Dawson passed on to Mitch and his siblings that helped Mitch handle the balancing act of peer leader: "Do what you're told, don't complain, show up on time, don't talk too much, and don't be a smart ass."

CHAPTER 3

MITCH AND HIS CREW

Mitch loved sports, so it made sense that he hung around with friends who did too—and in his neighborhood, there was no shortage of them. Whether you were trying to get a softball game put together or just wanted to go down to the playground to play some pick-up hockey, even if it's just a couple of guys throwing the football around, someone in the neighborhood was up for it.

All of Mitch's buddies were athletes, but Mitch's neighborhood in particular had a bonus: the girls were athletes too, and they played right alongside the guys in every sport without missing a step. Take Izzy Petri, for example. She was great at football, thanks to her brother Reno and her God-given abilities. They'd played catch for hours. Reno would fire that football at her and Izzy rarely ever dropped a pass. She wouldn't give Reno the satisfaction and she could rifle it back to him just as hard.

Eric Ziton was the name the Golyn parents bestowed on their son, Mitch's best pal. EZ-GO was the most natural nickname for this kid, and he wore it well. There are times when people get a nickname that becomes their identity; this was the case with Eric. He *was* EZ. He was a smaller dude, but he was also the funniest kid in town, the group's spokesman, and never ran out of the best ideas for all kinds of mischief.

All the parents in the neighborhood loved him because he was funny and asked thoughtful questions—like how someone's garden was growing or their vacation. And if he asked whether they were a Twins' fan? Forget doing anything else for a while—he could talk anyone's ears off about the Twins.

EZ was a running back in football and hockey line-mate with Mitch and Zack Deitz. In baseball, he played everywhere in the infield, and he caddied with the crew at Hillcrest Country Club. If anyone needed someone to climb a tree or scale a fence, EZ was the man to do it.

EZ had two sisters: Gloria, his older sister, and Joy, his little sister. Joy and Mitch's sister, Stephanie, were best pals. Unfortunately, Joy has a terrible stuttering problem that gets worse when she gets excited or upset. She does take speech lessons and has improved a little bit. Gloria had the same issue when she was younger, but she eventually grew out of it. She used to get in fights all the time because of her stuttering. You never would have known she'd had a stuttering problem by the way she speaks now. Gloria was fiercely protective of Joy because of their shared struggle with stuttering. If you ever picked on Joy, you would have to answer to Gloria. Almost everyone has seen Gloria in action, and you can be sure that if you mess with Joy, your punishment will come swift and severe.

To the crew, Gloria was "Glo." She was funny, smart, and tougher than a day in jail. Yup, Gloria Golyn was the toughest kid in the neighborhood. On top of her toughness, Gloria was impossibly pretty and mature for a girl barely sixteen. She had the body of a Playboy Bunny, and she knew full well that all of the boys had mad crushes on her and thus felt nervous around her. She never acted stuck-up, but she was known to use the boys' infatuations to her advantage.

Gloria was the clear leader in her band of girlfriends, which included Izzy Petri, whose real name is Isabella. She was a babe in her own right. Izzy's family lived right across the street from the Dawsons, and their dad, Enzo Petri, worked down at Hamm's Brewery.

Glo had to be tough. Older boys would cruise up and down her street in their cars looking for her or they'd chase her around the local playgrounds. Unlike the Finch sisters, who hung out with the crew because nobody else would tolerate them, Gloria hung out with the younger crew sometimes because they were only slightly less obnoxious than the kids her own age. She was a year older than her brother's friends, but she had the attention of all the high school boys. She played boy's hockey up until a couple of years ago because nobody offered girl's hockey anywhere—and damn was she good; she even led the peewee team in scoring one year. She's a champion swimmer, runs track, and can throw a softball through a brick wall. While she was at Hazel Park Junior High, she was already on the swim team at Johnson High School and ran varsity track there too. She achieved above her age group.

Gloria and EZ were always going at it about one thing or another. They knew how to get under each other's skin, as siblings do. Some of the funniest stuff between Glo and EZ was what he got up to with her dates when guys stopped by to pick her up. EZ made a point of answering the door and setting the stage for a night of embarrassment for Gloria, and he'd share with his friends all the best moments.

"Hi. Is Gloria home?"

"Yeah, she's in the basement washing her feet, I'm sure she'll be right up," EZ would say. Or "She's in the bathroom because Mom is helping her with that boil in her armpit."

On the occasions when EZ asked what the guy had planned for the night and it happened to be a movie date, he had a great line ready to use.

"So, what are you guys going to do tonight?"

"We're going to go up to the Plaza to see the *Planet of the Apes*," the guy answered.

"*Planet of the Apes*?" EZ answered. "Gloria saw that twice already this week with other guys, but I'm sure she won't mind."

During the summer, Mitch was at EZ's house pretty often. Gloria, as many girls did, was often in the backyard, laying out in the sun—which she knew drove the boys crazy. One time,

Mitch stopped by EZ and Glo's house on his way down to the field to play softball. Glo called Mitch from the yard.

"Oh, Mitchy-poo, you little shit, come here and talk to me."

All he could think was *ah, crap*. When it came to talking to Gloria in a bikini, there was no safe place to rest your eyes.

"So, what are you and the other dipshits doing today?" she asked.

Mitch had decided that staring at the sky was the best way to navigate the conversation.

"We're going to go down to the field and play softball. I think we got eleven or twelve people. Are you up for it?"

"No, not today Mitchy-poo. Today, I have a date with sunshine and baby oil." She paused. "Speaking of oil," she said with a little grin. "Mitchell, I think my skin needs a little attention. Can you, uh, oil up my back?"

For God's sake, Glo, this is torture. Why don't you just frickin' shoot me? Mitch thought.

He turned and headed into the house, Glo's laughter trailing behind him.

"By the way, when you go inside, you tell Eric that if you guys drink any more of my Fresca, I'm going to spend the rest of the afternoon kicking his ass."

When it came to Gloria, Mitch was both terrified and madly in love. She'd lay down on her stomach and undo her top, spending the afternoon oily and laid out in the sun, existing as the stunning woman she was. A combination of Ann-Margaret and Stupefyin' Jones from the *Li'l Abner* movie.

Reno Petri made the near-fatal mistake of trying to give her another nickname. It was a day nobody would forget: They were all walking back from the playground when Reno, who thought he was hilarious, said, "Hey Gloria! If Eric is EZ-GO, I guess that makes you... EZ-CUM." He roared with laughter, not immediately noticing that everyone had stopped dead in their tracks. Everyone looked at each other, then over at Gloria, waiting for the explosion.

After a bit of a pause to let Reno finish laughing his ass off, Glo slowly and calmly stepped in front of him, smiled, and softly asked,

"Torino, dear, would you mind saying that again?" He stared at her with a blank expression and didn't say a word. A few seconds went by.

"I thought so," she said, breaking the silence.

They all walked home without incident, and nobody ever brought up EZ-CUM again.

Just like Eric, Gloria was funny, but she knew how to pick a scab when she wanted to. All her girlfriends were pretty, but not one of them compared to Gloria. She's the one who would've stood out in a crowd of a thousand.

Reno had a great imagination for mischief. Fireworks were his specialty, but another favorite pastime was catching squirrels. He would bait a live squirrel trap with peanut butter, and when he caught one, he put the whole trap in a big plastic bag and gas them with ether. Once the critters were knocked out, he sprayed them funny colors and adorned them with doll hats—mostly from Izzy's old Barbie collection. He glued the hats to the squirrels' heads and called them "The Liberace Tree Rats." There were more than half a dozen of them.

Mitch once saw one of Reno's squirrels running through his yard—a squirrel painted with gold and purple stripes, featuring a little Vikings helmet. It was hysterical.

Reno got in huge trouble for doing this. Some of the neighbors saw these squirrels and didn't find it nearly as funny as the boys did. Once they found out that Reno was responsible, they went straight to his parents and raised hell. Reno quit catching the squirrels because of this. But every once in a while, you would catch a glimpse of The Squirrel General: painted orange with blue zebra stripes and wearing a G.I. Joe helmet.

Zack Deitz was called "Zitz." He lived right by the Hillcrest Shopping Center and was the best athlete on the kids' team. He was tougher than five bars of Turkish Taffy, which earned him a tough guy reputation. Kids looked for him when they wanted to pick a fight, which was always a mistake because Zitz was undefeated. He took on all comers and won, regardless of the age or size of his challengers. Zitz's fighting skills were unmatched. Holy shit, could he deliver a punch! For Zitz, it was all about balance—you couldn't knock him off his feet, and when he eventually got his opponents on the ice, he'd get in a few solid connections before the refs broke it up. Kids who took him on at the playground weren't lucky enough to have a ref step in. Zitz spilled a lot of blood on the hockey rink at Hayden Heights and lots of playgrounds in Saint Paul.

Every weekend, the crew went to open skating at Aldrich Arena in Maplewood near Shoppers' City. It was the only indoor arena nearby, so it attracted all types of people. There were always some kids who skated too fast and tripped other kids, knocking people down and acting like assholes. Once, there were two guys in particular who deliberately tripped Zitz because he was skating with two girls they liked from Maplewood. If they'd known who he was, they may have thought twice before tripping him. Zitz got up and caught one of them at center ice and proceeded to pummel this kid bloody in the face-off circle. The other kid made the mistake of trying to interfere, which earned him his own ass-kicking. There were rink guards posted to oversee the safety of those skating, but they didn't say a word or lift a finger when Zitz went to work.

After the beating was administered, the two girls rushed over to Zitz, grabbed him, one on each arm, and spent the rest of the hour skating with him. The grins on their faces and their grips on his arm proved just how proud they were of this enforcer who just beat up two nitwits to put them in their place. Everyone figured the girls were a package deal, as Zitz dated both of them at the same time for a while. That's what you'd call real talent.

In baseball, Zitz had an arm like a leg and could hit the living shit out of the ball. His speed would've made him a great pitcher, but he couldn't get more than one out of ten over the plate. Behind the plate, he had good receiving skills, and if a runner was stealing center field, Zitz could nail him every time. The boys' baseball coach put him in the outfield because he knew that if Zitz ever had to throw home, at least there was a backstop to rein him in. He quickly mastered his great arm and became a supreme center fielder, and by the time he got to Johnson High School, he was a starter for the baseball team as a sophomore, which was unheard of.

Hockey is king on the East Side—so much so it had a history of producing bona fide hockey stars. Zitz's older brother, Chet, topped that list. He was the best hockey player in the history of the neighborhood. He was better known as "Chetter Cheese," and he played for Johnson, led the city conference in scoring during his junior and senior year, and was all conference both years. Chet was fast, had great hands, and never stopped moving on the ice. As it so often is with brothers, Chet and Zack were a lot alike. They were good at everything. Chet was the shortstop on the Johnson Governors' baseball team and star running back for the Governors' football team. He made everything look easy, but the truth is that he worked his ass off. He could've played basketball or track, too; it didn't matter what he played. Chet was simply going to be the best at whatever he put his hand (or foot) to.

You could say that Hayden Heights Playground was the guys' "home ice." But Chetter had special privileges: When he was 16, he had his own key to the Hayden Heights warming house. He was a fixture at that playground. When Chet came home from college, he'd come down the playground and skate with the kids. He'd show them how to shoot: the wrist shot, the slap shot, the snap shot, and the wily backhand shot. Chet's main weapon was his snap shot, which was a kind of hybrid shot—somewhere between the wrister and the slapper. He was a true sniper with that shot and was so effective because he could get his shots off at full skating speed; he didn't need to wind up like a slapper or load up like the wrister.

Chet was twelve when he was selected for an all-state bantam team, which are usually composed of thirteen- and fourteen-year-olds. That's how good he was. There were players from all over Minnesota on this team, and they went up to Canada for four days to play in an international tournament. Teams from all over the world were playing, including teams from Japan and Russia. Playing in this tournament meant you were playing hockey at the highest possible level for your age. Chet not only played but shined.

A lot of kids are good on the rush down the ice; very few excel down low by the net where good stick-handling skills are a premium. Chetter Cheese was the best at both. He routinely flew past the other team down the ice, and when the game was down low by the net, he was a magician with the puck. He was so strong in his position that nobody could move him from in front of the net. If he had the puck behind the net or in the corner, he could make you miss and walk by you for a setup to one of his linemates.

When Chet was a senior at Johnson, the Governors played in the Minnesota State High School Hockey Tournament at the Saint Paul Auditorium. The place was packed. John Mariucci himself, coach of the Minnesota Gophers and part of Minnesota hockey royalty, was there—the only game he went to that year. He was there to see the highly touted goalie from Warroad. This goalie was being courted by the University of Minnesota, North Dakota, and every other hockey powerhouse college in the country. Johnson got Warroad in the first round, and nobody could have imagined that it would be Chet Deitz who won the day. Mariucci was quoted as saying he couldn't believe what he witnessed that day: "One of the most gifted high school hockey players I've ever seen."

Johnson hung a five spot on the hotshot goalie in the first period. Chetter got a natural hat-trick, and at that point, Mariucci left the building. Final score: 8-1, Johnson. Chet Deitz finished with four goals and six points for the Govies—two goals on breakaways, one goal where he stuffed the goalie, and the other one was a tip from the point. Johnson took third in the tournament that year. Andy Johnson, the Governor's stud goalie, got the shutout in nets in the third-place game. Warroad didn't win a single game, and their hotshot goalie was pulled midway through the second period and benched for the rest of the tournament. Chetter and Andy Johnson were both named to the all-tournament team, and it was Chet Deitz who went on to receive a full-ride scholarship at the University of Minnesota. He was a two-time all American, and if it hadn't been for an injury during his senior year of college, Chet would have played pro hockey.

The Warroad goalie never even played college hockey. The last anyone heard, he was the assistant night janitor at Marvin Windows in charge of sawdust. Chetter Cheese Deitz was the local hero.

For Mitch and his friends, everything revolved around sports. The Saint Paul playgrounds were the perfect place for kids to kickstart their sports participation—mainly hockey, football, and baseball. These were more than open spaces with monkey bars, swings, and a slide. The playground is where all the kids hung out. They all had warming houses and club rooms, and some even had gymnasiums. It wasn't entirely unusual for someone to get into a fight with other kids at the playground just to see how you measured up. Part of being an East Sider meant you'd play sports and get in a fight once in a while. It was part of the game.

CHAPTER 4

SNAG AND CRIME SCENE

Charlotte and Beverly Finch were Irish twins: siblings born within twelve months of each other. These two donkeys were the neighborhood's bad news duet. They were the same age as Gloria but tried to hang around with the younger boys because kids their age pushed them away. They lived on Utah Avenue, their backyard butting up against Mitch's backyard.

Char was big, mean, and had a mop of brown, frizzy hair. Bev was big and dumb with black frizzy hair, and she did anything Char told her, no matter how moronic or dangerous.

Char started school a year late to be with Bev. Char was six and Bev was five. Somewhere along the line, both of these brain donors got held back a grade, which made for some hilarious class pictures down the line. For their sixth-grade class photo, their mother dressed them up in matching sailor suits. In that particular class photo, they stood on each side of the teacher in the back row, making it look like the teacher was flanked by naval Military Police.

By the time they got to Hazel Park Junior High, Bev was thirteen and Char nearly fourteen—and the disparity between their age and maturity levels compared with their twelve-year-old classmates was obvious. A locker room of tiny twelve-year-old girls seeing these two fully developed, nearly six-foot-tall, hairy sisters of Bigfoot—it's a visual I wouldn't wish on anyone.

The sisters went on to high school at Archbishop Murray Memorial, the all-girls school up on Larpenteur Ave, three-quarters of a mile from Hill High School.

Char and Bev did everything and went everywhere together. The only time you'd see one without the other was when Char disappeared out on the golf course by herself at night—supposedly to take a break from her ever-needy sister and have a smoke. Just about everyone thought she was meeting boys out there to fool around with—though, it wasn't clear what kind of boy would want to fool around with a girl like her.

They were always up for a softball game or flashlight tag, though. The boys rarely had enough kids for two full softball teams, and Bev was competent enough to be the "everlasting pitcher." Actually, she was a pretty good pitcher.

In the 1960s, it was common to see boys walking around with a missing front tooth, but it was rare to see a girl that way. Charlotte was an exception to that rule, which earned her the nickname "Snag."

She came by her missing tooth via a collision with Bev and their brand-new Schwinn Varsity ten-speed bikes: one blue, one dark green. Despite their dad's strict orders, the Slobbsy Twins raced each other down a freshly paved Wyoming Avenue, ignoring kid rule number one: never ride your bike on a freshly tarred and sanded street for at least two or three days. The fresh tar wrecks your bike, clothes, and certainly your shoes. In this case, it wrecked more than that.

Bev, new to the science and complexities of the modern center-pull bicycle brake, tried to avoid a parked car by gripping the front brake as hard as she could to stop herself, but the bike responded so well that she stopped short and flipped clean ass over handlebars. As if on cue, Charlotte hit Bev's vacated bike and face planted on the pavement, busting up her teeth. There was sand and blood and tar and misery all over the place—in their hair, eyes, mouths, up and down their legs, and God knows where else.

Bev ended up with more than thirty-five stitches on her chin and forehead, which was how she earned her nickname,

"Crime Scene." Their poor mom dealt with the repercussions for days.

EZ was responsible for these girls' nicknames; it was his thing, assigning the perfect nicknames for people in the neighborhood. Some of these nicknames stuck with people for the rest of their lives. Mitch's nickname was Doc because his initials were "MD" for Mitch Dawson—there were others, but not all stuck and some stuck too well.

Crime Scene further solidified her moniker when she begged Snag to give her a do-it-yourself tattoo on her neck using India ink and a safety pin. It was supposed to be a little peace sign. Instead, it became an infection that hospitalized and nearly killed Crime Scene. They had to cut out infected tissue from her neck and give her a skin graft from her back that left her with a discolored, concave area on the right side of her neck. And, as if that weren't enough, Crime Scene already had five different speech impediments, which is why she never really said much. Every once in a while, EZ couldn't resist having a little fun at her expense.

"Hey Bev, say 'Crazy Rabbit.'"

She'd look puzzled.

"Kwazy Wabbit," she'd say, which always got a good laugh from EZ.

"You aw tho thupid Aewick," she'd say when she realized he was making fun of her.

The Finches were the neighborhood odd couple. Mr. Finch worked for Brown and Bigelow and always drove a Lincoln Town Car. He was a nice guy—and generous too. Mrs. Finch... Well, Mrs. Finch was head taller than her husband and seemed to always run a little bit fast for Mr. Finch. She always had a highball and a lit Newport going, and she liked to tell racy jokes. Mr. Finch always helped out when the other dads had a project going on or there was work to be done. Not only did they give away great candy at Halloween but they also gave out decks of cards, pens, and other cool stuff he brought home from his job. The Finch family had money, no doubt—they just focused on all the wrong things and had a terrible time performing any kind of maintenance. The Finches were the epitome of consumptive consumerism: a nice house with missing shingles and prominently featured broken windows along with a two-car garage with some siding burned away from the unfortunate barbeque incident of 1966. Their yard was huge and so overgrown that they tried to cut it back just a few times a year. They'd let the grass get a foot tall before dragging out the push mower. Snag and Crime Scene would commence efforts to push that lawn jalopy together down one side of the yard, only to jam it with the overgrowth, scream a couple times, blame each other for the problem, then go in and watch TV, leaving the mower where it was until their mowed path was grown over again.

They were lousy with pets too. At any given time, they had all manner of creatures at their house: lizards, turtles, snakes, fish, hamsters, gerbils. But all ended up dead, sooner rather than later. The only animal that enjoyed a long and healthy life at the Finch house was the woodchuck that lived under their old backyard playhouse.

Then there was the summer of the Finch family pool. The Finch parents decided to order the biggest aboveground pool in the Montgomery Wards catalog. It was something like twenty feet across and four feet deep. The Finch sisters wouldn't shut up about it; they bragged to the whole neighborhood that they would be the only ones in the neighborhood to have a private pool.

After a week of cleaning up the yard and getting the pool filled up, Char and Bev invited all the kids in the neighborhood over for a pool party. All the parents showed up too, with coolers and food aplenty—there must have been more than forty people in attendance. It was ninety degrees that day and a frickin' blast.

Mrs. Klaus made baked beans, Mrs. Petri made antipasto salad, and Mrs. Dawson made potato salad. Mr. Dawson brought a couple cases of Buckhorn, of course. Mr. Finch and Mr. Dawson were similar in that way: They could both drink Buckhorn Beer by the pallet. Mr. Klaus grilled burgers, brats, hot dogs, and Enzo Petri's homemade Italian sausage and peppers—a crowd favorite. The party stretched on all day and night.

Even Ike Tiller was convinced to come to the party for a swim. His parents never let him do anything or hang out with anybody, so he was understandably beside himself with excitement. His parents were strict due to religious beliefs, yet Ike knew a lot of the people at the party because he was their paperboy. He was a great kid and a good friend, but things weren't great at home for him. Nevertheless, Ike splashed and played and ate and hung out and had fun with everybody; so long as his dad didn't find out, he'd be fine.

In honor of the big bash, Char had told everybody that she and Bev were both planning to get new bikinis just like Gidget.

"Gidget?" EZ said. "They'll look like Gidget if Gidget was a pair of nine-foot-tall ape shits wearing fur underwear."

Nobody was sure if they would actually appear in new bikinis, but Gloria heard that Mrs. Finch had taken them downtown on the 14-B bus to Dayton's to shop for outfits. It was going to happen.

EZ was so excited at the prospect of "seeing these two swinging from tree to tree in bikinis." And he made sure everyone knew that he'd head home to think up a bunch of fresh insults.

Now, nobody could get under the Finch sisters' skins like EZ. He drove them absolutely nuts with the insults and digs he leveled at those girls, especially Char. He'd say things like:

"Oh, Snag, could you drag your knuckles over here and give us a baboon's perspective on the Vikings' chances this year?" She would get absolutely furious, and the group would break apart laughing. It was great entertainment. Once she got to her boiling point, it was go time. She outweighed him by fifty pounds, but she'd try to run him down to beat the hell out of him, but he was small and fast. Nobody could explain why the hate between EZ and Char was so intense, but it would come on just as quickly as it left. The day after a run-in, everyone could play softball together and hang out like usual.

The yard was filling up with people and food—and suddenly there they were, dancing out of the house one at a time with The Beach Boys blaring on the record player. These two girls, each with a face that looked like it had been worked over with a sack of lug nuts, had surprisingly nice figures and were not nearly as hairy as everyone had expected.

Even some of the parents stopped a second to notice—and who could blame them? But Mr. Ferdinand "Ferdy" Klaus was ogling them at a disturbing level of intensity. Maybe it was because Mrs. Klaus looked like Sergeant Schultz from *Hogan's Heroes*?

The Heidelberg Hound Dog, aka Ferdy Klaus, wandered over to the coolers to get a fresh beer, and then wandered over where the boys were sitting, all of them looking a bit dumbstruck by the reveal.

"Hey, you boys, come here." He dropped his head and lowered his voice once everyone got closer. "You know something, fellas? I tink Dat Charlotte Finch got di hugest set of blouse clowns I have ever seen."

Everyone fell on their asses, laughing. But he was right; they were huge.

The girls were always wearing lumpy old sweatshirts, even in the summer, so it's not a surprise they missed their true shapes. Or maybe it was the status quo for a bunch of goofy junior high boys to not notice one way or the other. Yet there they were, complexions so pale their skin was nearly transparent, except for their unrivaled crop of freckles: The two most awkward and obnoxious girls to ever haunt the East Side, complete with bods that were damn fine.

When Gloria and Isabelle finally showed up, though, they made Char and Bev look like Lurch and Herman Munster. Gloria never even went in the pool; she just took off her shirt and shorts and sat in her lawn chair the rest of the day, also wearing a new bikini. Izzy jumped in the pool long enough to cool down. Poor Snag and Crime Scene never even stood a chance. Now everybody at the party really had something to look at.

The pool was a lot of fun for the first few weeks, but then the shine came off—literally. They never cleaned the pool. Sometime in early August, Bev was flopping around in the pool during the day, and that night her parents rushed her down to Saint John's Hospital. Bev had developed a rash that was so severe you couldn't see her three zillion freckles. Bev spent the following week covered in pink calamine lotion—from her big head to her giant feet. Nobody had worse luck than Bev Finch. She was a disaster waiting to happen.

As expected, by the end of the summer, their pool looked like a failed science experiment. Deflated beach balls floated on a thick, dark green layer of scum, and beach towels that never made it to the clothesline were draped over the side. Perhaps it's better they neglected a pool instead of another cat.

One day later that summer, the guys were walking home from football practice at Hayden Heights and turned up the street only to see firetrucks and police cars up and down Utah Street. Everyone immediately knew it had something to do with the gruesome twosome.

Sure as hell, it turned out that Reno Petri had gone over to Char and Bev's house with some fireworks left over from the Fourth of July celebrations. He'd told the girls that the M-80 was designed to explode underwater, but he'd had a hard time convincing the two giants.

"No way, that's impossible," Crime Scene said. "You full of cwap, Weeno Petwee. Why would you thay thumthing that mental?"

Of course, everyone else knew that M-80s/Salutes/Cherry Bombs *do* explode underwater. That's the way they were designed. That was most of the fun.

"I'll prove they don't," Snag said. "Give me one. I'll light it, toss it in the pool, and we'll watch it fizzle."

"Forget it," Reno said. "You're not getting one of my last M-80s. These things are expensive as hell."

This was true, but they were totally worth it. They could blow up anything, including your arm.

Old Snag offered him a dollar for it to prove him wrong.

"A dollar? I can't get any more till next summer."

Reno was shrewd. He figured Snag could pay to entertain him.

"Five bucks," Crime Scene said.

"Nope."

Then Snag said the magic words: "Ten dollars."

"Sold," Reno said with a grin.

Snag went to the garage, where she'd stashed a pack of her mom's Salems, a book of matches, and a crumpled wad of small bills

Her parents weren't home, so she lit up a cigarette right there while she was at it.

After taking a few long drags off her smoke, trying to look cool, she handed Reno a ten, then grabbed the M-80 he held out to her. Snag made a hole in the scuz on the surface of the pool, and after several attempts, she finally lit the bomb and tossed it in the pool.

The explosive hit the water and began to sink… diagonally. Reno knew the fuses on an M-80 did not burn quickly, but even still, he started to slowly make his way away from the pool. Meanwhile, the "pyro experts" Snag and Crime Scene were laughing their asses off at Reno for trying to make them believe such a pile of bullshit.

"Fireworks exploding in the water," they laughed.

When it went off, Reno turned as gray as Snag's dead tooth. Disgusting water shot in the air, and the entire sidewall of the pool blew out. Nearly two thousand gallons of water rushed toward the house, and a lot of it made it into the basement. You see, Finch's yard was not entirely flat. When they set up their pool, they put it on the only partially flat spot in the yard, which was just eighteen feet from the house. How could anything go wrong, right? Snag and Crime Scene were caught in the torrent and knocked to the ground, instantly soaked to the bone. Their screams were heard for blocks, and Snag became hysterical. Naturally, Crime Scene did too. Neighbors must have thought someone was being murdered and called the authorities. It was an absolute disaster.

You could buy them a pool, put them in bikinis, and have a big party, but just like everything the Finch girls ever touched, the pool turned to crap. Arch and Jughead strike again.

CHAPTER 5

IKE TILLER

Isaac Tiller's family were strict Jehovah's Witnesses, and his parents were generally known as the most miserable people in the neighborhood. They didn't mix with anyone under any circumstances.

Ike's dad drove a delivery truck for *The Saint Paul Pioneer Press* newspaper and had no real friends in the neighborhood. The family had paper routes, and Ike himself delivered for the *Pioneer Press* every morning and *The Saint Paul Dispatch* every afternoon after school. Every dime Ike made went to his parents, and not because they were putting it into a savings account for Ike's education; rather, they kept the money because they needed it to live on. Ike did keep his tips, though.

It was common knowledge that the Tiller family rode the line of poverty, and they were not given to investing in a lot of material things or outside interests. Even still, their house was antiseptically clean, floor to ceiling—a doctor could have performed surgery in their kitchen. The windows shone at every passerby, and should you cross the threshold, you wouldn't see a streak of dirt on the floors. As poor as they may have been, they weren't living in squalor. As for Ike, he was rail thin and no slave to fashion, but his clothes were spotless and ironed, his shoes were shined, his hair was combed, and he had impeccable manners. Yet it all came at a cost when your father was Leon Tiller; Ike carried an air of sadness around with him.

Around 1960, Ike's dad built an underground doomsday bunker next to their garage. This shelter was the result of his obsession with the potential World War III and resulting nuclear fallout. It was full of canned goods, dry goods, weapons, and water. Everything was under lock and key. He was sure the cold war with Russia was coming. He hated the Russians, but he hated the Jews even more.

Ike could never caddy up at Hillcrest Country Club with the rest of the guys because of his father's antisemitism. Leon Tiller's hate had nothing to do with religion and everything to do with hating for hate's sake. The sick bastard hated the Getz brothers for their success and their money. He was a jealous and petty man toward anyone, but there was a special place in his dark heart for his hatred of the Getz brothers.

Ike's family had routine drills to practice retreating to the fallout shelter. His father was convinced that World War III was coming and that it would be God's way of cleansing the earth.

Yet the bunker did not serve as a refuge and storehouse alone. Ike's older brother, Aaron, used to get locked in the bunker overnight as punishment for the smallest of infractions. That came to an end when Aaron exacted his revenge on the backyard deathtrap. The next time his dad sentenced him to stay in the bunker overnight, Aaron chopped the living shit out of everything in that bunker with an ax he had hidden in the bunker. He chopped at all the cabinets with food and even put a few dents into the gun safe his dad had in there. He chopped his way through the door and then proceeded to chop the door into shreds from the outside. The next day, after seeing what Aaron had done, his dad nearly choked him to death.

Aaron was a regular at the Trestle and did all the stuff the other guys did: drink, smoke pot, chase girls, and watch disastrous stunts by guys like Dennis Pinder. This behavior earned him regular fights with Mr. Tiller.

Aaron had such a bad relationship with his dad that he left home and joined the Navy the same day he graduated from high school. He and some of his pals from the Trestle drove down to the Great Lakes Boot Camp near Chicago and were sworn in. Aaron did a tour in Vietnam at some point, and it's said that he got wounded while patrolling a river in a Navy patrol boat. He received a Purple Heart medal and was discharged after three years and never went back home to Minnesota. As far as anyone knows, he's out west somewhere.

Ike's sister Sarah was nearly deaf. She wore hearing aids and didn't really talk. She'd smile a lot and was very close to the younger siblings. There was a special school in downtown Saint Paul that Sarah attended—one equipped to handle kids who can't hear well and have trouble speaking too. By all accounts, Sarah was very bright, she just had difficulty communicating. Ike's little sister, Ruth, and his little brother, Jacob, were the polar opposite of Sarah: They would talk nonstop if you let them.

The fact that Aaron turned his back on the family and his faith was devastating for Ike's dad; it was an immense betrayal in his eyes. Jehovah's Witnesses refuse to participate in military service and vow to shun any member who leaves the religion, but especially those who join the service. Mr. Tiller was furious, and he took his fury out on poor Ike. The religion doesn't believe in national anthems or voting, and they don't celebrate holidays—no Christmas, birthdays, Halloween, nothing. Ike couldn't even have a best friend who was not a Witness. Ike was never allowed to come to birthday parties, and his parents made it very clear that they don't recognize such things. But every year, Ike would stop by Mitch's house the day after the party for some leftover cake and ice cream.

Mr. Tiller was from Wisconsin. To hear the neighborhood men tell it, Ike's family did not start out as Jehovah's Witnesses, but somewhere along the line, they got in... and they got in deep. Ironically, Mr. Tiller had been in the army before he became a Jehovah's Witness.

Mrs. Mary Tiller grew up down on lower Payne Avenue, close to where Mitch's dad grew up; in fact, they went to grade school together at Saint Patrick's. At high school, they split paths: Mr. Dawson went to Johnson High School and Mrs. Tiller went to Saint Bernard's.

According to beer-fueled sources, Ike's mom had a "checkered past." When the dads sat around the backyard, plowing through a case or two of Hamm's beer, stories about Ike's mom would come up at some point. The Tiller's absence from neighborhood goings-on was apparent, so it was inevitable that they be discussed. One of the dads described Mary as "wild" and a saloon favorite down on Payne Avenue for years. Just looking at Mrs. Tiller, no such thought would cross your mind. She was grim and withdrawn—anything but wild.

"When the neighborhood guys came back from World War II, Mary welcomed them home with open legs," Mr. Finch once remarked. "Leon married Mary to make an honest woman out of her."

"Yeah, that's true," Mr. Dawson agreed. "But he treats her more like a slave than a wife, and if she ever talks back to him, he smacks her around."

The Tiller family read the Bible a lot. They went to their temple all the time, and Mr. Tiller even did some ministry work. Ike's mom would walk around Hillcrest Shopping Center or up to Shoppers' City to hand out Jehovah's Witness pamphlets.

There were two other Jehovah's Witness families in the neighborhood. They lived with all the same restrictions, but they didn't treat their kids so God awfully. They seemed to be very happy and not at war with the world in any way. The Tiller family was a truly puzzling contrast to these other families.

All Ike ever wanted to do was hang out with the guys and play hockey, baseball, or whatever else there was to do. But, according to Mr. Tiller's interpretation and application, a Jehovah's Witness couldn't join any sports teams—which was bullshit. This rule was just another way Leon Tiller could deny Ike any kind of joy. Officially, Jehovah's Witnesses couldn't join the Boy Scouts, but they were permitted to participate in organized sports. To make matters worse, Ike was a good athlete and a pivotal member of the boot hockey team, which was something they could play any time or nearly anywhere. Boot hockey isn't an official team of any kind, so Ike wasn't really breaking any Leon rules by playing. Still, he never talked about it at home. There honestly isn't a more miserable way to spend your childhood. He couldn't do anything but deliver newspapers, do chores, and take beatings. It was less a childhood and more a slave's existence.

Maybe it was because Ike led a bit of sheltered life, but he was the most gullible guy in the neighborhood. Ike would believe anything you told him, no matter how outrageous. This was funny, especially when it came to playing Rock, Paper, Scissors. Ike lost every single game he ever played because he always chose rock, and the rest of them chose paper. He never caught on.

His mom let him hang around with the neighborhood boys a little bit and even let him go to the playground, but Ike would have to be very careful to keep the details of his activities vague, especially around Mr. Tiller.

Once, Ike spent all day at the playground watching Mitch and the guys play in a baseball tournament. He sat on their bench and kept score. When they needed a relief pitcher during the tournament, Ike would grab the extra catcher's mitt and warm up the relief pitcher. Ike felt like he was part of the team that day.

That evening, he was late for supper by a few minutes, and he really caught hell for it. His dad was not only strict but cruel. His tardiness was punished; his dad really hurt him that night, and, like usual, his mom didn't lift a finger to help. The neighbor kids always wondered whether she was every bit as bad as Mr. Tiller, an impression that was helped along by the stories the dads told about her wild side. She always had the look of misery on her face, though, and the parents in the neighborhood knew she was getting smacked around too.

On this particular occasion, Mr. Tiller threw Ike against the wall so hard that he dislocated his shoulder. He passed out from the pain and had to go to the hospital. A couple of days later, once everyone had found out what had happened, it took everything Mrs. Dawson could do to keep Mr. Dawson from going over to Ike's house and delivering Ike's dad a beating of his own. They'd already had some run-ins, so it wasn't hard to imagine a serious escalation. Such an encounter could only mean trouble, especially if Dad had had a few bottles of Buckhorn under his belt.

The beatings weren't unusual. Anytime Ike got out of line at home, it meant a beating—and sometimes even when he didn't get out of line. It got to the point that Ike began to measure the trade-off between the beatings and the fun he'd have doing kid stuff. If it was fun and all of the guys were doing it, he would gladly take the beating so that he could participate. But sometimes the beatings were so severe that he wouldn't come around for days.

When Mitch was about nine or ten, before anybody really knew who the Tillers were, he walked down to the Tiller house for the first time to see if Ike could hang out with him and some of the other guys in the neighborhood. They were all friends from school. When he got to the Tiller house, Ike's sister Sarah was in the front yard, and Mitch tried to ask her about Ike.

She was confused and started to wave her arms around. Mitch yelled louder about Ike, which was when Mr. Tiller came to the front door and yelled at Mitch.

"You stay away from her. You get out of my yard right now. You stay away from my kids."

Mitch didn't move quick enough, so Mr. Tiller ran out the front door at Mitch, chasing him out of the yard and into the street. Naturally, Mitch was terrified by this and ran home visibly upset. Once home, his father asked him what the problem was. When Mitch told him what had happened, Mr. Dawson grabbed Mitch by the hand and marched down the street to the Tiller house. Walter stood in the street and told Mitch to just go up and knock on the door and come right back to him. That's what Mitch did, and by the time he got back to the street by his dad, Leon Tiller had arrived at his door. Walter Dawson waved at him and asked him to come out.

"I need to speak to you."

Leon came out, walking down to the edge of his yard and making sure he didn't step into the street.

"I'm Walter Dawson, and this is my son Mitch. I think there's been a misunderstanding. Mitch came by to see if your boy could come out to play and I think maybe he frightened your daughter."

"My daughter Sarah is deaf."

"I'm sorry, Mr. Tiller, I didn't know that, and I'm sure my son Mitchell didn't know that either."

"I don't care what you know or don't know, our children aren't allowed to play with the kids around here. They can play only with kids from our temple because we all share the same values."

Walter Dawson was surprised by this and more than a little offended.

"These are all good families in this neighborhood with good kids."

"Not as far as I'm concerned."

This really got Mr. Dawson's Irish up. He turned to Mitch, motioning back to their house.

"OK buddy, head back home. I'm gonna chat with Mr. Tiller here for a couple more minutes."

"I have nothing more to say to you," Mr. Tiller stated.

"Don't worry, I will only take a minute."

Once Mitch was out of earshot, Mr. Dawson locked eyes with Mr. Tiller.

"Listen, asshole," he started. "You can believe whatever you want about the people around here, but if you ever chase my kid—or any kid—into the street like a dog again, I'm gonna come down here and beat your frickin' brains in. These are all good kids and they just want to include your boy."

Leon stood, unmoved.

Walter pointed at him.

"Just remember what I said."

Mr. Dawson turned and walked home.

The constraints on Ike mixing with kids in the neighborhood loosened a little over the years, but not by much. The key was to keep Mr. Tiller from finding out the details of Ike's activities, which wasn't all that hard because Leon Tiller didn't want to know anyway.

Mr. Dawson—and the whole Dawson family, really—had a special place in their hearts for Ike. Mr. Dawson knew horrible abuse when he was a kid, so that kind of thing really hit home with him. Ike may have been allowed to go to the playground, but his parents never bought him any skates, a baseball glove, or anything else that would encourage his participation. So, in some veiled act of solidarity, Mr. Dawson always bought two new Northland hockey sticks for Mitch, trusting one of them would make its way into Ike's hands. Luckily, both boys shot left. Mr. Dawson wasn't trying to undermine Ike's parents, he just felt bad for the kid. Like his dad, Mitch went out of his way to supply Ike with whatever he could—in this case, whenever Mitch got a new pair of CCM Tacks, he gave Ike his old skates, which he stored at the Dawson house.

Ike's dad couldn't wait for Ike to screw up. He was much harder on Ike than all the other kids in their family combined.

Ike's dad also never missed a chance to poison the minds of his children against their oldest brother Aaron. Any chance he got, Mr. Tiller ran Aaron's character into the ground and took every opportunity to hint that Aaron was somehow in league with the devil and influenced by Satan and his dark forces. He used everything he had, any unbelievable bullshit, to paint a vile picture of brother Aaron.

It was assumed that Ike's dad hated Aaron because Aaron turned his back on the church and went into the service, but truthfully the United States Navy was not the problem. The hate that Leon Tiller had for Aaron—and for Ike, for that matter—had a much deeper origin.

Ike took the beatings his dad wanted to give to Aaron. It wasn't Ike's fault, but he and Aaron were a lot alike. This severe level of abuse caused Ike to run away from home sometimes. When this happened, Ike's mother would call around to the other neighborhood moms, asking them to ask the kids whether they'd seen Ike. The worst part of running away was that returning home always meant more beatings. It was a hellish cycle for Ike; Leon Tiller was more a monster than a cruel man.

CHAPTER 6

HAZEL PARK

If one were to believe all the horror stories the older guys told the younger guys about Hazel Park Junior High, they'd think it was a Soviet gulag. Hazel Park was on White Bear Avenue, near Maryland Avenue, and the Trestle was behind it to the southeast.

They'd say that fights break out every day in the cafeteria and that gangs hang out at the north door, ready to rumble. And the "Rats"! Watch out for the Rats because they'll steal anything that's not nailed down. Who the hell are the Rats, you ask? They were the kids who lived in the Roosevelt Projects down on Maryland Ave. If you lived in those projects, you were a Roosevelt Rat.

But everything they said was bullshit.

There were a lot of good kids who had the misfortune of living down in the projects, and the neighborhood teams played boot hockey against them all the time. There also weren't any gang fights in the halls, except the occasional fight outside the "North Door" or up at the Trestle.

Outside the north door was the unofficial but designated student smoking area for Hazel Park Junior High. In between every class, a crowd of twenty-five or thirty kids gathered to have a heater. By the end of every day, the area outside the north door was littered with hundreds of cigarette butts.

What Hazel Park really was, was overcrowded. For a seventh grader, freshly arrived from sleepy little Hayden Heights

Elementary School, this was a major culture shock. My God, the hallways were choked after every class with great big ninth graders, getting-bigger eighth graders, dweeby seventh graders, and girls with boobs.

There were portable classrooms outside the school: two short rows in front of the school and two long rows in the back. They were even holding class in the auditorium, cafeteria, and anywhere else there was a flat spot—that's just how crowded it was.

The stories about the PE class were true and hilarious. PE was a scary thing because the gym teachers ran it like a Marine Corps base. All the students had matching Hazel Park uniforms, white socks and sneakers, and a towel with their name on it. No variations of this dress code were acceptable in the eyes of the PE overlords. If you forgot your uniform, you had to wear the uniform of *shame*: giant gym shorts and a sweatshirt that never got washed that had "I 4-GOT" written all over it. You'd spend the entire PE hour holding up the huge gym shorts.

There were strict rules, too. There was order. You had to go to this place at this time. You had to stand in a certain spot and keep your mouth shut. If you didn't do everything to the letter, they'd mete out punishment. One time, a gym teacher threw a basketball and hit a kid right in the back of the head. Another time, the kid standing next to me was chewing gum. Huge mistake. The gym teacher walked over to him, grabbed the kid by the hair, and walked him back to the locker room, shaking his head the whole way, then shaking it over the trash can until the gum flew out.

There were signs all over the locker room like:
STOP, LOOK, AND LISTEN
EYES OPEN, MOUTH SHUT
DO NOT BEG, BORROW, OR STEAL
KEEP YOUR HANDS TO YOURSELF

The awesome thing was that the longer you went to Hazel Park, the more fun PE became, as long as you followed the rules. It started out scary, but after a couple weeks, you'd find yourself sprinting down the hall to class. Whenever kids didn't follow rules, everyone got ready for a real treat of a show. The Hazel Park PE department's teaching methods were based on discipline, fear, and shame—and you loved it once you learned how to navigate the class. Once a kid got the hang of things, though, Hazel Park was a breeze—where everything was, where to go, and where not to go. If you were to ask anybody who'd ever gone to school at Hazel Park Junior High, they'd all vividly remember PE class and especially the PE teachers. They were tough and the kids loved it.

Hazel Park held great dances. Three or four times a year, a dance would be scheduled right after school. The bands were local high school kids, mostly from Johnson or Harding, and there were some surprisingly really good bands. The bands played a lot of Beatles, Stones, Animals, Zombies, and The Dave Clark Five.

The boys had a lot of fun dancing and hanging out with the girls during these dances. A couple weeks before each dance, some of the girls started to ask the guys if they were going to the dance, almost as though they were taking attendance and making sure certain guys were going. On the day of a dance, the girls always dressed just a little bit nicer, but it was much more casual for the guys, who showed up wearing T-shirts or whatever else they could get their hands on that morning.

EZ was the king of the dance floor, though. All the girls wanted to dance with EZ. While the rest of the crew was in their Red Ball Jets tennis shoes, EZ wore his special dancing shoes; he had all the style *and* the moves. He would dance to every single song. When the band played a slow song, EZ would grab up a seventh-grade wallflower and give her a twirl. He would actually teach them how to dance, too. Apparently, this was a big deal in seventh-grade circles.

There was one particular dance where EZ walked over to this tiny little seventh-grade girl who had a mouth full of braces and long, straight hair. When he offered his hand, she didn't know what to do. She looked terrified. Her friends urged her to stand up and take his hand. When she did, he walked her out to the middle of the dance floor for the slow dance. There, she became so overcome she began sobbing. When the song was over, she wouldn't let him go. Thankfully, EZ knew what was going on, so he danced with her for a few more songs so she could compose herself. When she went back to her chair, her friends mobbed her. That's my man EZ.

The best event at Hazel Park was the annual winter ski trip. They would take a couple busloads of kids out to Afton Alps or Birch Park to ski all day and hang out with the girls. If you didn't find somebody to make out with on the ride home, you just weren't trying very hard.

Mr. Sharky was the ninth-grade math teacher and wrestling coach at Hazel Park, so it wasn't unusual for students to chat with him about wrestling on a regular basis. Pro wrestling versus non–pro wrestling, and the pros and cons of wrestling. He was talking to Mitch one day and the fact that he had some open spots for next year's team came up. Heavyweight was his biggest concern. Mitch told him he should see about recruiting Manfred Klaus.

"Manny is big and strong as a horse, and when he makes a fist, it looks like a car battery," Mitch told him.

"Well, you bring him around, let me talk to him," Coach Sharky replied.

So that's what Mitch did.

Manny talked with the wrestling coach and was offered a spot on the wrestling team. Turns out, wrestling was made for Manny. He didn't just do well on the team—he absolutely dominated. He learned how to use his size and height to his advantage and how to leverage himself and implement maneuvers to give him an edge. He took it very seriously and began lifting weights and running, which was no surprise because Manny worked hard at everything he did. It didn't hurt that Manny had another growth spurt, too. He started the summer around 5'10", and when ninth grade started, he was 6'1"—a true powerhouse. He lost his first couple of matches of the season but then ran the string out the rest of the season with wins, mostly by pin-fall. Manny excelled at this sport and would go on to have a great wrestling career at Johnson High School. There was The Crusher and Dick the Bruiser—but now they had their own wrestling hero: Manny the Mangler.

CHAPTER 7

SPAGHETTI AND OLDSMOBILES

Growing up, everybody had a favorite car brand. Most guys liked Fords or Chevys, and some liked Mopars. But Mitch? He loved Oldsmobiles. This love was a family heritage, as his dad drove them exclusively. Whatever the car brand one liked best, it's safe to say they came by their fondness the same way Mitch did.

Mr. Dawson always described Oldsmobiles as just a little bit nicer, a little bit smoother, and a little bit classier than your average car. Overall, it was simply a better car. The Oldsmobiles were a little more expensive, but that was only proof of the better quality. He bragged about his Oldsmobile with its coveted Rocket 350 V-8 engine.

His buddies would tell him that an Oldsmobile was just a more expensive Chevrolet, but he challenged them on that: "Oh really? Let's take a ride then."

On a ride in a '66 Chevy Bel Air station wagon, it'd produce more rattles and squeaks than a wounded squirrel with a machine gun. But then came a ride in the Olds Vista Cruiser wagon. It was whisper quiet, the smoothest ride you'd ever have, and there was no way you could convince yourself the Chevy was on the same level as an Oldsmobile. It even had a cool window on the roof and air conditioning.

Every two years, Mr. Dawson would go out to the Oldsmobile dealer in Bloomington to buy a new car. The last two he bought were station wagons because a family of five had a lot of crap to haul around.

This year was an on-year. It was Saturday, when the day came, and Mrs. Dawson wanted to take Stephanie, Mitch's younger sister, up to Shoppers' City while Mr. Dawson, Casey, and Mitch went out to the Olds dealer to look at cars. When the family pulled up in front of Shoppers' City to drop the girls off, Mrs. Dawson pushed her door open, got out, and closed the door again.

"No need to pick us up," she said. "We're going to walk home."

This wasn't unreasonable as Shoppers' City was only about a half mile from home.

"What are we doing for supper?" Mr. Dawson asked.

"I thought I'd make spaghetti."

"Your spaghetti?" he sputtered. "What felony did I commit to deserve that? I'll get Chinese on the way home."

"Fine." You could hear the indignation in her voice.

The boys arrived at a very busy dealership. The showroom floor was packed with beautiful new Oldsmobiles: two Toronados, some Delta 88s, station wagons, and Ninety-Eight Regencies. Another station wagon had already been decided on, which was acceptable, but being surrounded by beautiful cars was just enough to get the gears turning.

Most of the cars were nice to look at, but there was one car in particular that drew all the attention. It was the centerpiece of the showroom floor and the most beautiful, sportiest, and coolest car the boys had ever seen: the 1968 high-performance 442 Cutlass Convertible in Flame Red. Mitch in particular fell madly in love; he couldn't look away. It spun slowly on a turntable in the middle of the showroom floor. Lights were trained on its smooth paint job, hitting the curves just right. This car had everything: a four-barrel carburetor, four-speed transmission, dual exhaust, and the Rocket 455 engine. This baby had chrome wheels and everything. Mitch and Casey stood there with a hot dog in each hand, watching the beautiful car spin, round and round. It seemed to get prettier the more it spun.

After watching the car for about fifteen minutes, Casey ran outside to Mr. Dawson, who was wandering among the station wagons and Delta 88s. You could see through the huge showroom windows that Casey was out there begging his dad to come in and look at automobile perfection.

Finally, after getting his third helping of a fresh donut and coffee, Mr. Dawson lumbered over to Mitch, with Casey trailing closely behind. Casey immediately began to try to sell the old man on this Cutlass, and the old man let him have some fun doing so.

Casey was not much of a goalie, but he was a born salesman. He could put on a feature and benefit presentation that would make a thirty-year car hustler blush. He didn't leave anything out. He mostly emphasized how cool his dad would look driving this car around Lake Phalen with the top down, along with other important visuals.

"Well, Casey old boy, how much?" Mr. Dawson asked.

Casey pointed to the sticker.

"Mr. Dawson, it's yours today for only $4,884."

Their father was laughing.

"There's a station wagon outside that is about half that price," he said.

"Yeah, but dad—"

After a morning of Mr. Dawson glad-handing and talking to car salesmen and of the boys slamming down free donuts and hot dogs, everybody was glad to head home with an array of color brochures. Mr. Dawson never made a deal on the spot. He always had to "think about it," excusing himself with the

"I need to check with my wife" line. The boys knew it was all crap because their father's buying tactics were familiar. He already knew when he was going to buy a car and which car he wanted; the trip to the sales floor was because he liked playing the game.

Later that afternoon, Mr. Dawson kept his promise and left the house in his quest for chicken subgum chow mein and pork fried rice, a family favorite, down at a Chinese food place on Payne Avenue. He'd always give himself a little extra time so he could stop in the Arlington Bowl or the VFW for a couple of beers, too. Mr. Dawson was all about tradition.

After school on Monday, the boys played softball down at the Curve Street field for a couple of hours before heading home for supper.

Mitch opened the kitchen door to the smell of dinner.

"Hey, lady, what's the hold up with the grub?" he asked.

"You won't have to worry about grub. It'll be too hard to eat with a split lip," she teased.

There was a comfortable connection in their teasing.

"But mom," Mitch rejoined. "When's supper for real?"

"Your dad's picking up the new car," she replied. "He said he'd be home by 6:30."

That was enough time to fill with something else, so Mitch went back outside to shoot pucks in the driveway.

Half past six came and went, and Mr. Dawson was nowhere to be seen. Mitch came back inside to investigate, and Mrs. Dawson preempted his question.

"Your dad just called," she said. "He said he's going to be a little late and that we should start without him."

"OK. What are we having?"

It turned out to be one of Mitch's favorites: a "loaf of meat" with a baked spud, some green beans, and a pie for dessert.

Mrs. Dawson was a solid performer in the kitchen. Some of her kids' favorites included date bars and lemon cut-out cupcakes, where she would cut out the cupcake top, fill it with lemon filling, then put the top back on and sprinkle it with powdered sugar. She was great with the cookies and the pies too—pretty much everything—but God forbid she make you a plate of spaghetti.

Just as the family was finishing up dinner, they heard Mr. Dawson rolling into the driveway. Casey and Stephanie were excited for the new car, but Mitch had seen plenty of station wagons already, so he wasn't all that fired up about it. Mr. Dawson bustled into the house with more excitement than either Mitch or his mom anticipated.

"Well, come on out and see the new car!"

Everyone filed out to the driveway and there it was: The gorgeous Flame Red Cutlass 442 Convertible from the show-room floor at the Olds dealer. Dad had bought the 442. Mitch couldn't believe his eyes.

That moment was one of the happiest days of Mitch's life. He could already see it: riding around town in the sexiest car God had ever made while all his buddies looked on in envy from their dads' lumpy old Plymouths and Fords.

Mr. Dawson already had the top down and was absolutely beaming. He was so proud of that car.

"Come on, everybody, let's take it for a spin around Lake Phalen!"

He looked expectantly at his wife, then his kids, and then his wife again—and it was in that last glance that he realized the car purchase may have been the dumbest thing he'd ever done.

Mrs. Dawson was livid.

"How could you buy something this Goddamn selfish?" she demanded, each syllable essentially spat from her mouth.

The whole point of getting a new vehicle was to get something sensible and comfortable to haul the knuckleheads and their stuff around. But, oh no, Mr. Dawson got put to sleep by a car salesman at the Olds dealership and bought the absolute worst choice for a family there ever was

"You are unbelievable, you know that? We never discussed anything like this. Why didn't you stop somewhere and buy a fifty-foot sailboat on your way home too? You take that damn thing back right now."

"You can't just take back a car," he tried to explain. "This isn't Shoppers' City; you don't return cars." Penny Dawson's fury was ramping up for the knockout blow.

"You better figure out something or I'm going to make spaghetti and meatballs every night for a month," Mrs. Dawson declared. Needless to say, there was no spin around Lake Phalen.

The very next day, there was a new Vista Cruiser station wagon in the driveway. Mitch's dreams were crushed, but it goes to show how effective Mrs. Dawson's threat of spaghetti was. All she ever needed to say was "spaghetti or else" and Mr. Dawson would tip right over. Mrs. Dawson didn't play that card very often, but when she did, she always got her way.

The ironic thing about her inability to make spaghetti and meatballs—one of the world's most basic meals—was that she worked across the street at the golf course part time and helped out with banquets on the weekends. EZ's mom and Gloria worked up there too doing the same thing. She was a great cook, in fact. She made great roast chicken, homemade pot pies, and she excelled at hotdish, especially chow mein hotdish and goulash. And her pork chops? Her family had the opinion that she made the best pork chops on earth—with cream of mushroom soup and mashed potatoes on the side. In fact, it was Mitch's favorite dish of hers. Pretty much anything she made was awesome, except the spaghetti and meatballs. Nobody could figure out why she was so bad at it. She tried dozens of recipes dozens of times, but it all tasted awful.

"How can spaghetti sauce that tastes like red paint somehow smell like feet and sadness?" Mr. Dawson remarked after one particularly bad attempt.

It wasn't just the sauce, though; the meatballs were problematic too. Mr. Dawson's favorite way to describe them was to say she had made her meatballs with only the freshest ground roadkill and sawdust. Every time she made the dish, Mr. Dawson showered his plate with a half-inch of Parmesan cheese and crushed red peppers, but even that didn't help. Mr. Dawson described her noodles as a "plate full of old skate laces," and he practically begged her to never make it because, ironically, spaghetti and meatballs was Mr. Dawson's favorite dish.

Once a month, the Dawson family went out to dinner specifically for spaghetti and meatballs. Because it was his favorite dish, Mr. Dawson was an aficionado. He could tell how much basil was in it, if there was too much garlic, and he knew which restaurant had the best meatballs. It didn't matter the occasion or restaurant—they'd all order spaghetti and meatballs. There were about a half-dozen spots on the East Side that Mr. Dawson liked to go to, and there was another fancier spot out in Little Canada that he loved too. But his absolute favorite spot was a place called Pasquale's down in Rochester, a little spot in a shopping center off Highway 52 about an hour and a half away. It was always a big deal to go down there. Again, the family order was spaghetti and meatballs, but such a tradition was tolerated because Mr. Dawson loved it. Once, Mitch dared to venture to ask to order a pizza instead, which just earned him a glare. You would have thought he'd asked for a kidney! The family went out for spaghetti and meatballs only.

There were a number of internal arguments about which place was best: Mitch didn't think Pasquale's was any better than the spot a couple spots down on Payne Avenue, but Mr. Dawson insisted that Pasquale's was the best. Every once in a while, when Mr. Dawson was feeling extra sporty, he'd order ravioli and Mrs. Dawson would get the fettuccine, but that's about as far as he would stray. Spaghetti and meatballs: Mr. Dawson's favorite meal in the whole world and Mrs. Dawson's kryptonite in the kitchen.

CHAPTER 8

THUNDER IN THE VICINITY

It was a typical Saturday evening in August: EZ, Manny, Ike, and Mitch were in EZ's cool basement watching AWA's All-Star Wrestling like they did every week, and a storm was brewing. The storm itself came as no surprise: The temp was in the upper 90s, and the humidity was damn near 100%—it was tornado season, after all. The intensity of the storm was surprising. Little did they know, they were about to weather the worst storm they'd had in years.

After every wrestling show, the boys would practice their signature wrestling moves on each other. Mitch was the Figure Four Leg Lock, EZ's was the Sleeper, Ike liked the Flying Elbow Smash, and Manny was fond of the Bear Hug. They were nothing but finishing moves and submission holds.

That night, Marty O'Neil told the TV audience that The Crusher and Dick the Bruiser, the boys' very favorites, were going to defend their AWA heavyweight tag team championship belts in a grudge match against—

BOOM!

The power went out.

A few minutes later, the tornado sirens went off. About twenty minutes after that, the power came back on, but by then the match was over. The boys had just missed The Crusher and Dick the Bruiser kick the living shit out of "Handsome" Harley Race and "Pretty Boy" Larry Hennig. EZ clicked over to Channel 4's Bud Kraehling, who was telling everyone to go to their basements and listen to WCCO radio for updates. Lucky for the boys, they were already in the basement. Bud Kraehling always gave sound weather advice.

The storm came up from the southwest like it always does. Someplace called Jordan had just been hammered, so everyone knew the storm would be in their front yards in just a little while. These big storms always tracked from the southwest to the northeast. All of Minneapolis and Saint Paul would get hit before the storm got to the northeast corner of Saint Paul.

It was funny to hear people describe where they boys and their families lived as the "Upper East Side"—as if that meant something in the world. It didn't mean shit. Maybe EZ's house was newer, but Mitch lived on the "Upper East Side" in a house that had a basement that ranged from wet and musty to flooded twelve months a year and they were only about fifty yards from the highest point in all of Saint Paul. The physics didn't add up.

To say that the guys were in EZ's basement was kind of funny because it didn't look like a basement. They had a newer house, the kind called a "split level." They had two living rooms in their house, two bedrooms upstairs, and two bedrooms downstairs (EZ's and Gloria's), as well as a bathroom on both levels. It was a pretty cool setup.

Despite Bud's advice to stay in the basement, the boys' curiosity got the best of them. They trooped upstairs to check on the conditions outside only to find all the neighborhood dads gathered in the street, staring up at the dark green sky and assessing the situation.

"I better get home," Ike said. "I'm sure we'll ride out the storm in the bomb shelter."

"I better go home too," Manny agreed.

They both dashed off toward their houses, hoping to beat the impending downpour.

EZ and Mitch walked to the end of the driveway to make sure Ike and Manny made it home. It was really blowing around out there. You could tell yesterday was trash pick-up day because Mitch had forgotten to retrieve their trash cans from the street, and now the two metal cans were chasing each other down Wyoming Avenue. The boys spun around and headed for the basement again, proving they had more sense than the collection of dads who remained standing in the street.

About the time they landed in the basement again and resumed looking outside, a lightning strike flashed through the sky and struck the giant cottonwood tree in the Petri's front yard. It sounded like a bomb had detonated. All the dads jumped about five feet in the air as the tree snapped in half like a dry wishbone. The dads tripped all over themselves as they ran for cover—it was like a scene from a Three Stooges movie, but in this case, there were five stooges. The top of that tree filled the Petri's entire front yard and still spilled into their neighbor's driveway

This storm didn't develop into a tornado, but it was a doozy. It knocked down trees all over the golf course. The power went out again, so everyone had to use the transistor radio and all the candles in the house. EZ's mom told Mitch to call home and ask whether his mom wanted him to run home or stay there. He called and she said that he might as well stay put, which is exactly what he was hoping for. He didn't feel like standing in nasty old basement bilge water at his house; it could get up to three inches deep. The water bugs liked it, too. They were all over the basement.

Mitch and EZ had some bottles of Bubble-Up and some chips and candles as they listened to WCCO for updates; they were good to go. But it was that explosion. That horrible explosion when lightning hit that cottonwood tree that shook the windows in the house and scared the hell out of all of us.

A few minutes after the lightning hit the cottonwood tree, the intensity of the lightning and thunder increased. You could tell the storm was close, maybe over the golf course.

Then suddenly, directly over the Golyn house was another flash of blinding lightning immediately followed by a clap of deafening thunder. The boys heard screams from upstairs, and Gloria came running down the steps, whizzed right past them, and slammed into her room. No hello, no hi, no "go to hell," no nothing.

"What's up with her?" Mitch asked EZ.

"It's nothing." EZ shrugged. "She just doesn't handle storms very well."

"What do you mean? Nobody likes storms," Mitch said, thinking the situation was funny.

"Glo is different."

At that point, you could really hear the wind picking up even from the basement.

Mrs. Golyn came running down the steps next, with Joy in tow, and followed Gloria into her room, shutting the door behind her. EZ's dad came downstairs and joined the guys in the living room. The whole situation was really peculiar: The three guys just sitting there, listening to the radio, and the girls locked away in Gloria's bedroom. Both EZ and his dad kept close eyes on Glo's bedroom door.

"It runs in the family," EZ's dad explained. "None of them handle big storms very well."

As it turns out, big storms absolutely paralyze Gloria, a condition known as astraphobia: the irrational fear of thunderstorms and lightning. This was not a little thing. At first, Mitch thought it'd be the perfect time to give her some shit and get her back for all the things she'd done to him, but that feeling came and went pretty fast. Something felt different about this.

After about an hour, the storm ended and the sun came out. Mrs. Golyn and Joy came out of Gloria's room and went upstairs, and EZ's dad stood up.

"Come on you guys."

He led the way upstairs and outside to assess the storm damage. After a few minutes of kicking around tree debris, Mitch realized he'd left his Twins cap on EZ's bed, so back he went to get it.

Mitch grabbed his hat from EZ's bed and turned to leave the room, but right then, Gloria stepped out of her room. Given the look on her face, Mitch was sure she'd thought no one was still in the house. She looked visibly upset, though not on account of Mitch's presence; it was obvious she'd been crying, so of course she lingered in her room.

At first, they both just stood there: Gloria looking down at the floor and Mitch glancing around, trying not to look at Gloria. The stairs looked like a haven, but Mitch couldn't quite make himself get to them. After a few seconds, her voice breaking up, Gloria spoke.

"Mitch, come here."

Come here? he thought. He was barely three feet from her. Come here for what? Then she yelled, half crying.

"Mitchell! You come here right now!"

Mitch quickly closed the gap between them, and she lost no time grabbing him and hugging him so tight it felt like she would never let go.

She began sobbing into his shoulder, and she was radiating so much heat Mitch broke out in a sweat. He didn't know what to do but stand there, so that's what he did, keeping his mouth shut and holding her in the most comforting hug he could manage. Maybe the embrace lasted just a minute or two—but it could have been as much as an hour, Mitch couldn't tell. After her sobs subsided, Gloria rested her head on Mitch's shoulder.

"Mitchell, is it over? The storm, I mean. Is it over?"

"Yeah, the sun's out."

"Don't leave me, Mitchell! Don't ever leave me," she begged.

Gloria had never called him Mitchell before, which only added to Mitch's confusion.

Just when he thought she was going to let go, she switched shoulders and cried a little more.

"I'm not going anywhere," Mitch said, not sure what else to say. "I'll stay here as long as you want."

The situation was odd. Mitch didn't feel like he was holding his best friend's older sister, the girl of his dreams. He was certainly feeling something, but he couldn't put his finger on it.

When Gloria finally broke away, she grabbed Mitch's hand and led him to the couch. They sat there together while Gloria tried to catch her breath and compose herself. She was still holding Mitch's hand, but there was no romantic element to it. Mitch just knew it was the right thing to do, to sit with her in her distress. She wiped her eyes.

"I'm so embarrassed to have anybody see me like this," she confessed. "Hardly anybody knows that I'm terrified of big storms. I don't know why this storm hit me so hard. I haven't acted this unhinged since I was a little kid, honestly."

Mitch listened.

"The fear makes it hard to breathe. I'm so damn mad at myself because I feel so—" Gloria stopped herself short to avoid crying again. After another minute, she continued.

"The only other person in the neighborhood who knows about this is Izzy, and she's sworn to secrecy. I guess if anyone had to see me like this, Mitch, I'm glad it was you."

Me? he thought. He searched for something profound to say, but nothing was coming.

"Uh, okay. Thanks?"

After a few more minutes of getting the adrenaline out of her system, Gloria grew serious.

"Now, this is going to be our little secret, right Mitchell?"

Mitch nodded.

"You know what will happen if you say anything about this, don't you?" There was a sharp undertone, a warning, in her voice.

"Yup, I know. A good old-fashioned Gloria ass-kicking.

She nodded to confirm.

"Bingo."

"Don't worry, I'm not as dumb as I look," Mitch said.

"I know, Mitchell." She said it almost too sweetly.

Mitch waited a beat before motioning toward the stairs.

"Are you ready?"

She looked a little bewildered.

"Ready for what?" she asked.

"Let's head out outside and help clean up this storm mess. It'll make you feel better."

"Ok, let's go." She punched Mitch playfully in the arm before springing up from the couch, almost as if nothing had even happened.

They went outside and joined the rest of the neighbors, picking up branches and straightening out the twisted mess of lawn furniture in the yard. The whole time, Mitch couldn't help but reflect on what'd just happened. Of all the older boys in their shitty old cars going up and down the street, all the jealous girls and bullies on the playground, the sports competition and her domination in those arenas—none of those things ever bothered Gloria. It turned out that she's just as human as the rest of the kids, and her biggest fear in life is thunder and lightning.

Maybe it was just good timing—Mitch just so happened to be in the right place at the right time when she walked out of her room. In that moment in the basement, Mitch wanted to believe that there was something only he could do for her that no one else in the world could. Whatever it was, Mitch was certain he did it right: he kept his mouth shut and was simply there. Lord knew that his mouth was the one thing that got him in more trouble than anything else.

CHAPTER 9

AFTERMATH

The next morning, chainsaws echoed from a distance, and people struck out into the neighborhoods to see where help was needed. The first among the work crew was no surprise: Mr. Dawson, Mr. Klaus, and Mr. Finch.

Mr. Klaus owned a chainsaw, Mr. Dawson brought along a really good bow saw, and Mr. Finch had beer. The other dads of the neighborhood were quick to join, and even Char and Bev Finch went out. It was not a surprise to see the two of them helping out, actually; they always wanted to be a part of whatever was going on.

The golf course was closed that day because of storm damage. Storm damage at Hillcrest Country Club—and every other golf course in the world for that matter—was a common thing golf course owners had to deal with every couple of years.

John Getz had a special job on the course that morning. He gathered some of the boys from the neighborhood—Mitch and his usual crew along with some other caddies—to help clean up the debris scattered on the course. He had most of the older caddies stay back and help clean up around the clubhouse.

John Getz hooked a flatbed trailer to the resident tractor and motioned for everyone to climb on. Manny fell off twice as John bumped over the hills on his way to the bottom of Devil's Hill. On the drive out, it was easy to spot the downed trees—there were a lot of them. There was even an uprooted tree laying right across the roof of one of the bungalows. It was kind of sad to see so many old-growth trees down. Luckily, no one had been hurt or stranded out on the course during the storm. The Getz brothers had a protocol for when storms like this came up: Everyone working at the course was required to jump in every available golf cart and go down to the other end of the course to herd all the caddies and golfers back to the clubhouse.

Devil's Hill was the prime sledding spot in the winter. It was a huge, steep hill; the top was the highest point in all of Saint Paul. At the bottom of the slope and to the left was a small grove of trees, which everyone mostly avoided sledding into.

About five or six huge trees had gone down in the grove, and there was another huge mess up by the twelfth tee box. Given the amount of work there was to do on the course, Mitch wasn't sure there would be enough manpower to get the job done. Could twelve guys get the job done?

John instructed the boys to pile all the limbs and branches as best they could and leave the big stuff alone. John had a crew coming the next day to haul everything away, including the piles the boys made. After explaining his expectations, John looked directly at Mitch.

"It's almost 10 o'clock," John said. "Mitchell, I'll be back at 12:30. That should be plenty of time to clear this mess and try to make smaller, more manageable piles instead of one giant pile."

Now, by specifically telling Mitch the time frame and scope of work, John was making him responsible for the outcome; Mitch understood that much. But Mitch wasn't too concerned— a 12:30 deadline was perfect because Izzy and Reno Petri had volunteered everyone on this crew to help clean up the cottonwood mess at their house, and Reno's mom, Mama Petri, invited everyone to stay for Sunday spaghetti and meatballs. She was serving at 1:00 pm "Affilato" (sharp). It was no secret:

Enzo Petri made the best spaghetti and meatballs this side of Sicily.

On his way to the golf course, it was impossible to miss the cottonwood in Petri's yard. It was huge, stretching from their garage all the way to the street—almost 100 feet. It was going to be a huge job for the neighborhood to get that monster cleaned up.

Things started out alright. The guys began to make a pile at the bottom of Devil's Hill, but Mitch had a feeling that this bunch of clowns wouldn't be able to sustain it. John's assignment was not complicated: gather the scattered tree branches into a pile. As expected, it didn't take long after John pulled away for the shit to start. Ray "the Rat" Munger, the local colossal asshole, was in the middle of it, acting like a tough prick and pushing the smaller kids around. He always picked on the smaller guys. Mitch certainly wasn't the only one who couldn't wait for the day when somebody finally gave the asshole a tune-up. He was just begging for it.

If he would have stayed back at the clubhouse with the other caddies, he would've had to do some actual work. Instead, he came out here to do nothing but cause trouble.

Things had unraveled into sword fights and spear-throwing—and even a goose chase. The only guys who did any work were Mitch and his closest buddies. A couple of the guys simply walked off the course once John left, never lifting a finger after they saw the scale of the job. Mitch tried to rally the guys once, reminding them that Mr. Getz expected a completed job by the time he got back. He was met with a couple of "Hey, Mitch, shut the fuck up" and a few other choice phrases. After that, Mitch knew that wrangling the guys into working together was a lost cause.

John promptly showed up at 12:30 with the ride back. By the way things looked, the boys hadn't finished even a third of the project, and they could all see John was not pleased with the effort.

"Pile on, boys, we're heading back," he said.

As everyone loaded onto the flatbed, he singled Mitch out.

"Maybe we needed more guys," he said flatly.

Mitch just knew he was going to get sat down at a later point.

Once they arrived back at the clubhouse, everyone jumped off the flatbed and went on their way. The five who'd been recruited to help down at the Petri's house were eager to get to the great spaghetti dinner and start work on that cottonwood tree.

But Mitch held back. Not being able to finish a simple job was bugging the shit out of him. Although Mr. Getz had mentioned that maybe he needed more guys for the job, Mitch knew there had been too many guys.

While the rest of the fellas walked over to Petri's house, Mitch walked back out to the bottom of Devil's Hill. He'd determined that the best course of action was to try to finish the job—or at least put a dent in it. He wanted to earn John's confidence. Mr. Dawson always emphasized one thing to Mitch: If he wanted to get anywhere in this world, don't screw up something simple. Mitch was only a teenager, but dammit, at least he was smart enough to know that. So, he went to work, dragging tree branches from the base of Devil's Hill to the pile by the twelfth tee box—about thirty-five yards. This kind of work goes super slow when you're doing it by yourself, but that didn't matter to Mitch at the moment; he was determined to do it anyway.

At about 3 o'clock, the absolute hottest part of the day, Mitch glanced up to the top of Devil's Hill as he hauled a big limb to the pile. He could see someone standing at the top of the Hill, making no move to help him or even wave in greeting. They just stood there, a silhouette with the sun at their back, so he couldn't see who it was. Mitch presumed it was Ike Tiller—Ike liked to wander around the neighborhood for hours when things were going bad at home. Sometimes he roamed the golf course with his dog, Buster, in the evening when it wasn't busy. But this silhouette was an oddity because Ike always had Buster with him. If that *was* Ike up on the hill, where was Buster? Mitch threw the limb onto the pile and brushed his hands off, shielding his face from the sun. He waved, but there was no wave in return.

Mitch shrugged and kept at his work piling tree limbs, and after a few minutes, Mitch noticed the person start down the hill. They weren't moving like Ike, and if it wasn't Ike, what kind of hell was Mitch in for now? The mysterious figure certainly took his time.

Mitch was over at the twelfth tee box when Mr. Mystery reached the bottom of the hill. He was walking back over for more branches and could suddenly see clearly who it was. His jaw hit the fairway. "He" wasn't Ike; "he" was Gloria.

What in the hell could she want out here? Mitch thought.

"Hey, where are all your pals?" she taunted. "Aren't they supposed to be out here helping you?"

"Don't give me that shit," Mitch shot back. "You know exactly where they are."

She smiled.

"I know." And at that, Gloria kicked off her sandals, reached in her pocket, pulled out a hair tie, put it up in a ponytail and began collecting branches.

Is she going to help me? Mitch was surprised.

They worked together for another few hours. The whole time, they spoke not a word about last night's storm or their moment outside her room. It was almost 6 p.m. when they called it quits.

"That's it, I'm done," Mitch conceded.

He plopped on the slope of the hill and laid back in the grass. He was exhausted, his arms were cut to shreds from all the branches, and sweat was pouring from his body. But it was worth it. He looked over at the bottom of Devil's Hill and could see it: The work was done, and they'd done it together. Gloria and Mitch had accomplished more work than the other twelve clowns put together.

Mitch was hopeful that his second effort at the tree branch project would mean something to John Getz.

Gloria walked over and sat down next to him. She was obviously tired and sweating like a horse, too, but somehow she still looked gorgeous.

"You know, you goofy shit, you missed a hell of a spaghetti dinner," she scolded. "Isabella and I played Frisbee with the guys, too."

"I know," Mitch admitted. "But this had to get done and I really didn't give myself a choice."

"Believe me, I get it." She paused. "I'm sure Charlotte will be upset about the condition of the golf course."

"What the hell do you mean?"

"I think it's right there in those trees at the bottom of Devil's Hill that Charlotte comes to smoke cigarettes and do whatever with whoever."

"Oh really, who do you think she's doing it with?"

Glo just shrugged her shoulders.

After a few minutes, she continued.

"So, tell me, Mitchy-poo, how's your love life? Any new cuties I should know about?"

"Well, let me see. Do you want the whole list or just the top ten?"

"Smart ass." She elbowed Mitch playfully.

She didn't say anything else about his "cuties" after that, though, which Mitch was glad for. He felt so far in the weeds when it came to girls; he didn't have the slightest idea how to begin to understand them. Yet there he was, evading questions about his love life that came from the love of his life, Gloria. Yet Mitch found some kind of satisfaction knowing that Gloria wondered about him and his "cuties."

He took the chance to change the subject quickly.

"How did it go with that big cottonwood tree in Izzy's yard?"

"Oh, it went great," Gloria reported. "There must've been twenty people there."

"I'm sure my guys worked hard when their dads were around. They sure didn't do much down here."

"Your 'guys'?" she prodded. "What are you, the neighborhood foreman?"

"Gloria, you know what I mean."

She smirked, pressing in.

"I do, Mitch," she said. "It seems like you're always in charge."

Mitch nodded and resettled himself in the grass, allowing the silence to settle between them again for a few minutes.

"Yeah, I think the guys did a pretty good job, all except for my brother," she broke in. "That kid can't shut up. He spent the whole day trying to be funny. It's exhausting. And you should have seen Char and Bev. They were the first ones to start working on that tree, and they didn't leave until it was done. They each ate two big plates of spaghetti and meatballs, they worked and didn't fight. Staying away from my little shit brother meant we had no major issues."

Mitch was comfortable on the hill when Gloria stood and commanded him to get up.

"Move your ass, Mitchy-poo. Let's go to the house. I'm going to make you some eggs."

"What?"

"You heard me," she said. "Eggs. Now. Let's go."

Mitch got up and moved his ass like his life depended on it.

A lot of thoughts went through his head as they walked back up Devil's Hill.

Why did she come down here? Why did she help me? What's with the eggs? Was she trying to somehow pay me back for showing her some kindness last night? And what was with the girlfriend question? Did she really care or was she just making conversation?

Mitch couldn't believe he and his "cuties" would be anywhere on Gloria's radar, so he chalked it up to her responding to her friend—Mitch—needing help today.

The past twenty-four hours had changed how Mitch thought of Gloria, so he wondered if maybe she felt differently about him too. There was a new tenderness toward her, the knowledge of her fear somehow humanizing her more than she'd even been in Mitch's mind. Storms aside, though, there were two things Mitch knew would never change: When it came to Gloria, he'd always be terrified and madly in love.

CHAPTER 10

THE CREEK

John and Sid Getz made certain that the crews started work by sunup the next day to clear the golf course of all the debris from the storm over the weekend. They spent most of the morning over at the bungalows, surveying the damage caused by the tree that fell across the bungalow with the porch. There was roof damage and a couple of broken windows—not bad, all things considered.

Despite the less-than-ideal state of things at the golf course, Hillcrest Country Club was open for business. The boys caddied at the golf course first thing in the morning to avoid the heat, but by 10 a.m., the temperature had already increased to 90 degrees. Though they worked at the Club, the boys weren't allowed into the pool at Hillcrest because it was reserved for members only, so once they'd finished their work, they set their minds to figure out a way to stay cool.

That morning, after Mitch had finished his loop, John Getz pulled him aside to acknowledge the work he'd done at Devil's Hill to the tune of an extra $20 bucks—he'd have had to caddy every day for a couple of weeks to make that! Mitch told him that Gloria Golyn had helped, but somehow John already knew about it.

"I'm sure you'll do the right thing by giving her a little taste... of money." John laughed. "At least take her out for some ice cream."

After the big storm, St. Paul was hit with a long string of days that reached temperatures in excess of 90 degrees, with high humidity to boot. The boys had few options to cool off. One, they could run through the sprinkler like they were six years old. Two, they could go over to Manny's house and fill up the fifty-five-gallon drum with water and dunk themselves like they were eleven years old. Three, they could ride the bus down to Lake Phalen, but then they'd still have to walk half-way around the lake to get to the beach. Four, they could ride their bikes to Phalen, which seemed like a great option at first because they wouldn't have to peddle the whole way there; it was an entirely downhill, three-mile ride from Mitch's house to Lake Phalen. Coming back, however, was the problem: all uphill. And in such high heat and humidity? Pass. The adults were at work, so they couldn't bum a ride anywhere. Wakefield in Maplewood had a little beach, but nobody really liked to go to Wakefield, and they'd still have to ride their bikes there and uphill the whole way back.

The simplest and best solution was what the boys affectionately called "the Creek." Now, what it really was was a rainwater runoff that came from Larpenteur Avenue through a half mile of wetland into a grated culvert. It sat about eight feet below street level, close to the golf course. There was plenty of tree cover, so nobody could see it from the road up above; they had plenty of privacy to construct their oasis. And, because of last night's rainfall, the boys knew the water would be running high.

Mitch, Manny, and EZ grabbed their bikes and goggles and rode over to Ike's house to see if he wanted to join in the adventure. When they got there, Ike's mom was already standing in the doorway.

"Hi Mrs. Tiller. Is Ike home?" Mitch asked.

She looked more grim than usual.

"No, he's not home, and if you boys see him, tell him to come home right away, you understand me?" She seemed somewhere between angry and worried.

The boys shot glances at one and other because they had a pretty good idea what was going on. Ike was on the run again.

"He delivered his papers this morning because we got ours," EZ offered. "But we haven't seen him either."

"If we see him, we'll let him know you're looking for him," Mitch reassured her.

The boys then hopped back on their bikes and rode to the creek.

When they got there, they found Ike and Buster, the former of which had already begun work on the creek. When Ike noticed them, he ran over to the pile of his stuff and pulled his t-shirt back on. Nobody thought anything of it. In fact, Mitch figured he was probably starting to burn up since he was pretty fair skinned. It was pretty common for Ike to wear his shirt while swimming.

But the first thing the rest of the boys did when they got there was take their shirts off. Even with a short bike ride, they were sweating their asses off.

"Ike, we stopped by your house on the way here," EZ relayed. "Your mom's looking for you and you're supposed to go home right away. She seemed a little worried."

"I'll bet she did." Ike didn't linger on the message. "Now, let's get this damn creek straightened out."

They'd all been burning up all day, so nobody protested either his evasion or suggestion.

"All I could think about on my route this morning was how much I wanted to jump in this damn creek," Ike said. "By 6 a.m. this morning, it was already in the mid-80s and humid as hell."

The water was more than a foot deep at the mouth of the creek when it ran high. The culvert itself was about two and a half feet across.

To enjoy the creek, however, meant putting in the work first. The boys set to work cleaning up all the broken beer bottles, old cans, debris, tree limbs, and at least one Shoppers' City shopping cart. The area was city property, not golf course property, so it wasn't tended well. They worked hard and piled up all the crap and trash right next to the sign that said NO DUMPING, KEEP OUT; they even convinced themselves that they were doing their civic duty by cleaning out all the debris. You would have thought they were doing the world a favor by cleaning up one hazard, just to create another. Yes, they were quite proud.

There were nine different kinds of tetanus waiting for you in that creek if you weren't careful. The boys kept their tennis shoes on the whole time—during cleanup and even while swimming in the creek—because even they were wise enough to know that they didn't know what they might run into. But they did a good job cleaning up. A little while and a little work later made all the difference. After cleaning, the next step was to collect enough boxes, cardboard, and whatever other material they could lay their hands on to plug up the culvert. This wasn't an easy feat, especially with the creek running fast, but they managed to find enough stuff to block it up. Within a few minutes, the whole mouth of the creek started to rise.

To no one's surprise, the first one in the water was Buster, Ike's goofy dog. That mutt loved the water. He ran up and down the banks of the creek and kept jumping in and chasing sticks. He'd even dive to the bottom and retrieve rocks. But after he'd spent his initial energy, Buster petered out and spent most of his time upstream hunting for frogs and collecting wood ticks.

By the end of it, they'd managed to create their own private swimming hole: twenty-five feet long, fifteen feet wide, and nearly six feet deep. This creek was right up there with the Trestle and Witches' Woods as one of their favorite places to be. The difference was that the creek was theirs alone. It was their own creation.

In the end, the boys knew the creek was basically a sewer runoff, but it was undeniably cleaner water than Lake Wakefield. The water was nice and cool and felt so good. Getting to the creek didn't require a long, hot trip to Phalen and back, and there was no funky smell and chiggers like there were at Wakefield. It was absolutely crystal clear rainwater that had been filtered through a half mile of wetland, straight to their own private oasis.

Naturally, they kept the creek and their swimming adventures very quiet. First, they didn't want the word to get out that they were basically swimming in a sewer, and second, they didn't want the word to get out in case somebody else wanted to swim in their sewer.

That day, the temperature rose to almost 100 degrees and stayed that way the rest of the week. Manny braved the heat to go up to a field over by the 14-B bus stop, where he'd spotted a car tire and wheel that was still inflated. He rolled it down to the creek, and the boys took turns floating on it. About every hour or so, Mitch dove down to the blockage to let a little bit of the water out to make sure the water didn't go up over the curb. Mitch was responsible for this because he could hold his breath the longest of all of them, so it was up to him to monitor the so-called culvert valve.

After a couple of hours, everyone started to get hungry, so EZ collected everybody's tip money from that morning and went up to the golf course to buy lunch. EZ's mom was working at the clubhouse, so she fixed the boys up good and proper. She probed EZ about where they were and what they were doing, but EZ was the king of evasion, and he got some really good deli sandwiches, chips, and pickles despite his mother's curiosity.

When EZ got back, the boys crowded around him to get their food. In the hubbub, Mitch noticed that Ike was actually hiding something underneath his t-shirt: he could only see the back of his neck plainly, but it was enough to know Ike had a huge bruise, no doubt from a recent beating by his old man. Mitch was tempted to ask him about it there in the open, but he remembered how fast Ike pulled on his shirt when they got there, so he kept his big mouth shut.

Does anybody do anything on behalf of the kids in Ike's family? Mitch wondered. *When is this stuff ever going to stop and who's going to stop it?*

Mitch noticed another bruise on the back of Ike's left arm but still didn't say a thing. The beatings were regular, and even though everyone knew about what happened at home, Ike didn't like to talk about it; if he wanted to, he would.

They enjoyed a nice creekside lunch and floated for the rest of the afternoon. There was a ball game that night, so they had to get going between 4:00 and 4:30.

"Ike, are you coming down to keep score for us tonight?" EZ asked.

"What time?"

"The game starts at 6:30."

"Okay. I'll have to see what kind of hell waits for me at home first," Ike said with a sigh. "With any luck, the old man will work overtime, and I won't have to deal with him, so yeah, if I can make it, I'll come down right after supper."

The boys were excited at the prospect of Ike being there with them. They felt a little more like a team when Ike was there. Even though he couldn't play, his scorekeeping and warm up drilling of the relief pitchers made it feel like he was part of the team.

Before they left, Mitch plunged to the bottom one last time and unplugged the culvert. Last year, they'd made the mistake of walking away without clearing the culvert grate. The water came up into the street after a big gully washer, and when a pond engulfed the entire intersection, a city truck was called. When the city guys dove down to unclog the culvert, the swimming hole had become more than eight feet deep. Hell, some little kid could have drowned. They never made that mistake again. As with everything else they did, they had to be careful not to screw it up for themselves—the good things the boys weren't supposed to do had a way of disappearing. They were really lucky that time the creek flooded the intersection—and that's just one example of something they were not supposed to do but couldn't wait to do any chance they got. As long as there was enough water running through it, the boys were at the creek: constructing, enjoying, and breaking down again.

EZ and Manny took off for home, but Mitch stayed back with Ike to help him round up Buster, who was still up the creek collecting wood ticks. Once they'd found the old dog, Mitch walked Ike back home, pushing his bike along. Mitch reminded him that he was supposed to have gone home if we'd seen him, a promise made hours ago.

"Don't worry about it," Ike assured him. "I'll straighten it out with my mom when I get home. I don't think she'll be too hard on me." He paused before continuing. "I had a blowout with my dad last night, and I took off. The funny thing is, I can't even remember what the old man was pissed about this time, but he still let me have it. Sometimes it's best if I just get out of there, so me and Buster went up to Witches' Woods last night."

Mitch felt a pit in his stomach. He was right. He'd had the feeling that Ike had had a tangle with his old man. Mitch hated being right about things like this.

"Ike, I don't know how many times I've told you, but you can come to my house. My dad has even said it was okay."

"I know, Mitch, but I think it's simpler if I just get out of there and let things blow over rather than get anyone else involved."

In the silence that followed them the rest of the way back to Ike's house, Mitch could tell Ike had thought a lot about it— and maybe he was right.

STANDING WATER

When Mitch got home from walking Ike back to his house, he found a different kind of storm rocking the house. Mitch's parents were going at it. He couldn't tell what they were arguing about at first, but then Casey came up from the basement, his shoes and socks soaking wet, and he quickly noticed that all-too-familiar stink: what you might imagine a well-decorated open sewer might smell like.

It didn't take long to figure out what they were yammering on about. Just like after every other heavy rainfall, four inches of standing water had seeped into the basement. It was hot and humid outside, and you could actually smell the musty basement when you walked in the front door of the house. Judging by her voice, Mrs. Dawson was on a war path. She was fuming at her husband.

"I want a new house! I'm embarrassed to live here, and I will not do another load of laundry down there until it's dry."

It was an empty threat of course because there was water down there every day of the year, though some days were worse than others. Of course, that's just what Mr. Dawson wanted to hear: how the house he'd worked his ass off for wasn't good enough.

Mr. Dawson typically met these battles with humor, and the funnier he got, the worse the fight got.

"What, no more laundry? How will we ever get all our whites gray again?"

As much as Mitch wanted to stay for the show, he had a baseball game to get to. He also knew that a battle that hot was going to last all night, so Mitch was sure he would catch the end of it when he got home.

By the time Mitch got home from baseball, the battle had moved to the silent treatment phase. When he rode up on his bike, Mr. Dawson was on the front steps, beer in hand, and some empties sitting alongside him.

"How did the game go?" he asked.

"We won, 6-2. I was two for three, and Zitz hit a dinger."

"All right, get inside and grab something to eat. Your mom is in the backyard with the other kids. You would do well to leave her alone and not ask her for anything." Sound advice.

The smell in the house had gotten worse while Mitch had been gone for the game. Even Beaver Lake didn't smell this bad. The water in the basement combined with the high humidity made the odor almost unbearable.

After a couple hours of more jabs, more silent treatment, and more than a couple of bottles of beer on Mr. Dawson's part, the whole family went to bed—and the Dawson parents made up with each other the way they usually did: loudly.

The basement fight was a longstanding element of the Dawson's marriage, but Mrs. Dawson knew they would never move, and Mr. Dawson knew he was never going to hear the end of it. So, he decided one day to fix the problem.

The following week, there were crews at the Dawson house, hired to do all kinds of stuff in an effort to transform the basement. Some jackhammered the basement floor, some were outside re-grading the yard with heavy equipment, and another set was putting new gutters on the house. There were seven guys forming a line from the basement to the dumpster to haul out the basement debris in five-gallon pails, one at a time. It was backbreaking work.

Mr. Dawson had the guys clear out a little garden area for his wife right next to her prized lilac bushes. This made her very happy as she loved flowers and gardening. But Mitch? He hated those miserable lilac bushes. They stretched about thirty feet along the side of the backyard, and he was responsible for cutting and trimming those damn things every year for five days of flowers. He pissed in those bushes every chance he got.

This basement project was the perfect excuse for all the neighborhood dads to show up every evening to drink beer and offer advice and opinions. At the end of it, the Dawsons finally had a dry, nonsmelly, laundry-producing basement, lightly perfumed with the cleansing aroma of Pine-Sol.

Every day for a week, Mr. Dawson went down to the dry basement just to sit on a folding chair. There didn't appear to be any reason for this daily adventure. It was cooler down there, sure, but that hardly seemed to be a reason to spend so much time in a basement with a few bottles of Buckhorn for company. As the rest of the family found out soon after, he did have a reason after all: Why not finish off the whole damn basement?

Now, there's something to understand about Mr. Dawson. He wasn't the type of guy to just do something; he overdid everything. If one was good, ten were better. The man typically did what he wanted to do, but Mrs. Dawson occasionally exercised her strength to keep him reined in the best she could. He always justified his decisions with the "I work my ass off" speech, coupled with "I do everything for everybody" plus "When I was a kid, we had nothing. Don't we deserve to have a few nice things in this world? That's not too much to ask blah blah blah." Mrs. Dawson knew her veto power was limited, however; whatever Walter set his mind to, he was going to do. He would always justify it with a speech—that was probably more for his sake than anyone else's—but it was good for the rest of the family to be aware of his reasoning anyhow.

This was all for show. Well, everything except for the part about how poor his family was when he was a kid. He grew up in absolute squalor down on Payne Ave; in fact, he lived all over the lower East Side, including Swede Hollow.

Swede Hollow, located at the end of Payne Avenue below Hamm's Brewery, was the true slum of the East Side. Years ago, businesses routinely used it as a makeshift dump. The people who lived down there scavenged for clothes, building materials, and anything else they could lay their hands on. There was no running water, no electricity, and no gas. It's hard to believe that an area like that existed in a place like Saint Paul, Minnesota, especially when you consider how deadly cold it often got in the winter. When Mr. Dawson lived there, he lived among an assortment of ramshackle houses and rickety old shacks that people built with discarded building materials. Their toilets consisted of outhouses constructed directly over Phalen Creek, and they got their water from springs near the brewery.

The city declared Swede Hollow a health hazard, and after seventy or eighty years, they finally decided to burn it out in December,of 1956. Mr. Dawson and a couple of his buddies bought a case of beer and went down and watched to celebrate. The city didn't have any plans after the burn, so once they got all the people out and razed the place, the city turned its back and left it. Soon after, the bums returned and erected their shacks once again.

The Dawson family is Irish, or Shanty Irish. It was one thing to be called "Shanty Irish" by others within the tribe, but if some Bohunk or Pollock called you Shanty Irish, they were considered fighting words. They used the term as a jab about being a poor Irishman, like they all were when they came over one hundred years ago.

Most people who call the Irish "Shanty Irish" use the term ignorantly, but the community knows. Shanty Irish was a term that arose from the fact that the Dawsons were a poor Irish family living in a shanty in Swede Hollow. It doesn't get more genuine than that—just don't call him Shanty Irish unless you want to get a painful lesson. Mel Johnson was an asshole who couldn't shut up and who used to work with Mr. Dawson. Mel constantly bragged about living in Bloomington—Bloomington had the Twins, Bloomington had the Vikings, and then the North Stars. If you didn't live in one of the southern suburbs, he considered you low class—and he wasn't afraid to say it to your face either.

He'd make cracks like: "You and the rest of your East Side Shanty Irish," or "That sounds like something the Shanty Irish would say." After work one night, Mr. Dawson and some of his coworkers from the office stopped at the Coney Island downtown for a beer. This asshole was there too, and he wouldn't let up on Mr. Dawson about the East Side "slums" and all of the Shanty Irish. He thought he was being funny, but he made just one more crack about the Irish after Mr. Dawson ordered a Jameson neat; then he punched Mel so hard that he sent Mel's nose over to visit Mel's left ear. Mr. Dawson tolerated a lot and had a great sense of humor, but he was sensitive about his heritage and could only take so much. He was a true Shanty Irish from Payne Avenue. You can ask Mel. Don't fuck with the East Side.

Poverty was the underlying reason Mr. Dawson and his friends joined the service as soon as they could. Some of those guys never graduated high school, some guys' parents signed them up when they were seventeen, but Mr. Dawson joined the Marines as soon as he graduated from high school, while he was still seventeen, to avoid an Army draft. To him, it was a sweet deal: They give you three square meals a day, clothes to wear, and a place to live. Sure, you had to go fight in World

War II, but it was better than living in abject poverty in Swede Hollow or in a cold water flat on the lower East Side of Saint Paul. In honor of his days of service, Mr. Dawson still wears his hair high and tight.

As a kid, Walter Dawson used to take a big canvas sack down to the railroad tracks and collect chunks of coal that had fallen off coal cars to heat their apartment during the winter. He also shined shoes on the Avenue for pennies and collected rags to sell to old Sol, the "Rag Sheeny." He knew hardship and the toll it takes on a person.

Finishing the basement was quite the process. When Mr. Dawson decided he wanted carpeting, boxes and boxes of carpet samples arrived for the family to test run. When he wanted paneling put up, they received dozens of paneling samples to pore over. He had a bar built, one that incorporated the family's old Kelvinator refrigerator, and rounded it out with some very cool Hamm's beer signs he got from John Getz. He had another phone installed and brought down the TV and the hi-fi from the living room. Of course, moving the big items from upstairs to adorn the downstairs left a few gaps, so he bought a big TV/record player console for the living room and a new Whirlpool fridge for the upstairs kitchen. The basement got the whole works: a bathroom, pool table, dart board, and cool new swivel bar stools.

He did overstep at one point, though. He said he could get a good deal on a couple of old pinball machines from his buddy at the Arlington Bowl that would really set the place apart. After a brief yet heated debate between the Dawson parents, the topic of spaghetti and meatballs came up and Mr. Dawson knew his spending spree for the rec room had come to a conclusion. Mrs. Dawson was drawing a line at lumpy old pinball machines stuck in her basement.

Aside from her veto power, Penny Dawson was still very much included in the proceedings. She went to Shoppers' City and bought furniture: a couch, chairs, lamps, ash trays, and highball glasses for the bar. After all, she enjoyed a nice Seven and Seven every once in a while.

In all this, Mr. Dawson was able to solve one of the truly great mysteries of his life on Wyoming Avenue: How many cases of Buckhorn bottles could the old Kelvinator refrigerator hold? The answer was two and a half cases, or more than four cases of cans. This was a huge burden off Walter's mind. He could sleep well now.

The Dawsons became the owners of the coolest, driest basement in the neighborhood, and it wasn't a close contest. Dad couldn't wait to show it off to his pals, so a party was planned. Mrs. Dawson made little sandwiches and two cas-seroles, and there was plenty of Old Dutch potato chips and French onion dip, Mitch's favorite. Mr. Dawson provided the beverages, which meant a lot of Hamm's beer and a big bottle of Seagram's Seven Crown Whiskey with lots of ice and a choice variety of mixers.

The morning of the big basement party, Mitch went into the kitchen right as his father hung up the phone, a huge smile on his face. He spent a better part of the morning walking around the house, just beaming. Mrs. Dawson kept asking him why he was smiling so much, but Mr. Dawson's answers were casually vague.

"Well, you'll see tonight. I've got a little bit of a surprise for everybody."

Of course, this was the kind of thing that drove Mrs. Dawson completely nuts. All day, she begged him to tell but he wouldn't budge.

"Just wait, you'll see tonight."

Enzo and Mama Petri brought a big kettle sauce with homemade Italian sausage and meatballs, which thrilled Mr. Dawson to no end. They also brought a couple loaves of Roma bread and two bottles of red wine.

Other guests brought appetizers like cheese and crackers and veggies and dip. A couple of the moms made desserts. All the food was served in the basement like a buffet.

After most of the guests arrived, there was a bit of a commotion at the front door—surprisingly loud enough to hear from the noisy basement. Mr. Dawson instructed the kids to go upstairs and give any help needed. So, Casey and Mitch went upstairs and, lo and behold, there were all three Getz brothers.

They were all in town and ready to party, and they'd brought box after box after box of all kinds of miscellaneous swag. But the coolest thing they brought was a small electric piano.

"This is the same kind of piano that Ray Charles plays," Sid Getz boasted.

They piled their coats on top of Casey, and Murray Getz put his fedora on top of Casey's head. Casey was instantly attached; he didn't take it off all night, which Murray loved. The very next day, Casey just had to have a fedora hat of his own, so Mr. Dawson went down to Goodwill and bought an old gray fedora for a buck. Casey wore that hat day and night for months

Everybody was thrilled to see the Getz brothers, and to make things even better, they had gifts for everybody at the party—mostly bottles of oddball booze. But their gifts to the hosts were really special: two bottles of bourbon from Grand Rickhouse Distillery in Kentucky. This was no ordinary booze. It was aged for fifteen years and came in decorative wooden boxes engraved with Mr. Dawson's initials. You know it's an important jug of booze when it comes in its own furniture.

"Walter, we got you two bottles of this select twenty-three-year bourbon," Murray Getz proudly announced. "One's for drinking tonight and the other is for a special occasion in the future. So, if you'll allow me, I'd like to give everybody a taste as we toast our host and hostess."

"Does this mean..." Mr. Dawson half-asked, trailing off.

"Yes, indeed! The Getz brothers are the new favorite sons of Kentucky," Murray confirmed. "We bought the distillery."

Everyone cheered.

Once everybody at the party got their bourbon for the toast, John Getz stepped forward and made a beautiful tribute to the Dawsons. Everyone raised their glasses and sampled the fancy whiskey. In turn, Mr. Dawson toasted to the three Getz brothers on their new venture in the whiskey business.

After another shot of bourbon, Mr. Dawson made Mrs. Dawson a Seven and Seven highball, and they got on with the party. It was a night and a party no attendee quickly forgot. The Getz brothers plugged in their electric piano, and Sid Getz sat down to play. They began with all kinds of funny songs like "Inkadinkado," "We're Off to See the Wizard," and "Zip-A-Dee-Doo-Dah." All these songs were peppered with perfectly timed, well-rehearsed jokes. It was absolutely hysterical and went on for hours. Mitch's favorite was "Blue Spanish Thighs."

At the urging of brothers Sid and John, Murray Getz did a twenty-minute stand-up comedy routine that was worthy of the Ed Sullivan Show. He had everybody in tears. The great thing about his humor was that it was funny but clean; no swear words at all. Now, that's not to say that it wasn't a little racy, but it was mostly innuendo and circumstance and veiled comments. Still, some of the funniest stuff the audience had ever heard in their lives.

People took turns going up to sing with the brothers. Another big highlight was when Barb Finch sat down at the piano and started to play. Mitch had no idea she was such a great piano player—turns out she used to play in saloons all over the Twin Cities years ago and was how she met Mr. Finch.

She was amazing. This revelation opened up even more entertainment opportunities: The Getz brothers could sing some of the classic songs because Barb Finch knew them all. They sang songs like "Sentimental Journey," "Paper Doll," "Glow Worm," and Mrs. Dawson's favorite, "Stardust." Sid Getz could sound just like Nat King Cole. They also did some Sinatra songs and some more tunes from The Mills Brothers. It was fantastic.

The unapologetically goofy Casey Dawson danced the jerk, Watusi, and mashed potato all by himself to every single song. While some people will only dance when no one's looking, Casey was someone who would dance anywhere, anytime. He didn't care who's looking or what they thought. This crowd thought his dancing was hysterical.

By the time 4 a.m. rolled around, only Mr. Dawson, a couple of the other neighborhood dads, and a few of Mr. Dawson's Payne Avenue buddies were left. The basement warming had meant so much to Mr. Dawson for a lot of reasons: to show off his new basement to the neighbors and to shut my mom up about a wet basement—but at the end of things, he was happiest to have spent time with his veteran buddies. They drank a lot of beer and shed a few tears; there was something pretty special about having his guys be able to come hang out in his very own basement saloon.

Most of Mr. Dawson's friends served in World War II in one capacity or another. Some of them experienced unspeakable things and others never left the States. It was just luck of the draw. When they got together, they never sat around and told war stories; that's just not done. Somebody might share an anecdote about basic training or life when they got out of the service. Mr. Dawson had a notion that those who talked about their service the most probably did the least.

Mr. Dawson himself was in the South Pacific. He saw combat in the Philippines, and he also built bridges. If the enemy blew up a bridge that crossed a river or ravine, his outfit was responsible for assembling a "Bailey Bridge" to replace the span. He'd told his boys that they could snap together a hundred-foot bridge in a week. Shorter spans took only a few days. This experience in the military was how Mr. Dawson got into the bridge and road inspection profession with the state of Minnesota after he'd come home.

Walter had only one pal who was never in the service: Carl Leary. He'd tried to participate, but Carl had been thrown out.

"Carl was a great guy when he was sober, which was rare," Mr. Dawson shared.

Carl started drinking as a kid and never stopped. If Walter ever spotted Carl down on Payne Avenue, he tried to help him out with a few bucks, even though he knew where the money would go: straight into Arlington Bowl or the nearest liquor store. Carl spent all day mumbling and staggering up and down Payne Avenue, panhandling for beer money.

"He became a Payne Avenue piss bum who never amounted to a damn thing in his life. That D-horn could have been anything in the world. He was smart and he was funny." Mr. Dawson would shake his head at the memory. "Instead, Carl was a wet brain drunk."

Carl ended up drinking himself to death.

Mitch and his siblings didn't hear a lot about the wars their father participated in, but Mr. Dawson did once share that Mrs. Dawson's older brother, Wayne, saw the bloodiest battles of the South Pacific and was the most decorated man he knew. His awards included two Purple Hearts, and he saw more action than all the guys my dad knew put together.

Uncle Wayne was in the Navy and piloted Higgins boats, the landing crafts that transported troops from a ship to shore.

Each boat held about thirty-six troops, a Jeep and eighteen troops, or a good load of supplies. It's been said that the Higgins boats were a pivotal piece to winning the war because it was near impossible for the enemy to defend miles of beach compared with a single port.

"Uncle Wayne told me a story long ago," Mr. Dawson said, describing what he remembered. "At Guadalcanal, he would leave a ship with his Higgins boat and hit the enemy shore under heavy fire from the Japanese. When the ramp went down, of the thirty-six Marines, only about twenty would get off the boat and make it to shore. He would raise the ramp, back off the shore, and take the dead and wounded back to the ship, only to have it emptied and filled again with more young Marines heading to the same fate. This happened over and over for days."

Wayne was a hero but a distant guy. When he visited for holidays or get-togethers, he was pretty quiet and reserved but very nice and very kind. He spent most of his free time volunteering at the Fort Snelling Veteran's Hospital. Uncle Wayne never got married, never had kids, and never talked about the war.

CHAPTER 12

WITCHES' WOODS

For Mitch and his pals, one of their favorite spots in the whole world was Witches' Woods. Witches' Woods was on McKnight Road and across from the golf course, bordered to the east by Century Avenue. Beaver Lake was only a few blocks south.

The Woods were legendary. The people who had owned and lived on the property in the Woods around fifty or sixty years ago—two old spinster sisters and their mother—gave it its name. They built a big house right in the middle of the woods. As the legend goes, the neighbors realized one day that they hadn't seen the mother of the sisters in quite some time. In fact, after that point, no one ever saw the mother again, and it was rumored that the daughters had killed their mother and buried her somewhere in the woods. However, she was never found, so nobody knows if there's any truth to that story.

Eventually the Ramsey County Sheriff along with firefighters were called to the old house and they broke down the door. The sisters were taken straight to the old Ancker Hospital by ambulance because they were in such bad condition. Deputies found the house filled from floor to ceiling with garbage. Five tons of trash got hauled away in one day.

The boys found out later that their Witches' Woods was not the original Witches' Woods from which the sisters were hauled. They had been taken from a wooded area north of Larpenteur Avenue over near Beebe Road, a half mile away from the legendary Witches' Woods. That area had been fully developed with homes and streets, so the current Witches' Woods must've adopted the name and legend over time.

Twice every year, once in the spring and once in the fall, the boys "camped" in the Witches' Woods. They called it camping, but it wasn't really much of a trip; the boys arrived there early in the morning, telling no one where they were going, and left by the time it got dark. There was no overnight camping. They weren't supposed to be there in the first place, but let's be real: that was the best part about the experience. Just like with the Trestle, parents and other authorities urged all kids to stay out of Witches' Woods, but in truth, they were probably more concerned about what would happen if something went wrong in the Woods. If someone got in some real trouble deep in the woods, there was no way to get to them because it was too thickly wooded.

Like the Trestle, kids still went in there all the time, though, whether on foot or mini bike, the latter of which made the trek faster, lucky bastards. Also like the Trestle, Witches' Woods was a big party site for the older kids at night. With more than one hundred acres of woods and trails and ponds and swamps, you could spend days in the Woods having a blast. They couldn't resist the call of adventure!

Manny and Zitz were still in Boy Scouts, so they were in charge of setting up the camp. These two came correct. They had their backpacks full of camping gear, camping shovels, little saws and stuff to make a fire, and cooking utensils. They had everything, including, and most importantly, a first aid kit. Someone always got banged up or scraped on these misadventures. Mitch's job was to bring hot dogs and buns. The other guys brought pop and chips. The most exciting part was the hot dogs and marshmallows over the campfire.

Building a campfire in the Witches' Woods was a colossal no-no, but who was going to stop them? They certainly didn't care. Besides, Manny and Zitz could build a textbook, Boy

Scout–approved fire pit every time. They dug a hole, put rocks at the bottom, surrounded it with two layers of rocks, and made sure water was close at hand. The rest of the boys had to go out and collect firewood and kindling, making sure it was all very dry. Zitz said the dry stuff creates less smoke, which was the enemy of wayward campers like them.

One weekend in early fall when the boys were in ninth grade, they got up there early like they always did, set up camp, and then went adventuring through the woods, looking for remnants of the creepy old lady's house and the spot where they buried their mother. They never found any sign of the mother or her grave—no one ever did. Though, that's not surprising since the old lady was never anywhere close by to begin with. The boys' search involved tipping over old logs and looking through abandoned cars and other crap that was scattered around the woods.

Ike knew the Woods the best because he spent the most time in them. He didn't wait for camping trips to come to Witches' Woods. He'd bring Buster and spend hours exploring. It was a place of refuge for him when things were really bad at home. Ike didn't have other activities in his life like the rest of the neighborhood kids did with hockey and baseball and going to dances or even Scouts. He had Witches' Woods, the Trestle, and Buster. He knew every little creek and pond in the whole place.

Ike even had his own secret place, and it wasn't just a campsite; Ike had built his own shanty. It wasn't easy to get to. About a month before their fall camping trip, Ike brought EZ and Mitch to his hideout. It was situated next to a pond on the side where there was a hill, and it looked like you couldn't walk around the pond on that side. You had to get off a trail and climb a steep slope until it leveled off again. There was a kind of a depression back into the hill with a lot of cover. You could stand right next to this spot and not see it, and that's what made it so cool.

He'd built his shack with old pieces of plywood, and it measured about eight feet long and six feet wide with tar paper on the sloped roof. All that was covered with tree branches. It even had a plywood floor with a rug on it. Ike showed his friends a hole beneath the floor where he kept all of his supplies. Everything was wrapped in heavy plastic. He had a blanket, pillow, some canned goods, beef jerky, tools, candles, and a couple packs of smokes. He even had a plastic picnic jug for fresh water. On top of these vital supplies, he'd also gathered some reading material: some Mad magazines and a couple of old Playboys. He decorated the walls with nudie pictures and car pics from hot rod mags.

He found things for his shack by roaming through the neighborhood on trash day. There were loads of things to be found in the trash behind Hillcrest Shopping Center, especially the hardware store; Ike made it a point to never steal anything.

"Holy shit, Ike, you could practically live here," EZ said.

Ike lit a cigarette.

"Yeah, well, sometimes I have to. I've slept in here lots of times. Sometimes I think they don't even notice I'm gone. I've had a few places up at the Trestle too, but somebody always finds them. It's not like here. I always feel safe here." Ike paused. "Isn't that funny? I feel safer in the middle of the woods in a plywood box than at home with my own family."

He knew what he was doing, and he knew that, realistically, he could be holed up for a couple of days at a time, so he even had dog food for Buster. When he retreated back to his house in town, he made sure to completely cover his hideaway with branches. You wouldn't be able to see it unless you knew where to look. Mitch and EZ were pretty sure they couldn't have found their way back to town even if they wanted to.

"I don't know what to do, you guys," Ike confessed. "Things are really bad at home. If my dad's not beating on me, he hits my mom. I run away, but she stays there and just takes it. She takes it and I hate her for it."

"We had a bad fight on Sunday after church. I threw a coffee cup at my dad's head when he smacked my mom in the mouth. I started screaming at him. He screamed back at me some Bible bullshit about a wife submitting to her husband as to the Lord and some other crap I don't understand. Then he called me an unholy bastard. I don't know how much longer I can take it. I spent Sunday night here, then got up Monday morning and went right to school from here. I got called down to the office during homeroom because my mom had called school looking for me. I got sat down by the guidance counselor. She asked me what was going on and if I needed anything. I sure as hell don't need Hazel Park sticking their nose in. I didn't say much else and they let me go to class. Luckily, I have PE first period so I could catch a shower."

"Have you heard from Aaron?" Mitch asked.

"No!" His tone warned Mitch away from the topic.

"OK, OK, I won't bring it up again."

Ike paused.

"I didn't mean to snap, Doc."

After that exchange, they all sat there without saying a word for a while until Ike broke the silence.

"It's hard to think about," Ike said. "I was pretty young when Aaron left. I can remember some things as if they were yesterday. Mostly the screaming matches, the yelling, the arguments he had with my dad. It feels like I can't remember any good times at all, if there even were any to remember. I also know that without Aaron I feel completely alone in my house and afraid all the time. When I was a little kid, Aaron used to stand up to my old man for me. He would take the beatings meant for me."

"What are you going to do, Ike?"

"I don't know, but I gotta figure it out because it's going to end up very bad for somebody in that house, and it's not going to be me."

"You're talking crazy, Ike, you know that? Why don't you go tell somebody or call the cops?"

"I asked my mom that once. She said that all that would do was get us more beatings."

"You can always come over to my house," Mitch said, reiterating what he'd told him when they walked home from the Creek together not so long ago.

"I know, Doc, and I appreciate it."

"You can't come to my house, asshole," EZ announced. "I see the way you look at my sister."

Ike smiled.

"Sometimes I think about old Hack Helvik and how I'd like to just walk up to the Trestle and disappear someday, never to be found."

"You realize everybody's pretty sure Hack is dead, right Ike?" Mitch reminded him.

"Well, then, his misery is over."

"Jesus Christ, Ike, that's bleak," EZ said.

Ike reassured him.

"I'm just thinking out loud."

A month later after visiting Ike's shack for the first time, they were back for the biannual camping trip, ready to relax at the big pond catching turtles when they heard a train coming up from the west. The same railroad tracks that ran past Hazel Park and under the Trestle also ran alongside Witches' Woods. They all got up quickly to go down to the tracks to fire off a few rounds at the boxcars with wrist rockets. Wrist rockets were lethal; you wouldn't want to get plunked by one of those.

Everyone was loaded up and ready to shoot when Manny screamed.

"Hold your fire!"

Mitch thought, "Hold your fire?" "What, are we advancing on an enemy position?"

"Look, that train is full of cars."

He was right. The train cars were loaded with new Fords from the Ford plant.

"Those are the new Thunderbirds and Torinos," Zitz marveled. He was from a Ford household, so naturally he knew exactly what each car was. The train was moving slowly as was typical for a loaded-down train, so the boys waited until they saw some old box cars before they took aim and peppered the train.

After an exhausting day of old lady corpse hunting, turtle wrangling, and boxcar assaulting, it was time for a well-deserved dinner.

When they were outside of the woods, the boys teased and razzed the living shit out of each other, but the Woods forced a different dynamic on them. It was important to have your head on a swivel in there, and there was an added responsibility to look out for yourself and your pals. Getting in bad trouble in the woods meant Maplewood cops or Ramsey County Sheriffs and no more camping trips, and just like with the Creek, the boys couldn't risk spoiling that.

There was real danger in Witches' Woods: bums. These vagrants would wander in the woods and build small shanties and live there for part of the year. If you went past Witches' Woods at night, you could see campfires off in the distance through the trees if you looked hard enough. The bums knew they could have a fire and the cops couldn't do anything about it. There was no way to get to them at night if they were deep enough in the woods. They came up from Swede Hollow and other spots like the River Flats down along the Mississippi on the D-horn express slow freight to Witches' Woods and lived there until it was time to move on. Every time the boys ventured into the woods, they would invariably find one or two of these shanties—one time they actually saw someone sleeping in one of the shacks. That finding ended their camping trip pretty quick that day. But of course, it wasn't enough to keep them away for good. Just like the Creek and the Trestle, the Witches' Woods was a sacred place where the boys could sit around the campfire and really talk about stuff—mostly girls, sports, and fart jokes—but those were the things that mattered most.

CHAPTER 13

SHOPPERS' CITY

It was Christmas Eve morning—the perfect time to do some Christmas shopping. EZ and Mitch headed down early to Hill-crest Shopping Center, with a plan to join up with Manny on the way and meet Zitz at Hafner's Bowl to roll a few games. Ike and his family were at church, otherwise he might have come along just for something to do. Christmas was a non-factor in Ike's house.

When they got to Manny's house, EZ rapped on the door. Every encounter with Mr. or Mrs. Klaus was a treat. His mom welcomed the boys in and chatted with them about Christmas, but quickly she hushed them.

"Keep it down, boys. The old man's a little hung over dis morning. He got drunk last night down at the 'Cats Paw.'"

"The Cat's Paw?" Mitch asked. "Where's the Cat's Paw?"

She grinned.

"It's on Arcade Street, two joints from the Cat's Ass."

It only took a second for them to land on the floor laughing.

Mr. Klaus came into the kitchen just then.

"You fibbing old Christmas goat," he said lovingly. "Vhy do you tell da kids lies like dat. I vas home last night clipping your toenails vit my bolt cutters so you don't make dat click-clack sound on da kitchen floor." He laughed at his own joke. "Manfred is coming, boys. He's getting dressed."

Manny arrived in the kitchen shortly thereafter.

"Let's get the hell out of here," he moaned. "I can't take these two anymore. This has been going on all morning."

His parents chuckled as they ushered the boys on their way.

Mitch had all his tip money from the golf course and a fist full of pages of Holiday Station Stamps that he'd stolen out of his dad's glove box. Mr. Dawson always collected them but never used them.

After about an hour of bowling, they made their first shopping stop at the Eighty-Eight Cent Store where EZ did all his shopping. Cheap prick. He bought gifts for four people and didn't even spend ten bucks.

Mitch wasn't much better. At the Holiday Gas Station, you could buy anything for under $1.99 and four pages of stamps. It was a cool place. They sold gas and oil, but they also had knives, guns, ammo, tools, clothes, hardware, and sporting goods.

Mitch purchased a pair of gloves and wool socks for his dad, a stocking hat and scarf for his sister, and slippers and mittens for his mom. Their next stop was the Mother Goose, the novelty shop by Snyder's Drug Store to pick up something for Casey. He liked funny stuff, so Mitch got him a rubber dog turd and whoopee cushion so he could fart to his heart's content.

"Manny, what are you getting today?" EZ asked.

"My dad said he wants a new snow shovel," Manny replied.

"Yeah, how about your mom?"

"My mom wants something to hit my dad with."

"Seriously, are you going to get your mom something?" EZ pressed.

"Yeah, she wants a new ironing board."

EZ complained about the gift choices.

"You're going to walk around all day with an ironing board and a snow shovel? We're going to get your stuff last."

"Yeah, that's fine, I don't care. I figured I'd get them both up at Shoppers' City anyway."

"I'm going to get all my stuff up at Shoppers' City too," Zitz said.

"Cool, that'll help us save time," Mitch reasoned.

Shoppers' City was the superstore of its time. They had absolutely everything. At Christmas, they really went all out. They were giving away stockings full of candy and little toys for the kids, carolers sang Christmas songs, and Santa had a line going all the way around the store.

After battling the crowd and picking away at their Christmas lists, the boys stopped at the record shop to pick up a couple new 45s. Mitch got "Midnight Confessions" by The Grassroots and "Magic Carpet Ride" by Steppenwolf. EZ got "Dance to the Music" by Sly and the Family Stone and "I'm a Believer" by The Monkees. Zitz' brother, Chet, got Zitz into The Rolling Stones, so that's all he would ever buy. Zitz got the last copy of "Jumpin' Jack Flash."

It was well known that you couldn't go to Shoppers' City without a visit to the pet store. Who doesn't love puppies and kittens and lizards and fish and all manner of critters?

They boys also made a stop at the bakery to grab something to eat. Mitch got a cinnamon roll about the size of a manhole cover, and the other guys got Christmas cupcakes.

They sat down in the cafeteria to enjoy their goodies. They dug in enthusiastically and stopped to take in their surroundings only when they'd cleaned up their treats. They looked around the cafeteria and noticed some girls from school a few tables over: Melanie, Renée, Carolyn, and two other girls they didn't recognize. They too must've been doing some last-minute Christmas shopping, and boy, oh boy, were they cute.

Melanie looked up and saw the boys.

"Hey guys!" She waved. "Merry Christmas! Come join us over here."

EZ moved first, darting over and making himself comfortable in a spot right between the two cute stranger girls.

When it came to meeting girls or breaking the ice or setting the tone, EZ did all the heavy lifting; the rest of them only had to sit back and enjoy the fruits of his labor. EZ had a complete arsenal of opening lines, funny stories, impressions, and the occasional but tasteful dirty joke

Introductions were made. It turned out that the two new girls were Renée's cousins from Virginia, Minnesota. Della was Mitch's age, and her sister Maggie was a year older.

It was only about 12:30 p.m., according to the big Coca-Cola clock in the cafeteria, and the girls announced that they had just been about to order lunch. The guys were doing pretty good for time; by 3 o'clock, they were running home to make it in time for the Christmas Eve celebrations.

"It's only 12:30, guys," Mitch said. "Why don't we have lunch now too?"

Everybody agreed, despite their recent consumption of pastries. They all got the Shoppers' City Lunch Special: a cheeseburger, small fries, and a Coke for $0.79. All except for Manny. He got the "Extra Special": double cheeseburger, super fries, and a large Coke for $0.99.

Coming to the cities and going to Shoppers' City was a big deal for Maggie and Della. They didn't have anything like it up where they lived. The closest thing they had was a Ben Franklin store that Maggie said wasn't much bigger than the cafeteria everyone was eating in. They must've arrived pretty early because they already had bags full of stuff and were done shopping for the day.

While they were eating, the topic of hockey came up. Mitch mentioned to the girls that he and the guys were all playing in a big tournament the day after Christmas down at Phalen Playground. This piqued Della and Maggie's interest because, where they come from up on the Iron Range, hockey is a religion. They both played hockey when they were younger, like EZ's sister, Gloria. In fact, Maggie reminded Mitch of Gloria just a little bit... but in more ways than one. Mitch couldn't take his eyes off of her.

This was both good and very bad. It was good because she was gorgeous. It was very bad because she was out of reach. She'd be gone in a couple of days, and Mitch would have to deal with one more heartbreak. So, he tried not to think about it—which turned out to be a useless endeavor, especially while she sat nearby. If you asked him, Mitch wouldn't have been able to tell you why he put himself through this type of thing.

Sitting in the cafeteria, the kids had a front-row seat to all kinds of people, many of whom they knew from one place or another: kids from school and some kids from church, community leaders and friends' parents. They even saw Ray "the Rat" Munger pass by with his mom. Everybody must've had the same idea: last minute shopping at Shoppers' City. There was even a lady who walked by with a couple of bags of groceries and a set of snow tires in her shopping cart. Boy, what a great gift for her hubby.

Carolers walked through the store singing Christmas carols; there must've been a dozen of them. At one point, they came into the cafeteria and sang a few for us, which was pretty cool. The day was going so well, with hardly any hiccups.

Just when they thought the day couldn't get any better, it did. In this instance, the entertainment came in the form of Char and Bev Finch, stumbling down the aisle from the furniture department, followed by Mr. Finch. Old Snag and Crime Scene had a huge rolled up rug lodged on their shoulders. It must've been twelve feet long at least. It could've been a scene out of a Laurel and Hardy movie.

Char was in front, and Bev was in the back, like always. Mr. Finch was yelling at them the whole time. The problem was, every time he said something, Bev stopped and tried to turn around to listen, but knocked stuff over every time she did so, which elicited even more yelling from Mr. Finch. Right in front of us, they swung around, knocked over a mannequin, a display of Christmas ornaments, and nearly took the head off an old lady.

It was like their very own little Christmas comedy. It was hysterical.

"Come on." EZ stood up and walked to the edge of the cafeteria to get a better view.

The whole scene was epic. Mr. Finch yelled at them again and growled. At this point, nearby shoppers were starting to notice.

"Why don't you two idiots use your heads?"

Right then, Char threw her end to the floor, and Bev and the other end went down with it. Bev sprawled in the middle of the aisle, struggling to prevent the huge rug from unfurling.

"Then go ahead, Dad," Char screamed. "You carry Mom's stupid Christmas present yourself."

Not aware that Mitch and the guys had seen the whole thing, Char was understandably shocked when EZ, her arch enemy, sounded off.

"Well, Merry Christmas, girls," EZ said. "Are you two rein donkeys going to pull Santa's sleigh tonight?"

Christmas flames shot out of Char's eyes.

"I'm going to beat your ass, Eric," she hissed.

"I'll tell you what," EZ fired back. "In the spirit of Christmas, let's find some mistletoe. I'll bend over and you can give it a little smooch instead."

Char stormed off into the pet store, and Bev followed, probably to choke some kittens. By this time, two guys from Shoppers' City had run over, grabbed up the rug for Mr. Finch, and taken it over to the cashier.

Mitch and the other guys were laughing so hard their sides started to hurt. Mitch had to sit back down. Then, the unexpected happened: Maggie sat down next to him. He felt like a drooling idiot, sitting there and wondering in silence. Mitch wanted to say something, but he couldn't think of anything. It was like his brain had been rendered inoperable. Maggie broke the silence.

"I hope you know those girls," she said.

"Yeah, they're from our neighborhood. This is nothing out of the ordinary for them. This kind of stuff happens to them all the time."

Maggie looked at him and laughed. What's funny is, Mitch was not trying to be funny; he was just telling the truth, at which she laughed. Could it be that Mitch was learning a thing or two about talking to girls?

The two of them got to talking, and as Mitch nodded along as she talked about her and Della's lives up on the Iron Range with the iron ore mines all over the place, he wondered if he was learning how to listen better. He was really enjoying hearing Maggie's stories, and she was just as interested to hear about his life. She asked about him and the things that he liked. It was a really cool experience, sitting there with a bunch of girls hanging out and having fun talking.

As Maggie and Della were talking, Mitch couldn't quite pinpoint what was different about them, but he knew it was something in the way they talked. Like when they said the word "Minnesota" it sounded like "Minnesooda" and when they said they lived "on the Range," it sounded like "un da raynch." Then it came to him: They actually had an accent. Later, Mitch asked his mom about it.

"Oh sure, the people up on the Iron Range have a distinct accent," she said. "There's a lot of Finlanders and Bo-hunks and other ethnicities from all over up there."

Shoppers' City had become even more crowded since they'd arrived. Everyone hung out for a little while longer, until Renée broke up the fun.

"We've got to get going," she said. "My mom is going to pick us up in a few minutes."

Mitch looked up at the big Coca-Cola clock over the menu board of the cafeteria.

Holy crap, he thought. *It's already 3:30.*

"OK girls, we still have to get some stuff done around here."

Manny and Zitz hadn't bought anything yet, so they said their goodbyes.

"I hope we see you guys before we go back up north." Della smiled.

"Yeah, that would be great," Mitch replied, truly meaning what he said.

We headed back out into the store, but not before glancing back one time at Maggie. To his delight, she met his glance.

CHAPTER 14

IKE GOES MISSING

Last weekend, Mr. Dawson bought the family Christmas tree from the tree lot at the A&W root beer stand by Aldrich Arena. The stand is closed for root beer sales this time of year, so they sell Christmas trees instead. He got a big Scotch pine, which the family decorated in no time, and aside from a couple of incidents with Woodrow the useless cat getting frisky with some of the low-hanging ornaments, everything was set for Christmas.

For the two weeks it stood in the living room, Woodrow was on alert—so much so it seemed that he didn't take his eyes off it once. His perch on top of the TV set was the perfect viewing spot.

Most years on Christmas Eve, the Dawson family went to visit an aunt and uncle from Mrs. Dawson's side who lived south of the Trestle. Hanging out with the older cousins Herman, Bob, and Dick was a rare treat. Those guys had the teenage trifecta: jobs, cars, and girlfriends. However, the Dawsons changed plans this year; they stayed home Christmas Eve to get ready for Christmas day, which they were hosting. All sorts of family would be at the house, and all of the Dawsons were excited. Mr. Dawson wanted to host every event at their house now that he had the big, beautiful finished basement. He couldn't wait.

Mr. Dawson stopped by Jerry's Drive-In after work to pick up some chicken and onion rings so Mrs. Dawson didn't have to cook on Christmas Eve. When Mitch and his buddies had passed

Jerry's earlier in the day, he'd said a little prayer requesting that his old man would get some bird and rings for dinner.

The whole family was in the living room watching the Andy Williams Christmas special when the phone rang, right after 8 o'clock. It was Ike's mom. Mrs. Tiller wondered if anyone had seen Ike; he'd left his house a couple of hours ago but he hadn't returned and it was getting late.

It was common for Ike to take off, but only in the warmer months and always to either Witches' Woods or the Trestle. Looking back, Mitch couldn't remember a time when he'd run off in the winter. This was really strange.

Mitch's mom asked him if he'd seen Ike that day.

"Nope."

"Ike's mom is on the phone and she sounds a little frantic," she reported.

"I haven't seen him since we played hockey down at the playground yesterday," Mitch said.

His mom went back to the phone to report to Mrs. Tiller.

It was Christmas Eve. Everybody would be busy with family, so Mitch figured he was probably out walking around. Surely he'd be home soon.

Mr. Dawson did not share Mitch's optimism.

"This is bullshit," he said after Mrs. Dawson had left the room. "It's after 8 o'clock. No kid is going to be out walking around in the dead of winter, not to mention on Christmas Eve. Nothing's open."

Mrs. Dawson was working away in the kitchen, getting ready for tomorrow, while Mr. Dawson and the kids sat in the living room. There was an uneasy feeling in the air now. They'd been watching Christmas shows on TV all night, but Mitch found it more difficult to focus on the shows after Mrs. Tiller's call, and Mr. Dawson watched the clock above the TV more than he watched the TV. Mitch could guess what was going through his mind: "How much longer am I going to sit here before I go out and look for Ike myself?" The answer? Not long.

After about thirty minutes, Mr. Dawson stood suddenly from his easy chair.

"I'll be right back." He grabbed his jacket, pulled on his boots and hat, and headed out the door.

He came back in after driving around the neighborhood for forty-five minutes. He got his stuff off, came back to the living room, and sat down in the easy chair with an uneasy look on his face. He shook his head when Mitch looked at him expectantly. He would've been surprised if his dad had come home with any info on Ike.

Ike's welfare was especially important to Mr. Dawson because he saw a lot of similarities between Ike's situation and the problems that had plagued him as a kid.

Mr. Dawson didn't say a word the rest of the night. Everyone except Mr. Dawson went to bed at 10:30. He sat in the living room in his easy chair next to the lighted Christmas tree, the TV off. He may have even sat there all night.

It must've been zero dark early the next morning when Stephi came bursting through the door, waking both Mitch and Casey.

"Come on, come on," she urged. "It's Christmas, let's go! We've got presents to open, let's go!"

There were groans all around, but the boys stumbled into the living room anyway. Sure enough, it was still dark outside. Stephanie didn't care. Casey turned on the Christmas tree lights, and Stephi tore in. Wrapping paper and bows flew everywhere; there were skates and dolls and new boots and hats and mittens and all kinds of things that needed to be opened. As Mitch reached over to grab a present, the doorbell rang, scaring the ever-loving daylights out of the kids—Casey might've even pissed his pajamas.

Mitch got off the floor to look out the window, only to see two cops standing on the front steps.

"The cops are here, get Dad," Mitch yelled.

"Huh?" Casey said, half-listening.

"Casey, you idiot, it's the cops, get Dad."

Casey started down the hallway only to be met by a pair of bleary-eyed parents.

"What the hell is going on?" Mr. Dawson demanded.

"I don't know, but there's cops outside," Mitch replied.

"Look out, get out of the way," Mr. Dawson grumbled, stepping over the minefield of Christmas presents and wrapping paper. When Dad opened the door, he invited the cops inside.

"Come on in, Harold."

Both came in and stood at the front door.

One of them was Sergeant Harold Botnich, who Mr. Dawson knew. Mitch knew Sergeant Botnich's daughter, Carla, who went to school with Mitch and lived across from Beaver Lake. Her parents got divorced last year when Mr. Botnich caught his wife playing grab-ass with the guy from the liquor store on McKnight Road.

"Sorry to bother you on Christmas, Walter. Good morning Mrs. Dawson."

Mrs. Dawson blinked at him in response.

"It's 6:30 on Christmas morning, Harold," Mr. Dawson said. "What's this about?

"Ike Tiller didn't come home last night."

Mom gasped.

"Oh my God, no."

Sergeant Botnich asked Mr. Dawson if it would be OK to ask Mitch a couple of questions. His dad looked Mitch dead in the eye.

"Harold, you can ask my boy anything you want," he reassured him. "Penny, take the other kids downstairs. Now."

Officer Botnich waited for Mrs. Dawson and the other kids to clear the room before addressing Mitch.

"Ike's mom says you guys are friends and you might know where he is."

Mitch was still kind of shocked. He didn't know what to say, but still managed to blurt out "Witches' Woods."

"The Woods?" He shook his head. "We had twenty inches of snow the other day, I doubt he's in there."

"Or maybe the Trestle?" Mitch suggested, running through their usual places. "Those are the only places I can think of."

"OK, is there anybody else who might have some information about the whereabouts of your friend?"

Mitch just kept looking at the floor and shook his head. He could feel the burn of oncoming tears, so he said "no" to keep them at bay.

"Do you have any idea why Ike might not come home?" The sergeant pressed in and Mitch kept staring at the floor, shrugging his shoulders in response to the sergeant's question.

"OK, we'll check the neighborhood and see what we can find," Sergeant Botnich assured him. "Hey, Mitchell, it's going to be OK. I appreciate you being honest with me." He patted Mitch's shoulder, "Can I have a word with your dad now?"

"Head downstairs." Mr. Dawson pointed the way. "I'm sure your mother could use you for something."

"OK."

The grown men waited until Mitch's footfalls on the stairs stopped.

"Walter, when we have a situation like this, we always call Maplewood Police and the Ramsey County Sheriff's Office," the sergeant explained. "They'll be checking places like Witches' Woods when it gets light out, though I highly doubt they'll find any tracks going in or out of the woods. We'll be checking all the corner stores tomorrow when they open."

"As for the Trestle, we'll be checking up there, too, but let's hope he's nowhere near it. The Trestle is a bridge full of crazies this time of year. People congregate up there at Christmas, building fires and drinking and carrying on."

"I had no idea," Mr. Dawson replied. "That really happens up there?"

"No matter how cold and shitty it is, they're up there every year," the sergeant warned. "Let's just hope the Tiller boy steers clear of it. A couple of the worst calls I ever answered were up to the Trestle on Christmas. Both were suicides. People go up there because they have no place else to go. They go there so they won't be alone on Christmas. Misery loves company, especially at Christmas, and we certainly don't need another Hack Helvik story on our hands."

"Isn't that the kid who went missing from the Trestle years ago?"

"Yup. We never found him." The sergeant paused. "Here's the problem, Walter: This kid is either holed up at someone's house... or not. That means he might still be outside someplace, so we gotta work fast."

"You know this kid has it bad at home, right?" Mr. Dawson asked.

"Yeah, the mom said the boy and his father had had a fight before the boy ran off. We hear this scenario all the time."

"This case might be a little different. Ike takes regular, severe beatings, and this is not the first time he's disappeared."

Nodding slowly, Sergeant Botnich acknowledged Mr. Dawson's input.

"All right, I appreciate the info."

"No problem, Harold, keep us posted."

"Remember, if you hear anything, let us know right away. Once we find out anything, I'll be sure to let you know," Sergeant Botnich reminded him.

Right after the cops left, Mr. Dawson went downstairs to rejoin his family.

"OK, you two," he said, pointing at Casey and Stephanie. "Get upstairs and get back to opening your presents." He didn't have to ask twice. They darted upstairs. Mitch stayed put, getting the sense that his parents weren't done with him yet.

"Mitchell," his dad inquired, "Are you telling us everything?"

Mitch kicked at the carpet a moment too long.

"Hey, quit staring at the floor and look at me," Mr. Dawson barked.

"Dad, I told the police everything. I don't know where he is and I don't know why he ran away."

"Alright, let's go upstairs," Mrs. Dawson said calmly. "We hear you Mitch. Can we get on with the Christmas festivities and let the police do their work?" She looked at both Mitch and his father pointedly.

They trooped back upstairs, re-entering the Christmas morning fray.

Casey and Stephanie had trashed the living room. There was crap everywhere. Stephanie was already wearing her new hat and mittens, and Casey got a new Winnwell goalie mask and hockey helmet. Mr. and Mrs. Dawson sat down and started opening their own gifts, but Mitch just felt like shit. Here was Christmas, and even though Mitch was surrounded by everything he could ever want in his own living room, he was finding it difficult to enjoy, despite his mother's request.

In that moment, Mitch felt so damn mad at Ike he could've killed him. Mitch tried to wrestle through it as he absentmindedly opened a gift. Why was he mad? Was it because Ike had wrecked Christmas? No. Was it because of how worried Mitch was for him? Mitch had never felt like this before. Then, another realization hit: Mitch wasn't mad at Ike; he was mad at Ike's parents.

Mrs. Dawson went to the tree and picked up another present. After reading the tag, she walked over and put it in Mitch's lap. All he could do was sit and stare at it for a minute. He already knew what the box contained, and given the circumstances, it was going to kill Mitch to open it. Sure enough, when he opened it, there was a brand-new pair of CCM Tacks. Mitch did the best he could to hold back his tears because it was Christmas, but getting a new pair of Tacks meant giving the old skates to Ike, just like he did every Christmas. Seeing the new skates made everything worse. What if there was no Ike to give his old skates to?

Mrs. Dawson treated the family to a hearty breakfast of homemade caramel rolls that morning, hoping to tide their appetites over until after church and Christmas dinner. After that, everyone pitched in to clean up the house and get ready to go to the 8:30 a.m. mass over at Blessed Sacrament.

Just as the five of them were walking into church, Mitch looked over at Casey and about died. He elbowed his dad and nodded his head in Casey's direction. Mr. Dawson turned around and looked at Casey, who was wearing his new goalie mask. He couldn't do anything but laugh and tell him to go put it back in the car.

"It's Christmas, you little shit," he chuckled.

Just like every Christmas, mass at Blessed Sacrament was a packed, drawn-out affair with the communion, the Latin, and the choir. It took almost two hours, which gave Mitch plenty of time to wonder about Ike. He even prayed for his safety; he'd never prayed for a friend before.

On the way home from church, Mr. Dawson made it a point to drive extra slowly through the neighborhood to look for Ike. Mitch and his mom kept their eyes peeled for him too; the other two were just happy it was Christmas. Casey and Stephanie couldn't wait to get home to start playing with all their stuff.

When they turned up their street, the first thing they saw was a group of four Saint Paul police cars and two Ramsey County Sheriff's cars at Ike's house.

That can't be good, Mitch thought.

As they drove slowly past the house, they could see Ike's dad in the back of one of the Saint Paul police cars, and right then, another siren blared as it approached. All the kids looked out the back window of the car and saw it was an ambulance heading toward Ike's house. Mitch felt sick to his stomach. His parents did their best to reassure the kids that everything was going to be ok, but the arrival of the ambulance sure didn't make it seem ok. Mr. Dawson pulled over and parked when he saw Sergeant Botnich. He got out of the car and walked over to talk to the sergeant. At that point, Mrs. Dawson was getting a little frantic. Mr. Dawson came back a few minutes later.

"No Ike yet," he announced. "But Botnich is going to call later when he knows more. Ike's mom is going to the hospital but is going to be fine, and they arrested Ike's dad. There's nothing more anyone can do for now, so let's get to the house and get on with our Christmas. We've got company coming, OK everybody?"

This was meant to redirect everyone's attention for the rest of the day and keep bad feelings at bay so Christmas wouldn't be spoiled for everyone else.

"By the way, Mitch, where is your tournament tomorrow?" Mr. Dawson moved the car back into the middle of the street.

It was a distraction conversation as much as a practical one.

"It's at Phalen Playground."

"What time?"

"We play a Forest Lake team at 10:00."

"Am I driving you and the guys?"

"Yup. And can you pick up Zitz too?"

"Sure."

Mrs. Dawson had prepared a big glazed ham for Christmas dinner, another one of Mitch's all-time favorites. She served the great big Christmas dinner in the newly finished basement, and to set the mood, the kids helped adorn the place with Christmas lights and decorations to enhance the festivities.

One of the other presents Mitch had received was an NHL rod hockey game. The teams were the Bruins and the North Stars, Minnesota's new NHL team. Mitch, Casey, and their cousins played rod hockey all day long, Casey wearing his new goalie mask the whole time. This distraction helped them keep their minds mostly off the Tillers.

There were many moments during the Christmas celebration when Mitch felt himself starting to have fun, but the process was arrested every time he sat down, reality hitting him in the pit of his stomach. Mitch was very aware, again, of how alien this feeling was to him, the feeling of helplessness. Helpless because he didn't know where Ike was and he couldn't do anything to help him.

The Dawson parents put on a pretty good show that day, only briefly mentioning to the aunts and uncles that Ike was missing. Mrs. Dawson was especially great at keeping her spirits up. She was cheerful, fun, and festive like usual. Mr. Dawson, however, had moments where he struggled to hide his distress. He was distracted all day—you could see it in his face. He was hosting a large family gathering in his newly minted, custom-finished rec room and bar with all the amenities, yet he kept going upstairs to look out the window by the Christmas tree. If he did it once, he could've done it one hundred times that day. He still managed to have fun with the kids, and he shared more than a few beers with the adults, but deep down he was hurting just like Mitch.

CHAPTER 15

CHRISTMAS DESOLATION

The Ramsey County Sheriff's Department, the Maplewood Police, and the Saint Paul Police checked everywhere for Ike, including the Trestle and Witches' Woods. The one place they didn't check was the golf course, which was where Ike was, forty yards from Mitch's house. When Ike left his house, he had his jacket, hat, boots, a pocket full of change, and a terrible cold. Ike felt awful. He walked out to Larpenteur Avenue to start the hitchhike to nowhere. He had no idea where to go.

He should have gone straight to Mitch's house, but he was understandably scared and uncertain. He didn't want to put a damper on their family's Christmas Eve celebration. Ike knew he had a standing invitation to the Dawson house if things ever got rough, an invitation that Mr. Dawson had himself offered.

Once he got out to Larpenteur, it was obvious it was Christmas Eve. There were no cars traveling anywhere, so he walked up to McKnight, hoping for a bus, when he chanced a glance over at the clubhouse at Hillcrest Country Club. The windchill was icy, his joints and head were aching, and he just wanted to get out of the wind for a couple of minutes, so he walked up to stand in the side doorway with the hope that a bus would show up eventually.

There were no footprints in the snow leading up to the clubhouse. There were no footprints anywhere, in fact. It looked like no one had been there since the last big snow last week. After standing in the doorway for a few minutes, he caught sight of what would end up saving his ass: the pair of warm and furnished bungalows.

Ike trudged through the snow down to the bungalow with a porch, hoping that it might be open. He turned the handle and thanked his lucky stars: There was no lock on the screen door, and the porch was filled with lawn furniture. Ike started to build himself a fort on the porch with the lawn furniture and cushions, hoping that this construction would be enough for the night. However, it didn't take long for Ike to realize that it was too cold for the porch to be his safe haven. He had to get indoors.

He surveyed the bungalow and decided his best point of entry would be to simply bust out the window of the door. So, he scrounged around the porch, found himself a short 2x4, and on the first attempt, shattered the small window, reached in, and unlocked the door, making his way inside for the night.

Once inside, he plugged up the broken window with a chair cushion from the porch. He took his boots off and left them on the porch so as to not drag in snow and dirt. He was careful not to upset anything inside the bungalow. Even though there were two bedrooms, he decided to sleep on the couch. That way, he didn't have to make a bed in the morning. The only food he found were some saltine crackers and the world's worst cookie: Fig Newtons. At the very least, he was warm and out of the weather for the night.

Now that he was safe indoors and out of the elements, he finally had time to try and understand what had happened at his house earlier that day. Usually, there was a pattern to the encounters with his dad, and somehow, it always seemed worse right after church. But this time, it hadn't started with Ike; it'd started with Ike's younger brother and younger sister. Ike's dad was enraged about absolutely nothing, and he threatened and terrorized the younger siblings. Ike's younger sister crawled under her own bed because she was so scared.

Of course, when Ike spoke up and tried to intervene, Mr. Tiller really let him have it. He hit Ike several times and called Ike "A vile unholy bastard," announcing that "a bastard has no place in the house of the Lord" and other biblical bullshit. Mr. Tiller quoted the Bible when it was convenient for his cruelty. Ike let fly plenty of curse words of his own, and that's when his dad exploded and told Ike that he's a filthy unholy bastard like his brother and to get the hell out of his house and never come back. Like usual, Ike's mom was useless.

Ike stretched out on the couch with a blanket that night. He was exhausted yet barely slept at all.

The next morning, Ike was thinking a little more clearly, but he still couldn't bring himself to go to the Dawson house because it was Christmas. Of all days to go to a friend's house when you're in need would be Christmas Day, right? Wrong. The Dawsons would've taken him in with open arms and kept him safe, warm, and fed, but Ike had spent too many years in a house that showed him no care. Could he really ask the Dawsons to help him in his hour of need when they were already so busy with their holiday?

But it was more than just concern about disrupting the holiday that kept Ike away. Underneath it all, he was afraid of what Mr. Dawson might do. Here he was, a kid who had been kicked out into the cold on Christmas Eve. That alone might push Mr. Dawson's rage right over the edge. Ike was no idiot; he knew Mr. Dawson felt a certain way toward his own father, and all he needed was a reason to go full-on dad mode. Mr. Dawson knew cruelty and desolation; he knew all about being cold on Christmas. He knew misery down on Reaney and Payne Avenue, and he knew the real darkness of days lived in Swede Hollow. He would not stand for a kid to suffer like he did.

Mr. Dawson never tried to hide the fact that he did not like Mr. Tiller, and he wasn't alone in his feelings. None of the dads in the neighborhood liked Mr. Tiller. To hear the guys talk about it over beers in the backyard, Ike's dad wasn't a real man's man. They said that anybody who hits women and children isn't worth a shit. Besides, he never came around the neighborhood to lend a hand to anyone. Everyone was sure that one of these days, that asshole would get what's coming to him—either by one of their own hands or fate's hand.

Ike saw that the buses had begun running again, so he made sure the coast was clear as he left the bungalow behind and headed back to Larpenteur Avenue. Ike caught the number 9 bus. For ten cents, you could ride the bus all day, and that's almost what he did.

He rode the bus all Christmas morning, but as he came back through downtown, he noticed a crowd outside the Union Gospel Mission, which Ike knew meant food. They were giving out free Christmas dinners.

Ike jumped off the bus, ran over to the Mission, and got in line. He didn't know if he would have to tell them who he was, but as soon as he got to the food line, they cheerfully served up a great big turkey dinner, no questions asked. He sat down in the mission hall and looked around the room to get a sense of how bad some people had it.

Because Ike's religion doesn't celebrate Christmas, he really didn't understand what he was seeing. All these people—young, old, and everything in between, including little children—were both destitute and happy at the same time.

All the people were very nice, both the people serving and the people receiving, but a few of them started to ask questions about why this teenage boy was here by himself, so he thought it'd be a good time to go.

Ike went back out to the bus stop and waited for the next bus, not sure where he would go next.

As he boarded the bus, Ike could feel his cold becoming something worse. He felt feverish, even sweating a little bit, and he was aching all over.

The bus came up East 7th Street from downtown and turned on to White Bear Avenue. There were probably about twenty-five people on the bus with Ike, and when the bus pulled up in front of Blessed Sacrament Catholic Church, everybody got off the bus for Christmas mass. Everybody looked happy, the streets and buildings looked festive, and Ike was left alone on a bus, so he decided to get off too.

People were congregating for the noon service, also known as the hangover mass, at Blessed Sacrament. Had the Dawson family gone to the later mass, they probably would've seen Ike.

The first thing Ike noticed was how packed the church was. It was standing room only, so Ike stood in the vestibule for a while. But then he noticed the steps leading up to the balcony. He climbed the close stairway with others looking for a seat to enjoy the mass. Once in the balcony, he looked out over the congregation. He could see some kids he knew from school and their families. The balcony was just about full at that point, so Ike went up and found himself a seat in the back by the choir.

Ike really enjoyed what he saw and heard that day. The Blessed Sacrament choir was decked out in their best finery to sing for the service. When mass was over and people were filing out of church, Ike thought he'd stay for a while.

And stay he did. He filed downstairs with everyone else, and then, when no one was looking, managed to creep back upstairs to the balcony. He grabbed a missal on his way and sat on the floor between two pews in the back to read for a while and digest that big Christmas dinner from the Mission. Predictably, Ike nodded off, the missal slipping from his hands as he fell into slumber.

CHAPTER 16

B.S. AND FATHER O'DEA

Like he did after every mass, Father O'Dea walked through the church, looking for hats and mittens and anything else his congregants may have left behind. There was always a call later in the day for one thing or another. It was during this survey that the good father stumbled upon Ike on the balcony.

Father O'Dea rapped Ike on the foot to wake him. Ike awoke afraid, sick, and confused. It took him a minute to remember where he was and what he was doing.

"Son, what are you doing here?" O'Dea inquired. Ike was bewildered.

"I must've fallen asleep."

"Just the endorsement a Roman Catholic priest prays for," O'Dea chuckled. "Someone falls asleep during his Christmas mass and doesn't even wake up to go home. I know my Latin isn't very good, but to put someone asleep? That's pretty bad." The priest spoke in a thick Connemara brogue.

"It's not like that, Your Highness," Ike pleaded.

"Your highness, indeed," chuckled the priest again. "I'm Father O'Dea." He paused before continuing. "You're asleep in a church, son. On Christmas day, no less, and I don't recognize you. Be straight with me, boy, and tell me what's going on."

It took some time, but Ike finally confided his situation.

"My family is Jehovah's Witnesses, Father, we don't celebrate Christmas."

"Well then, that leads me to my next question. What then are you doing here in the Church of the Blessed Sacrament?"

"It's a long story, Father," Ike lamented.

Father O'Dea sat down in the pew in front of Ike and twisted around to face him.

"Would you care to tell me about it?" O'Dea asked.

Ike knew he couldn't keep everything bottled up any longer. For the first time in the entirety of his odyssey, he broke down and bawled his eyes out.

"They don't want me, Father, nobody wants me," Ike snuffled out. "I don't know what I did. We fight all the time. My dad hates me. He calls me horrible names and says the most terrible things to me, all in the name of God. Last night, on Christmas Eve, he threw me out of the house and told me to never come back." Ike wept.

He spent a couple minutes getting it out of his system, at which point two nuns filed up into the balcony to collect the choir song books.

"Don't be afraid, son," O'Dea said, noting the look of panic in Ike's eyes upon seeing them. "They're ok. Now, tell me, young fella, what's your name?"

Ike paused, so the father coaxed.

"Come on, son, out with it."

"My name is Isaac Tiller," Ike told the priest. "But my friends call me Ike."

"Isaac, is it? My son, that is a grand name. Do you know how they describe Isaac in the Bible?"

Ike shook his head.

"No, Father. I mean, we read the Bible all the time, but I guess I never asked."

"Isaac is the 'one who laughs' or the 'one who rejoices,'" Father O'Dea proclaimed.

Ike found this ironic.

"'Laughs and rejoices, huh? Holy shit, Father, do *they* have the wrong guy." Ike scrubbed some of the tear stains from his cheeks. "I can't remember the last time I laughed or rejoiced."

That got a smile out of Father O'Dea.

"Well, young Ike, again, my name is Father O'Dea, and we have to get you home."

"Please, no, Father, I can't go home. They don't want me."

O'Dea reassured him.

"I really don't believe that," he said. "I think tempers flared, things were said, but I'll bet it's all blown over by now. Your parents will probably be worried sick."

"Oh, Father, if that were only true," Ike lamented.

Father O'Dea paused for a second before venturing on.

"Isaac, a moment ago you mentioned something. You said that your father would say terrible things to you in the name of God. Is that right? Am I remembering that correctly?"

"Yes, Father."

"And your father knows the Bible, correct?"

"Oh yes, Father, he does some ministry work at our temple of the Jehovah's Witness."

"I see." He pursed his lips in thought. "Isaac, can you tell me what your father said to you last night?"

"Do I have to, Father?"

"No, Isaac, you don't have to do anything, but I am interested to know what your father tells you 'In the name of God.'" Father O'Dea's patience was a balm to Ike's heart. Ike thought for a second, closed his eyes, and recalled the previous night.

"My father refers to me as an 'unholy bastard.'" And just like that, Ike started to cry again.

"Go on, son."

"My dad warned me that 'a bastard shall not enter the congregation of the Lord.' He must have said it ten times. I don't know what any of it means, Father."

After this revelation, it was now Father O'Dea who closed his eyes and shook his head.

"Isaac, you're sure he said those exact words? 'A bastard shall not enter the congregation of the Lord?'"

"Yeah, he says it all the time," Ike affirmed. "He used to say it to my brother Aaron before he left home and joined the Navy. He also always says 'The woman will bear the consequences of her sin.'"

Father O'Dea noticed the missal next to Ike's feet for the first time.

"Isaac, were you reading that?"

Ike nodded.

"That's good," Father O'Dea said. "It says a lot about the love of children in the Bible—there are a great many passages about children."

Father O'Dea extended his hand toward the missal, and Ike gave it to him. Father O'Dea paged through, looking for something.

"Here, this is one I want you to always remember." Father O'Dea cleared his throat. "Now, listen carefully. In Mark 10:16 it says, 'And he took the children in his arms, placed his hands on them and blessed them.' Isaac, I want you to recite this with me, okay?"

Ike looked a little bewildered, but agreed.

"All right, Father."

"Look here," he said, pointing at the verse in the missal. "Ready, boy?"

Then the two of them said the verse in unison.

"That's fine. Nicely done, my boy," the priest encouraged. "Isaac, I want you to listen to me very carefully, okay? This is the most important thing: You are loved by the Lord, you will 'Enter the congregation of the Lord,' and you will be welcomed at the gates of Saint Peter. This is a certainty, my son." The priest waited for his words to sink in. "Do you understand me, boy?"

"Yes, Father."

"I may need to have a little talk with your dad," Father O'Dea continued. "Isaac, has your father ever hit you?" Father O'Dea asked the question, but he already knew the answer.

Ike looked up at the priest and paused for a while before answering.

"Yes, Father," he confessed. "My dad hits me all the time."

"Your brothers and sisters, if you have them? What about them?"

"He doesn't hit my younger siblings, but he does terrify them," Ike replied. "And as far as my older sister, I've never seen him hit her. My oldest brother and my mother, well, that's a different story. Before my brother left home, he caught beatings on a regular basis just like me. I've seen my dad hit my mom on many occasions too."

Ike could see the gears turning in Father O'Dea's mind as he searched for the right things to say.

"Yes, my boy, I'm definitely going to have a word with your father. And, in any event, what are we to do with you? You have to go home." He paused before continuing. "Here are my options: I can call your parents or I can call the police. If you've been gone now for a while, there's no doubt they're looking for you."

No doubt, indeed. Ike didn't realize it at the time, but while he was at Blessed Sacrament taking counsel with the good priest, a serious area-wide search for him was underway.

"You can't stay here, to be sure," said Father O'Dea. "Unless you want to go across the street and bunk with the old nuns?" He laughed.

Even with Father O'Dea's kind words and reassurances, Ike knew he had to get out of that church before the priest made his phone calls because, either way, it meant going home. At this point, it was less about Ike not wanting to go home and more about the fact that he'd been told directly to never come home again.

"Let's go down to my office and we'll get you squared away," said Father O'Dea. Ike nodded in agreement.

Once they were downstairs, Ike could see the place was filling up with more nuns.

"Oh my, look at the time! Here they all come."

Ike looked a little bewildered.

"The sisters are coming in for their Christmas mass before early dinner," Father O'Dea said.

Right when they reached the priest's office, Ike paused.

"Could I please use the restroom?"

"Certainly. It's right down the hall."

Ike couldn't have planned a more perfect exit because not only was the bathroom right down the hall, so was the exit. Ike walked down the hall, straight out the door, and took off running down Ames Avenue toward the Trestle.

In the space of a few minutes, since realizing he had to leave the church but also knowing that he had to find some sort of stability, Ike decided to do what he should have done last night: go to the Dawson house, which was about half a mile away. The quickest way was to go down and cross the Trestle. When he got down next to the 3M warehouses on Hazel Street, he walked three blocks north to the bridge.

One reason people were warned to stay off the Trestle at night was because there's no light source up there. But that night, as Ike walked up Hazel Street, he could see that wasn't the case that evening. There was a huge fire at the Trestle inside what looked like a big steel barrel. This should have sent Ike running the other direction, but he kept moving up toward the bridge, making sure to stay out of sight. As he went past the flower shop and greenhouse, which were situated right before the Trestle, he could hear people carrying on. This must've been some kind of Christmas party.

Once he got closer, he could see that there might be a dozen or more people up there drinking and partying. He didn't know if they were just older kids having fun or some bums. At that point, he'd begun to feel even sicker, so he'd turned around and started to walk away from the Trestle. Because of the snow, there was no way to pass under the Trestle to the other side. His walk of a few blocks had just turned into a mile and a half, a daunting task for someone under the weather.

When Ike passed behind the flower shop on his way back up to White Bear Avenue, he noticed the greenhouses anew. If there was any chance Ike could get in there, even for a little while to keep warm, maybe he could wait out the Trestle party for a couple hours and then head to the Dawson house.

He went to the door of the greenhouse, which was unlocked. Ike slipped in. It was dark, warm, and smelled wonderful. It was Christmas in Minnesota and yet flowers were in bloom. Ike sat down on a pile of fertilizer bags. He couldn't make any noise because the flower shop was only about thirty feet from the house where the shop owners lived. But when the trains came rumbling through under the Trestle, you could make all the racket you want. The greenhouse was less than fifty yards from the tracks.

Within a few minutes, Ike could see car lights heading up the path to the Trestle. Then he saw a spot light. It was the cops, and they weren't there to bust up the party, he realized. They were there looking for him. His heart raced. Father O'Dea had made the call. Ike sat quietly and waited for them to leave.

Ike made himself comfortable on the bags of fertilizer and began to replay in his head everything that had happened to him in the last twenty-four hours. It seemed like the fight between him and his father had happened a month ago, but the pain of it all was still very fresh.

Ike began to process the things that Father O'Dea had said to him at Blessed Sacrament—how he was not alone in the eyes of the Lord and that he was loved. While these words gave him some comfort, it also compounded the confusion that he felt. Why did this have to come from a complete stranger, a Catholic priest no less in a church he'd never been to before? Why couldn't he ever feel this way in his own house with his own family?

The only affection that Ike had ever felt in his house came from his dog, Buster. Ike realized with a pang how much he missed his dog. Hopefully one of his siblings had taken it upon themselves to feed Buster and make sure he wasn't put out in the cold like Ike had been. His mind then moved to his brothers and sisters and the cruelty that they would endure in his place. His dad would surely find someone else in the family upon whom to unleash his wrath. All these things swirled in Ike's mind as he fell asleep on the fertilizer.

When Ike went down, he went down hard. The night was fraught with fever dreams, and he never made it across the Trestle that night. When Ike woke up the next morning, he stood up and looked outside, then sat back down and noticed he was soaking wet: His fever had broken overnight. The warmth of the greenhouse probably had something to do with it. Ike was feeling better than yesterday but still wasn't feeling great, so he laid back down on the fertilizer to close his eyes just for a couple more minutes, hoping he wouldn't be discovered by the flower shop folks first.

When Ike woke up next, it was the middle of the afternoon. He'd just had his first real sleep in days. The flower shop must've been closed for Christmas because no one had bothered him and it looked like the shop itself wasn't open. Luck had shone on Ike again. Ike left the greenhouse as quietly as he'd come, looked around to make sure the coast was clear, and made his way toward the Trestle.

Ike hadn't eaten since the meal at the Mission on Christmas day and was starving. He still had some change in his pocket, so once he crossed the Trestle, he headed toward Lou's Food Market on White Bear Avenue and Maryland Avenue for something to eat.

Ike didn't make it a block down Maryland before he was met by three Saint Paul Police patrol cars. He stopped dead in his tracks. Sergeant Botnich got out of the first car and approached Ike.

"Hey, Ike, we've been looking for you." His voice was steady as he took a few steps toward Ike. "Come on over here and we'll get this figured out."

Ike knew the journey was over, so he went over and climbed in the backseat of the sergeant's squad car.

"How much trouble am I in?" Ike asked. "After my dad threw me out, I couldn't go back home."

"You're not going home now," the sergeant promised. "Nobody's there."

"I don't understand," Ike said, puzzled. "Where are they then? Are they OK?"

"I'll explain everything to you soon. But first, let's talk about you."

After the sergeant asked him some questions of his whereabouts over the last couple of days, he reassured Ike that he wasn't in any kind of trouble, except for maybe breaking into the bungalow at the golf course.

"Now listen, Ike, you're going to have to answer for the damage at the golf course, but I wouldn't worry too much about that. I'll talk to Sid Getz and let him know what happened."

Ike's stomach gurgled loudly.

"When did you last eat, Ike?" The sergeant was concerned.

"Yesterday at lunch time."

It was decided that Ike needed to get some food in him right away before taking him to the hospital, so they headed to Lou's for a sandwich.

TOURNEY TIME

Manny and EZ were at the Dawson's house by 8:30 a.m. the morning after Christmas, ready to head down to Phalen Playground for the annual Christmas hockey tournament. Every year, Phalen Playground would put on a hockey tournament for the neighborhood teams during Christmas vacation. All they had to do now was pick up Zitz and head over to the playground.

Once they picked up Zitz, Mitch told them about Ike not coming home. They all wondered aloud about what may have happened to him.

"Hey, you guys should start thinking about playing hockey," Mr. Dawson encouraged. Don't worry about Ike, he'll be OK."

Mitch didn't know if his dad really believed it, but that's what a dad says with a carload of kids going to a hockey tournament.

When they got to Phalen Playground, it was obvious how huge a production this tournament was. Every playground has lights for their ice rinks, but the lighting they brought in for this tournament looked like something from Met Stadium, with huge generators to power the lights.

A-midget, B-bantam, and A-peewee hockey teams were participating in the tournament. The tournament hosts had two rinks going day and night, and they used a truck with a big roller brush on the front to clean the ice between games. To re-surface the ice, they flooded the rinks using a contraption with a big water tank on it. They even had portable warming houses teams could use as locker rooms.

The rinks had freshly painted lines, and the ice was just like glass. And, while the ice may have looked nice, it chipped up easily. The funky Zamboni contraption they used laid on the water too heavy, which made the ice brittle. If there was anything the guys learned from years of flooding the hockey rink at Hayden Heights Playground, it was that "a lot of thin is better than a little thick." Hayden Heights had the best ice in the city, and the tournament coordinators could have learned a thing or two. They'd have been better off spraying the surface lightly several times.

The weather was perfect for this year's tournament. The temperature was in the mid- to high twenties for the whole tournament—perfect outdoor hockey weather.

And good for Ike, wherever he was, Mitch thought.

Oh, the beloved Phalen Playground, the *darling* of the Saint Paul playground system. If your playground got something new, Phalen already had three of them. Phalen had it newer, better, and sooner than anywhere else, which is just one of the reasons nobody liked Phalen Playground. The other reason? Phalen teams were very good at every sport.

To the Minnesotan hockey world, Phalen Playground was considered the cradle of East Side hockey. A lot of great players came from the Phalen neighborhood specifically, but there was a lot of great hockey being played all over the East Side—up at Hayden Heights and playgrounds like Lockwood, Prosperity, Wilder, Hazel Park, and Conway.

Mr. Dawson dropped the guys off at the building and then went to find a place to park. They walked down to the warming house to find the rest of their team. After a few minutes navigating the tournament chaos, Mitch spotted Randy McKay, their goalie, and some of the other guys. He'd moved up by Mitch's house a couple years ago, which was the best thing that had ever happened to their hockey team. Randy was a fantastic goalie, and his dad was their coach.

Once the guys caught up with Randy and his dad, Coach McKay had a little Christmas surprise for the whole team: new Hayden Heights stocking hats, each with their jersey number pressed on. The boys tried them on—they almost looked like an official team. The hats were compliments of the team sponsor, Jerry's Drive-In on White Bear Avenue. Jerry's had the best fried chicken and onion rings in the history of chicken and onions.

There were teams from all over the Twin Cities, but besides the Phalen team, Hayden Heights was the only other bantam team from the East Side. You could walk around in the blue and gold uniforms of Hayden Heights, and a lot of people recognize the team, but they wouldn't actually know where Hayden Heights was.

"You boys are from Hayden Heights, right? Is that near Anoka?" one hockey mom remarked. Hayden Heights was like Shop Pond. "Where the hell is Shop Pond?" one may ask. Hardly anyone knew where the Shop Pond gang was from. Truth is, they were from the North End and mostly Rice Streeters—and, as it would turn out, they were the best team in the tournament.

That's the thing about Hayden Heights. It's technically in Saint Paul, but just barely. It's hidden in the farthest northeast corner of the city, just past Hillcrest Shopping Center. Even people who lived in Saint Paul proper couldn't tell you where the neighborhood was on the map.

There were two reasons the Hayden Heights team got into the tournament at all: One, they were a good, solid hockey team, and two, Randy's dad, the coach, used to coach at Phalen, so he knew the guys who put on the tournament. It was an opportunity for the boys to show their skill, so they were determined to have a good showing; otherwise, Hayden Heights might never be invited back.

It was common tournament practice to place the host team in the weakest bracket to ensure an easy path to the championship game. Phalen was no different, so of course their matchups were slated to be the easiest. They were the only good team in their bracket, paired against weak sisters like Fridley, Columbia Heights, a team from West Saint Paul, and a couple other tomato cans. Hayden Heights, on the other hand, was in the strong bracket, slated to play teams like North Saint Paul, South Saint Paul, Shop Pond, Minneapolis, and Forest Lake.

When the boys emerged from their warming house for the first game one hour after arrival, the crowd had doubled. The place was buzzing. Winter Carnival Vulcans showed up to wreak havoc among the crowd and smudged the faces of all the females who would let them. The Saint Paul Fire Department had built a blazing bonfire by the monkey bars.

As the rest of the guys on his team skated down toward the rink on the ice path, Mitch stayed up by the warming house a few seconds longer to look over the crowd, hoping to catch a glimpse of Ike. Ike had no reason to be down there watching a hockey tournament of all things; he was probably somewhere trying to stay warm. But Mitch couldn't help himself. He hoped that he might see his friend.

As Hayden Heights began their warm-ups on Rink 2, a nice crowd began to line the boards to watch the game. There were a lot of parents and other familiar faces—like Gloria, Joy, and Izzy who had come down with EZ's mom and dad. Snag and Crime Scene's presence was a real surprise. The team was missing a couple of guys because of Christmas vacation, so they had decided to run with two forward lines and two sets of defensemen. Coach McKay moved Mitch back to defense, a position he loved to play because he could see the rink better and got to unload his shot more often.

In the first game, Mitch had two assists: one on EZ's break-away goal, and the other when Zitz tipped his shot from the point. Manny unleashed a bomb in the third period to seal it. Forest Lake pulled their goalie with a minute left, and Zitz got an empty net goal. Randy was stellar as usual. Hayden Heights beat Forest Lake, 4-1, and would face the winner of the Shop Pond vs. South Saint Paul game. You always knew when South Saint Paul was playing because of the frickin' annoying cowbells their fans were always clanging.

At the end of the game, Hayden Heights shook hands with the other team and then skated back to the warming house. Another game had started on the other rink: East Side Midgets vs. North Saint Paul. All the guys on these teams were huge. Reno Petri, Izzy's brother, played for the East Side Midgets. They were good every year.

The dream of every kid in this part of the East Side of Saint Paul was to one day play hockey for Johnson High School. On their way to playing for the Johnson Governors, the kids wanted to play for the East Side Midgets, whose home rink was at Hayden Heights Playground.

Once Mitch got his skates off, he found his dad over by the concession stand. His dad bought him a hot dog and a pop to re-energize him.

"You guys don't play again until 2," he informed them. "Do you guys want to go home or stay here?"

"I want to stay here and watch some hockey."

"That's fine," his dad agreed. "I'm going to go up to the parking lot. Merv Chambers wants to show off his new work van."

Merv was Dave Chambers' dad, and Dave played for Mitch's team. Mr. Chambers had a plumbing business and never went anywhere without a case of Hamm's beer in his van.

If this were any other day, Mr. Dawson would be set: watch some hockey, have a few beers with the other dads, grab a hot dog here and there, and even take a couple of pulls off the bottle of peppermint schnapps he often had in his jacket. This could've been a perfect day for the old man, but because he had to drive the guys, there was no beer and no schnapps for him—just a lot of coffee.

The guys walked over to watch the midget hockey game for a while. It was a barn burner. They caught up with Gloria, Izzy, and Joy, all of whom had their skates on. They had been taking shifts watching the games and flying around the general rink. Gloria knew a lot of the guys on the East Side Midgets. Mitch and the guys happened upon the girls in the middle of a conversation about Snag and Crime Scene.

"Charlotte told me that Bev has the hots for one of the guys playing for North Saint Paul," Gloria said. "He went to Hill High School, and they jumped on the 14-B bus and rode down here for the day."

Well, that explained their appearance—they weren't there to watch the Hayden Heights team play after all.

Final score: 5-2, East Side Midgets.

Gloria had all the high school guys sniffing around her at all times, which made Mitch mad as hell. He hated seeing guys milling around her.

But, there were plenty of girls skating around, so he tried to distract himself by watching them swoop around in their white figure skates and fuzzy mittens. But the queen, Gloria, was ever present; she skated circles around them with her Bauer Supreme hockey skates and Cooper hockey gloves.

Every time Mitch turned around, the crowd was bigger. Even some girls from Hazel Park Junior High were there. The place was just rockin'. If you lived on this side of Lake Phalen, you went to Cleveland Junior High, but if you were up by Hillcrest, you'd go to Hazel Park Junior High.

"Hey, Mitch!" Renée's voice broke Mitch from his reverie.

"Hey, Renée," he said, turning around to locate her. "What are you guys doing here?"

"You told us about the tournament, remember?" Renée grinned. "We came here to watch you guys play hockey, you idiot." She waited a second. "Good game, by the way."

All the girls from Christmas Eve at Shoppers' City, including Della and Maggie, were there.

"You came all the way down here for hockey?"

"You know we all live just on the other side of the lake, right?" Renée pointed out.

"Oh, no, I didn't know that." Mitch shrugged. "So did you walk around the lake or did you get a ride?"

"Neither," she answered proudly. "We walked across the lake."

"No shit, that's cool," he declared, impressed.

Maggie sidled up to Mitch. He was surprised by this move, but she made him feel comfortable right away.

"Renée's right: You played a really good game out there," she said with a smile.

"You sound a little surprised."

"I guess I was a little," she confessed.

"What time is your next game?" Melanie asked.

"We play at two o'clock, and it looks like we're going to play Shop Pond."

"What the hell is Shop Pond?" Renée asked, puzzled.

"Never mind, it's not important." Mitch waved off her question.

Mitch hung out and talked with the girls for a while. They caught up on Christmas, and Mitch told them about Ike, even though most of them didn't know him. He was a quiet kid on all accounts and not very popular.

Every once in a while, Mitch would shoot a glance around the grounds to see if he could spot his teammates; he wanted to keep tabs on them as their next game approached. The last time he looked up, he saw Gloria glaring at him with a look of disapproval. What could he have possibly done? He looked further, about ten feet from Gloria, and spotted EZ and Randy holding court with some girls he didn't know. EZ waved him over just as Renée and her crew decided to go warm up in the warming house.

"We'll be out to watch your game in a little while," she said, shivering.

"Alright."

Mitch went over to join up with EZ and Randy. It turned out that the girls were from Cleveland; Randy knew them growing up in the area surrounding Lake Phalen. EZ had them all laughing, surprise surprise. He wanted to introduce Mitch.

"Ladies, this is my pal, my best pal in the whole world, Mitch Dawson," he announced, throwing his arm around Mitch's shoulders. "We call him Doc. He's the Mayor of Hazel Park Junior High." He laughed in his hearty way.

"Ah, um, hi," Mitch fumbled.

"The girls told me there's a dance tonight at Arlington Playground, and they've invited us to go," EZ relayed.

Mitch was pleasantly surprised.

Wow, this came out of nowhere.

"By the way, I'm not the mayor of anything," Mitch clarified. "My boy EZ thinks he's hilarious."

After talking with the Cleveland girls for a while, Mitch noticed the time.

"EZ, Mac, we gotta get ready for the game."

When he turned around, all the girls from Hazel Park were standing right behind him, which made him feel a little uneasy. He's talking to these new girls from Cleveland, *and* there's a bunch of girls from Hazel Park who had come to see his team play—plus Della and Maggie. All of them were busy giving each other dirty looks when Gloria and Izzy walked up, barging right past all the other girls. Talk about timing. Gloria looked Mitch right in the eye but directed her words to EZ.

"Eric, don't you guys have a game coming up?"

Why was she looking at Mitch? He was so far in the weeds, he had no clue what was happening.

All the Hazel Park girls were friends with Izzy and Gloria, whereas the Cleveland girls only knew Gloria by reputation. They gave her a wide berth.

EZ gloated.

"Well, ladies, we gotta go prep for the next game. So, on behalf of my teammates, I'd like to thank you all for coming out to see me today." The girls groaned and rolled their eyes with a laugh.

"Come on, guys, let's head in," Mitch urged. "We'll talk about the dance later."

"Dance?" Gloria exclaimed. "What dance?"

The guys just kept walking.

Once they'd made it some distance away, EZ poked fun at Mitch.

"Hey Doc, I gotta hand it to you: You're about as smooth as a head-on collision."

"Kiss my ass, EZ."

As Mitch walked into the warming house, he was trying to get a grip on what the hell was going on with the opposing groups of girls. He'd gotten up that morning expecting to play in a tournament, net himself a few sweet goals and assists, and that's it. He had no clue he was going to get tangled up in any of this drama shit—and he wouldn't admit it to anyone, but it was kind of fun.

CHAPTER 18

NICE HATS

Hayden Heights was playing their best hockey of the year against Shop Pond, but after two periods, they were down 1-0. These guys had shut out South Saint Paul, 4-0, in their first game. These cats were tough, and they just kept coming.

Mitch and the guys lucked out on the timing of their best hockey performance. There was a great crowd watching their game, and there was no game on the other rink, so this was the only show.

Between the first and second period, Mitch looked around. He saw his parents, the warring factions of girls—Cleveland on one side and Hazel Park, including Della and Maggie from Hibbing, on the other. Gloria was standing next to Maggie and served as the anchor for the Hazel Park girls. It was almost too much to see them standing side by side. They were both stunning. It was a scene Mitch would never forget.

There must have been a hundred people watching. Even the Sasquatch sisters, Char and Bev, were still skulking around, scaring small children.

Some of the South Saint Paul parents had stayed to watch the game just to cheer against Shop Pond.

The Channel 5 news truck had just rolled in to cover an evening peewee game: Phalen vs. Hastings, two of the top peewee teams in the state. This was the premier game of the tournament. The Channel 4 truck arrived shortly after.

Near the end of the second period, Zitz made a rush down the middle and unloaded a slap shot just inside the blue line.

It hit the goalie right between the eyes. The SOB went down like a ton of pucks. True to form, all the South Saint Paul fans cheered and rang their stupid cowbells when the goalie went down, and they booed him when he got back up. Class act.

Some of the other parents, including Walter Dawson, started yelling back at the idiot bell ringers. There was a lot of shouting, and someone even threatened to ram a cowbell up someone's ass. It seemed the crowd might get really rowdy, but it calmed as fast as it came up. Shop Pond's original goalie went out of the game and they sent in their other goalie, the one who threw the shutout against South Saint Paul. Shop Pond was one of the only teams in the tournament that had two goalies. The rest were lucky to have one.

Randy McKay must've seen forty shots by the end of the second period for Hayden Heights. They were playing tough, but those guys were flat out good.

The Cleveland girls were standing behind the net, cheering Randy on. Right near the end of the game, there was a face-off on Hayden Heights' end, and when Mitch looked behind the net at the girls, four of them were wearing Hayden Heights stocking caps, just like the ones Coach had given the team before the tournament. Mitch certainly knew he was playing a hockey game at that moment, but he couldn't help but wonder where the hell they'd found those hats. Then he realized what they must've done: They had gone into their warming house and taken them. Those were their hats.

Just before they dropped the puck, one of the girls yelled.

"Hey, boys, how do you like the hats? If you want them back, you better come to the dance tonight."

Final score: 1-0, Shop Pond.

Shop Pond would play Phalen tomorrow for the championship, and Hayden Heights would play South Saint Paul for third place.

When Mitch and the rest of the team came out of the warming house after the game, there was no sign of the Cleveland girls. Gloria, Izzy, Joy, and the rest of the Hazel Park girls hung around and gave them a couple of atta boy whacks on the back, and Renée and Melanie even provided some hugs

You could see that the whole crowd had migrated over to the other rink to watch the featured Hastings vs. Phalen peewee game. It was cool to see the camera crews from the TV stations at work. Hal Scott from Channel 4 was interviewing a coach from Phalen about ten feet from Mitch and EZ, who took the opportunity to stand in the background waving like little kids. Channel 5 was talking to Hastings. It was a really good peewee game, so the guys stayed and watched for a while. It was 2-1 in favor of Hastings after the first period when Mr. Dawson found Mitch.

"Find your buddies, Mitch. It's time to roll."

It didn't take long for Mitch to find the other guys; they said goodbye to the gals and headed for the Dawson's Olds wagon. As they were pulling out of the parking lot, Mr. Dawson held his nose dramatically.

"I think I'm gonna take you guys to Como Zoo," he howled. "You guys smell like a carload of damp gorillas."

The boys all laughed.

They drove in silence for a few minutes while Mitch calculated what had happened with the Cleveland girls and their hats.

"You know, I can't figure it out, guys," he started. "How'd the Cleveland girls know which four hats to take?"

The other guys looked at each other in confusion and Mr. Dawson started laughing.

"You mean you haven't figured it out?" he teased. "I told them."

"You what?" Mitch yelped.

"Yeah, they were milling around and giggling outside of the warming house. I said, 'Hi girls, it looks like you're up to no good.' One of them blushed and nodded. They told me what they wanted to do, so I took them into the warming house and pointed out all your guys' stuff, and they grabbed your hats. I thought it was funny as hell. How about you guys?" Mr. Dawson laughed some more.

"Well, that's funny, Dad, but we know how to get them back."

"What do you mean?" he asked.

"They told us that we have to go to the dance tonight at Arlington Playground to get our hats back."

"Is that so?"

"Oh, by the way, Dad, I wonder if I could go to a dance down at Arlington Playground tonight?"

"Well, that all depends," Mr. Dawson said with a chuckle. "What time is your game tomorrow?"

"We don't play till 1:30."

Mr. Dawson nodded.

"OK, that might work."

"Well, we'd need a ride too. Could you take us?"

"Your mother and I are going to Hafner's Bowl tonight with Eric's mom and dad, so you'll have to find another way."

"We can take the 14-B bus," EZ suggested. "It goes right to the playground."

"That's a good suggestion, Eric," Mr. Dawson said. "Let me talk to your mom, Mitch."

After driving around the lake, they turned up Maryland Avenue and headed up toward Lou's for a couple loaves of Roma bread. As they got closer to the store, snow began to fall hard and fast.

The guys weren't talking about the two really good hockey games they'd played that day' they were talking about going to the dance tonight—what time they should meet and should they call some of the other guys. Just as they approached the entrance of the parking lot, an ambulance came up behind them. Mr. Dawson pulled over and the ambulance went right past them into Lou's parking lot. There were already two cop cars in the lot.

Mr. Dawson drove slowly and found a spot a safe distance away. Naturally, they all wondered about what was going on; they could see people were still coming in and out of Lou's, so it must not be *that* bad. Mr. Dawson left the car running.

"OK, you guys sit tight," he instructed. "Stay here and I'll be right back."

They all went back to talking about the girls and going to the dance.

About ten minutes later, Mr. Dawson came out of Lou's with the loaves and got back in the car.

"What's going on, Mr. Dawson?" EZ asked.

Mr. Dawson turned and looked at Mitch, then paused.

"It's Ike Tiller."

"What?" Mitch's heart began beating faster immediately. "What do you mean 'it's Ike Tiller'? What's going on?"

"Ike is in there right now and he's going to be OK," Mr. Dawson stated calmly. "Apparently he came into the store a little while ago with the police."

"Where has he been? Can we take him home, or to our house?" Mitch began a barrage of questions but was stopped short.

"Mitchell, listen to me: He hasn't eaten in a while, and he's probably dehydrated. They're going to take him to the hospital and make sure he's OK."

The boys all sat back and took a collective sigh of relief. It was quiet in the car for a good minute. Mitch didn't like the look on his dad's face, and he certainly didn't like the tone of his voice. It worried him. Mr. Dawson had turned back around and was staring straight ahead, the car running but still parked.

"I talked to Sergeant Botnich," he told them in a low voice. "He told me that the Saint Paul police and Ramsey County are looking into the situation now."

"Dad, I don't understand," Mitch pleaded. "What does all that mean? Did Ike break the law? Is he in real trouble?"

"I'll fill you in later. We better get going. It's really starting to come down."

"Fill me in later?" Mitch erupted. That was complete bullshit. He'd been worried to death about Ike for the last two days; he thought he might be dead.

Mitch slammed open the car door and ran up to the store. Mr. Dawson rolled down the window.

"Mitchell, get your ass back here!" he yelled.

Mitch went into the store anyway. He had to see Ike with his own eyes.

Ike was sitting on a stool, his back to the door, eating a sandwich Lou had made for him. A blanket had been draped over his shoulders. Lou, the cops, and the paramedics were all talking together.

"Hey, Ike."

Ike turned toward Mitch. He looked rough. The boys waved at each other, which was really all Mitch needed. He turned around and walked out, almost bumping into Father O'Dea from Blessed Sacrament. Mitch paused outside and saw the priest walk straight over to Ike. *That's odd*, Mitch thought.

His dad honked the horn, which made Mitch move back to the car, expecting a good tongue thrashing because he'd just ignored a direct order from his old man.

Mitch got back in the car tentatively, but his dad just looked at him in the rearview mirror and didn't say a thing. He backed out of the parking spot and headed home.

It was snowing a lot heavier by the time Mr. Dawson pulled back out onto the street. Mitch hoped that the peewee game had finished so they wouldn't have to postpone it until tomorrow. That was the tough thing about outdoor hockey tournaments— or baseball tournaments for that matter. If the weather got bad, it'd screwed up the whole tournament schedule.

It was quiet in the car the rest of the way home until EZ piped up.

"What time are we going to meet for the dance?"

It felt funny for him to mention it. In the short period of time since seeing Ike, Mitch had forgotten all about hockey and the dance.

"Let's do a call later to figure out when to leave," Mitch suggested, his focus entirely on Ike at the moment.

Mr. Dawson dropped each guy off, driving through slush. There were already plows coming down White Bear Avenue, and by the time Mr. Dawson pulled into their own driveway, they couldn't see across the street the snow was coming down so heavy.

CHAPTER 19

WINTER DRIVING

"Listen, Mitch," Mr. Dawson said, shifting the car into park once they'd reached the driveway. "About Ike. According to what he told the police, he didn't run away from home... his dad threw him out of the house. This is going to get very bad for them, and there's no telling what's going to happen." He sighed. "But anybody who throws a kid out onto the street in the dead of winter, on Christmas Eve no less, has to answer for it."

Mitch's dad waited for his words to sink in before he continued.

"This is serious business, pal, and I want you to do me a favor: I don't want you talking about this to all your friends and speculating and trying to figure out what's going on. We don't know for sure, so let's just hold off on the rumor mill for now. Just concentrate on hockey and what we know: Ike is safe, and they're going to get him help."

Mitch nodded, grabbed the bread off the car seat, and got out of the car to haul his stuff from the back of the station wagon.

Mr. Dawson went straight into the garage to try and fire up the snowblower. With a big yard comes a long driveway, and he wanted to get a head start on the snowfall. He'd bought the used snowblower a couple years ago, though he couldn't say it'd served him well. He always had it in the repair shop because he hardly ever got it started. In moments like this,

Mitch knew his dad would be best left alone, so he walked past him into the house.

Mitch went to the basement to hang up his stuff so it could dry out overnight. Mrs. Dawson was already down there doing some laundry.

"Well, how did the big tournament go?" she asked.

"We did pretty good," Mitch reported. "We're one and one, and we play for third place tomorrow."

"Oh, that's great," she celebrated. "Where is your dad?"

"He's in the garage wrestling with the snowblower."

Penny shook her head.

"That'll be a while."

"But we saw Ike!" Mitch exclaimed.

"What? Where?" Her eyebrows shot up.

"We saw him at Lou's Food Market. The cops were there, and there was an ambulance to take him to the hospital."

"Oh my God! What happened to him?"

"I didn't talk to him, but Dad said that they said he's going to be all right. He talked to Sergeant Botnich and has more details about the whole thing. I know they're taking Ike to Saint John's just to check him over."

Mrs. Dawson grabbed her laundry basket and headed upstairs.

Mitch was absolutely beat, and hungry too. He couldn't wait to dig into some ham sandwiches, but first: a big glass of Tang. Then he remembered suddenly there was a dance to attend.

He went back upstairs to figure out the details, but just as he got to the top of the steps, his mom was going out the back door all bundled up. This was unusual. Mitch knew she was not going outside to shovel snow; she must mean to ask his dad about Ike. Mitch went into the living room and stretched out on the couch. He wanted to watch the 6 o'clock news to see if he'd made it on TV at the hockey tournament.

Mitch must have dozed off for a few minutes because he woke to Casey begging him to play rod hockey in the basement.

"Shove off, Casey, I'm hungry."

Mitch got up off the couch and went into the kitchen. A glance at the clock told him it had *not* been just a few minutes—he'd been out for over two hours. It was 8 o'clock!

Damn, I forgot to talk to the guys about going to the dance.

Right then, his mom came into the kitchen.

"Oh, you're up finally. Randy McKay called and said that a girl had called him to say they canceled the dance tonight because of the snow."

"Okay. Are we still on for ham sandwiches?"

"Yes, indeed, Mitchell," his mom said with a nod. "Everything's in the fridge, and I can heat up some other leftovers too?"

"I'll take it all, I'm starving."

Mitch looked out the window and saw his dad working the driveway with the snowblower—surprisingly, it looked like it was going pretty well.

"How did Dad get the old snowblower going?" he asked his mom.

"I have no idea. Maybe he put gas in it this time." She chuckled at the memory of the last time Mr. Dawson had pulled out the snowblower.

"Mom, are you and Dad still going out tonight?"

"No, we're going to stay in. Your Dad is going to keep that driveway clear if it kills him."

Almost as if by magic, ham sandwiches and an assortment of leftovers were warmed and ready for his consumption.

"Thanks, Mom."

Mitch took the food and sat down in front of the TV. He had two big ham sandwiches, a pile of potatoes, a bowl of Jell-O, and some Christmas cookies. He'd have to wait until the 10 o'clock news to see his TV debut.

After he ate, he laid back down on the couch and didn't get up until 8:30 the next morning.

Over a foot of snow had fallen overnight. One of the benefits of living near the bus line was that it was the city's first plowing priority after a storm. Whenever it snowed, Mitch knew he'd have a clear driveway and a clear bus line down at Curve Street—the problem was getting from one to the other. The path would take you down Wyoming Avenue one block, and that itself was an adventure because Mitch's neighborhood was almost always the last neighborhood in the city to get plowed.

It usually took about three or four days for the plows to do the side streets, and by that time, the streets had developed deep ice ruts, which made driving absolutely horrible. If you didn't have your car moved off the street by the time they plowed, they would plow your right in, giving you the pleasure of spending the next two days digging yourself out, compliments of the city of Saint Paul's Snow Plow Division.

For the second day of the tournament, the Dawsons didn't have to pick up any of the other guys, so the whole family piled into the Olds wagon and took the mostly sideways run down Wyoming Avenue to Curve Street, where the 14-B bus ran. Thankfully, Mr. Dawson was an old pro at sideways driving, and he'd put brand-new snow tires on the Olds wagon right after Thanksgiving, so they had a good chance of making it.

When they got to Curve Street, though, Mitch's dad hit the brakes and slid right through the intersection and thirty yards down Wyoming Avenue toward White Bear Avenue, snow tires be damned. The only thing to do was keep going down the hill because there was no way to turn around and go back up the hill to Curve Street. So, Mr. Dawson floated that station wagon three more blocks all the way down to White Bear Avenue, where it was cleared curb to curb.

The Phalen folks did a fantastic job clearing all the snow and plowing the parking lots to get ready for the final day of the tournament.

Earlier that morning, the East Side Midgets won their tournament. Hayden Heights was up next, and then Phalen would play Edina for the peewee tournament championship. The day would end with Shop Pond playing Phalen for the B-bantam title.

All the girls from both schools had come to see the hockey games again: seven Cleveland girls, four of them sporting the boys' new stocking hats, and the girls from Hazel Park, including Maggie and Della.

Hayden Heights smoked South Saint Paul, 4-1, for third place. Mitch got a goal and an assist, EZ got a goal and an assist, Zitz got two goals. It was a pleasure to shut up those bell-ringing assholes from South Saint Paul.

The Hayden Heights team really proved themselves in the tournament. They proved that they're a solid hockey team and that Hayden Heights is no tomato can. The best part was that they showed up and played great hockey in front of a big crowd and made an impression on a lot of girls. Mitch never expected *that* to happen.

The winning teams received their trophies and then went to get changed—there was still a lot of hockey to watch and social mingling to do. In the space of about twenty minutes, the Cleveland girls re-invited Mitch and the boys to a make-up dance at Arlington Playground the following week. A very cute girl from Cleveland gave Mitch her number and his hat—to stay in touch. Mitch also learned that Renée and the girls had a lot of stuff planned while her cousins were in town, including sledding, some skating, and a New Year's Eve party at Melanie's house that everyone was invited to. What a great way to end the tournament.

A couple days after the tournament was over, EZ, Manny, Zitz, and Mitch joined Renée, Maggie, Melanie, and the rest of the girls at Aldrich Arena for a couple of high school hockey games: Hill vs. Cretin and Johnson vs. Washington. Maggie and Mitch sat together the whole time, and Mitch quickly found out that Maggie and her sister knew every bit as much about the game of hockey as he did.

His mom volunteered to drive them all home from the hockey games at Aldrich. On the ride home, Maggie asked Mitch if he was planning to go to the party at Melanie's house on New Year's Eve.

"Sure, all the guys are going," he said.

What she did next surprised Mitch.

"Well, how about we go together?" she asked.

Mitch didn't respond quickly enough.

"I don't want any confusion from any of the other girls," she said hurriedly. "I want it to be clear that you're at the party with me. Exclusively."

"Abso-frickin-lutely."

Then they kissed right there in the Olds wagon as it rumbled down Larpenteur Avenue, Mom be damned. The only drawback to going with Maggie was that Mitch wouldn't get to swap spit with every girl in the room, but being that Maggie would be the prettiest girl in the room, that wasn't really a problem.

For Mitch, the coolest part about getting to know these girls—but especially Maggie—was that they did all the talking. They asked questions, they talked about themselves. It was very unlike EZ's way, which was to entertain the girls. Mitch didn't have that kind of personality, so when Maggie did all the heavy lifting, Mitch was there for it. And wherever they went and whatever they did that whole week, Maggie and Mitch ended up sitting next to each other, and not by accident.

Mitch saw Maggie every day of that vacation, and when he wasn't seeing her, he must've filled in the time talking to her on the phone.

"Are you talking to that Maggie again, Mitch?" his mom asked one day. "Isn't that the sixth time today?"

Mitch was pretty sure she was becoming his girlfriend, but at the same time, it was hard to know with these things. Do they just happen? Mitch didn't know, but he was determined to find out.

During the holiday vacation, Maggie and Mitch played pick-up hockey down at Hayden Heights Playground together, went sledding down Devil's Hill with his friends and her cousins, and met for hamburgers at Henry's on White Bear Avenue. After every meeting, Mitch got more excited about New Year's Eve.

Then the day arrived. Izzy had convinced her brother Reno to take her to the party, and she called to ask if Mitch and the boys would like to ride along both ways.

"Hell yeah, that works out perfectly," Mitch agreed. Especially since EZ had let the guys know his plan to bring a couple six packs of Hamm's beer and Zitz had a pint of peppermint schnapps, a bottle of Night Train, and a jug of MD 20/20. Did anyone know where or how they'd procured the drinks? Nobody could (or would) tell.

The girls went all out for their party. They decorated Melanie's basement and served all kinds of food, and they'd planned party games for everyone. There were probably twenty people there. Mitch felt Maggie's presence instantly, and he stuck by her side all night.

My God, Mitch thought. *Maggie is just gorgeous.*

The events of the New Year's Eve party left little doubt that Maggie was now Mitch's girlfriend. She didn't let him go for one second from the moment they got there—except for the couple of times Mitch had to throw up in the stationary tubs in the basement. Mad Dog 20/20, never again. Thankfully, Mitch had a roll of Wintergreen Lifesavers in his pocket because Maggie found a nice corner in Melanie's basement with a little love seat. Maggie, the Iron Range vampire, proceeded to leave a trail of hickeys all over Mitch. By the next day, he looked like he'd been battered half to death with a sack of door knobs, but he happily wore the dozens of *love contusions*, even if he was compelled to wear turtleneck sweaters for a week. The damn things were unbearably itchy, but to Mitch, they were well worth it.

Thus began the long-distance love affair.

CHAPTER 20

GARAGE TALK

A month had passed since Mitch saw Ike at Lou's; he'd never gone home after visiting the hospital to get checked out. Mitch thought he might see him after Christmas break was over, but Ike and his siblings had been sent to live somewhere while the authorities sorted out the business between his mom and dad. The Ramsey County Sheriff's Office got involved, and so did the State of Minnesota Child Welfare Office. Ike's dad got in a lot of trouble.

Ike's mom had lied to the police about what had happened on Christmas Eve. When she had reported him missing that evening, she told the police that Ike and his dad had had a fight and that Ike had run away as he usually did. But by the end of January, everyone knew that wasn't true; Mr. Tiller had thrown Ike out into the cold that night after he'd rained down a flood of verbal and physical abuse.

On Christmas Day, Ike's mom called the police and told them the truth about the whole thing. Within ten minutes of that call, Ramsey County sheriffs arrived at the Tiller house to get the family around noon. In those ten minutes, Mr. Tiller had beaten Ike's mom pretty badly. He viciously cut off all of her hair for ratting him out and even threatened to kill her. When the sheriffs arrived, they separated them as they waited for the paramedics to arrive and take her to Saint John's hospital. The police took Mr. Tiller to jail while the kids watched on from a Ramsey County Family Service's van. Sarah, Jacob, and Ruth

Tiller were put under the protective care of Ramsey County, and anyone who knew the story could easily imagine just how terrified Ike's brother and sisters must have been.

Before they took her away, Mrs. Tiller told the authorities to search the house and to make sure they checked the bunker by the garage. She noted it was locked, but they had her permission to break the lock. Inside they'd find a gun safe. Mr. Tiller didn't know that his wife knew the combo. She gave the police that combo, and it was noted that she'd said, "You'll get to see what I have to live with, what haunts me day and night. Now, you'll meet the real Leon Tiller."

Mr. Tiller did not go quietly. He'd bellowed and ranted to the best of his ability.

"Don't you dare enter my house," he'd screamed. "You have no right. No authority. That's private property. I do not give consent to a search. You will all pay for this; you will all pay."

That was the normal stuff. Then he really went nuts, going on about the "Spawn of Satan" and "the unholy bastards in my house" and "a whore is a bottomless pit."

"Hell is empty and all the devils are here," he'd shouted. "Hell is empty and all the devils are here."

The cops eventually got him to the ground, cuffed him, and dragged him away, kicking and screaming.

They had entered the bunker in the Tiller's backyard, and what they found was very disturbing. There were the usual canned goods, dry goods, and water that one would expect in any fallout shelter, but what they didn't expect were the thousands of pieces of literature on the apocalypse and the end times. There were countless books about the signs of the end of the world and large-scale war, famine, disease, and crime.

They also found Leon Tiller's arsenal, just as Mrs. Tiller had promised. There were lots of handguns, rifles, shotguns, and all the ammunition needed for an armed revolution. The other thing they noticed was how poorly the shelter was constructed.

In reality, it was a death trap. There was no ventilation and no electricity; it was basically a hole in the ground with an extension cord coming from the garage.

"It sounds like Leon Tiller wasn't afraid of the end of the world—more like he was hoping for it and certainly planning for it," Mr. Dawson remarked as he shared details with the family.

It was also discovered that Leon Tiller had been in the middle of an expulsion from his Jehovah's Witness temple. Basically, he was being thrown out of his church because of his behavior toward his family, as well as the terroristic threats he'd made to other members of the temple. His actions were considered detrimental to the health and welfare of the temple and its members. It was determined that he would be shunned and thereby would realize the deepest of dishonor. Ike's mom was treated and released from the hospital after a few days of Mr. Tiller's arrest.

It had been a little over a month since Mr. Tiller had been arrested and the kids taken into Ramsey County's custody passed, but finally, Ike and the rest of his siblings were finally back home. Ike called Mitch to let him know and was eager to tell Mitch that his dad, on the other hand, was in jail down in Saint Peter, Minnesota. He didn't know for how long he'd be locked up.

"Why would they send him all the way down to Saint Peter, Minnesota, when Ramsey County has a perfectly good jail in downtown Saint Paul?" Mitch wondered to his dad.

"He got sent to Saint Peter?" Mr. Dawson seemed surprised. He paused for a minute as if to choose his words carefully. "Mitch, Saint Peter is a kind of combination jail and hospital, though for right now, you don't need to worry about that. Your buddy's home. That's what we're celebrating, right?"

"It sure is, Dad. Our boot hockey team has stunk so far this year without Ike."

The first chance he got, Ike went to visit Mitch. He banged on the door before Mitch could open it, and when he did, the first thing Mitch noticed was how great Ike looked. He looked healthy and almost happy, for once. Mitch let him inside, where he was greeted with a big hug from Mrs. Dawson. By the look on Mr. Dawson's face, Mitch bet he was just as happy to see Ike as Mitch himself.

After chatting with Mitch's mom and dad for a few minutes, Ike and Mitch went out to the driveway to talk and play a little boot hockey. Mitch remembered the pair of skates and new hockey stick from Christmas, compliments of Walter Dawson. There were some upcoming boot hockey games, and Mitch needed to get Ike up to speed. Mitch's team had gone 0-2 since Ike had been gone, and those pricks over on the other side of the Trestle reminded Mitch of it every day in school.

Ike was open about what had happened between him and his father, and Mitch mentioned how he'd heard that his father quoted the Bible during his abusive tirades.

"Yeah," Ike confirmed. "He says awful things to me and my mother. Terrible things about whores and bastards and the devil. I'm telling you, Doc, just before all this happened, he was raving more about my brother Aaron than ever. Aaron's been gone for a few years, yet my dad can't seem to let it go. Something's really wrong with my dad, and I think I'm starting to figure out why."

Mitch always thought that Ike's dad was just an unreasonable asshole. A mean, rotten, cruel asshole, but the way Ike talked about him made it sound like there was something else more sinister involved. Mitch didn't ask what Ike meant, though. He figured if Ike wanted him to know he would tell him.

Ike moved on, telling Mitch that Ramsey County had sent the younger kids to a family over by Lake Gervais in Little Canada and that he and his older sister, Sarah, went to live with a family by the state fairgrounds.

The reprieve had done him a lot of good. He'd eaten well and had had the best sleep he'd had in months, but he had really missed his little brother and sister. Despite the separation, the family was able to speak to each other on the phone every day, and the younger kids bore the whole thing surprisingly well.

Ike emphasized how obvious the changes were in his mom since they'd all been reunited.

"She seems happier," he said. "She doesn't have that constant look of dread on her face—and she even laughs sometimes."

They shot the puck around a bit before Ike continued.

"Can you guess who called every couple of days to check in on me and my sister?"

"I have no idea."

"Father O'Dea from over at the Blessed Sacrament."

"How in the world did that come about?" Mitch was shocked. For a kid kept far away from other faiths, Mitch was surprised he even knew Father O'Dea's name. Ike proceeded to tell Mitch about his time at the church on Christmas Day and how the good father had tried to help him—and had continued even though they were all home.

By the time Ike had finished filling Mitch in on the details, Ike and Mitch had moved on to working on their one-timer shots. Before long, out came Casey, adorned in his ever-present new goalie mask, ready to get in the nets. Mitch actually enjoyed having Casey playing with them, now that he was actually getting better at the game. Maybe it was the mask?

After about a half an hour more, Mitch's dad came out of the house with a beer in hand and went into the garage, closed the door, and turned on the heat. A little while later, he poked his head out the door.

"Hey, you two," he said, looking at Mitch and Ike. "Get in here."

When they got into the garage, they saw that Mr. Dawson had three chairs pulled out. Of course, Casey came in too, but Mr. Dawson told him to go back into the house. The old man wanted to sit them down for a little talk—and Mitch could tell this was less of a pep talk and more of a get-your-head-out-of-your-ass talk.

Mitch wondered how long his dad had been waiting to share his thoughts with them, but he was relieved when he made his point in a quick fashion.

"If you two knuckleheads haven't noticed, you're not little kids anymore," he explained. "Everything you do now has consequences, and the decisions you make now will affect more than just you."

"Ike, look at me," he demanded. "I want you to be crystal clear on this: If anything ever happens like this again—I don't care if it's Christmas or my birthday or the second coming—you come here. You come to this house, day or night, whatever the hour. You don't go wandering around the East Side like a frickin' piss bum. That's how people get killed. You have no idea how lucky you were for those two days. Any little thing, slipping on the ice, hitting your head, running into the wrong people, any of that stuff could have had some seriously bad consequences. And like I told you, those consequences wouldn't affect just you but everybody else around you. Do you understand me? That this is where you come?"

Ike nodded.

"This is all a part of growing up, fellas," Mr. Dawson continued in a slightly calmer tone. "Before you know it, you guys will be driving and going to high school, and your parents won't be around every split second to think for you. You're going to have to make decisions for yourself. Ike, we're all just thankful you and your family are OK. Now, you two get out of here."

Mitch didn't often hear his dad take the tone he did for the first part of their conversation; he could've sworn the old boy was getting emotional about the whole thing. Maybe it was an adult thing.

Ike and Mitch went back out to the driveway for a little more boot hockey with Casey.

Later, Mitch went inside and called EZ, Manny, and Zitz to come over to see Ike and hang out. The boys played rod hockey and shot the shit, and Mitch was able to brag about his new girlfriend, Maggie. The Dawson's cool new basement was the perfect spot to hang out with the guys; Mitch finally understood just a little bit of the pride his father felt.

In the middle of it all, more people came through the door: Gloria, Izzy, Reno, along with Mr. and Mrs. Petri, who had brought over a big kettle of spaghetti and meatballs. The party was on!

"Walter, my Pisano," Mr. Petri rejoiced. "I make-a so much sauce and meatball. When I look arounda my house, is nobody here. I look out the window. I see everybody youra house, so I bring."

Mitch thought his dad might cry. Someone made a few more calls, which led to EZ's parents' arrival, along with the whole Finch family—which wasn't so bad, actually. The Finch girls could be borderline tolerable so long as they didn't get into it with EZ. They had fun that night playing darts and listening to the music and just hanging out with all of us. The one major drawback was Snag's awful perfume. She'd got it for Christmas and wore so much it smelled like she practically bathed in the stuff.

"It's called 'White Shoulders,'" Gloria lamented.

You couldn't get within five feet of her without choking on it.

Each time more parents arrived, Ike was summoned up to the kitchen to be showered with hugs, kisses, and reassurances from the moms and knowing nods from the dads. The last two guests to arrive were Sid and John Getz, which sent a shiver down my spine. After all, Ike had broken into one of their bungalows at the golf course. As it turned out, though, they weren't mad; on the contrary, they came with bags full of stuff for Ike and his siblings in the way of sweatshirts and mittens and hats. They even presented Ike with his very own Minnesota Vikings football jersey, signed by the team. The lucky prick.

It was an oddity, but one or more of the Getz brothers always showed up at the right time. They didn't have any kids who could play with the neighbors, and none of them lived in the neighborhood, yet they were always there when they were needed. They went out of their way to help people.

The Dawsons had a full house. Mitch's sister Stephanie loved to hang out with the adults in the kitchen, and she had a partner in EZ's sister Joy. Casey, the nut job, wore his new goalie mask all night, played rod hockey until his hands were tired, and slipped his whoopee cushion under the cushions of the unsuspecting. He got Crime Scene twice. Each time, a large fart and a lot of laughs followed. Everyone all took turns shooting pool.

Later on in the evening, Ike, EZ, and Mitch were sitting on the couch when Glo and Izzy walked over. Without saying a word, Izzy looked at EZ and Gloria looked at Mitch, gazing just long enough to convince them both to get up and move. Granted, it took Izzy a couple more seconds before EZ moved, but he understood what was going on: Those girls were going to sit down on either side of Ike and stay there.

The look on Ike's face was priceless. There he was, terrified while flanked by two beauties, and there was EZ and Mitch, once again trying to understand what motivates girls to do the shit they do. It had to have been Gloria's idea. Ike seemed to have himself sorted, so EZ went and shot some pool while Mitch went to find his dad and ask to get the Polaroid because he wanted to get a picture of the moment. Gloria and

Isabella made it a point to sit with Ike the whole evening, as if to say, "Ike, you're here, you're safe, we're not going to let anything happen to you." Ike didn't know what to do with himself and the sudden abundance of beauty. They all made polite conversation, and Ike talked to them about his odyssey, but you could tell he felt out of place. Ike was relatively quiet to begin with—even before all this happened—and he didn't really mingle much with anybody else but Mitch and a couple of the other fellas, so this level of connection among Gloria, Izzy, and Ike seemed unprecedented. Maybe the events around Christmas had shifted something.

After a while, Penny Dawson brought out one of her specialty desserts: a raw apple spice cake, another one of Mitch's favorites. Mitch couldn't help but look over at Ike and the girls on the couch every once in a while to make sure Ike wasn't *too* overwhelmed. It was odd enough for him to get so much attention, and even more strange for that attention to come from beautiful girls.

They were all having a great time, but in one of his glances over to the couch, Mitch could tell there was some serious conversation taking place. You could see Izzy starting to cry, and Gloria's eyes welling up a little bit—but no tears escaped Ike's eyes. Mitch wondered if he must have been all cried out.

Nothing like this had ever happened to anyone Mitch knew. Beatings, abuse, jail? Maybe it's because he lives in this little sheltered part of the world up in the far northeast corner of the East Side, or maybe it's because people are just good at keeping secrets, but what Ike and his family were enduring was completely foreign to almost everyone... except Walter Dawson.

The conversation among the parents centered on Ike's family for most of the night. Early on, Mitch's dad wondered out loud about their financial situation, and Mr. Finch thought a call to their Jehovah's Witness temple might be in order to see if they were in a position to help out. The moms decided they would contact the other families in the neighborhood about delivering food to Ike's house in the way of hotdish, meat loaf, or fried chicken—whatever anyone could bring.

At one point in the evening, they must have got to talking about some really bizarre stuff because anytime one of the kids walked into the kitchen, the room got quiet, and the collective parents waited for the kid to leave the kitchen before any talk resumed.

The dads inevitably filed outside to look at John Getz's new Cadillac and talk shop about their own cars. Just like Mitch's dad buys a new station wagon every two years, Mr. Getz buys a new Caddy every year. There was no love lost between the Getz brothers and Leon Tiller. Leon never hid the fact that he was a raging antisemitic asshole. He'd refer to the Getz brothers as those "Christ-killing Jews" and he'd rail against their "private kike club." The Getz brothers have done so much for so many people in the area and beyond; they've been the unsung heroes for the city and neighborhood—and all Leon Tiller gave the world was nothing but hate in the name of God.

At one point, Mitch could sense his dad's temperature rising by the tone of his voice. Even from the basement, he could tell he was getting fired up about Leon Tiller.

"If that son of a bitch Tiller ever hurts those kids again, he'd better hope to God the cops get to him before I do," he stated, just enough Buckhorn Beer encouraging his bold speech.

"He hurts his wife and kids, dat Strunze," Enzo Petri piped up.

Back in the basement, Mitch thought about the Christmas he felt he had missed a month ago. It was a Christmas shrouded by the specter of a missing friend. Now, as he looked around, it seemed as if nothing had ever happened. All was right with the world again.

The words from the talk Mitch's dad had with him and Ike earlier in the garage were still fresh in his mind; words about growing up and being responsible and not being little kids anymore. Mitch knew what he said was true. Mitch could see it happening right before his eyes. Here they were, a bunch of neighborhood kids sitting around, almost acting like adults. It wasn't that long ago that the room would have been filled with insults and put-downs and threats of violence—usually EZ spouting them at Charlotte. Maybe they all realized, just for that evening, how important a moment it was that they ought to rise above childishness. Maybe tomorrow they'd be right back to the same bullshit, but for tonight, Ike was back and they were all together.

Ike was home. He's safe and happy, and two stunning girls were talking to him for some reason—plus, Mitch's friends were all there. This was better than Christmas!

And at that thought, Mitch winced at a sudden realization.

"Oh, shit. I forgot to call Maggie tonight."

CHAPTER 21

THE MOMS

The following Sunday, the neighborhood moms made their march on the Tiller household. The Dawson kitchen was filled with food: Hotdishes, cakes, dessert bars, loaves of fresh bread, and more hotdish. Penny Dawson, Mrs. Golyn, Mrs. Klaus, and Mrs. Petri assembled everything and planned to take it all up to Ike's house in support of Mrs. Tiller and the kids. The Tiller house was only half a block away, but there was so much stuff they had to pile it all into the back of the Dawson station wagon and drive it down. Mrs. Finch had promised that she would be over shortly, once her sister came by. Penny called Mrs. Tiller ahead of time to let her know they were on their way and that she could expect the neighborhood gals. Mitch's mom said that Mrs. Tiller sounded excited to see everyone and that she would make coffee. All the gals were still dressed up from church, which seemed only right given the circumstances: This is what it looks like when people come in support of a family when someone dies. It looked just like that.

When Mrs. Dawson rang the doorbell at the Tiller house, they couldn't have been more surprised when Mary Tiller answered the door. Gone was the meek, timid, and withdrawn mother of five; instead, she was dressed up—even wearing make-up—with her hair done. She looked great.

"Hello, Penny," Mrs. Tiller greeted them. "Please, come in, ladies."

After everything was brought in, Mary served coffee, and they all went into the living room to sit down.

"Mary, I think you know everybody here," Penny started.

"Yes, that's right."

All the gals nodded politely.

"I thank you all for your kindness and generosity," Mary said. "Yes, I know all of you, and I know all your children, too. I've admired you all for years, I couldn't be more grateful that you're all here."

EZ's mom complimented Mary on her bold new hairstyle.

"Short, but very cute," she said.

"Well, you have Leon Tiller to thank for that," Mary responded. The gals looked puzzled.

"What do you mean?" EZ's mom asked.

"Well, just before they took Leon away, he pinned me down, beat me, and hacked off my ponytail with a kitchen knife."

Nobody made a sound.

"Isn't Leon just the sveetest ting?" Mrs. Klaus said sarcastically.

Just as everyone was finishing their cups of fresh coffee and had endured twenty-five minutes of walking on eggshells to hear about the events that led to Leon's arrest, Barb Finch and her sister Lorna arrived with their signature bouffant hairdos freshly schlacked with a couple of cans of Aqua Net. Mrs. Tiller welcomed them at the front door.

"I hear there's a party of some kind here," Mrs. Finch teased.

"Ladies, you are certainly welcome, but we're just having coffee and delicious date bars."

"Well, we can fix that!" Lorna said, presenting Mary Tiller with a couple of bottles of chardonnay.

"I hope you don't mind, Mrs. Tiller, but I thought maybe you could use a glass—or a couple—of wine."

Mary stretched out her arms and folded Mrs. Finch into a big hug.

At that point, Penny Dawson asked if she could use the phone. With Mary's consent, Penny excused herself to the kitchen to make a call to Mitch's dad, and within minutes, he'd delivered a jug of Canadian Club and some 7-Up to the back door.

When Walter Dawson dropped off the booze, he brought Casey and Stephanie to the back door for the sole purpose of inviting Ike's little brother and sister, Jacob and Ruthy, down to the house for the afternoon. He told them he was planning to have hot dogs for lunch and wondered if they would like to join. Both kids were quite shy, but being that Casey and Stephanie were there, it wasn't too difficult to convince them to go with Mr. Dawson.

"By all means, the kids would love to go," Mrs. Tiller said.

It was a "two birds, one stone" scenario. With the little kids away, the gals could speak a little more freely, and the kids themselves got to interact with some neighborhood kids, something they should've been doing all along. Everyone hoped this would be a new chapter for those two—the whole family, really—finally being able to mix and mingle with other kids their age in the neighborhood.

Good move, Water Dawson.

The Tillers didn't keep any wine glasses in the house, so the gals made do with tumblers for their wine and highballs. The coffee cups were quickly replaced, and the neighborhood gals were settled in with a good supply of beverages and date bars.

Most would describe the East Side neighborhood as tight knit, with the Tiller family always having been the outliers. But not today! Many friendships among parents are generated through their kids, living in the same neighborhood, or playing sports or scouts or any number of activities together. When the kids get together, the parents get together, so it's an inevitable sort of coincidence. This had never been the case for the Tiller's, however, until that day. After all the years of watching the neighborhood gals interact and live life, today was Mary's first date with them.

With some booze at the ready and new friends eager to listen, Mary was quite open about the events that had led up to the police dragging Leon Tiller away. The neighborhood gals wanted to hear every last gory detail, and to their dread and delight, they got their wish.

"Leon and Isaac had a big fight, and Leon ended up throwing Isaac out of the house... on Christmas Eve. My boy was left to roam around in the cold on Christmas Eve, and I didn't do anything to stop it." Mary's depth of her shame poured out in her words, a shame that had been eating away her soul for years. Looking around at the room full of nearly complete strangers, she felt a barrier going up. No mother in this room would ever let such horrors happen to one of her children. Was she right to share so freely? Mary feared that these women would judge her as an unfit mother.

"I had to go to the hospital for treatment and evaluation, and at the same time, the sheriff's department took my kids away. I had no say," she continued, quiet tears blinking at the edges of her eyes.

"Mary, please," Penny soothed. "You don't owe anyone an explanation. You don't have to tell us anything."

"I know that," Mary confessed. "But I've never told any of this to anybody. It's truly a relief to finally say it out loud. I just hope you all are willing to listen with open hearts..."

"Oh, honey, you're among friends," Mrs. Finch piped up. "We're not here to listen, judge, and leave. But before you proceed, would you mind if I made myself another highball? I want to be prepared."

Chattering in agreement, all the moms marched into the kitchen to crack some new ice and made fresh cocktails for a story like they'd never heard before.

"I'm sure you all know my husband hits me," Mary lamented once they were all settled again. "But I should clarify that he doesn't beat all the kids; just Isaac. Before Isaac, his brother Aaron. He has never touched my oldest daughter or the two youngest kids."

The moms nodded, some looking down into their cocktails. They'd known, but how does one respond? Gretta Klaus knew her own mind, though.

"For God's sake, vhy does he do dat, Mary?" she asked.

"He beats me because I'm a sinner." Her response was simple and quick, and it was met with another long silence, broken periodically by ice clinking in glass as the mothers sipped uncomfortably.

"My dear, vee, all of us, sinners," Gretta said.

"That may be so, but I'm being punished for the sins of my past," Mary responded. "I'm being punished for the sins of my youth and because Leon likes it."

The moms were glued to Mary at this point, hanging on every graphic word. But Gretta didn't let up.

"I'm sorry, Mary, I don't qvite understand dis," she said.

"Let's just say this: When I was younger, before I was married, I—"

Mary paused to choose her words carefully.

"I kept company with a lot of fellas down on Payne Avenue."

The rest of the gals knew right away what Mary was talking about, but it took Gretta a few extra seconds for it to sink in.

"Oh, yah, I see," she said with a nod. "You vas da fun girl."

"I guess that's one way to put it," Mary agreed. "Or you could say I was a—"

"Now, wait a minute, honey," Mrs. Finch cautioned. "Don't be too hard on yourself. Me and this one over here"—she pointed to her sister Lorna—"worked in saloons up and down University Avenue and Rice Street when we were younger, and believe me, we had our share of 'Fun.'"

She chuckled as if remembering something fondly.

"In fact, that's how I fell for my man," she continued. "While your husband punished you for your past, my husband celebrated me. I can't speak for anybody else in the room, but believe me, the story of your youth has been told a million times by a million girls."

"I was trying to find love back then," Mary confessed. "But all I found were a lot of back seats. I was a fool and drank too much. The boys were coming home from the war, and all the guys wanted was a good time. They all had their sweethearts. I was just some distraction."

The ladies murmured softly, encouraging her to go on.

"I was so sick and tired of getting my heart trampled on, and that's when I met Leon. He'd moved here from Wisconsin to go to seminary school at Bethel College. My girlfriend and her fiancé set us up on a double date. I'd gone through Catholic school my whole life—Saint Pats then on to Saint Bernards—but it wasn't until I met Leon and we talked about life and religion that I really felt God come into my life. We dated for about a month and then got married."

"Leon became more and more distant from the teachings at seminary school. He kept thinking there was something else, and that's when he discovered the Jehovah's Witnesses. We started going to the temple to learn more about their teachings. The more time I spent with Leon and the more we went to the temple, the more I forgot about my life as a wild girl down on Payne Avenue."

"Looking back at it, I see now that Leon looked at me more as a human reclamation project and some sort of modern-day Mary Magdalene. He was going to save me from my 'familiars' and certain ruination. He claimed he would spend his life in service to God to save my soul. He really believed that he, Leon Tiller, could absolve me of my sins."

"Once we got married, we jumped in deep with the Jehovah's Witnesses, and early on, it was the happiest I'd ever been. But even then, if I ignored him for two minutes or disagreed with him, he would blame it on my past and the influence of Satan. I even started to believe it myself. I could hardly speak without his permission. I remember vividly one time, when we were at Temple, I openly disagreed with him about the most innocent, innocuous thing that had nothing to do with religion, and when we got home, he beat me senseless. We were one year married, and that moment was the beginning of him quoting scripture over me as he beat me. It was always about whores of Babylon and harlots in the home. When I woke up after that first beating, I went back to my parent's house for a time, not knowing what else to do. That led me back to the saloons down on Payne Avenue and the comfort of a different way."

"Of course, I went back to him eventually. He promised it would never happen again. He had just got a new job with the Saint Paul Pioneer Press and was looking to buy a house. It was a good job, too, a union job, and that's when we bought this house."

"Our oldest son, Aaron, was born two years after we were married, and then our first daughter came along a year later. And once every couple of years, early on, if I wasn't in absolute lockstep with his opinion on the most trivial thing, he would beat me in the name of God. Each time, I went back to my parent's house, and each time I would wander back down to Payne Avenue, and each time I would go back to him under the same promise that he would never do it again."

"This went on for years. I lived a life where I hated myself for what I was, hated myself for what I had become, and hated Leon for what he did to me. I remember wondering where the hell God was in all of this."

"Those times I went back to Payne, I always ended up hanging around with the same fella. He was really something before booze got a hold of him, but he's dead now."

"As time passed, Leon became a crazed zealot. Thinking himself as some kind of prophet, he became increasingly involved in the Jehovah's Witness temple, but he was so over the top with the harshness of the Bible and the vengeance of the Bible. He never spoke about anything that had to do with the light and goodness. He started referring to Aaron and Ike as bastards, godless bastards." Her voice choked as she pressed on. "And, according to the Bible, Leon is right. He was right all along. Those boys are bastards. Both were born out of wedlock because Leon Tiller is not their father. Their real father is a guy who found his life at the bottom of a bottle. Their real father was just another tragic story down on Payne Avenue. Leon found out that those boys are the result of his cruelty to me. Still, he thought that with enough punishment, I would be cleansed of my sins. I know Aaron figured out the truth. He never said so, and he never asked me. He never acknowledged it, but sometimes a mother just knows."

The room was gripped in stunned silence.

Mrs. Finch, always very direct, asked Mary a simple question.

"Where is Leon now?"

"He is down at the mental hospital in Saint Peter," Mary said. "They're trying to help him.

"Saint Peter? You mean…" Mrs. Golyn remarked then faded out.

"Yes, the one and the same," Mary confirmed. "They are evaluating him to see if he is a threat to himself or others. I go to visit him once a week."

"Why on earth would you visit this bastard?" Mrs. Finch asked for everyone else in the room.

"They have to determine if he's getting any better," Mary replied. "And by all accounts, he is. He seems like he's in much better spirits. They're giving him medication now, but I know all the medication in the world can't change the fact that he's not Aaron and Ike's father."

"What's it going to take for them to release him?" Mrs. Dawson asked.

"They're trying to get some of the charges against him dropped, so I don't know at this point," Mary stated. '

You could almost hear the wheels turning.

"When I first tried to tell Leon that Aaron and Ike were not his sons, he didn't really want to know the truth. However, once the truth was known, hell at the house began. Leon prayed on it, Leon took counsel with other members of the temple, trying to forgive, trying to come to grips with it. When he punished someone in the house, whether Aaron, Ike, or me, it made him feel better—but it didn't last. Then, if he'd had a bad day at work, he'd take it out on the boys."

"Leon walked a tight line between being mean and being cruel, and in some cases, he dabbled in torture. Like when he would lock Aaron in that bomb shelter in the backyard. Locking a kid in a hole overnight isn't punishment, it's torture."

"That animal drove Aaron away. Aaron joined the Navy after high school, and we haven't seen him since. It's been years now. Aaron was a bit on the wild side, but he certainly didn't deserve the abuse he got from Leon. I'm just as much to blame, though. I did nothing to stop it."

"Leon swears he will never divorce me. I really believe he won't divorce me because he wants to keep punishing me, and I can't go anywhere because I still have four kids at home and my daughter has special needs. Both of my parents are gone now, so I have nowhere else to go."

"But Mary, how can you live, fearing for your life every day and fearing for the lives of your children?" Penny asked, incredulous.

"Well, Penny, this is my hell."

As the afternoon wore on, Mary was able to sit back and listen to stories from the other moms. There were some tears shed, but also laughs. Mrs. Finch and her sister talked about some of their escapades down on University Avenue and Rice Street, which was reassuring for Mary. She was among friends now, especially knowing for a fact that not everybody was an angel like she thought they must have been. These gals knocked the hell out of the wine and were well on their way to finishing off their jug of booze as they bonded. The neighborhood moms came shoulder to shoulder in support of their new friend: the erstwhile wilted flower, Mary Tiller.

CHAPTER 22

WINTER CARNIVAL

The Hayden Heights hockey team was on an absolute tear. Going into the bantam tournament for the Saint Paul Winter Carnival, their overall record was 11 and 3. Next weekend, the tournament would be held at the State Fair Hippodrome and Saint Paul Auditorium. Mitch, Zitz, and EZ had really discovered their scoring stride, but the biggest team improvements arrived with the younger guys on the team. These guys were not very big yet but they're fast as hell and tough little shits, and Randy has been stellar with the net, as usual.

Manny Klaus was living the life of the two-sport athlete; he had a big physical presence on the ice and was a terror in the squared circle.

Their very own heavyweight wrestling champion, Manny the Mangler, dominated the ranks of the high stake's world of junior high wrestling. All the boys cheered as they watched him rise.

Compared with how he was at the beginning of the school year, Manny was a changed guy. Not only was he bigger but he'd begun to lose his baby fat and replace it with muscle. He'd got a set of weights for Christmas and had access to his dad's collection of workout equipment whenever he wanted. Manny also had a bench press, about 200 pounds of weights, a curling bar, and half a dozen dumbbells. And, according to Manny, his dad had to keep buying more weight because Manny kept maxing out with the weights he had available. It's tough to keep up with Manny.

Mitch started working out with Manny as something to do for fun after Christmas, but it became kind of a regular thing. Which was a good thing. Even Mitch started to notice changes in himself—two inches over the past year—and it wouldn't kill him to get a little stronger.

Zitz has weights too and a basement full of other workout stuff that his brother Chet collected. Chetter got Zitz started working out a while ago, and anyone could see that Zitz is strong as hell. EZ, on the other hand, is not the kind of guy to make the extra effort. He's pretty sure that he can get by on bullshit and smart-ass remarks, and his experience thus far has only reinforced that belief. It's served him pretty well so far, but it would be a lie to say that the guys didn't wonder if that would change next year in high school. It's said that everything changes in high school; everything gets bigger, stronger, and faster.

"Every time I feel like exercising, I just lay down and take a nap until that feeling goes away," EZ has said, time and time again. That's EZ for ya.

Manny hasn't lost a match since the first two of the season. Some of the guys Manny faced have been even bigger than him—some of them weighing over 230 pounds! The difference is that Manny is a much better athlete than these bigger guys. He's faster and stronger and wins just about every match by pin fall.

But football is where Manny might be the most effective. All the guys play football down at the playground, and Manny is a lineman on the team. But Manny is no clubfooted immobile clod. During drills, he can keep up with everyone, even though he outweighs the heaviest of them by seventy-five pounds. The guys couldn't wait to get a look at him in action next year in high school.

Despite the physical changes, the biggest difference in Manny is his confidence. He just seems more at ease and not afraid to speak up. He's even talking to girls of his own volition.

In preparation for the tournament for the Winter Carnival, Coach McKay got the team an hour of ice time down at Wakota Arena in South Saint Paul. This was important because anybody who's played hockey knows about the world of difference between outdoor ice and indoor ice. The guys were excited for the practice until they found out it was to happen at 6 a.m. on a Sunday morning. Still, it was pretty cool because most of the guys had never played a hockey game on indoor ice—though it is a common activity to skate up at Aldrich Arena during open skating. Manny's dad volunteered to pick up the guys and take them to practice. It was Mitch, EZ, Manny, Zitz, and one of the younger guys, Georgie Porter.

Georgie centers the second line, and he's easily the most improved player. Georgie is not very big, but what's funny is that he started the season an inch shorter than EZ, and now he's an inch taller. That's what happens to a kid during a hockey season, though, especially at the junior high school age. Everybody grows and matures throughout the year. The way Georgie skates, and with his low center of gravity, trying to take him down is like trying to knock over a fire hydrant on the ice. He's only a few goals behind Zitz for the team lead in scoring.

The first fifteen minutes of practice were horrible. Everyone found out fast that their skates were dull. When you're skating outdoors, you only get your skates sharpened a couple of times a season; everything is kind of rough and you make it work. The indoor ice, however, was rock hard, especially first thing in the morning. The guys' dull skates did nothing for them: They could barely do their drills, they couldn't catch a pass, nothing. Coach McKay had a particular strategy for this tournament because all the teams were going to be good; luckily for Hayden Heights, the other teams didn't usually play indoors either. Despite their skates, the team did everything based on ringing the dashers, which is to say they threw the puck down along the dashers on one side and let it ring around and send players into the offensive zone on the other side. This is something you just can't do outside because, with the way the boards are set up kind of square in the corners, you lose the puck half the time. But it was a solid strategy for indoor rinks, so they worked on it for the rest of the practice. The real lesson, though? Get the damn skates sharpened.

After practice, Manny's dad took them all out for breakfast to his favorite diner on Concord Street. Going out to breakfast was a rarity for the boys, so they took full advantage. The place was busy that Sunday morning, so there was a wait for a table, but they had a menu board at the entrance so you could decide what you wanted to eat while you were waiting. Everything was numbered one through nine, and each item was a variation of the same thing: eggs and bacon or sausage, toast, and other typical breakfast stuff.

Mitch ordered the #1, which was just a couple of scrambled eggs, toast, and some bacon. Zitz got the #2, which was the same as the #1, just with sausage instead of bacon. Georgie and EZ both got #4, which was a stack of pancakes. Mr. Klaus got the house special, steak and eggs. When it came to Manny, he sheepishly looked up at the waitress.

"I'll have the 59," he muttered.

"What the hell is the 59?" Mitch whispered to Manny.

"It's a combo of the #5 and #9," he said. "Oh, and can I get a short stack with that?" he added in the direction of the waitress.

"You got it," she said, jotting down the order details.

Manny ended up with the #5, The Cattleman's Omelet, which had everything—four eggs, three kinds of meat, veggies, hash browns and cheese—as well as the #9, biscuits and gravy, with a short stack of pancakes on the side. That was Manny. His food alone took up half the table, which was funnier than all hell. He made quick work of breakfast that morning, despite the stunning amount of food.

The city of Saint Paul was at full Winter Carnival fever. Every day, the newspaper published clues to the location of the Winter Carnival Medallion, a tradition started back in the fifties as a hunt for a treasure chest. After a few years, the prize was changed to a medallion. The point of the hunt was to show the world how hearty people from Saint Paul are, that they would go out and hunt for a prize in the dead of winter. Last year, it was out in Highland Park. It was too early to tell where it was this time around, though it was usually at Phalen, Como, or someplace down by the river. If the medallion isn't found by the last day, the newspaper would publish precise directions to its location. "Go to this park and walk three feet left of the swing set while facing the teeter totter, look at your feet, and there's the medallion." It's a cool $2,000 to the finder.

A few years ago, they hid the Saint Paul Winter Carnival medallion on the home plate of the Babe Ruth baseball field at Beaver Lake. Treasure hunters ripped that place to shreds looking for the prize, and it took the city months to rebuild the entire park. That year was the closest it ever got to Mitch's house.

The team's tournament game was good but not great. All of the competitors were A-bantam teams as well as the best B-bantam teams in the Twin Cities. There were never any tomato cans in the Winter Carnival Tournament. Hell, they were lucky to be invited to begin with. The overall game may not have been the best hockey the team had ever played, but for Mitch it was a good tournament, with two goals and four assists. Zitz had a good tournament too, with four goals and three assists, and the goalie, Randy, let in only four goals the whole tournament.

The saloons all over town are being haunted by the Winter Carnival Vulcans. Volcanus Rex and his Krewe were the arch enemies of King Boreas and the rest of the Winter Carnival Royalty. They were the ones who brought a little mischievous fun into the Winter Carnival. While the Carnival ran, those guys didn't pay for a single drink. They go from bar to bar, lightly terrorizing the women and putting smudgy black shit all over their faces. The locals acted like these loons were celebrities, and while it's all good fun, too many free cocktails can lead to things getting out of hand.

King Boreas was usually some downtown businessman muckety-muck or a car dealer or somebody who knows somebody. His royal company is filled with other guys—the East-wind, Westwind, Southwind, Northwind—and they each have their Queens and Princesses, all of whom are about thirty years younger than the men. They ride in parades all over and make public appearances as ambassadors for the city of Saint Paul.

The Winter Carnival also features a Junior Royalty, and teenagers from every playground in town run for the titles. Each playground has a Prince and Princess title, and all compete for the King or Queen title.

Dozens of kids run to represent each playground. The kids sign themselves up, usually after being coaxed by the playground director. It's a nice feather in the cap to have the winner come from your playground. The Winter Carnival officials go around to the playgrounds to interview each candidate. They ask each one about their sports and activities at the playground, what school they go to, and other general stuff like that.

At Hayden Heights Playground, nine girls and eight guys were in the running. And, to the disappointment of the other seven girls, Gloria Golyn and Isabelle Petri were two of the contestants. The results were predictable; Gloria was crowned the Princess and Izzy was her Lady in Waiting.

Gloria represented Hayden Heights Playground along with the Prince, Mason Devers, a kid who plays for the East Side Midgets and was a fixture down at the playground.

There was a big coronation event downtown at the Saint Paul Auditorium to crown the winners. This was a huge deal. The Dawsons went early to grab good seats near the stage because they knew the place would be packed.

In honor of her new role, Gloria's mom took her to the Pink Lady Beauty Parlor on White Bear Avenue, and they gave her the works. She had her hair all done up with little flowers, and for the first time ever, Mitch would see Gloria wear makeup. She could have been Liz Taylor's prettier younger sister.

Even as a teenager, Gloria's splendor put the actual adult Queen of the Snows to shame. As for the rest of the contestants in her group, Gloria was a woman among girls. When their names were announced, each girl and their guy counterpart had to walk the entire length of the Saint Paul Auditorium to the stage. The rest of the girls came clomping down the runway wearing their sensible Buster Brown shoes, but Gloria wore heels and walked that distance like a fashion model on the red carpet in Hollywood. There was no question of who was going to win the crown for the Junior Royalty group.

When Gloria was crowned, the place erupted, and everyone was hugging and screaming. It was pretty cool that somebody they all knew well had won.

Yet somehow, to Mitch, her win made her feel like she was a million miles away at the same time. It's funny what goes through one's head at events like this. It all seemed like a movie. One minute she was reigning queen of the neighborhood, and the next minute, you were sitting out in the audience with all these strangers, watching the world fall at her feet. Was that how life would be from now on? Mitch wondered. She'd live her life in the limelight, with the rarefied air of celebrity, and he'd be down at the playground, scraping and flooding the rink.

She was Gloria, Queen of the Snow Drift—or Snow Tires or whatever they called it. She'd beaten every girl from every playground in Saint Paul. The city was hers.

All three TV stations covered the event. She was interviewed by Mel Jass from Channel 11 while hundreds of cameras flashed. She made the front page of the paper; they basically dedicated the whole spread to her win.

After the main event, everyone went down to Matt and Genes on 7th Street for pizza to celebrate. There were fifteen people, and EZ and Mitch got to share a whole pizza. The Dawsons were set up to take him and his sister Joy home because the Golyn parents had to escort Gloria. As part of the honors, she was whisked away to some fancy reception at the Prom Ballroom with the rest of the Winter Carnival Royalty, including the Vulcans and a couple hundred new admirers.

The next day, Mitch stopped by EZ's house to see if he wanted to skate down at the playground. As soon as he walked in the door, however, Gloria came up behind him.

"What's up, Mitchy-poo?" she asked. She put Mitch in a headlock and pounded his head with a few knobbies.

What is this bullshit? he thought.

Tightening her hold, Gloria complained.

"I heard you guys went out for pizza last night. I got stuck *(thunk, thunk, thunk on Mitch's head)* eating stale crackers and drinking warm Hawaiian Punch."

Finally escaping the headlock, Mitch tried to catch his breath and smooth his hair.

"Oh, poor Gloria," he taunted. "What's the matter, Your Highness? Didn't the royal feast meet the standards of her majesty, 'Glorious Queen of the Snow Shovels?'"

Gloria moved to re-engage the headlock.

"I'll show you 'Glorious,'" she growled. "And it's 'Snow Flakes,' a-hole. Queen of the Snow Flakes."

"Royal highness, my ass."

"Now, you listen here, you little shit. If you think you're going to get away with calling me Royal this or Queen that, you got another thing coming... in the way of a 'Royal' ass kicking."

Her warning complete, she backed off.

"At least I got some leftover pizza when I got home. I was starving."

At that point, EZ came into the kitchen, and Gloria lightened up.

"Hey, Mitchell, mom's driving me and the Izz up to the Plaza later to see the new *The Love Bug* movie if you and numb nuts Eric want to go with?" she asked.

The way she was acting, one would've thought she'd stayed home last night and watched TV instead of becoming the teenage Queen of the entire city of Saint Paul. The fame didn't do anything to her; she was the same old Gloria, just the way she's always been.

She did countless parades and appearances over the next year, but besides that, she never said a word about being Her Royal Highness "Gloria, Queen of the Snow Plows."

CHAPTER 23

HOCKEY SEASON ENCORE

By the time the Winter Carnival tournament was over, there were just two more games left in the season, and they were just makeup games for those the team missed because of bad weather earlier in the year. As soon as those games were over, the boys arrived at the dreaded Dead Zone—that time in Minnesota between hockey season and baseball season, which is half of February and all of March and April. It was the time of year they occupied themselves down at the playground with stuff like floor hockey, dodge ball, and ping-pong tournaments. To keep themselves as fresh as they could, they'd arrange a number of boot hockey games to play with their arch rivals from Hazel Park. It was all they could do to keep busy because there was nothing else to do outside.

Mitch was the commissioner of the five-team boot hockey league, and Hayden Heights was the reigning champion of the league. They'd been defeated only a couple of times during seventh and eighth grade, so everybody was gunning for them.

The kids over by the 3M warehouses near the Trestle had the best place to play boot hockey: newly punched-in streets with no houses. The streets were perfectly flat with no traffic. Those guys even built their own nets and were really organized. The players on the two teams were good friends and, ironically, Hayden Heights' favorite team to beat. The rest of the teams played in parking lots or in alleys.

The toughest team to play against were the kids from the projects. These guys didn't have a lot of talent, but they were tough as nails and refused to give up anything without a fight. The boys played against everybody they could find. These unofficial league games were fun, but they sometimes came at a cost.

There were always scrapes, cuts, and bruises, and every once in a while, somebody got a tooth knocked out. In a game against the Frost Lake boys, somebody got a pretty serious cut over the eye, so the boys tried to keep their heads up and stick down after that. When the games got cheap and chippy, fights would break out—and believe it or not, there were some beauties. The best one was the time Zitz squared off work with Arnold Swayne from Beaver Lake. Arnold had been hacking Zitz the whole game, trying to provoke him. He finally managed it, and after they jawed at each other for a couple of minutes, they dropped the gloves and Zitz beat the living shit out of Arnie. That's the last time Arnold Swayne ever played boot hockey for the boys of Beaver Lake. Zitz got the Gordie Howe hat trick in that game: one goal, one assist, and one fight.

But before the Dead Zone really had a chance to hit, there was the big Valentines Day dance at Hazel Park. All week, the girls were talking about it, and the school was buzzing with excitement.

True to form, EZ showed up wearing his best duds, dancing shoes ready. The real anticipation was knowing that this was one of the last dances the guys were ever going to have at Hazel Park. There would probably be one very last dance right before school let out. It was a bittersweet moment for Mitch and his friends.

But the bitter part of the moment didn't last long. The girls were all dressed up and ready to rock 'n' roll, and the band was outstanding. They played everything from The Beatles and Cream to Steppenwolf and The Doors. In all of the anticipation, Mitch had failed to consider something: He had a girlfriend. He'd get to enjoy the music but wouldn't be able to dance with anyone because of that girlfriend—a long-distance girlfriend, at that. Furthering his problem was the fact that his girlfriend's cousin was at the dance. He knew that if he danced with anybody, Maggie would get a full report by tonight. Mitch was torn by his desire to stick with his girl and the desire to enjoy one of the last dances he'd have at Hazel Park. It was one of those situations that made him wonder if all of it was worth it. He'd only seen Maggie one other time since they'd met—and would hopefully see her again soon—but he couldn't tell you how or when. They still talked on the phone just about every night, but it wasn't the same thing as being in the same town and going out like regular boyfriends and girlfriends do.

Adding to the problem even more, Mitch had started to notice the girls in school had begun to get prettier over the past year; Maggie didn't stand out quite like she used to. He himself had shot up in height and filled out a little more. As odd as it was, it seemed like girls were starting to notice him more than they used to, too.

Mitch has his problems, but EZ steals the show at every dance, and the Valentine's dance was no different. He danced every single song and managed to draw out another wallflower for the thrill of her life. He was a showman and a half. Most songs, he was dancing with three or four girls at a time.

When Mitch got home from the dance, it was supper time, which looked like chow mein hotdish, which perfectly suited Mitch. Just as he was getting all his stuff off and putting away his boots, Mr. Dawson came into the kitchen and motioned toward the phone.

"You had a phone call, and the message is on the counter," he said.

Who the heck would call and leave me a message? Mitch wondered. He got up to see what his dad was talking about, and as it turned out, it was a message from Clete Paris. Mitch thought the name sounded familiar, but he couldn't quite place it.

"Do you know who this guy is?" he asked his dad. "It sounds familiar, but I can't figure it out."

"Yeah, I've got a pretty good idea. Give him a call back after supper. We're about to sit down and eat here in a minute."

All the way through dinner, Mitch couldn't stop trying to figure out what this business with Clete Paris was all about. Once he, Casey, and Stephi got the kitchen cleaned up, Mitch grabbed the phone and called Clete Paris. He learned that Clete Paris was the head coach of the VFW-sponsored Anderson-Nelson VFW hockey team, which was the powerhouse A-bantam team on the East Side. All the guys had had the opportunity to try out for them that year, but they'd collectively decided as a group to play together one last year. Most of the guys on that team were from down around Payne Avenue.

This VFW-sponsored team was a top-level team that played as many as seventy games a year. They were in two different leagues, and they even practiced indoors sometimes. Their season was way longer than the high school hockey season. Both Mitch and Zitz thought they could play with those guys, but it was a tough team to make. Some of the team members had been playing together as long as Mitch and his guys had been playing together.

Mitch talked with Coach Paris for a little while and then hung up the phone and looked at his dad, who was waiting to hear his news.

"So, what did he want?" he asked.

"Well, we talked about hockey," Mitch replied. "He said he saw me play a couple times and he congratulated me on a good season. He said that he talked to some people like Coach McKay and the Phalen head coach, and then he asked if I would like to join the VFW team for the rest of the season for a pretty heavy tournament schedule. He said they have three tournaments coming up, some games, plus scrimmages, and a full schedule of practices." I had to catch my breath. "And get this: He wants me, Zitz, and Randy to join the team. He told me they have three kids out for the year."

"Out for the year?" Mr. Dawson wondered. "What did he mean?"

"He said one had his appendix out, one got hurt skiing, and one got in trouble at school."

"So what did you tell him?"

"I told him I wanted to play but that I had to talk to you."

"Well, I don't think there's much to talk about," Mr. Dawson said with a grin. "You do want to play, right?"

"Hell yes I wanna play."

"See, that wasn't hard."

"The coach said that if I decided to play, they have practice tomorrow morning at 10 o'clock at Aldrich Arena." Mitch was beaming. "Can you take me?"

"I think we can make that happen."

"He also said that they'll give me my uniforms then."

"Uniforms, plural?"

"Yup, they have home and away uniforms."

"I've been a member of that Anderson-Nelson Vets Club on Payne Avenue since I got out of the service in 1946," Mr. Dawson mused. "I used to take your mom dancing there years ago."

Holy shit, was Mitch excited. Lucky for him, there was practice the very next morning. Otherwise, he might've driven himself nuts in anticipation. Here was his chance to play more hockey and avoid the dreaded Dead Zone. What's even crazier was that this team actually had a following. People who didn't know the players personally follow them around and watch their games.

A little while later, Mitch got another phone call. It was Randy McKay, and he was pretty fired up too. He said his dad was going to come along as an assistant coach for the rest of the season, which was great news for Mitch too. He loved Coach McKay, and Coach McKay knew how to work with him. Then, Randy dropped the best news of all. There were three tournaments coming up: one in Rochester, one in Duluth, and one on the Iron Range in Eveleth. They were going to travel and stay in hotels and play hockey—and to top it all off, Mitch would get to see Maggie while he was away playing hockey.

The next thing Mitch did was call Maggie to tell her the news. She was so damn excited that she could hardly contain herself. She was telling him about all the things they could do and the places they could go when Mitch had to gently remind her that he was going to be up there to play hockey. He didn't know how much time he'd have for extracurriculars. Even better than getting to see her at Eveleth, was the possibility of seeing her at the Duluth game too. She offered that she might be able to figure out a way to go down to Duluth, as it wasn't too far away. Everything that had happened just that evening was awesome. Mitch didn't know, realistically, how much time he'd be able to spend with Maggie, but just knowing that his girlfriend would be in the stands and that he was probably the only one who had a girlfriend in the stands was a huge deal.

And, as if that weren't enough, she told Mitch that she and her sister were going to be in Saint Paul for Easter. In the end, over the next month and a half, Mitch would get to see her at two hockey tournaments and over the Easter weekend.

After he finished up his call with Maggie, Mitch's next mission was to run over to EZ's house to tell him the news. But just as he hit the door, Mr. Dawson cleared his throat at him.

"Where are you headed?"

"To Eric's house to tell him that I'm going to be playing more hockey."

"Come here," his dad commanded.

Mitch complied and stepped away from the door.

"Do you think that's the smartest thing to do?"

"What do you mean?"

"It's one thing to be selected for this team, but it's another thing to go around bragging about it."

Just like that, all the excitement he had for all the plans he'd been concocting, everything he could think of that might happen in the next month, was gone. Leave it to his dad to pop his balloon.

"So what are you saying," Mitch asked. "That I can't tell anybody?"

"That's not what I'm saying and you know it," Mr. Dawson noted. "But it does sound like you're gonna go rub it in his face a little bit."

"Yeah, that's half the fun," Mitch confirmed.

"Well, maybe between here and there you'll be able to grow up a little bit." Mr. Dawson rubbed his temples. "Now, get out of here."

Grow up a little bit? Nah, he had to go tell his boy EZ all the news.

When Mitch got to EZ's house, he found him downstairs half-watching TV, half bragging about his performance at the dance earlier that day. Gloria and Izzy were there too—Mitch's timing could not have been better. EZ was in the middle of naming off all the girls he'd danced with at school that day and all the phone numbers he'd received, and all the jokes that he'd told.

"I had all the girls wrapped around my little finger," he crowed. "And old Doc, my best buddy, sat on the sidelines like a cold turd." He was careful to emphasize how Mitch, his best pal, hadn't danced with one girl that day.

Oh, Mitch could not wait to give this asshole a tune-up. Then, of course, Gloria piled on, never one to miss a chance to give him shit.

"What about it, Mitchy-poo, no dancing for you?" she jabbed. "Can't be seen swinging other cuties around the dance floor, huh? Just your Sweety?"

Mitch didn't think it was possible, but somehow this was going to get better. Now he had both EZ and Gloria giving him shit.

Then Izzy defended.

"Shut up, you guys. Mitch is being true to his girlfriend. I think that's sweet. Good for you, Mitch."

Finally, an ally in the room.

"So, how *is* your Iron Range honey?" Gloria probed. "Mildred or Mazzola or whatever. Have you talked to her lately?"

"It's Maggie." He delivered the line matter-of-factly, managing to hide the fact he was stunned by her question. He knew they'd met at his hockey tournament a couple months ago, but he didn't think Gloria would remember or care who he was dating. "Why do you care, Gloria?"

"What do you mean, why do I care? I'm always looking out for you, Mitchy-poo." She fluttered her eyelashes dramatically. "So, answer the question: How is the lovely Maggie from the Iron Range?"

"Well, she's great. I talk to her every night."

"I bet you don't get to see her very much, though?" Gloria responded with a certain amount of dastardly satisfaction.

"I don't see her as much as I'd like to."

"When are you going to see her again?"

"Yeah, Doc, when are you going to see this so-called girlfriend again?" EZ added. "I mean, really, you could've been out there dancing with every girl in school today, but instead you're clinging to some phantom that you pretend is your girlfriend. I'm telling you, Doc, it's really quite sad."

Mitch might've felt bad about what happened next, but he didn't because EZ walked right into it.

"Well, as a matter of fact, EZ old boy, I just got recruited by the East Side VFW A-bantam team to play for them the rest of the year."

EZ's face was satisfying enough, but Mitch went on.

"My first practice is tomorrow morning, which is when I'll get my new uniforms."

"What?" EZ's mouth was practically on the floor.

"Yup, we're going to play three tournaments, and this is where Maggie comes in. One is in Rochester, one is in Duluth, and one is in Eveleth. Eveleth is right next to Virginia, where Maggie lives. I just talked to Maggie, too, and she's going to be at the tournaments in Eveleth and Duluth. The team will be staying in hotels the whole time and getting free food and everything. As an added bonus, Maggie's going to be down here for all of Easter vacation."

Nobody spoke after Mitch spilled it all out.

"So, does that answer your question, smart ass?"

"What the hell do you mean you got recruited?" EZ pushed back. "You're full of shit, they don't do that."

"Eric, they just did. Me, Zitz, and Randy are all going to finish out the season with the VFW A-bantam team."

The mood in the room noticeably cooled. EZ was not used to being bested when it came to tit-for-tat match-ups.

"So no tryouts, no nothing?" EZ inquired. Mitch was beaming.

"The coach, Clete Paris, saw us play a number of times this year and they needed to fill some spots, so we all got a call."

EZ was sitting up on the couch now, a furrow starting to crease on his forehead.

"So, you see, for the next month and a half, my *dance card* is kind of full." It was the perfect cherry-on-top remark, and Mitch lost no time sealing that TKO of a moment.

Izzy walked over and gave Mitch a hug.

"That's awesome, Mitch," she encouraged. "Reno played for them when he was a bantam player. Those guys are good and they played tough competition from all over."

"Yeah, I'm a bit worried about that," Mitch admitted. "I hope I can keep up."

"You're going to do great," she assured me.

Mitch waited to hear from the Queen of the Snow Banks herself, but she said nothing. No words, just a big smile and a slow shake of the head.

Less than five minutes into practice the next day, Mitch could really tell the difference between a team like this and the team he'd played on that year. The new team had more talent across the board, but what really struck him was how tight and fast they were and how they could do everything at a much higher level. It was impressive but not enough to make him feel overwhelmed, thankfully. He'd played a lot against some of these kids coming up through squirts and peewees, so Mitch knew he could play here.

Coach Paris put Mitch back at defense, and they had Zitz on the second line—and boy was that something to watch. Zitz had two more thoroughbred horses to run with and you couldn't tell any difference between the first line or the second line. The first line was centered by the team's top guy and captain, Mario DiMucci. Mario was pretty well-known and was generally considered the top hockey player in his age group on the East Side. While Mitch and the guys were rink rats at Hayden Heights, Mario was at Wilder Playground day and night. Not only was Mario good but he was damn tough too—after all, he was a Golden Gloves champion. Mitch couldn't recall whether

Mario and Zitz had ever scrapped, but it was safe to say it's a good thing they're both on the same team now. Mario was a welcoming captain, going so far as to skate around and swat Mitch in the ass with a stick to give him a little uptick to his game. Mario was a vocal leader on the ice, and that's saying a lot for a fifteen-year-old kid.

A couple of the guys on the team knew me, but every guy on the team knew Zitz. His reputation as a tough guy preceded him wherever he went, and this team was no exception. All the team members made the three new guys feel welcome; they felt part of the team right away.

By the end of practice, Mitch had been paired with Dylan Paris on the first power play unit, and Zitz was on the first penalty kill unit; Zitz was a forechecking demon. Dylan was the coach's son and was only in the seventh grade, yet he'd been playing above his age level his entire life. He was almost as tall as Mitch and would never have been able to guess he was only thirteen years old. He's calm with the puck and never gets rattled or makes bad plays out there.

Mitch and Zitz were both a boon to the team; however, the one guy to make the biggest impact was Randy McKay. The team's top goalie had just had his appendix out, and the remaining goalie was a first-year player who'd been their only goalie for a couple of weeks. Randy had gone to school and played hockey with all the guys on the VFW team before he moved up by Hayden Heights. He made believers out of everybody during warm-ups; he didn't allow one shot.

After practice, Coach Paris pulled the three of them aside and told them he really liked what he'd seen out there.

"Here are your schedules, boys."

They glanced through to see what they were up against: a whole bunch of practice, all at Aldrich Arena, some remaining league games, a handful of scrimmages, plus the dates for the three tournaments. Mitch was going to be on the ice every day.

The very best part of it all was when they received their equipment. Mitch had expected to get the other players' jerseys, but that wasn't the case at all. Everything was brand new. Each guy got a brand-new helmet, breezers, gloves, socks, a bag, and two NHL-quality jerseys and a practice jersey. On top of all that, they also provided brand-new VFW A-bantam jackets. Mitch had no clue where the heck they got all their money, but he could tell the team was well funded.

"Guys, we didn't qualify for the Minnesota A-bantam tournament in South Saint Paul this year because we had three guys out for the season and a couple of other guys were sick, so we're really happy that you're here to help bolster up our roster going into these other tournaments," Coach Paris said. "Zack Deitz, I'm leaning on you to add some grit upfront. I know you can put the puck in the net, but we gotta get a little bit tougher, especially when we start playing the teams from Chicago, Canada, and Michigan. These teams are all good. They're big, they're strong, and they're fast. Especially Canada. They play a lot more physical than we do down here. Mitch, if you stay steady on D and move the puck up ice the way you showed today, you'll do great. I think you've got a good vision on the ice. You might want to think about new shoulder pads, though. Yours look a little small on you."

"OK, I'll talk to my dad."

He turned to Randy and swung his arm around Randy's shoulder.

"Our new backstop here is going to carry us quite a ways," he stated. "Randy, I like the way you call out to your teammates when the puck is thrown into our zone, letting them know if they're covered or not. I also like the way you get out of the crease and set up the puck behind the net. A team will always play their very best when they have confidence in their goalie. But I think you know that."

Randy just nodded politely.

Once Coach Paris finished up, Mitch grabbed his new gear and uniforms and headed up the steps to get out of the arena. Just as he reached the top, he looked around for his dad and spotted him sitting in a row next to EZ, Manny, and Ike.

"What's going on, guys?" Mitch asked.

They all jumped out of their seats and started jostling him around and giving him shit. They said they got there about five minutes into the practice because they'd wanted to see what all the fuss was about.

EZ was the one Mitch least expected to say anything positive, but he walked right up to him, looked him in the eye, smiled, and declared some hearty advice.

"Listen, Doc," he started. "Keep your 'head up, stick down' and you'll do alright." Manny agreed, and Ike pointed out what he'd observed of their speed.

"Holy crap, Mitch, they're fast—like high school fast. And when are all these tournaments with fancy hotels that you're going to take me to?"

Mitch laughed, but on the way home with all the guys in the backseat, he wondered how good an idea it was to bring Ike along on a tournament. Had he been anywhere? Of course, Mitch wasn't exactly a world traveler, but maybe they could bring Ike to Rochester with them. Definitely not the other tourneys. Those were reserved for him and his dance partner, Maggie Kuula.

CHAPTER 24

THE IRON RANGE

When you're used to playing teams from places like Conway, Lockwood, Edgecumbe, or other playgrounds in Saint Paul, it really shifts the game when you see names like Chicago, Madison, Two Rivers, and Green Bay on the tournament schedule. This is some fast company, and this was who the VFW-sponsored team saw in their first tournament in Rochester. After ten days of practice and two scrimmages, the team couldn't wait to play. They had a bunch of set plays ready—mostly breakouts, forechecking coverage, and stuff like that.

Though Ike had teased Mitch about taking him on a tournament, the Dawsons took him seriously and brought him along to Rochester. Ike had an absolute blast on the trip. First, he just loved the idea of taking some kind of trip that involved an overnight stay in a hotel, but more than that, Ike had the most fun at the hotel after the game Friday night.

Coach Paris limited the team to one hour in the pool per day, and never before a game. Lights out was at 11:00 p.m. But after the pool and before lights out, it was nonstop knee hockey. Every guy on the team brought two sticks for the tournament, but in their gear bags they also brought a sawed-off stick for knee hockey tournaments in the hotel hallways. Mitch fixed up a couple sticks for himself and Ike, cutting them down to about eighteen inches long and cutting the end of the blade off. To play, the team set up goals in the hallway and played each other one on one, up to five points. All the parents were down at the bar, and what they didn't know couldn't hurt them. The boys had most of the third floor to themselves and tried to keep the screaming to a minimum. Ike did great in his knee hockey games; he won most of them. He even beat Mario two out of three games. After their game, Mario grabbed Ike and picked him up.

"Who the hell brought this guy?" he joked.

Coach Paris had everyone ready to go for the tournament, and when it was time for their first game, they burst out of the gates flying. They were up on host team Rochester, 2-0, after the first period and then beat them 4-0 on Friday night in the opening round. On Saturday, in the semifinal round, a team from Two Rivers, Michigan, got the win, 1-0; honestly, the score should've been more like 5-0, but Randy McKay was unbelievable in nets. That was not a particularly good game, except for the fights. Mario and Zitz won both their battles, but that also meant they were both in the box for five minutes each. It's tough to win when your best players are serving penalties.

After the semifinal game, the team got back to the hotel, had a meal, played a little knee hockey, and then took a dip in the pool. It was the end of a long day, so everyone was shot and checked in well before curfew. On Sunday at noon, they played the third-place game against Madison—and it was the best and cleanest game of the tournament that day. They earned one penalty, and it happened to be on Mitch for roughing. The Madison team, however, took six penalties, and the VFW team scored on four of them. Their power play unit was an absolute machine. Final score, 5-1. Mitch made no goals in the tournament, but he did get three assists, all three of which were on the power play. Chicago played Two Rivers in the championship game later that day. Final score, 4-1, Two Rivers

Before leaving Rochester on Sunday, Mr. Dawson took Mitch and Ike to Pasquale's, Mr. Dawson's favorite spaghetti spot in the whole world. The Dawson family usually went once a year, so this extra visit was a real treat, especially for Mitch's dad. He always said that Pasquale's spaghetti was the best. The family had a really good meal, and Mr. Dawson ordered more spaghetti sauce and meatballs to go.

The next tournament was up in Eveleth, Minnesota, in a couple weeks, and Mitch would finally get to see his honey.

Growing up in Saint Paul, especially on the East Side, you'd have no choice but to believe that the area was the center of the hockey universe. Every playground had hockey teams, and the Johnson High School team had won state championships multiple times. In fact, Johnson was in the high school hockey tournament almost every year, and when they weren't, schools like Washington, Monroe, Murray, or Harding would pop up and make an appearance. Of course, nobody's dumb here either; places like South Saint Paul and Edina were also powerhouse programs too, but the East Side of Saint Paul had always had an amazing hockey tradition.

But then you'd go to a place like Eveleth, Minnesota, on the Iron Range and find out that maybe Saint Paul wasn't the center of hockey. They certainly had a great history on the East Side, and those high school championships were nothing to shake a stick at, but Eveleth had earned more state titles. They start with names like Mariucci, Mayasich, and Ikola and go from there. The place is all hockey, all the time.

Zitz and Mitch got out of school early for the tournament and rode up together. Once they arrived at the Iron Range, they drove straight to the arena in Eveleth. The first game was at 6:00 p.m., and as luck would have it, they were slated to play Virginia, Maggie's hometown team. Maggie, her sister Della, and three other girls were there in the lobby to greet them. As soon as Maggie saw Mitch come through the door, she ran over to give him a great big hug. A handful of Virginia guys weren't too happy about the reunion, based on the looks Mitch and Maggie got from them. Maggie looked gorgeous, and of course Della was a doll too, and their three girlfriends were just as pretty. Mitch was pretty sure he caught one of them eyeing Mario DiMucci when he came through the door.

As soon as you walk into the old Eveleth Hippodrome, countless banners hang from the rafters to greet you: five high school state championships, plus third place and consolation championship banners. Then there were the youth hockey championship banners. It was endless. In fact, the first banner in the arena was won by Eveleth's A-bantam state champs a couple of years ago. They were runners-up last year.

Edina won the A-bantam state championship last week and last year too. They weren't in the tournament this year, but Greenway is—and so is Hibbing, Bemidji, Warroad, Thunder Bay, and Virginia.

The official name of Mitch's team is Anderson-Nelson VFW, but if you were to look up at the brackets for the tournament, the tournament organizers had the team listed as Johnson. This misnomer was not an accident and likely done for rivalry purposes. After all, it's a lot easier to hate a Johnson team than a nondescript VFW team. These people took hockey very seriously.

If you check the record books, you'd find that back in the 1940s and 1950s, a lot of the state high school tournament games were between Eveleth and Johnson. Understandably, when any team that's even barely affiliated with Johnson High School shows up in Eveleth, it's cause for the locals to come out in numbers, and this game was no different. It was a little bit like David and Goliath—the great big city team taking on the little town of 4,000. It'd be an easy bet to say over one hundred people showed up for the game against Virginia, Eveleth's next-door neighbor and arch rival. Eveleth didn't like Johnson but they despised Virginia. The Eveleth people were actually rooting for us, which was pretty cool.

Even though the people in Eveleth considered Johnson a significant rival, the boys didn't know a thing about it. As soon as Mitch entered the arena, he could tell there was tension in the air. With that said, they were awesome hosts. They provided food tables for the teams during the whole tournament—so Mitch and his buddies helped themselves to lots of hotdish, pasties, and porketta. The people were actually super nice, too.

In the locker room before the first game, Coach Paris reminded them of what they could expect from this tournament. There was a lot of talent on the ice but also a lot of really physical play—and he was absolutely right. As soon as they dropped the puck in the first period, Mitch spent the entire game getting hacked, hooked, slashed, boarded, tripped, and cross-checked. It felt personal. And maybe it was—maybe the local boys didn't like the idea of the hottest girl from their school getting tied up with some clown from the cities like me. Anderson-Nelson still beat Virginia, 3-1, with stellar play from Randy in the nets, as always, and a goal and an assist for Mitch. When Virginia pulled their goalie with just a minute left in the game, Mitch was able to drop an empty net goal.

After the game, the team hung out with the girls, watched the next two games, and ate three different kinds of complimentary hotdish. Mitch even had porketta for the first time, and Zitz wasted no time helping himself to seconds. They also took some good-natured ribbing about Johnson playing the Eveleth powerhouse teams of the forties and fifties from some of the old timers.

Mr. Dawson took the hockey gear and headed over to the Coates Hotel in Virginia, where the rest of the team was staying. The next game was a real barn burner and about the most entertaining game Mitch had ever seen. It was Eveleth vs. Warroad. Warroad showed up with ten players, and what's really interesting was that three of their ten players were goalies. They don't dress three goalies for every game, but three different guys played nets in this game. When you have that small of a roster and they're all really good, a lot of times they're matched up against the weaker guys on the other team. This Warroad team had a ton of talent and they just kept coming after Eveleth until they wore themselves out and sent the game into overtime. Eveleth won, 2-1, but all three of the Warroad goalies were outstanding. Warroad didn't have big numbers, but man could those guys play hockey.

The last game was a blowout. Thunder Bay crushed Bemidji, 8-0, though it could have been much worse. With a running clock in the third period, the game was over in forty-five minutes flat. The East Siders would get Thunder Bay tomorrow afternoon at four, and after their performance against Bemidji, Coach Paris was proved right: The Canadians are really physical. Bemidji was the weakest team that they'd seen in this tournament and even compared with the teams in the last tournament. They just didn't look like they belonged. Zitz and Mitch rode back to the hotel with Coach Paris and Dylan. Maggie promised a surprise for tomorrow, and Mitch just couldn't wait.

When the Dawson car arrived at the range the night before, it had been dark, so nobody really got a real sense of the landscape. However, on the way to the arena in Eveleth the next day from the hotel in Virginia, the boys saw clearly what iron ore mining actually looks like. Surprisingly, the iron ore mines are not out in the middle of nowhere. One of them is right next to the cities of Eveleth and Virginia; the one they call the Thunderbird Mine basically connects Virginia to Eveleth, and it looks like the Grand Canyon. This mine is over three miles long and a mile across. They use monster machines to get the ore out of the ground. Mr. Dawson pointed out the big dump trucks, which are called production trucks, they use to carry the ore. The wheels alone on those monsters were twelve feet high.

Maggie's big surprise was evident the second they walked into the arena. Maggie, Della, and their girlfriends made a huge banner that must've been ten feet long. They hung it right behind the net at the far end of the rink. It read: "The Pride of the East Side." It had all of the teammates' names and jersey numbers on it. It was really impressive, actually, and it earned Mitch a lot of atta-boys from his teammates.

Anderson-Nelson was up 2-1 after two periods against Thunder Bay. Those guys were big, they were tough, and they hit hard, but the East Side boys outplayed them in every aspect of the game. Dylan Paris scored both goals: one on a breakaway and the other one on a power play. The kid's instincts were unbelievable.

Thunder Bay outshot them by a pretty wide margin, but again, Randy McKay was brilliant in nets. Thunder Bay kept taking stupid penalties for things like hooking and tripping, penalties that you take when you're not hustling, not working hard, and frustrated. In the third period alone, they played shorthanded just about the whole time. These guys were break- ing their sticks over the net they were so pissed. By the third period, Thunder Bay had made a point of trying to neutralize Dylan, but in doing so, they left Mario and Zitz alone, which gave them all the opportunity in the world. Both guys got a goal in the third period. Final score, 4-1.

It wasn't until the whole tournament was over that Mitch's team found out that Thunder Bay had only lost a few games that year. They were the top-rated bantam team in all of Ontario, Canada, which is a pretty damn big province, so getting whipped by a team from the East Side of Saint Paul was a monster upset—which explained the postgame brawl.

As everyone was skating through the line, shaking hands after the game as usual, one of the Thunder Bay players got to Dylan Paris. He shook hands with his right hand and then blasted Dylan on the side of the head with his left hand. Thus commenced the brawl. Every kid on the ice was in a fight. In fact, Mitch was in two—and he wasn't the only one. The parents from the Thunder Bay team were screaming bloody murder, and a couple of dads climbed over the chicken wire and ran out on the ice. The biggest problem was that the refs were already gone. The coaches ran out there too to try to break it up. It was a mess, but it was a lot of damn fun. Zitz squared off with the biggest kid on their team and beat the living shit out of him. He had the guy's jersey up over his head and managed to pound him right into the ice. The refs had to come back and get everything straightened out. It was a prime example of what it looked like to be sore losers.

After it was all over, Mitch had a black eye and Mario had hands that were bloodied by someone else's blood. Randy McKee managed to get in a couple of shots, and even Dylan got back into battle and held his own. Overall, it was a huge team victory. That night back at the Coates Hotel, all the girls came over to hang out. Coach ordered a bunch of pizzas, and they even had another little knee hockey tournament, injuries aside. Mitch sat out of the tournament so he could sit on a couch with Maggie the whole night and just relax. Mario disappeared with Maggie's girlfriend, Trudy—they must have found a quiet place to play a little grab-ass.

On Sunday, the East Side team beat Greenway for the tournament championship, 2-0. Randy McKay was easily the tournament MVP. Even though Greenway outshot the East Side in the game, Randy would not have it. He absolutely won the game for the team. The tournament organizers gave out one big team trophy, and then each player got an individual trophy. When it was all said and done, the folks of Eveleth could not have been nicer. Rivalry or not, those folks treated the opposing teams well. It must have been some form of mutual respect—from one legendary hockey culture to another.

Three weeks later, the last tournament was in Duluth and was organized as a four-team round robin: Anderson-Nelson, Duluth, Cloquet, and Hermantown, each of which was a stud team. Anderson-Nelson won one game and tied two games. Somehow, based on the way they scored it, they took second place. The team got to add yet another trophy to their collection playing some really solid hockey against some of the best teams in the state. Maggie even made it down from Virginia for two of the games, to Mitch's delight.

As much as Mitch loved his team over at Hayden Heights Playground, the hockey Mitch had been playing with the VFW guys for the past six weeks was the best hockey experience of his life. In that short time, Mitch felt he'd improved a lot, and he even made a lot of really good new friends. Playing on the Anderson-Nelson VFW team also provided a lot of opportunities to help at the VFW club, which was, surprisingly, almost as much fun as the hockey.

CHAPTER 25

THE VETS CLUB

It didn't take a genius to figure out how the VFW could afford to give their sponsored teams all the equipment and uniforms. The teams worked for it, and the VFW held fundraisers so they could buy bundles of hockey sticks. It wasn't complicated.

On the weekends when they didn't have an away hockey tournament, the guys from the A-bantam team worked at the VFW post on Payne Avenue. One weekend, they worked the Friday fish fry, and Sunday morning, they did a pancake breakfast. They all had to show up in their uniforms to clear tables and help with the dishes, which wasn't a glamorous job, but it did afford them some good team perks. On the bright side, tips were provided sometimes. Working at the VFW was a lot like working up at the golf course, and it was the same guys doing all the work—or not. Some of the guys worked harder at not doing work. These clowns were outside walking around and bullshitting all the time. As for Mitch, as much as he hated some parts of it, he preferred to do the work and get it over with. At the golf course, he'd established himself as a trustworthy guy, and he wanted to do the same at the VFW. One way the VFW was different from the golf course was the guys who worked the fundraisers who hadn't played for the VFW team in years. Some of the guys were out of high school but still took time to volunteer.

Another difference between the golf course and the VFW were the people. Oh my God, the people. Holy buckets.

Hundreds of people came through the events every weekend. There was no ban on smoking inside, which meant working in a thick cloud of smoke that very well might choke ya. Beyond that, anything a guy might wear would inevitably smell like smoke by the end of a volunteer shift. It was awful, but the guys really had no choice. Thankfully, the work itself was easy.

There were some veterans from the Korean war, but most were from World War II. There were a few of the old timers from what they called the great war, World War I. But there were two really old guys who had been in the Spanish–American War and fought with Teddy Roosevelt. Mitch didn't know the first thing about that war, but everyone knew about Teddy Roosevelt. He's on Mount Rushmore, for Christ's sake.

There was always a specific group of five or six guys who sat together at a table in the corner. Any time you'd visit the VFW, no matter the time of day, those guys would be there. They were the Vietnam guys. The war was still going on, so you'd think there'd be more of them. A couple of them wore their army uniform shirts, but most of them turned into hippies who grew out their hair and decorated their skin with tattoos. Two of the guys had been pretty badly injured over there—one was missing an arm, and another guy was in a wheelchair. It didn't take many days of volunteering for Mitch to notice that everybody else seemed to ignore the Vietnam guys. They weren't celebrated or honored at the VFW at all, not like the other veterans. Mitch had heard some of the Vietnam War commentary: People hate the Vietnam war and they treat its veterans like villains. All the evidence pointed to that being true.

Mitch and the rest of the team were slated to work at the VFW's biggest fundraiser of the year: the annual spaghetti dinner. This was no ordinary event. It was an all-you-can-eat affair of spaghetti, meatballs, salad with homemade Italian dressing, fresh Italian bread, and dessert for $2.00. Every dinner sold was pure profit because all the labor was on a volunteer basis, and everything else was donated, including all kinds of prizes for the raffle drawings. This event took a couple of days of prep and was where they made most of the money for their team. And there was a reason this dinner was a monster success every year: The guy who made the spaghetti sauce was none other than Enzo Petri. Mr. Petri had the production down to a science. He'd bring in a crew of guys who'd worked on the dinner for a couple of days—cooking the sauce, meatballs and pasta—including Mario DiMucci's dad, Carlo. On the eve of the event this year, Mario asked Mitch and Zitz if they wanted to come down and roll meatballs on Saturday, and they were happy to agree. How tough could it be to roll meatballs?

The first thing they heard when they arrived in the kitchen Saturday morning was Mr. Petri.

"OK, you boys, you go wash upa you hands and get started," he directed.

What a production it was. The kitchen had two huge commercial stoves, both of which had two giant kettles of Enzo Petri's famous homemade spaghetti sauce.

After washing their hands, Mitch and Zitz followed Mr. Petri into the walk-in cooler. On a shelf next to the kegs of Hamm's beer were boxes of meatball mix, each box weighing about twenty-five pounds. In total, there were almost two hundred pounds of meatball mix.

"Did you mix all this by yourself?" Mitch asked Mr. Petri.

"I no makea meatball, Mitch, this comes froma Sammy de Angelis," he said. "Sammy makea meatball mix and Italian sausage for many markets in town. It take me two weeks if I do this. He makes a very good meatball, you try later."

Mitch tried to do the math in his head to calculate how many this might serve, but he came up blank. Mitch had to remember to ask Mr. Petri later because there was a more pressing matter at hand: they had loads of meatballs to roll.

The meatball-making process started with Mr. Petri scooping out the meatball mix with an ice cream scoop. Doing so meant the meatballs were the perfect portion every single time. But that was the easy part. After scooping, the meatballs had to be rolled, and the five meatball rollers needed some coaching. After a few minutes of loading their meatballs onto the big commercial sheet pans they would use to bake them, they surveyed their work and could immediately tell they didn't know what they were doing; some of the meatballs looked like eggs, some looked like bricks, and some looked like hockey pucks.

"Oh, Marone, dis is all-a wrong," Mr. Petri mumbled. "Isabella, you teach, I go check da sauce."

Izzy rolled her eyes and shook her head, taking her father's place in the room.

"Mitch, you and Zack get a pass this time, but Mario, you should know better, you Strunza," she threw out the insult like her father. "You're a Pisano, for Christ's sake."

They were all a little embarrassed.

"OK, you guys, let's pretend for a couple of minutes you're not complete morons. This isn't difficult. These big sheet pans can each hold 150 meatballs. That means ten across and fifteen down, all right? All we have to do is roll them—but don't overroll them. The key is to roll them gently and make them perfectly round so that they can all fit. If there aren't exactly 150 on this sheet, Papa Petri will raise hell." She pointed at the half-filled sheet pans.

"OK, everybody, let's re-roll these meatballs. We'll probably do ten or eleven sheets today."

"How many people are they expecting?" Mitch asked Izzy.

"We're gonna be making over 1,500 meatballs." She was beaming. "And it looks like there's probably over sixty gallons of sauce. There could be more than 1,000 people if the weather's decent."

Enzo Petri stood over those kettles of spaghetti sauce for eight hours that day, so naturally the sauce was simmered to perfection. It took the meatball team all day to roll, bake, and store those meatballs. Before everyone finished cleaning up for the night, Enzo Petri made them all meatball sandwiches. He had a couple of fresh loaves of Italian bread on hand—and truth be told, he was absolutely right about those meatballs. They were so like his that you would never know that he hadn't made them himself. Certainly the best meatball sandwich Mitch had ever had.

The next morning, Mr. Petri was there by 6 a.m. with the rest of his guys to boil up the pasta. The bakery delivered fresh bread, and a couple of the moms were mixing up salad. When Mitch got there at nine, he, Mario, Zitz, and a couple of the other hockey guys started setting up banquet tables and fitting them with plastic tablecloths.

When noon hit, the place started to fill up with people coming from church. It didn't take long for the place to become packed, and it stayed that way all day. People were even showing up with containers to buy sauce to go, including Mitch's dad. The Dawson family arrived at noon, and while Mrs. Dawson and the kids stayed for a couple hours, Walter hung out all day, ate twice, and had a few beers with John and Sid Getz. Mitch was kind of surprised the brothers even showed up, as he'd never known them to be the type to hang around Payne Avenue.

At one point, Mr. Dawson waved Mitch over to say hello. As Mitch approached their table, he noticed a spread of some kind of paperwork they were showing his dad. Once Mitch got to the table, they shuffled all the paperwork and stuffed it into a folder.

"Mitch, I'm going to ask you a question," John Getz announced. "I know you're a straight shooter, so I want you to give me a straight answer."

"Sure," he agreed, a little nervous because he wasn't great with being put on the spot.

"Who do you think has the best spaghetti sauce?" he asked. "Your dad says it's Pasquale's down in Rochester, but I want to know what you think, son."

"My favorite spaghetti sauce is right here, made by Enzo Petri," Mitch admitted.

They all laughed.

"We agree," he said, still chuckling a bit. "Your dad thinks Pasquale's is best, so the three of us are all going to go down there to find out next week."

Mitch felt like he was missing some kind of inside joke. Why would they go all the way down to Rochester for a plate of spaghetti?

His dad changed the subject.

"Mitchell, guess what? John and Sid invited your mother and me to fly down to the Kentucky Derby next month. We'll all be guests in Murray Getz's suite at the race track. How about that?"

"We're going to take your mom and dad down to Kentucky to have a good time," John Getz said.

"You see, Murray, John, and I own a horse that's in the race, and we're also taking a private tour of our whiskey distillery to drink some really good bourbon," Sid revealed.

"It sounds like a lot of fun," Mitch said half-heartedly, not sure why he needed to know all the details. Nor did he have the slightest clue of the scope and scale of what it meant to own a racehorse that ran in the Kentucky Derby. It sounded like a big deal, but he had no idea how big of a deal it really was.

"Now your dad has to take your mom out shopping for a big hat," John said with a chuckle. Dad and Sid laughed right along with him. Apparently big hats are a big deal at the Kentucky Derby?

"Mitch, we've got some stuff to go over, and you better get back to work," Mr. Dawson said.

Sid then slid a five-dollar bill across the table at Mitch, who looked down at it and then looked over at his dad, who gave him the nod. Mitch picked it up and put it in his pocket.

"Gee, thanks Mr. Getz!" As he scurried back to work, they got back to their paperwork.

The funniest moment Mitch experienced during the big spaghetti dinner happened when he was helping Coach Paris man the table selling tickets for the dinner. A tiny old lady hobbled in on her cane, working her way down the long hallway to the banquet room to Mitch and Coach Paris. Both of them watched her work her way toward them, and it pained them to watch her move. It took the poor old lady forever, but she finally arrived at the ticketing table.

"Well, hi there, young fellas," she said.

"Hello."

"Young man, can you get me a chair so I can sit and catch my breath?" she asked me.

"Sure can!"

Mitch thought she must've been 114 years old or something. He wasted no time getting her a chair and helping her sit down.

"Thank you very much," she said. "Do you fellas mind if I wait here a few minutes? My mom's parking the car." Then she let out a cackle that could've raised the dead. She laughed so hard at her own joke, and Coach Paris and Mitch nearly cry-laughed along with her. She reminded Mitch of Manny's mom and dad, always the jokesters.

Mitch's mom came back to pick him up at 6:30 p.m. He didn't have to hang around to clean up because he'd got there early to help with setup. It was such a fun event that he couldn't wait to do it again next year—and show Izzy how much he could improve with his meatball rolling.

CHAPTER 26

SHOWDOWN ON WYOMING AVENUE

With school almost over for the year and Hazel Park Junior High in the rear view mirror, it was time to get on with the summer. EZ and Mitch had their gloves and bats in hand and were headed down to the playground, planning to pick up Ike and Manny on the way as they always did. It was time to see if they were going to have a baseball team this year.

The guys always got a kick out of going to Manny's house because Manny's mom and dad were the funniest people in the neighborhood. It was a running joke that they would say the most horrible things about each other—in jest, of course. Like the night they went to Manny's house to watch a Twins game on TV and Mr. Klaus answered the door.

"Come in, boys, I get Manfred for you," he'd said. "But be quiet. Ve don't vant to disturb ze creature. She hasn't been fed today."

Right away you could tell he'd been into the schnapps.

"Mr. Klaus, how *is* Mrs. Klaus today?" Mitch had asked. "Vell boys, you know da old sayin'? If it wasn't for Mrs. Klaus, I wouldn't have a piss to... no... I mean a pot. I couldn't... I don't... oh, ya. I wouldn't have a pain in the ass."

It was priceless.

Mrs. Klaus answered the door when the boys knocked for Manny.

"Hello, Mrs. Klaus."

"Hi boys, come in."

"How's Mr. Klaus today?" Mitch asked.

"Well, you know, boys, he's better than nuttin," she professed in her thick German accent. Which was hysterical because Mr. Klaus walked in the kitchen just as she said it.

"Oh, my dad wanted me to tell you guys he's gonna swing by later to see if he can borrow Mr. Klaus' power drill. His is on the fritz," Mitch stated.

"You bet, no problem for old Walter," Mr. Klaus said.

"Ferdinand, Your drill is out in da garage on da verk bench," Mrs. Klaus chimed in.

"Woman, I know right vare is it mine power drill, I'm not as dumb as I look."

Mrs. Klaus paused, a mischievous grin on her face.

"Ferdinand, you couldn't *possibly* be as dumb as you look."

Mitch almost pissed himself.

On their way to Ike's house, Snag and Crime Scene appeared out of nowhere, coming up the street toward them. When they got close enough to talk, they stopped.

"What are you guys doing?" Snag inquired. "Going down to play softball?"

"No, we're heading down to the playground," Manny told them. "We're going to hit some fungos and play 500. Zitz and a couple of other guys are going to meet us, and we're just going to hang out down there today."

"How about tomowow fow thoftball?" Crime Scene asked.

"Yeah, try to find some more people," Mitch said, after noting Manny and EZ's nods.

"Can we play flashlights tonight?" Snag asked.

EZ looked a little disgusted.

"No, we're not playing flashlight tag tonight," he said. Snag seemed surprised—and a little more upset than one would expect—by this response.

"Why not? Why can't we play tonight?" Snag insisted.

EZ glared at her.

"What the hell," he shot back. "Do you need some kind of explanation? How's this: I don't feel like it, I'm not in the mood."

Snag stood there looking a little dumbfounded. Crime Scene had her arms crossed, annoyed for her sister's sake.

After about an hour of playing 500 at the playground, it started to drizzle. No big deal; they kept playing. They had nothing else to do. But after another twenty minutes, it started to pour, so they hightailed it over to the main building. In their hurry to get out of the rain, they'd forgotten their stack of balls. The boys played a quick game of Rock, Paper, Scissors to see who had to go back out in the downpour and grab them.

"OK, ready guys? Rock, Paper, Scissors, Shoot," Mitch said.

There were four papers and one rock.

"See ya, Ike!" EZ teased.

"I never win," Ike said.

"Did you remember your umbrella, Ike?" EZ continued ribbing him.

"Ike, if you hurry up, I'll buy you a bottle of pop," Manny offered.

As Ike dashed back out into the rain, the rest of the guys retreated further into the playground building to get their pops. They saw Connie, the playground director, through her office window, screaming at that jerk, Ray Munger. It was hard to understand them at first, but once they got a little closer, they could make out her words. By the sound of it, Ray had been caught smoking in the boy's bathroom, driven inside because of the rain. He was in there with a couple of other kids until one of the baseball coaches who had been down at the playground for baseball sign-ups walked into the can. A big cloud of smoke came billowing out as soon as the door opened.

Connie was letting Ray have it, but he was yelling back at her and trying to claim innocence.

"It was the other kids," he tried. "They were smoking, not me."

"I've had it with you, Ray," Connie shouted. "You're out of here for a month."

"A month?" he argued. "You're crazy. I'm telling you, it wasn't me. It was those other kids."

"Get out, Ray. Get out right now and don't come back for a month, I mean it."

It looked like Ray was going to start to cry, which is what assholes do when they don't get their way.

On his way out the door, Ray threw a shoulder into EZ, who wasn't looking, and knocked the bottle of pop right out of his hands. It smashed all over the concrete floor.

"Hey, asshole, you owe me a dime, you Rat," EZ shouted.

Ray stopped short, walked over, grabbed EZ by the arm, and swung him right into the pop machine. EZ hit that pop machine face first. After that, Ray dropped EZ and ran out the door and into the rain, crying like a pussy.

Connie had seen what'd happened and ran out the door after him.

"That's it, Ray, never come back here. You're out for good," she yelled. As she walked back up to the boys, she gasped. "Eric, your nose!"

When EZ's face bounced off the Bubble-Up machine, his nose burst. There was blood everywhere. Connie grabbed some towels and told EZ to lay down on the mat in the gym to try to stop the bleeding. His forehead above his right eye was banged up too.

Connie was an old retired Army nurse, so EZ was in good hands. She managed to get the bleeding to stop, and she had enough experience to tell his nose wasn't broken.

"Eric, I'm going to call your parents," she said.

Fighting back tears, EZ shook his head.

"No, it's okay, Connie," EZ pleaded. "My mom is out of town with my sister, and my dad probably isn't home yet. He took my other sister and her friends roller skating in North Saint Paul."

"You sure?" she asked, searching his face.

"I'm fine, thanks."

With EZ's bleed-out averted, Mitch changed the subject to distract from the situation.

"Is Ray really out for good?" Mitch asked. "Connie, are you serious?"

"Yup, that's the end of it," she confirmed. "He's outgrown this place."

After years of terrorizing all the little kids, especially the girls on the general skating rink, it had finally happened: The Rat had been given the playground death sentence, a lifetime ban.

Only one other time in known playground history had such a punishment been handed down. It happened a few years ago, when the cops caught Terry Hubble trying to break into the playground building one night. Now, the Rat joins Terry Hubble in the hall of infamy, and they couldn't be happier.

Besides, Ray was sixteen now and would be going to high school at the end of the summer. There weren't any sports for him to play down at the playground anymore. He'd aged out. He really didn't have a reason to hang around Hayden Heights Playground, except that he had nowhere else to go, and he sure as hell couldn't make any teams at Hill High School. Those guys were good at everything. The Rat was just big and lazy. He'd played all the sports but was never any good, just big and lazy.

Remembering their original mission, Manny piped up.

"Hey, Connie, how are we looking for a baseball team this year?"

"Not good, guys, not good," she said. "I've got no coach lined up, and right now, we're sitting at six guys, maybe seven. I'll make some calls around to the other playgrounds to see if they're going to field a team."

Their disappointment was obvious, and she did her best to reassure them.

"The problem is, by the time guys get to your age, they start playing VFW or doing other things. There aren't many teams out there with guys your age. I'll let you all know what I find out, though. Now that I think of it, the VFW tryouts are this week down at Phalen Playground if you guys want to try that."

It sounded like they were aging out around the playground, too.

EZ was a prideful little shit, but he was hurting and wanted to get out of the playground building as quickly as he could before he really started to cry. Conveniently, the rain had stopped pretty soon after the whole incident. Connie jammed a couple wads of facial tissue up his schnoz and handed him a clean towel before they headed home.

On the walk home, they talked about what they'd like to do to Ray Munger if they ever had the chance and the guts. His actual size rivaled how big a prick he was, which made it even more important that somebody get a hold of the guy and slap the living shit out of him. EZ, of course, had the most creative idea.

"I'd like to lock him in a room with Snag and Crime Scene," EZ said. "I'd throw some Twinkies in the room and let them tear each other apart. That would be a three-birds-one-Twinkie sort of solution."

He got a few shoulder slaps from that joke, but the merriment didn't last long.

After walking on for a few minutes, EZ stopped and moaned, holding his head.

"Guys, I gotta sit down for a second. My head hurts, and I think I might be sick."

Ike knelt down in front of EZ to look at him closer.

"You might have a concussion," he suggested. "Eric, we've got to get you home."

EZ looked up at Ike and argued.

"What the hell do you know about—"

He stopped when he remembered that Ike had probably had one or two concussions of his own at the hands of his father. They all sat there in silence for a few minutes until Eric felt well enough to keep walking.

By the time they turned up Wyoming Avenue, EZ was looking terrible. You could even see the swelling starting around his right eye. Just then, as it was when they'd left for the playground, Snag and Crime Scene appeared out of nowhere again. They all knew EZ was going to get an earful from Snag. Her timing couldn't have been better... or worse.

EZ always held the upper hand when it came to his and Snag's snafus only because he was just wittier than she was. She was a better target than him too because of all her odd features and habits. As she approached and noticed his condition, she became obviously curious to find out what had happened, but more than that, she seemed delighted it was Eric who was suffering.

Just before the girls caught up to them, the roar of motorcycle engines floated down Curve Street, getting louder as the seconds passed. Sure enough, four rode past us, coming up the street toward the golf course. Those four Harleys sounded like fifty.

Though they were loud, they drove by pretty slowly. Mitch wondered what they'd want up this way. When they got to the end of the street, they cut down Winthrop and went out to Larpenteur. Maybe they'd found a new shortcut. Mr. Dawson would not be happy if that was the case.

Complete with long hair and leather jackets, hippies on motorcycles would cruise up and down the Dawson's street, which infuriated Mr. Dawson and the rest of his buddies in the neighborhood. The curious thing was there's nothing of interest in the neighborhood. They shouldn't really have a reason for coming up this way only to maybe cut over to Larpenteur Ave, but half of Winthrop Street isn't even paved. It didn't make a lot of sense, but one or two rode up the street every couple of days. These bikes were outfitted completely with ape hangers, sissy bars, and saddlebags. The riders had goggles and helmets on so nobody could get a good look at them, which was probably just the way they wanted it. They didn't seem to want anything, either. They didn't make any trouble. They were just loud. The Harleys looked pretty cool though. One had bright red and orange flames painted on the gas tank.

Once they'd passed the kids and disappeared from view, Crime Scene pointed at EZ.

"What da hell happened to you?"

The boys continued their trek up the street without a word.

"By the looks of that bruise, I'm sure it'll be an improvement," Snag remarked.

They still kept walking.

"Hey, Char, Eric might be really hurt," Manny said over his shoulder.

That didn't stop Snag, though. She took the situation as an opportunity to finally give Eric the endless ration of shit that he usually gave her. She'd be the one to relentlessly hammer the insults on him for change. Alas, if it were only that simple. Little did she know what was coming.

The two sisters were following close behind, with Snag giving Eric the needle. Insults like, "Hey Eric, have you been chasing parked cars again?" and "What happened? Were you staring into the mirror too long and your face blew up?" and "Did you smart off to the wrong third grader and she kicked your ass." She had some pretty good digs in there, but it wasn't the time for them. They were wearing down the crew. Manny finally turned around and explained.

"That asshole Ray Munger bounced EZ's head off the pop machine down at the playground."

"No shit," Snag said. "Well, I hope your face didn't wreck that pop machine, Eric, it would be a shame to have to get a new one just because your ugly face was printed on it." She cackled. "Maybe you finally got what you deserved."

Before Char could savor her one and only victory over Eric "EZ" Golyn, Eric stopped, blew the blood out of his nose, and turned to let her have it with both barrels.

"Really, Charlotte? This is what you think I deserve, after all this time, you really feel this is what I deserve, you mangy ape? I got my face smashed in, Charlotte."

That was odd. He never called her Charlotte. She looked surprised; they all were, in fact.

"So, I wanna be clear on this," EZ sniffed. "You're happy that the Rat, the most hated piece of shit in the neighborhood, did this to me? You're happy for him and you're happy I've got a smashed-in face?"

He wiped the crusted blood off his face the best he could, looked at Snag, and paused for a moment—just long enough for Snag to turn white as a sheet. She knew she'd poked the bear. She knew that in her glee she'd pushed too far, and now she was about to get it like never before.

But Eric didn't do anything. He simply informed her of how it'd be.

"How's this, Charlotte: No flashlight tag for you. Not tonight, not tomorrow night, not ever. You hear me? Not ever."

Snag shook her head.

"No flashlights?" she said, her voice rising a pitch. "You can't do that. I want to play flashlights, Eric, goddamn you." Her voice was choking up a bit.

"Well, you should've kept your big alligator trap shut," Eric snapped.

Snag yelled at him.

"Well, you're a big pussy!"

At this point, EZ and Snag were standing toe to toe, with EZ looking up at Snag. Mitch was afraid she might throw a punch right at his mouth—a nice fat lip might complement the other distorted facial features he was sporting.

"I'm telling you right now, Charlotte, keep your mouth shut or you're gonna be sorry," EZ warned.

"Sorry for what? Sorry that you're a short, rotten, lying little prick?"

That did it. First, Ray the Rat had humiliated him down at the playground in the unfortunate encounter with the Bubble-Up machine. Now, literally adding her insults to his injury, the last person in the world he needed to deal with was Snag. Maybe it would have been okay if she'd taken a few jabs at Eric and let it go, but she made EZ feel that she was actually glad that the Rat had hurt him that day. She wasn't actually glad of it, but she was so far down the tracks in her mess that she couldn't walk it back, so she just kept piling it on—a classic mistake when you're overmatched in an insult battle.

"Rotten little prick, am I?" EZ asked. "That's it." Eric stepped back and took a deep breath.

Even though he was wounded and bloodied, EZ summoned a litany of insults that would've made Don Rickles sob.

"Listen, you slack-jawed, knock-kneed, lazy-eyed, pigeon-toed, snaggle-toothed, hairy-lipped orangutan. I wish I was born with a dozen more middle fingers just to let you know how I really feel about you."

Snag started to wilt.

"Your face can make an onion cry."

"You shut up, Eric!!!"

"Seriously, Charlotte, how does it feel to be twenty-six years old in the tenth grade?" He didn't wait for any answer. "You fuckin' brain donor. I heard they held you back in grade school twice because you couldn't figure out which crayons tasted best."

The tide had swiftly turned against Snag. EZ had her on the ropes, and then he delivered the knockout punch. Crime Scene looked on, speechless.

"Now, do us all a favor and climb that tree, so you and your big muscular feet and hairy nipples can swing from limb to limb all the way home."

The guys looked around at each other. Where the hell did "hairy nipples" come from?

Snag backed away from Eric, both hands covering her mouth as she started to cry. Now, understand this: Snag doesn't cry. Scream hysterically? Yes. But she doesn't cry. Yet now, for the first time, she cried. There was no denying that EZ had cut deep enough to really hurt her. This was different from the days past when they would give each other shit. Somehow, this was different.

"Eric, how could you?" she pleaded. "I can't believe you would say that."

"Why not, you big, nasty fur-bearing creature?" EZ took a step closer to make his point. "Let's see. I'm in the middle of the street, bleeding like a stuck pig, and my eye is swelling shut. Remember, Charlotte, you started this shit, not me."

There it was again; he'd called her Charlotte.

Usually, after roughing Snag up verbally, EZ would be beaming with pride. But nothing like that happened this time.

Eric's nose started bleeding again, so he turned and continued home without another word, and the rest of the guys slunk after him. Only a few steps later, Snag ran up behind Eric, and for a second, Mitch thought she was going to slug him.

"Eric, I hate you," she sobbed. "I hate your guts."

EZ turned around.

"Yeah, and you smell like pork and beans," EZ responded.

Snag took off in the opposite direction of the main group. EZ watched her go, and then turned to Mitch.

"Doc, it may not look like it, but I've never felt better in my life."

Joy and EZ's dad got home from roller skating about half an hour after the guys got to Eric's house. By this time, the bleeding had stopped again, but Eric's face was an absolute mess. His right eye was swollen shut. Joy took one look at him and nearly got sick, and naturally his dad wanted to know what the hell went on, so Eric filled him in.

Gloria and EZ's mom rolled in shortly after that. They'd been up in Duluth for a couple of parades over the weekend—part of Gloria's duties as the Saint Paul Winter Carnival Queen of the Snow Cones.

Eric's mom was understandably upset when she saw her son's face. Glo, on the other hand, was torn between razzing Eric like Snag did or hunting down The Rat and going after him herself. Nobody would put it past Gloria to go looking for Ray. If you dared to put your hands on someone in her family, you'd better be prepared to meet the full wrath of Gloria. Glo had no fear... of anybody.

EZ's dad was about to go up to the golf course and have a little talk with Mrs. Munger, who worked in the kitchen at the golf course, but Eric begged him not to go. That's not how things were done. Kids were supposed to settle the shit between themselves, not get the parents involved. EZ's dad wasn't convinced, but EZ managed to talk him out of getting in the middle of it.

Eric's mom and Gloria worked up at the golf course part time, too, so Eric's mom said she'd take care of it. Mrs. Munger was the nicest lady but had absolutely no control over her son. Somebody would gain control over him one day and hopefully kick the living shit out of him once and for all.

The mood settled down after a bit, and after Gloria got all of her stuff put away, Mitch filled her in on the showdown between EZ and Snag. At first, she didn't seem to think anything of it; it was the normal course of business in the neighborhood, after all. But then I gave her a more detailed account, relaying specifically some of the things that were said. She got a kick out of a lot of them.

"There is something weird between those two," Mitch noted.

Gloria smiled and agreed.

"Oh, it's weird alright."

Of course, there was no love lost between Glo and the Finch twins. They too had had their battles over the years, usually during softball games. She's had to endure those two imbeciles all of her life, through school and neighborhood stuff, and they'd finally learned to leave each other alone.

CHAPTER 27

ROUGH START

If you want to talk about a rough start to summer, picture this: It was the day after school let out for the year and everyone was excited for a fun summer. But then Bobby Kennedy was assassinated in California. He was in the running for president and probably would have won.

Mitch was only about nine or ten when President John F. Kennedy was shot and killed, and he could remember it being a big deal to everybody—especially his parents—but he didn't remember much beyond that. Bobby's assassination felt like a much bigger deal; maybe because Mitch was old enough to understand things a little bit more and everybody was rooting for Bobby Kennedy to be the next president. He could remember how upset his mom and dad were when President Kennedy was killed in 1963. This time around, his mom seemed to be just as upset; she was watching the television day and night.

Despite everything, Mitch was learning that no matter how big the tragedy and no matter how many people it affected, life goes on. He still had to go to the golf course and work. His dad had to go to work. The buses were all still running. Life wouldn't stop for him or anybody else. It seemed that in the wake of everything that had happened, Hubert Humphrey, the vice president from Minnesota, would run for president. Mitch's mom was a big Humphrey fan—his dad, not so much.

Over the following week after the showdown between EZ and Snag, it wasn't uncommon to see the twins skulking around the neighborhood, looking for something to do. Whatever they planned to do that summer certainly wouldn't involve a swimming pool in their backyard. Last summer's pool disaster still gets a lot of laughs every time someone brings it up.

They kept coming around, looking to play softball or flashlight tag, or to just hang out. But the guys all found themselves in a different place than last year. They were all getting older and had started to do their own things. None of the guys had played a game of softball or flashlight tag once this year—and it didn't seem like a big deal because they all had so many other things going on. Yet those two had nothing, and they seemed oblivious to the general shift away from neighborhood games. They'd already stopped by Mitch's house twice this week. Ideally, someone would put them out of their boredom and give them jobs.

As Connie promised, she'd called around to see about a baseball team, but she couldn't get enough guys for a team at Hayden Heights. This sudden space in Mitch's schedule gave him a chance to put in a lot more hours at the golf course; Manny too.

Zitz and EZ had both tried out for the VFW baseball team and they both made it: Zitz the starting center fielder and EZ, smashed face and all, an infielder, probably second base. Baseball was EZ's best sport, even though hockey is the sport that had his heart. His skills as a good hitter and a great fielder make a big impact on the baseball field. He just makes things happen when he's in a baseball game, especially when he gets on base. He'll drive the other team nuts. EZ had speed, but more than that, he had a knack for stealing bases and could stretch a single into a double.

EZ and Zitz got the same kind of treatment from the VFW baseball team as Mitch did with the VFW hockey team: pro-style uniforms, bags, jackets, warm-ups, and a pretty heavy schedule that included quite a bit of travel. Mitch was still beat up from the extended hockey season and, frankly, he didn't think the VFW could use another light hitter with no real position like him. He could pitch some, but the VFW guys were loaded with pitching studs, mostly from the Babe Ruth League over on Larpenteur Avenue by Presentation Church.

With Leon Tiller still "away," Ike wasn't delivering newspapers anymore. Honestly, he didn't even know if his dad was still employed at the Pioneer Press. Mitch asked him if he wanted to come up to the golf course for some work, a suggestion that lit Ike up like a pinball machine. He needed to make some money, and he remembered the kindness that the Getz brothers had shown him a couple months back at Christmas. Mitch brought up the idea to John Getz, who loved it. Ike still had to clear it with his mom, but after talking to her, he was able to start work the very next day.

Considering Leon Tiller's proclivity toward antisemitism, the whole situation could be explosive should Leon Tiller ever find out. Knowing Leon's steep hatred of the Getz brothers, Mitch wondered if they found any great satisfaction in the fact that his son was in their employ. Of course, there is no telling when or if Leon Tiller would come home, and Mitch was fairly convinced that the world didn't care; it was as if it had gone right on spinning without him, like he had never existed. Life moved on, no matter what.

Mitch noticed that Ike and his siblings had been happier since their dad's arrest. He'd even see Ike's mom go out for walks with the kids—sometimes with some of the other moms in the neighborhood. This never would have happened if Leon Tiller had still been around.

Summer had only just begun, but Mitch, Zitz, and Manny knew that summer vacation would be cut short because they wanted to play high school football. Mario DiMucci from down at Wilder would probably be the quarterback for the junior varsity squad. During his time with the VFW hockey team, Mitch had the chance to watch the guy a lot, and he proved himself the best guy on the ice, no matter the opposing team. Just a great athlete all around. But Mitch had heard rumors that football might be his best sport—and he's a kicker too. Zitz is a fullback/linebacker. Manny might even make varsity as a lineman; wrestling brought out Manny's natural athleticism. Mitch was a receiver/defensive back with good speed and good hands.

Manny and Mitch spent some summer evenings that year running around the golf course after work. The course was about two and a half miles around, and you'd need to stay close to the edge because that's where it's most level. The boys wore their football spikes, and they sprinted up Devil's Hill as fast as they could at the end of every run. Then they'd walk down the hill and sprint up backward as fast as they could manage. Once in a while, Gloria and Izzy would run and drill with them. Surprisingly, the girls kept up every step of the way, and every once in a while, Gloria would beat them at their own drill.

After their runs, Manny and Mitch put on work gloves and tossed bricks back and forth till they couldn't take it anymore. This exercise was designed to help a ton—Mitch as a receiver and Manny as a lineman. They shook hands as hard as they could at the end of each workout, but Mitch always won, which showed he had the upper hand over Manny in one way: Mitch had a stronger grip.

Captain's practice would start in August, then two-a-day practices with the coaches. According to Reno Petri, the coach practices could be brutal, especially in the heat. The worst part about being new to the team had nothing to do with weather or the game itself—yes, it was the hazing rituals. The upperclassmen had done everything from shaving a guy's head or taping him to the goal post to locking him in their locker or throwing him, bare-assed, into a full girls locker room and holding the door shut. Reno told them about one guy who got his eyebrows shaved off. Unlucky for him, the damn things never grew back. If you've ever seen anyone with their eyebrows shaved off, you know how creepy it can be.

With all the football practices and Maggie working at the fair every day, Mitch was looking at a summer of seeing Maggie hardly at all, which was just another reason the long-distance thing was wearing him out. Mitch had stopped calling her every night; they ran out of things to talk about weeks ago.

All kinds of things happened that summer. Reno Petri got a car, a 1959 Ford Fairlane, which was a pretty big deal. Mitch didn't know anybody else who had a car, and the thing was huge. He and his dad bought it at an auction for pretty cheap. He said it'd been an old highway patrol car and had heavy-duty everything, including the reminiscent look of an old highway patrol car. The car was not pretty, but it cruised nicely enough.

Izzy turned sixteen and got a job at the A&W drive-in over by Aldrich Arena. Reno gave her a ride to work sometimes, which worked out pretty well because he was working right across the street at Shoppers' City. Izzy also picks up some hours at the golf course. Reno said he'd be able to drive Mitch, Zitz, and Manny to football practice some days, even. Gloria was sixteen too, and she worked at the golf course just about every day—in the dining room, and then sometimes on the weekends she would drive around in a golf cart, serving golfers beer and cocktails. To hear her tell it, she was making a fortune in tips. Talk about an easy job.

It wasn't unusual for all of them to be there on the weekends, and it often ended up being a lot of fun.

A week after the run-in with Ray the Rat, EZ's face still looked pretty bad. It didn't phase EZ though. Even if the chances of running into The Rat at the golf course were pretty high, EZ wanted to grab a bag and do some caddying to start making money.

On their way up to the golf course one day, Ike, Manny, EZ, and Mitch saw Charlotte off in the distance, standing on the corner as if waiting for a bus. Since the 14-B bus stop was a block away, they figured she must've been waiting for something else. As they got closer, they noticed she looked a little different than usual. She'd combed her hair, and when they got even closer, they could tell she was wearing makeup and that dreadful perfume. She put on her best smile when she saw the crew. She must have been waiting for them, Mitch figured, so he braced himself for a renewed deluge of EZ/Snag snark. But he was wrong.

EZ acted as though he could see right through her.

"Hey guys, are you going up to the golf course?" Snag asked. She fell into step with them. "Are you guys gonna be around tonight? I was wondering..."

Everyone kept walking without a word. She ran ahead of the group at that point, sensing the need to be dramatic, and stopped right in front of EZ.

"I thought if you guys would be around tonight, we could hang out and play flashlight tag."

EZ looked at her for the first time that day, his eyes steely.

"Charlotte, do you remember this face, the one that got smashed in? And how you thought it was so funny?" he spoke directly to her, his gaze not straying for a second. "I told you before, Jug-Head, your flashlight tag privileges have been permanently revoked. You will never play again. I'm I clear? Never."

Having said his piece, EZ sidestepped her and walked away. Snag stood motionless there on Winthrop Street, speechless as she faced the reality EZ had imposed. The rest of the boys waited a beat before following EZ—and even as they passed the driving range and turned up toward the clubhouse, they could still see Snag standing there in the distance. Even more creepy was the fact that she was still standing there twenty-five minutes later as they passed by in the other direction while they were caddying. She provided her most hate-filled glare as they passed. EZ didn't acknowledge her at all as they walked by, and once Snag saw she was getting nothing else from them, she turned and ran away.

"What is it with you two?" Mitch asked. "She just wants to play flashlights."

EZ growled.

"She can kiss my ass. Between playing baseball this summer and working up here, who has time? Besides, I'm going to hang out at my new girlfriend's house tonight."

"Get the hell out of here, you got a new squeeze? Who is it?"

"Remember Linda Meeks?"

"You're shittin' me," Mitch said. "From North Saint Paul, the figure skater?"

"Yeah, she lives up by Silver Lake."

"No shit." They were all incredulous. "When did you start tangling with her?"

"Jesus Christ, Doc, you ask a lot of questions." EZ sounded exasperated. "You don't need to know everything. Let's just say I've been working on this one for a while. She'll be the perfect girlfriend for the summer. They have an in-ground pool and a cabin on the Apple River in Wisconsin. To top it all off, she just got her driver's license. Besides, you've seen her; she's a babe."

"Yeah, we've seen her skating up at Aldrich almost every weekend."

"Has your new summertime honey seen your face since your encounter with the Bubble-Up machine?"

"Nah, but I called her and told her about it. No big deal." EZ shrugged and changed the subject. "Now, get this, Doc, she's going to train out in Colorado with the same figure skating coach who trained Peggy Fleming. She's even met Peggy Fleming, and they think she has a real future. Who knows, maybe the '72 Olympics?"

Mitch felt a little jealous of EZ: a gorgeous potential Olympic figure skater, in-ground pool, and a frickin' Apple River cabin? Leave it to EZ to work all the angles.

Ike spent his day at the driving range while the rest of them caddied two loops on the golf course, absolutely dragging ass. As if that weren't enough, they had to deal with Ray the Rat that day. He'd been picking on the new caddies again, so naturally, some of the new kids refused to come back to work—why would they? If it was between a chance at a decent tip or a chance at a decent tip (or not) while also putting up with the Rat, nobody could blame them for staying away.

The boys were sitting by the clubhouse at the end of their rounds, finishing a few bottles of pop before heading home, when Ray came bolting up toward them. Anytime the Rat comes toward you, he rushes at you like he's going to hit you or something, so you've always got to be on guard. For Ray the Rat, it's all about intimidation. In this situation, he intended to ambush Mitch, all while bitching about caddy assignments. He knew that John Getz relied on Mitch to keep the caddies straightened out, and he hated that.

"Hey Dawson, why did I get only one loop today? I heard all you guys did two."

He was talking to Mitch but his eyes were trained on Ike.

"If you keep pushing around the new caddies, you won't get any, so go take it up with John, Ray," Mitch defended.

"Why don't you come back tomorrow and maybe they'll put you to work scrubbing goose shit off golf balls," EZ chimed in. "Meanwhile, go home, put on your ballerina shoes, a little lipstick, and tell yourself some knock-knock jokes."

The rest of them just about cried from laughing so hard.

"What did you say?" Ray barked back.

"Go piss up a rope, you fucking clown," Manny remarked.

Manny's words shocked Mitch more than they did The Rat—Manny never says anything and Manny never picks a fight, but there's only so much shit you can take from a bully. Ray knew this too.

"Oh, so you're a big hard guy now, Manny, is that it? You're some kind of hard guy now that you're going to high school, huh? Decide it's finally time to grow a sack?"

Manny wasn't a fighter by nature, but he'd been working out almost every day, plus he's learned a lot about wrestling. If those two actually squared off, Manny might have a chance, but that's the thing with Ray—there's no squaring with him. It's all about sucker punches and cheap shots, and what he did to EZ down at the playground was a prime example. Eric wasn't even looking when Ray grabbed his arm and smashed him into that pop machine.

Manny stood up suddenly, and when he did, the Rat took a couple steps back. Now that was a telling sign if ever they'd seen one. When Ray got a little bit of real push back from a real opponent, the first thing he did was give ground. Ray had a funny look on his face, like he was either surprised or scared, but that changed to resolve a second later. He charged Mitch again and stuck his finger in his chest.

"Listen, I'm not done with you, Dawson. I'll see you real soon."

Right then, Ray's mom drove up toward their group in her old, yellow rust bucket station wagon, a cloud of blue smoke following her. When she pulled up, Ray turned around and got in the car, pretending that they were all pals.

"OK, guys, I'll see you later." His mother didn't see the sneer on his face.

Mrs. Munger, clueless, waved goodbye and took her little angel home.

What an asshole Ray was.

CHAPTER 28

BOILING POINT

As Mitch, Manny, Ike, and EZ walked home from the clubhouse, Mitch could see his brother Casey running toward him. His usual reason was to try to mooch a quarter so he could go down to the store, but there was something different about the way he was running this time.

As Casey approached, EZ yelled toward him.

"What's up, Casey Jones?"

Casey ran up and paused to catch his breath before launching into his news.

"What did you guys do to Charlotte?" he asked.

"What do you mean?" Mitch asked. "We didn't do anything to Charlotte."

"Well, Joy and Stephanie were playing in the backyard when Charlotte came over, screaming at them about you guys."

"Screaming at them? What was she saying?"

"I don't know, I wasn't there," Casey continued. "But both girls came in the house all hysterical. Joy was crying, and with her speech thing, you couldn't tell what she was saying, and Stephanie didn't sound much better."

Mitch looked over at EZ and tried to get a read of his face. Unsuccessful, he sighed hard.

"God damn it, Eric, what's going on?"

He didn't answer the question.

"Come on, let's go." EZ picked up his pace and jogged toward the Dawson house.

Everyone was quiet the rest of the way home. Mitch's mind raced, occupied with two things: What was the best way to tear Charlotte a new one for terrorizing my little sister, and figuring out what the hell was going on between Snag and EZ. It was evident that something else was going on. Had all the insults finally brought them both to a breaking point? Or was it the sudden lack of insults?

When they guys got to Mitch's house, Joy had already gone home, so EZ left to check on his sister. Mitch asked Manny and Ike to wait outside. Mitch and Casey went inside and headed to the basement. Stephi was in the basement with Mrs. Dawson and seemed to be OK now. Mrs. Dawson was trying to get the full story, and Stephi was doing the best she could given the circumstances. The way it sounded, all the screaming had been directed at Joy. But beyond the screaming, there was another issue: It sounded like Snag had grabbed Joy and pulled her hair.

"Charlotte was screaming about Eric, over and over, and she called Joy a 'stuttering little retard,'" Stephanie relayed, sniffling back tears.

Mitch couldn't understand it. Why would the giant cave dweller suddenly decide to pick on a little eleven-year-old girl? He knew his mom would not sit still for such shit; you could see it in her face. She'd be having words with Mr. and Mrs. Finch, no doubt. If they weren't going to control those apes, someone else would.

A few minutes later, there was a knock on the door. It was EZ, Gloria, and Joy. Joy was still visibly upset, and Gloria seemed calm—but Mitch had seen that look before and he knew there was no calm beneath her demeanor. Both Manny and Ike were still hanging back in the yard, too curious to go home.

The Dawson kids went outside by the garage, everyone gathering to consult. Inside, Mrs. Dawson was trying to get the Finch's on the phone.

"Mitch, Mitch, look at Charlotte. What's wrong with her?" Casey asked, finger pointing.

You could see the Finch's backyard from the Dawson's driveway, so when everyone looked over, they could see Snag standing in her backyard, her stance and expression defiant. She'd obviously been bawling her eyes out, but she was ready and waiting for something to happen. With all the adrenaline pumping through him, Mitch realized that he was too.

While Mrs. Dawson was on the phone raising hell with Mrs. Finch, her absolute best friend, Gloria sat Joy and Stephanie down on the steps to get the whole story. Between the two of them, they were able to convey that about half an hour ago, Charlotte came up behind them in the backyard, scared the shit out of them, and then started screaming at Joy.

"Now, think carefully. I want you to be very sure about this," Gloria said steadily. "She was yelling at Joy about Eric?"

"Yeah, well, she was yelling about all of the guys, really," Stephanie confirmed. "But mostly about Eric. She said Eric was a big fat liar, and she said Joy was a stuttering little retard." Stephanie paused and looked at Gloria for a second longer before continuing. "And, Gloria, she called you a horse."

"A horse?"

"Yeah, she said 'Gloria is a nasty horse.' Then she pulled Joy's hair."

It's doubtful Snag actually said "horse."

"She did that? She put her hands on you, Joy?" Gloria asked, her voice rising a bit in pitch.

Joy started to tear up again, but she nodded. Gloria took a breath and opened her arms.

"Come here, darling." She embraced Joy and reassured her. "You'll be OK. I'm going to take care of all of this right now."

Gloria stood and put a little distance between herself and the little girls before exposing her fury at her brother.

"'Whorse,' am I?" she muttered.

Oh, shit. Here we go, Mitch thought.

Gloria looked at Eric in disgust as she reached into her pocket, digging around for something.

"Well, dumb ass, is this about what I think it is?"

Eric stared at the ground like it was suddenly the most interesting thing.

"I don't know." He kicked a rock.

Manny, Ike, and Mitch looked on, dying to see what would happen next.

"Don't lie," Gloria barked. "It is, isn't it? Well, I hope you're happy." She pulled a hair tie out of her pocket. "You couldn't just walk away, could you? You just had to keep giving in. Now, Charlotte's heartbroken, and she beat up on your little sister." Gloria was telling it as it was, shocking the rest of the guys in the process. "You moron."

EZ slowly looked up from the ground and gave the guys a kind of side-eye; he didn't want to make eye contact.

Charlotte, heartbroken? It all started to fall together. Ka-frickin-boom.

"Oh, no. Oh, no, no, no," Mitch mumbled in disbelief. "It's not possible."

EZ turned beet red with embarrassment, and his shoulders shrunk down. His eyes were trained back on the ground again, trying to make himself as small as possible in the face of his humiliation. Mitch felt like he'd been kicked in the gut. Thanks to Gloria, the nature of what had been happening between Eric and Charlotte was now obvious. Mitch just couldn't believe it. EZ was one of his best guys. How had it happened right in front of him with no detection? Through all the fighting and misery and insults and horrible treatment they served to each other, Snag wasn't out on the golf course meeting randos to play grab ass—it had been Eric all along.

"Manny, how in the hell didn't we see this?"

"See what?" Manny replied.

"EZ had a secret thing with Snag. That's what this is all about. We actually watched the breakup the other day without realizing it."

There was a moment of stunned silence as Manny and Ike started to piece it together too.

"Wait a minute, you mean like a secret love affair?" Manny said.

"Yeah, can you believe that shit?"

"No, I uh, I really can't believe it," Manny admitted. "EZ and Snag?"

EZ was cowering.

Ike howled in realization.

"Oh shit, I'll bet this had something to do with when Eric got his face smashed up the other day and Charlotte's hairy nipples."

"And the way he kept saying 'Charlotte,'" Mitch noted. "Yup, it was all happening right in front of us."

You couldn't have found two people in the world who despised each other more than EZ and Snag, and yet there they were, involved in some secret love affair, an unholy union. Holy shit, Mitch still couldn't wrap his mind around it.

Gloria kicked off her sandals as she put her hair in a ponytail. Mitch saw a look in her eye, and he knew it was payday for the somebody who had hurt her little sister. And that somebody was Charlotte Finch.

Today was the day everything boiled over. Even though Snag called Gloria a "whorse," Gloria was set on punishing Snag for putting hands on her little sister. Nobody messes with Gloria's family, and she was going to make sure to reinforce that message.

After tightening up her pony tail so that it was in an optimum fighting position, Gloria sprinted toward Snag's house and hurdled the backyard fence by the lilac bushes with ease. Everyone followed her over there to watch the fight, and Snag—who was a head taller than Gloria and outweighed her by sixty pounds—stood her ground in her yard as Gloria approached. Gloria covered the distance in a blink at full stride, and with both feet seemingly off the ground, Gloria delivered a punch to old Snag's mouth that solved some of Snag's dental issues and created some new ones.

That one, perfectly executed punch knocked out Snags dead tooth, the broken tooth, and loosened up a few more on the bottom. It also split her lip wide open, splattering blood everywhere. Snag was knocked clean to the ground. Gloria wasted no time jumping on her to deliver more punches, battering her head like it was a speed bag. Beverly came out of the house screaming, running to her sister's rescue. But that was a huge mistake. Bev jumped on Gloria's back, but Gloria flipped Beverly over and began beating her next. She slapped Bev's face back and forth, like she was painting a barn. She looked like a mountain lion tearing up a couple of donkeys. The whole thing lasted less than a minute. The guys had all just beheld—or experienced—the full wrath of the one they call Gloria, Queen of Snow Storms.

The thing is, Gloria was quickly getting out of hand. She wouldn't let up and kept delivering blows. Manny and Mitch jumped the fence too and ran over to break up the fight. Manny instinctively wrapped his arms around Gloria and pulled her up off of Beverly. Her feet were two feet in the air, but she still fought to get loose. At some point, though, she gave way to physics; Manny was just too big and strong for her to fight off. He carried her over to the fence and set her down by Joy and Stephanie.

Both Snag and Crime Scene were a hideous mess of blood, bruises, less a couple fistfuls of hair that had ended up on the patio. Their mom and dad both came outside to assess the situation, and while you could see their mom was upset, their dad was shaking his head. He knew his girls had been asking for it, and they'd finally got what was coming to them. The Finches helped their girls up and ushered them inside to affect repairs. What a way to blow up summer vacation, man.

Mitch looked around to snap himself out of the post-fight fog and noticed that EZ had disappeared. Given everything that had just happened, Mitch knew he would've done the same: get the hell away from everybody before the questions started to fly. Manny, Gloria, and Mitch jumped back over the fence and headed back to the Dawson yard.

Seeing Gloria in a fight upset Joy quite a bit, but Gloria stepped to the task of calming her sister down again. Gloria was not taking a victory lap around the yard; in fact, she seemed upset too. Meanwhile, Stephi had a different reaction. She cheered for Gloria and patted her on the back, as if to say "good job." Stephi spun around and sparred playfully with Casey, landing a few shots of her own. Stephi clearly thought the whole thing was awesome. At that moment, Mrs. Dawson came out to the driveway stretching the phone cord with her, with no idea of what had just happened. She probably thought Mrs. Finch was still on the line.

After hanging out a little while with Ike and Manny and recounting the incident in the Finch backyard a couple of dozen times and the diabolical and unthinkable relationship between EZ and Snag, the guys headed home and Mitch went inside for the night.

Even though Charlotte and Beverly got the beating of a lifetime, Gloria did not come out unscathed: Her hands had swollen up like boxing gloves, so her parents took her to the ER that night. It turned out that she'd dislocated two of her fingers wailing on those two cement heads.

Mitch laid in bed that night thinking about the whole Snag and EZ affair, and even though he'd had enough time to process it, it was still hard to believe. Mitch thought back on all the interactions between them that he could remember, trying to pinpoint when it could've started, but he couldn't determine a single time there had been any clues that something was going on between them. It seemed like the farthest thing from reality. They had everybody fooled. Might felt like a complete idiot, not knowing that his best friend had a secret love affair with his arch enemy, the she-devil, Snag.

CHAPTER 29

THE SNAGGLE-PUSS REGRET

EZ avoided everybody over the next few days, knowing full well that he was going to have to answer for the Charlotte Finch romance. He had a couple of baseball games during the week that kept him away, and he didn't caddy up at the course. He'd eventually have to come clean; none of the guys would let him off the hook for this. They all wanted answers. How could it have possibly started? And when? It may seem kind of sick, but they needed the gory details.

Since late the night before, it had been pouring rain, but Mitch didn't care. Today was the day he'd finally break EZ's silence. So off he went. Mitch wanted to see how EZ would try to bullshit his way through this one.

When he got there, Gloria answered the door with curlers in her hair and a hand still wrapped up from the battle the other day. She seemed a little frantic.

"Where the hell have you been? Get in here."

In keeping with her natural ability to completely confuse and bewilder Mitch, she grabbed his collar and hauled him inside. He never knew what she was doing or thinking.

"Yeah, all right, I'm here. What's going on?"

Just then, a rumble of thunder sounded in the distance, and Gloria closed her eyes and bit her bottom lip until the thunder passed. He remembered.

"Is he down in his room?"

"Yeah, probably," she said, closing the door behind Mitch. "Good luck getting anything out of him, though. He hasn't said two words to me all week."

"So, how are you doing?"

"Oh, me, the so-called Queen of the Snow Flakes, I'm just freaking peachy," she said, clearly exasperated. "I've got parades tomorrow and Sunday, and I've got this—" she held up her sore hand—"plus, we're supposed to have thunderstorms all weekend, so I'm a little freaked out."

"Can I say something here?" Mitch asked.

"What?" she snapped.

"I know I'm not supposed to speak of it, but you do seem to be doing pretty good with the weather."

She looked at him with a hint of humility.

"Well, I'm doing OK now," she confided. "I just hate being alone when a storm hits." Every minute or two, you could hear some more thunder rumbling off in the distance, and Mitch could sense Gloria's uneasiness with it all. Mitch realized she was probably making conversation with him so he wouldn't leave her alone. Mitch didn't mind that at all.

"How's the hand?" he asked, to keep the conversation going.

"It's still sore, but I'm working, so it's not too bad."

"Have you seen Bev or Char since the fight?"

"No, and I'm not looking forward to it either. Talk about being uncomfortable." She sighed. "When you live that close to somebody and some bad shit goes down like what happened on their patio, it's hard to pretend that nothing ever happened. And if anybody thinks I enjoyed fighting with those two, they're dead wrong."

"Gloria, it wasn't much of a fight."

"I know, but I've grown to hate that shit." There was an edge to her voice now. "That's not the kind of crap the Queen of the Snow Flakes is supposed to participate in. Still, you can't let anybody bully your family."

"So you're telling me that you didn't enjoy pounding on those two just a little bit?" Mitch was prodding her, and he was rewarded with a small smirk.

"Well, maybe I did *a little* bit," she confessed.

He chuckled and started to make a move toward the stairs, but she stopped him.

"Hey, Mitch, what's your hurry?"

"No hurry."

They both knew what was going on, and Mitch knew Gloria had too much pride to simply ask him to stay with her in the kitchen until the storm blew over. Mitch might've looked like a dumb kid, but he really wasn't. Mitch was glad to hang out with her for a little while longer and talked about her parades and other bullshit. After exhausting all the small talk topics, Mitch looked outside and noticed that the rain had stopped.

"It's clearing up."

Gloria looked out the window and confirmed.

"So it is."

She walked over and hugged him for what seemed like an extraordinarily long time. Her curlers nearly poked him in the eye, and Mitch nearly... poked her in the thigh. "Mitchy-poo," she whispered. "It seems like you're my port in a storm. I still remember what you did for me last summer during that bad thunderstorm." Then the blissful moment passed. "Now, go downstairs and find that dumb ass brother of mine."

Mitch would never forget holding Gloria in his arms that day last summer. Never.

Mitch went downstairs, and just as he raised his fist to knock on EZ's bedroom door, EZ opened it. He must've heard Mitch come downstairs. Mitch smiled at him, and they both retreated to the family room

"So, what's new pal? How's your love life?"

"How's my love life?" EZ responded. "My love life is fabulous, couldn't be better! Linda and I are making plans for the county fair."

"Asshole, you know what I mean, you little prick. Tell me about your other love life."

"Mitchell, my friend, whatever do you mean?" he said sarcastically, flopping down onto his bed.

"You're going to tell me everything," Mitch demanded. "And whatever you don't tell me, I'm just going to make up.

"Alright, alright. Sit down, shut up, and I'll tell you all about it."

That was surprisingly easy, Mitch thought.

"I'm not kidding when I say that the hardest thing for me in this world is keeping my big mouth shut," EZ started. "I've been dying to tell somebody about this forever, but I just couldn't. Not even you."

How can I be this lucky to be the one person in the whole world who's going to get the full story right from the horse's ass? Mitch thought.

"OK, OK, let's hear it."

Rolling his eyes and shaking his head, EZ began his confession.

"All right. It started last summer—"

"Last summer?!" Mitch howled. "It's been going on that long?!"

"Are you going to just shut up and listen?"

"Fine."

"So, last summer, we were all playing flashlight tag on the golf course one night. It was hotter than hell that night; so hot and muggy you could hardly breathe. I went into that clump of trees down at the bottom of Devil's Hill to hide for a little while, but somebody was already in there, so I flashed them with my flashlight. It was Snag. She had her sweatshirt off and was standing there in just her bra, smoking a cigarette.

"What the hell?"

"That's exactly what I thought. But, like I told you, it was hot that night, and she was sweating like a mule, so she'd taken her sweatshirt off to try to cool down. You know how she and her sister are always wearing those big old sweatshirts, right? She saw me and I saw her, and I don't know—something kinda just happened. She stood there, didn't even try to cover up, and I didn't look away. Then she asked me something like 'what do you think' or 'how is this' or something. I didn't make fun of her, she didn't make fun of me, and all of a sudden, we're just two people standing in a little clump of trees where nobody could see us." EZ was flushed across the face just remembering the moment. "You know those knockers are huge, right? When I turned off my flashlight, I thought she would just put her sweatshirt back on, but instead, she walked toward me and stood right in front of me as if to present them to me. And, with her height, those warheads were staring me right in the eye."

"Doc, I didn't even think about it. I had zero issues with her at that very moment, and I instinctively reached out to grab one of them. But then she slapped my hand away and barked 'What the hell do you think you're doing?'"

Mitch caught himself holding his breath.

"Doc, I swear I didn't know what was going on. I was embarrassed as hell that I even wanted to touch old Snag. I thought I hadn't read the situation right at all, and then there I was, standing there like an asshole in the trees with Snag."

By that point, Mitch had found a seat on the couch, clutching a pillow, horrified about what might've happened next. He was waiting for EZ to deliver the next terrifying moment like one would wait for the monster to break through the door at a Frankenstein movie.

"She turned her flashlight on like she was searching for something on the ground. Finding her sweatshirt, she went over and spread it on the ground, right between two trees. I was about to turn around and get the hell out of there then she whispered, 'Come here.' I just froze. Then she walked over, grabbed my hand, and led me over to where her sweatshirt was on the ground. She laid down on it and pulled me right on top of her."

"We rolled around and made out without saying another word. It was so weird, Doc. I didn't think about Snag and all of her obvious faults and how much I despise that imbecile the whole time, none of that not once. The bugs ate us alive, but she didn't say one mean thing to me and I didn't say one mean thing to her; we just did what we did."

"OK, EZ, but what did you 'did'?"

"We just made out and maybe a little bit more. Had a cigarette, but that's it, and that's the way it's always been." He paused to think it over. "Oh, yeah, the other thing is that I have to call her Charlotte when we get together."

"Holy shit, I thought it was so strange the other day when you were calling her by her actual name," Mitch said. "This is all really starting to make some sense now."

"Any questions?"

"Yeah, about a thousand."

"OK, out with it. What do you wanna know?" EZ asked. "Remember, this will be your only shot. After this, we're not talking about it again."

"Ok, here goes." Mitch drew a deep breath. "EZ, this is the Snag we're talking about. I can't even hardly say it, but you were making out with 'the Snag.' She's two years older than you, over a head taller than you, and she's way out of your weight class by over fifty pounds—and plus, this is frickin' *Snag*. How could you bring yourself to tangle with the diabolical Snag?"

"Doc, I don't know what to tell you. When our little 'meet-ings' are over, I don't think about it for a while. I don't think about her, and then after some time passes, it just happens again. I know that's not much of a reason, but I can't think of anything else to say to explain it."

"How often do you have these 'meetings,' and where do you go in the winter? Do you just meet up on the golf course in the summer?"

"Those are fair questions," EZ noted. "It usually happens about once a month, mostly in the summer." He considered his words before continuing. "It was always up at the golf course, but twice in the winter, we went downtown to the Strand The-ater and watched a movie."

"Oh, so you guys went on dates?"

"They weren't dates," EZ defended. "We didn't even ride the same bus to the theater. You know how they're always missing their pets over there? She'd come by the house in the winter, asking if anyone had seen her cat or dog or whatever. That's how I knew she wanted to meet at the movies. After leaving my house, she'd walk to the bus stop and take the first 14-B, and then I'd take the next one. Same on the ride home. We walked in separately, and we walked out separately. We didn't even sit together until we could make sure no one we knew was there."

"Wow, this is unbelievable, EZ." Mitch shook his head in disbelief. "I couldn't even begin to make this shit up. Now, here's something else that I can't figure out: Where the hell was her goofy sister Beverly in all of this? You never see those two without each other."

"I don't have the slightest idea," EZ said. "I'm telling you right now, when we did this, we never talked. We didn't chat. We didn't catch up. We didn't ask about each other's day; we just did what we did and that was the end of it."

"Well, then, how did you two come up with a plan to fake it in front of everybody by still calling each other names?"

"Doc, you're not getting this," EZ said, rubbing his temples. "We didn't talk *at all*; we didn't come up with any plan. Everything you saw, everything that we said to each other, was the real deal. We weren't pretending to hate each other then secretly getting together. We really do hate each other. But I can tell you this, after the first few times, I started to get pissed off at myself for doing it, and I kept promising myself that I wouldn't do it again." EZ shrugged. "What can I tell you, Doc? I'm weak."

"You're an idiot."

I thought about how Gloria had handled Snag and laughed.

"Gloria found out, didn't she? What happened? Did she catch you guys?"

"No. One time I came home after we'd met up, and I must've stunk to high heaven from that nasty perfume Snag uses. As soon as I walked in the back door, Gloria could smell it."

"What did she say?"

"She said, 'You smell like that great big Snaggle-Puss jackass, Charlotte,' and in that moment I knew I was busted. She laughed at me and was grossed out at the same time. Gloria asked me straight out about it, and I couldn't lie. She busted me." EZ sighed, remembering the interaction he'd had with his sister that night. "Right there in the kitchen, she told me exactly what was going to happen, and I'm so pissed at myself because she was 100% right. She implored me, 'I know Charlotte. She's nuts, and one day you're going to have to stop this and it'll be ugly.' I told her we were just fooling around. She said, 'Yeah, but I'll bet Charlotte doesn't see it that way. I'll bet she thinks you're her secret lover boyfriend.'" EZ groaned. "Boyfriend, my ass."

"As far as I know, the only other person who knew about this was Ike."

"Ike? Why the hell did you tell him?" Mitch pressed.

"I didn't. He actually *did* catch us, or at least he saw us both go into the trees at the bottom of Devil's Hill and figured it out. He never said anything, though."

"Wait 'til I get a hold of him," Mitch grumbled.

"Don't you think he has enough shit to worry about?" EZ said in Ike's defense. "Leave Ike alone."

"Okay, fine. So jump ahead to this bullshit the other day."

"Alright," EZ said. "But then we're done talking about this for good, okay?"

Mitch nodded.

"The last few times we got together, Snag was pressuring me to do more stuff."

"What, like more dating?"

"No, you idiot, she wanted to do more stuff together, like DO IT."

"Oh, you mean the big DO IT. But you didn't?"

EZ shook his head.

"What stopped you?"

"First of all, a place to do it, and second, I didn't really want to go through with it. I mean, I did want to, but I didn't know if it'd be worth it, you know? Making out and playing a little grab ass is one thing, but doing the big deed? That's a big deal. But, like I said earlier, I'm weak, and I eventually gave in. I told her that some night or maybe the next time we played flashlight tag, we could wander off and do it."

"Okay, now where was this revolting event going to happen? By Devil's Hill?"

"No, that's actually where Ike comes back into the picture."

"BACK into the picture? What do you mean?"

"We were going to use Ike's shack up in Witches' Woods. You've been there. You know you can't get more secluded than that. I even went up there and made sure the place was straight and clean. He has blankets and pillows and everything. It would've been perfect, and there was no chance of getting caught. I made sure there was bug spray and water, and Snag said she wanted to bring candles and a bottle of wine, and I don't know what else, but she wanted to make this a really big deal, so Devil's Hill was out."

"She got obsessed with the idea of going up to Witches' Woods. She was coming by the house almost every day, looking to see if I was around. When she did see me, it was always, 'Are we going to play flashlights tonight?' Or 'Let's all do something tonight.' She was driving me nuts. A part of me wanted to do it to get it over with, but a bigger part of me was looking for any reason to get out of it. During all of this, I was starting to get together with Linda, and I completely lost interest in having anything to do with Snag. I didn't want to screw it up with Linda before it really got started, which brings us to the day we were walking up Wyoming Avenue when she confronted me and my bloody face. And there it was: my way out."

"Well, Pussy Cat, I am no expert here, but she sure didn't react like you were two people just fooling around," Mitch observed. "She acted like her boyfriend had broken up with his girlfriend."

"Dammit, Doc, don't say that shit."

"I don't know, EZ," Mitch said, sarcasm practically dripping from his words. "Like I said, I'm no expert, but what everybody saw was a big, good, old-fashioned break up of 'Lov-vers.'"

"Kiss my ass, Doc," EZ rebuked. "That's it, fun's over."

"Oh, come on, lover-boy! Lighten up. In thirty years, everyone will have forgotten all about it."

EZ covered his head with a throw pillow.

"I knew this was going to happen," EZ said. "I knew it. And what's worse, Gloria knew it. I'll never live this down."

"Honestly, EZ, how did you think she was going to react?"

"I don't know what I actually thought about that," EZ muttered. "I feel like such an asshole because Joy got mixed up in it and got terrorized by the Snag, and then Gloria proved she knew what she was talking about and stepped in and beat Snag's brains in."

"See, Eric, right there," Mitch observed. "There's the silver lining on the dark cloud you get to drag around the rest of your life: Those two idiots took a beating, and I got to watch it. See, it worked out for everybody."

"Again, Doc, kiss my ass."

CHAPTER 30

HOME FROM SAINT PETER

Mitch hadn't started high school yet but he felt like he was already working a full-time job that summer at Hillcrest Country Club. Ever since school had let out for the year, he'd usually do one caddy loop on the weekends, but during the week they had him working in the clubhouse, out on the course, the driving range, or at the pool. All the guys had more drive to make some money that summer, especially with the Ramsey County Fair coming up and the Minnesota State Fair at the end of the summer.

John Getz made sure that whenever a couple of big shots came to Hillcrest to shoot a round, Mitch got one of the bags. Most of the time, this made for a bigger tip, but every once in a while, one of the pricks stiffed him. John always wanted to know what some of the big shots were tipping, and if one of them was a little extra tight with the buck, well, John would put them on *his* list—and maybe they wouldn't get a tee time next time.

Mitch got most of his cash on the side from John Getz, which was fine for him, but he did work for tips. The side money came with a lot more responsibility than last year: He had to keep his eye on the rest of the caddies, especially the new ones who were just as lazy as the old ones. They were all trying to find the easiest way to do nothing for something.

Part of Mitch's responsibility included regular check-ins with John and Sid Getz, who'd routinely pull Mitch aside to chat about what was happening on the golf course, among the caddies, and whether there were any improvements they could implement. They specifically wanted to make sure Ike was thriving. How was he doing, how he liked working at the Club, and whether he seemed to be happy—all questions Mitch was happy to attempt to answer. They were very aware of the home life Ike had had, and it almost seemed like they were taking a protective interest in him.

Ike was doing great, though and seemed to be very happy. He was a hard worker, and folks at the golf course treated him well, so it looked like a win on all fronts. It's easy for people to warm up to Ike because he doesn't say much, and he's a vast improvement over the local asshole Ray the Rat. Ray Munger was burning his last bridge at Hillcrest Country Club that summer, even though his mom still ran the kitchen and handled all the events. She wouldn't be able to protect him from the consequences of the bullshit he pulled, like lying, taking off early, and picking on younger caddies. Ike was basically getting all the duties and jobs that Ray normally got, all paid on the side. They'd still use Ray once in a while to caddy, but as far as other work at the course, he just wasn't worth it. And there's no doubt that the downgrade made The Rat furious—to think that a guy like Ike could come in off the street and replace him without breaking a sweat. The brothers kept Ike mostly at the driving range and the tennis courts, where he could make some pretty good tips. They tried him on the course as a caddy once, but because he didn't know the first thing about golf, they decided to keep him off the course as much as they could, maybe only use him in a pinch.

It was hard to believe, but Ike had never been to either fair. The Ramsey County Fair was within walking distance of the neighborhood, set up right behind the old folks home on White Bear Avenue near Aldrich Arena. Mitch went every day it was open. The Minnesota State Fair was a much larger event, which meant the guys went less often but would spend more money—food, rides, games. Mitch had to make sure to save up a lot of money, and the best way to do that was to work his tail off. This year was special, however, because Ike would be able to experience the fairs for the first time. To say that Ike was excited for the experience would be a huge understatement.

Mitch had asked him before why he'd never gone to the fairs, and Ike said it never really came up. It was a non-subject in their house.

"My dad just said that fairs and carnivals are where evil lurks, so we'd have no part in any of it."

Day one of the Ramsey County Fair was a day Mitch would never forget. With Ike along, it felt like he and the other fellas were taking a little kid to the fair for the first time, that's how excited Ike was. He wanted to do everything, see everything, and eat everything. If there was one mission they did pretty well, it was probably the mission to eat everything. If he ate one Pronto Pup, he ate three. He also had two bags of mini donuts, a great big cotton candy, and a snow cone. As soon as he got off the Tilt-a-Whirl, he ran over and got in line for the Scrambler, then the bumper cars, and then did it all over again. They had some cows and goats and other farm animals, which Ike just loved. He got some feed so he could treat the pigs and the other critters. He wanted to ride on the ponies, too. Even though most of the kids in line for the pony ride were four or five, fifteen-year-old Ike didn't care; he wanted to ride a damn pony. All of Ike's friends had so much fun watching Ike absorb the fair that they didn't feel the need to do much else besides what Ike wanted to do.

It was hot as hell, though, so they took a little break in a shady spot next to the beer garden, grabbing ice cream cones on their way. If it weren't for the fair, they'd probably have been dunking each other at the Creek. But Ike didn't care how hot it was; he wanted to keep going. Mitch had to remind him that they had all day to explore, plus the fair would go on through the weekend. After a few minutes of cooling down, Gloria and Izzy walked by. They spotted the boys and came over.

"When did you guys get here?" EZ asked.

"Just now."

"How do you like your first Ramsey County Fair, Ike?" Izzy asked.

He grinned.

"What do you think? I could do this every damn day."

"Have you ridden the Ferris wheel yet?" Izzy asked.

"Nope, that's next."

"Come on, then, I'll go with you."

"You mean together?"

"Yeah, together, you goof ball," Izzy declared. "Come on, let's go get in line."

Ike shot up like he'd been sitting on a spring, a huge grin on his face.

While Ike and Izzy headed back toward the midway, Gloria came and sat down in Ike's spot in the shade. We'd all been bullshitting about work, baseball, and the fair before the girls showed up and had resumed doing so when Gloria broke up the party.

"Shut up, you guys, and listen," she demanded. She looked serious, so everyone quieted down quickly. "Ike's mom was calling around the neighborhood to find out when you guys were coming back from the fair."

"She knew we were going to be here all day and night," Mitch said. "I was standing there when Ike told her this morning, right before she left to go see Ike's dad."

"Well, when she came home today, Ike's dad came with her."

A sudden chill ran through Mitch's body.

"Ike's dad is home?"

"Yup. Mom told us to find you guys at the fair and emphasized that Ike was to come home with us right away."

"Ah shit, Ike is having the time of his life. He already said once that this was the most fun day he's ever had." It was hard to think that the best day of his life might also be the worst day of his life. Ike's dad had been gone for more than six months, and as far as anyone could tell, the family had settled into a new normal.

"So, what's with the Ferris wheel ride?" EZ asked. "Was that some sort of deception ploy?"

"No, not really," Gloria said. "Izzy told me she wouldn't come unless she could ride the Ferris wheel at least once and get some corn on the cob. We're both coming back tomorrow for the day."

After two turns on the Ferris wheel, Ike and Izzy walked back to the shady spot, each with corn on the cob. Ike was smiling ear to ear, all kinds of corn stuck in his teeth.

"You guys keep your traps shut, especially you, Eric," Gloria warned. "I'll tell Ike about his dad. My mom's over at Shoppers' City, and I told her once we found Ike, we'd meet her there so she can take us home."

When Ike and Izzy sat down with their corn cobs in the shade, Gloria moved to sit next to Ike. With Izzy on the other side of him, Ike turned redder than the candied apples for sale over by the duck pond. It was eerily reminiscent of the time they'd sandwiched him in the Dawson's basement last winter. They all chatted for a few minutes, and then Gloria told him about his dad's homecoming. Ike just shook his head.

"Well, I knew it was going to happen sooner or later," Ike confessed.

"I'm sorry I have to ruin your day," Gloria admitted. "But we do have to head back, Ike. My mom's waiting."

Ike said his thanks and goodbyes and walked away with Gloria and Izzy. The whole proceedings put a real damper on the day. Mitch didn't feel like being at the fair anymore, but then again, they hadn't hit the arcade games yet and he had a whole pocket full of dimes for just that reason. The drag line machine, ring toss, and shooting gallery were just begging for it. Plus Mitch knew Ike—he'd rather them have fun than waste the day feeling sorry for him. As the trio walked out of the fairgrounds, the roar of Harleys came within earshot. Some of the local bikers had arrived.

They guys ended up staying at the fair until it got dark. They saw a lot of kids from school, and EZ met up with his new gal, Linda—and she was something else. Not only was she a great figure skater but she's in all the school musicals and plays. Linda was there with a couple of her girlfriends from North High in North Saint Paul, and Mitch couldn't help but notice that one of her girlfriends was eyeing him up pretty good. She asked him to go on rides with her, but he told her he had a girlfriend. Some girlfriend, though. As much as he liked Maggie, he felt like he was missing out on a lot of summer fun all kids have a right to. He'd only seen her a few times since his tournament games at the end of the season, and while every time was great, the time apart was horrible. The state fair was coming up, so he hoped they could get together when she wasn't workin—but until then, there was nothing but waiting.

By the time the guys were walking out, you could see and smell that the crowd at the county fair had changed over. Gone were the families and the kids, replaced by the older teenagers and a lot more bikers and hippies of various sorts. The smell of pot hung heavy in the air. The bikers were mostly just hanging out by their Harleys, but you knew it was time to get the hell out of there when they showed up in force.

Bikers were still coming by Mitch's house. You could hear them roaring up and down Curve Street, and every once in a while, they'd come up Wyoming Avenue. It seemed like there were five or six of them coming up Mitch's street all the time. Walter Dawson and the rest of the neighbors sure as hell don't like it, but Mitch's dad especially.

Mitch didn't see Ike for a few days after Mr. Tiller arrived home. Then, one morning, he showed up at the golf course for work. Mitch was surprised to see him because he thought working at the golf course would be out of the question as soon as his dad came home. But, to hear Ike tell it, his dad was not aware of much at present.

"It's so weird at the house right now, Mitch," Ike remarked as they walked out to the practice putting green. "Everything is so quiet. There's no yelling. That's part of how things have to be from now on. Quiet, so we don't upset my dad. When I think about it, it's not that much different than before. Always on eggshells at my house."

"There are all kinds of new rules, too," he continued. "We don't talk about the past. We don't talk about why he got sent away or anything else that might set him off. My mom drives him to the VA hospital for appointments, and they have him on all kinds of medications. He twitches a lot, he gets dizzy, and he sleeps a lot. Sometimes I don't think he even notices I'm in the room. He hardly ever talks to me."

They kept walking, Mitch listening to Ike talk.

"It's like he's a kind of zombie. He reads and quotes his Bible all day, and my sister Sarah sits with him for hours. He seems to like that, actually. The other kids are restricted to their rooms most of the time so they don't make any noise when he's around."

"What about working here?" Mitch asked. "Can you stay?"

"I haven't told him about it, and he hasn't asked." Ike shrugged. "I'm sure my mom hasn't mentioned anything either. I'm hopeful that what Leon doesn't know won't kill us. My mom said he has a meeting at work with the union next week to determine whether he is disabled from work. I'm not sure what that means, though. My mom seems to be doing OK, but she's starting to look like she did before: miserable. She said that my dad has 'issues' and that they're trying to get him better with the right medication. I'm not going to kid you, Mitch, he's creepy. I keep finding myself waiting for the rage and the violence, but there's nothing there. He just looks like he's a million miles away."

When Mitch got home from the golf course that day, his dad had the grill going. It looked like burgers and his mom's neighborhood-famous potato salad for supper—one of Mitch's favorite summer combo meals. Casey has a baseball game down at the playground, so they're going to eat a little early at the picnic table tonight. Mitch's mom had it all set up and ready to go.

"Hey, Dad, can I have grilled onions on my burger?"

"Mitchell, my boy, you and me both."

Mitch asked his dad if he knew that Ike's dad was home.

"Yeah, I heard he was. Ike's mom called your mom the other day, and they talked for quite a while."

"What's the deal?" Mitch asked. "Ike said his dad has changed a lot..."

"By the sounds of it, that's a good thing, right?" his dad contended.

"I guess. Ike doesn't seem too sure. What did they do to him?"

Mr. Dawson was flipping burgers, toasting the buns, and drinking a beer—everything except answering Mitch's question.

But Mitch wasn't going anywhere without some kind of answer, so he just waited. Finally, Mr. Dawson looked at Mitch.

"You know how he was down in Saint Peter?"

"Yeah, so?"

There was another pause.

"Mitch, Saint Peter is more of a hospital than it is a jail. Make no mistake, he was locked up, but if you go down to Saint Peter, there's a lot more going on than just breaking the law."

"You've lost me, Dad."

Mr. Dawson pursed his lips.

"Mitch, Saint Peter is a criminal mental hospital."

Mitch felt a kind of sick yucky feeling when he heard the term "mental hospital." The mind immediately moves to images and thoughts of people in straitjackets chained to their beds, screaming in agony like they do in horror movies.

"What were they doing to him down there in Saint Peter?"

When his dad stopped and looked at him, Mitch could tell his dad knew what they did to him, but he also knew there was no way he was going to tell him, especially since Ike probably didn't know himself. He was wise at that moment, his dad. He knew not to tell Mitch anything because it'd get right back to Ike, and that's the kind of information that should come straight from your mom. If she hadn't told Ike, then it was best not to say anything at all.

"They're trying to help him. The fact that they let him out of that kind of hospital must mean he's doing much better, alright? The mental hospital in Saint Peter is no joke, Mitch."

Just then, you could hear the Harleys roaring in the distance, the sound getting closer every second; the biker crew was coming up the street again. Mr. Dawson handed Mitch the spatula in a hurry.

"Watch these burgers for a minute, yeah?"

He went to the end of the driveway to glare at the bikers as they passed.

Mitch knew his dad wasn't telling him everything, but he also knew his dad didn't want him to worry about this stuff. It was just impossible to not wonder about what was going on in Leon Tiller's head.

CHAPTER 31

CASEY DAWSON, SPACEMAN

Casey's birthday was a couple of weeks ago, but because of a baseball tournament up in Elk River on his birthday weekend, the Dawsons had to postpone the birthday party.

Casey's baseball team had made it to the playoffs and ended up doing great. When Casey stepped to the plate for his first time at bat during the tournament, he was wearing his goalie helmet and mask. Mitch just about shit himself, but his parents were laughing. Shouldn't they die of embarrassment? Knowing Casey, you kind of get used to his antics; he's just one of those kids who's funny and doesn't even know it. He'd developed into a really good ball player and a good goalie, too; Mitch was a proud brother, despite Casey's goofiness. Casey ended up putting on a regular batting helmet and went three for three in his tournament game, with a walk, and he struck out two in two innings of relief. Casey's team won the Elk River Tournament and were runners-up for that year's Saint Paul City Championship.

Casey's birthday was always a big summertime staple. Mr. and Mrs. Dawson always used it as an excuse to put on a big barbecue and invite the family and the neighbors. With all the excitement about the Apollo program and landing on the moon next year, the Dawsons decided to have a NASA/space-themed birthday party for Casey, the Spaceman. Casey knew everything there was to know about the U.S. space program—who flew what mission and when and on what spacecraft. He even knew all about each astronaut. Mr. and Mrs. Dawson picked out the perfect presents, too: a realistic astronaut helmet, space boots, and a NASA jacket. As was so common with any type of new head adornment, it seemed Casey didn't take off that helmet for the rest of the summer. And, thank God, it replaced his goalie mask and his nasty old fedora. He insisted that everyone call him Buzz, as in Buzz Aldrin the astronaut.

The whole neighborhood came to Casey's party. Even though this was a party for a twelve-year-old, all the little kids, big kids, and their parents showed up.

Just like every year, Mr. Dawson had coolers filled with Buckhorn for the adults and several gallons of Tang, the official drink of NASA, for the kids. This was Casey's only request for the party.

Mr. Dawson pulled Mitch aside before the party.

"You remember what the two rules are for tonight, don't you?" he questioned.

"Yup! We can't drink any beer and no pissing in Mom's garden because she will have my ass," Mitch said confidently.

"That's right."

"But can we still piss in the lilac bushes?"

"Get out of here before I put my foot in your ass," he growled.

Mr. Dawson made burgers and dogs, and Mrs. Dawson made a bunch of other stuff to eat. Normally, she'd bake a cake too, but with more than thirty people attending, she bought a big cake from the bakery at Shoppers' City instead.

Good ol' Enzo brought over homemade Italian sausage links that Mr. Dawson happily grilled up with the capable help of his right-hand grill man, Ferdy Klaus. Those three were clearly enjoying their cold beers and jokes at the grill, and Mitch felt it might be a good time for a few laughs.

"Hey, Mr. Klaus, how are you today?" Mitch asked.

"Good, Mitch. Hows about you?"

"Fine. And how's the lovely Mrs. Klaus?"

"Well, Mitchell, she's probably in da house eating her weight in potato salad."

Everyone at the grill had a nice chuckle at Mrs. Klaus' expense. What a jokester!

The notable no-shows were Snag, Crime Scene, and Ike. Nobody had seen Bev or Char since the battle in their backyard, which is pretty understandable. Who could blame them? The real mystery was Ike's whereabouts. His mom and siblings had already arrived, but Ike was nowhere to be found. Mitch knew he wasn't at work because they'd already worked together and left together earlier that day. Mitch's timing was good because Ray the Rat showed up right as they were leaving the clubhouse. They all knew that asshole had Ike in his sights. He regularly makes these little comments and threats about Ike because Ike is doing the work that he used to do. Stuff like, "I better not catch Ike down on the driving range or out by the bungalows" or "Don't let me catch you, blah blah blah blah." Truly, if the Rat ever starts anything with Ike—well, let's just hope Manny is somewhere close by.

When Mitch was leaving work at the course that day, he mentioned the party to Ike, and Ike said he knew all about it. Most probably, Mrs. Dawson had called Mrs. Tiller and invited them. Way to go Mom Dawson!

"Everyone but my dad is planning to be there," Ike had told Mitch.

"No shit. How did that go over with your dad?"

"Not good. Have I told you the zombie is gone and the screaming maniac is back? He and my mom had a big fight about the party last night. He got mad as hell, but my mom wouldn't back down. She told me after he stormed off that she's just not going to take his crap anymore. She wants her kids to have a life."

"Holy shit, Ike. Did anyone get hurt?"

"Nope, he didn't lay a hand on her. I think he knows what will happen if he does." Ike was silent for a moment, and there was a sudden air of sadness that surrounded him. "Doc, I thought this medication was supposed to help him. First, there was the zombie, then the maniac appeared again. Where's the help?"

"My mom was awesome though," Ike noted. "For the first time ever, she's fighting back and standing up to my dad. And you want to know the funniest part about all of it? I don't think he knows what to do. I'm sure he thought he was going to bulldoze right over her again. Through all of this, my dad hasn't changed; I think it's my mom who has changed the most."

"When did all this start back up with your dad?"

"About a week ago. He got a letter in the mail from his union saying they won't let him go back to work. They say he is disabled because of his condition."

"Condition?" Mitch asked, remembering his previous conversation with his dad.

Ike walked in silence for a moment before speaking.

"It's got a long name, Mitch. I can't remember it, but as soon as he found out about their decision, my mom said he stopped taking his medication."

"What about working here, Ike?"

"I don't know, Mitch." Ike sighed. "Sooner or later, he's going to figure it out."

"Ike, you really should stop working here." Mitch was concerned about Ike's safety.

"Yeah, I know, but really, the damage is done," Ike explained. "He's talking about paper routes again, and we already know what he thinks of the Getz brothers. He despises those guys. Whether I stop now or later won't make a difference; when he finds out that I've been working for the 'Jews,' there's going to be hell to pay."

"OK, well, I'm going to head home to help set up the party. I'll see you tonight."

Ike stuck around work to get in a few more hours.

Ike's brother Jacob and sister Ruthy were hanging out with the other younger kids, and Ike's mom stayed in close proximity with the other moms. Mrs. Finch wouldn't leave her side. From Mitch's vantage point, it seemed like the moms were all taking turns standing guard over Mary Tiller. She looked nervous again, like she was just waiting for something to happen. Maybe she thought Ike's dad might show up and start trouble. That would be a treat. Mitch would just love to see him come and try to start some shit. Mitch's dad would tear him apart with his bare hands, kiddie birthday party or not, and who knows how many other dads would pitch in. Mr. Dawson hated that prick before he went to prison, but he hated him even more afterward, if that was even possible. Figuring she'd probably have a good answer, Mitch walked over to ask Ike's mom where he was. She looked confused.

"I thought he was going to be here with you boys. I haven't seen him since he left the house this morning."

"I haven't seen him since I left work earlier."

After mingling a while at the party and trying to get Ike off his mind, Mitch went down to the basement to call Maggie and try to get an idea of when she planned to come down so they could visit the state fair together. He quickly found out, however, that Maggie and her sister would have to work every single day of the state fair, open to close. They might get a morning off here or there, but they were going to be behind the counter at the French fry stand for the entire ten days. Mitch kicked himself. What kind of idiot must he be to think that just because Maggie was working at the fair that he'd be able to see her a lot? When adding in his football practice, Mitch realized he was an even bigger idiot than he thought; he'd been saving up and planning on this all whole summer, but now his hopes were dashed. He felt deflated, and he got the feeling that Maggie thought the same. It now seemed painfully obvious that their relationship just wasn't working out, especially now that he was just a couple of weeks away from starting high school.

When Mitch went upstairs into the kitchen, his mom and some of the other moms were still prepping food.

"Mitchell, here, you take some of dis food outside vit you," Mrs. Klaus commanded.

"I'd be happy to."

"By da vay. Da old man has been in the schnapps since about noon, so you let me know if I have to go home and get da veelbarrow."

When Mitch walked back outside, chuckling at Mrs. Klaus' jokes, he could see EZ, Gloria, and Izzy had made it to the party. EZ was walking toward Mitch and the kitchen door with a plate full of food, and Manny was close behind with a second plate. And the two girls, well, the two girls were just standing there in their peak summer glow, both wearing tube tops and cutoff jean shorts, both tanned and gorgeous, though Izzy was darker than Gloria. Izzy has that olive complexion; she could get a tan just walking past a candle.

Mitch noticed that Gloria had little flowers in her hair. Little flowers? Come on. It just wasn't fair to a poor sap like Mitch. Gloria knocks him on his ass every time he sees her, especially during summer. She slays Mitch and she knew it. But especially tonight.

Gloria broke his reverie.

"Mitchell, is Ike here?"

"No, why? I was just looking for him myself."

"Something really weird happened earlier and I want to make sure he's okay."

"Oh, Christ, now what?"

Gloria grabbed Mitch's arm and walked him over to the garage. Izzy, Manny, and EZ followed.

"When me and Izzy finished up in the clubhouse dining room today, we were just starting to head down Winthrop when we saw Ike come out of the clubhouse, so we stopped to wait for him. Then, Ray Munger came out of the building and ran up on Ike pretty hard."

"He did?"

"Yeah, the Rat kept walking toward Ike and Ike kept backing up, trying to keep his distance."

"Really? What else?" EZ urged.

Gloria continued.

"I started walking back toward Ike and Ray, and then my old pal Izzy here grabbed me and tried to stop me. We were close enough to hear Ray tell Ike to get another job and to never come back to the club again. Ray said that if Ike did come back, he would beat the living shit out of him. I thought he might beat the shit out of him right then and there, but one of those Harley guys came cruising down Winthrop and stopped right next to them when he saw Ray threatening Ike. The guy revved up his motorcycle really loud and then he said something to Ike. We couldn't hear what he said, though. The motorcycle was too loud."

"What did the guy look like?" Mitch asked.

Gloria shrugged.

"I don't know. I couldn't see him clearly. He was wearing a helmet and goggles like they all do. Oh, but he did have a long ponytail."

"Was he wearing a black leather jacket, and did he have a sissy bar and really cool bright orange and red flames painted on the gas tank of his bike?"

"Yeah, I think he did," Izzy confirmed. "The guy on the motorcycle must've scared the piss out of the Rat."

Izzy prodded Gloria.

"Glo, you better tell them what else Ray said."

Gloria paused, rolled her eyes, and recalled the Rat's words.

"He said 'What are you looking at, Gloria, you stuck-up bitch?' Then he turned and ran back into the building."

Smiling now, Izzy begged to differ.

"Can you imagine Ray saying that to Gloria? Everybody knows Gloria isn't stuck up."

Gloria looked at Izzy and challenged her.

"So what are you saying? I'm still a bitch?"

They all got a laugh out of that one. The whole time the girls were telling this story, Mitch couldn't help but stare at Gloria—he couldn't get over how gorgeous she looked. And it wasn't just the hair; she'd put on some makeup too.

"After that, I grabbed our warrior here," Izzy said, pointing to Gloria, "and we skedaddled down Winthrop Street."

"Well, what the hell happened to Ike?" Mitch demanded.

"He was talking to the guy on the motorcycle when we left, and since we didn't know how long he'd be, we left."

"Why would a biker stop and talk to Ike? Guys, this is not making any sense at all."

"You said it, Mitchy-poo," Gloria chirped.

They all turned and started to walk back toward the party, but Gloria called Mitch back.

"Mitchell, come here."

Somehow, those words sounded familiar. Mitch turned and walked back toward her.

"What's up?"

Gloria was looking at Mitch as if she expected him to say something else. After a few moments of silence passed, she spoke.

"Well... you didn't say anything about my hair. Do you like it?" she asked. "I fixed it special for a big parade in Minnetonka today."

Dumbfounded, Mitch shrugged.

"Huh? What do you mean?" Mitch could feel his face warm. He'd been noticing her since she'd arrived.

"What do I mean?" She sounded like she was getting frustrated. "I mean, I fixed up my hair with flowers, and I want to know if you like it or not. Is that so damn hard?"

"Well, no. It looks nice, I guess. Why do you care what I think?"

Gloria muttered something under her breath.

"Mitch, you know, you're so goddamn dumb I'm surprised you walk upright."

She punched him in the arm—hard—and then stormed off.

What the hell was that all about? Honest to God, Mitch just couldn't understand her at all. Did she want him to gush over her hairdo? Couldn't she just let him suffer in silence? In that moment, Mitch felt a strong desire to go make a damn bonfire.

Mitch spent some time puttering around the party, thinking about what Gloria had shared about Ike, Ray, and the motorcycle rider. Nobody knew what the deal was with these guys on the Harleys. Mr. Dawson and the rest of the adult neighbors considered them a menace to society, but so far, no one had seen them cause any trouble—other than the loud engines making things noisier than usual. All they seem to do is just kind of cruise through the neighborhoods on streets that don't really go anywhere. They must know someone who lives around here, but Mr. Dawson thinks that they're up to "No damn good."

Around 6:30, Zitz showed up to the party with Mario DiMucci and Mario's sister, Gina. Gina had driven Zitz and Mario up to the Dawson's house, knowing she could hang out with Gloria and Izzy. Gloria knew Gina from school. Gina and Mario live down by Wilder Playground, and their dad works at Hamm's Brewery with Izzy's dad. The two families have known each other since Izzy and Reno were little kids. As a matter of fact, they think they might be distant cousins, which isn't surprising.

"All the Dagos on the East Side are related one way or another," Mr. Dawson had commented, on more than one occasion.

Since playing VFW hockey together a few months ago, Mitch, Zitz, and Mario had become pretty tight, but now that they were all in football camp together, they'd become even closer. Mario and Zitz are a lot alike: tons of talent and tough as hell. Just ask the Canadians, especially the team from Thunder Bay. Those guys fought back-to-back on the ice more than a couple times during their run with the VFW bantam team.

Just as everyone expected, Mario became the quarterback for the junior varsity team at Johnson, Zitz was getting tons of reps in the backfield, and Manny was dominating the line on both sides of the ball. Mario told Mitch that he was his new favorite receiver because he could get open and actually make catches. Mario has an arm like a leg, and he puts a lot on the ball when he throws it downfield. Mitch didn't have any problem making catches from Mario, and working on his hand strength had been paying off. All four of them would start on the defensive side of the ball this year.

"Are we still in Saint Paul?" Mario wondered. "I mean, I've never been up this way before. Is that a golf course?"

"Yeah, that's Hillcrest Country Club," Mitch confirmed. "That's where a bunch of us work."

"Holy shit, Doc, I didn't even know this area existed."

EZ chimed in.

"Mario, welcome to the home of the 4-H club," he proclaimed.

Mario looked really confused.

"The 4-H club? What the hell does that mean?"

"The 4-H club: The Hayden Heights Happy Hackers," EZ boasted. "That's us."

Mario nearly split a gut laughing.

"You know the 14-B bus that runs up Payne Avenue?"

Mario nodded.

"The end of the line is right down the block, and the end of Saint Paul is about a block that way." EZ pointed north.

"So, this is the upper East Side, huh boys?" Mario clipped. "Pretty nice from what I can see. Are we close to Shoppers' City?"

"Yeah, kinda," Mitch said. "You can walk there from here. Aldrich Arena, too."

Mario marveled.

"You know, when I look around, the one thing I can't get over is how big your yard is. Is everybody's yard this big?"

Mitch beamed like he owned the place.

"Some of us have double deep lots and no alley. My house sits on two lots. So, we're a double-double."

Mario seemed impressed, but his mind shifted gears.

"Doc, is my guy Manfred here?"

Mario and Manny had met at football captain's practice.

"Oh, yeah. Manny's probably over by the grill waiting for more food," Mitch said, pointing in the direction of the grill.

Just then, Gina broke away from Gloria and Izzy and walked up to the guys.

"Mario, come on, you can talk to these guys later," she demanded. "We have to go say hi to Isabelle's mom and dad."

"Okay. But we gotta say hi to Mitch's mom and dad, too," Mario asserted.

Mario knew Mr. Dawson from hockey earlier this year. He and Randy McKay even roomed with Mitch and Zitz for two of their VFW tournaments. As they walked away, Mitch laughed.

"Hey, Mario, don't come back empty-handed."

"What?"

"Get some food on your way back," Mitch yelled.

"You got it, Doc. I can smell the Italian sausage on the grill already."

Once the two of them were gone, Zitz probed.

"So, what's been going on?"

"Ike's in the wind again," EZ piped up. "Nobody has seen him since work today, and it sounds like things are back to crazy at his house."

"Really? No shit," Zitz said. "What happened?"

"My sister and Izzy saw him after work at the golf course. I guess Ike had a run-in with Ray the Rat, and some biker on a Harley was involved."

"Wait, what? A biker was involved? What the hell is that about?" Zitz asked.

As EZ retold the story about Ike, Mitch took a minute to survey the party and noticed that Ike's mom and siblings were gone. He thought briefly about walking down to his house to see if he was there and wanted to come up to the party—but what if what he'd told Mitch about Mr. Tiller was true? What if things were back to their usual at the house? Mitch thought maybe he'd better leave it alone. Mitch rolled over in his mind what Ike had said earlier about his dad changing or not and how his mom had changed. No, the one who had really changed was Ike; there was plenty of evidence for it every day.

Even still, Mitch wished he knew where Ike was, which was a familiar and shitty feeling. However, it didn't sound like his dad had chased him off this time. Chances were, Ike was up at the Trestle or the Woods, and he'd probably come home tonight. Then again, maybe he'd wait until tomorrow.

As the night wore on, it all happened just the way Mitch had imagined it. There were ten of them around a bonfire, including EZ's new girlfriend, Linda, and Izzy's brother, Reno.

The dads were in the garage drinking beer, the moms were mixing highballs in the kitchen, and Stephi and Casey, aka Buzz the Spaceman, were all over the place. EZ was in top form as he usually was when he had a new audience. Mitch was sure Linda hadn't seen EZ work a crowd, so she was in for a treat. He was just killing them with his impressions and one liners. Mitch even thought Mario was going to die laughing.

Sitting around the fire, Mitch found it difficult not to stare at Gloria once again. One time, Mitch glanced over at Gloria and caught her glaring back at him. She made a grimace and gave Mitch the finger. Mitch really must've struck out with the hairdo question.

CHAPTER 32

A COLD BEER AT THE TRESTLE

The next morning, the Dawson kids were on the after-party cleanup crew, as always. Mitch got up early to start cleaning up the yard. Stephi was the next one out of the house to join him, and then Spaceman Casey, complete with his space helmet and moon boots, came out to put away all the chairs and throw away the trash. It was a great party. The cleanup was involved enough that the kids all got a dispensation from church. Mrs. Dawson trudged around the kitchen in her slippers and muumuu, regretting her last two highballs, and Mr. Dawson spent time returning neighbors' borrowed tables and chairs. Mitch was motivated to get the mess cleaned up because he could still do two loops at the golf course if he hustled, and two loops meant pretty good tips on a Sunday—not that he needed to save for anything anymore.

After about half an hour, Mrs. Dawson stepped outside and waved Mitch down.

"Ike is on the phone!"

Mitch bolted to the house and grabbed the phone.

"Hello?"

"Hey, I was hoping to catch you before church."

"No church today. Where the hell are you?"

"Well, where the hell do you think I am? I'm at the course."

Mitch was relieved. And then frustrated again.

"I'm planning to go in later because I'm cleaning up after the party. Where were you last night?"

"Never mind that now," Ike said, brushing off his friend's concern. "I got some things I want to talk to you about. You're planning to caddy today?"

"Yeah, I'm going to try to do two loops."

"OK, I'm not going to hang around that long. Can you come up to the Trestle after you're done?"

"What's going on, Ike?" Mitch asked, highly suspicious now.

"I'll tell you later. Can you meet me up there or not? I've got a new spot down on the warehouse side of the bridge."

"Yeah, sure. And tell Sid or John I'll be there later, okay?"

"OK. And Mitch?"

"Yeah?"

"Ray the Rat got flushed yesterday."

"What do you mean?"

"Just that. John Getz hauled him into the office, and about a minute later, Ray came out and didn't have a job here anymore."

"No shit."

"Yup," Ike affirmed. "You remember that little scene down at the playground when he got thrown out of there? It was similar. And he blames you for getting fired."

"I'm sure he does," Mitch mused. "But what could I do? John asked me the other day why we're losing so many caddies, so I told John the truth: it was because of Ray. I'm not going to protect that asshole."

" I don't blame you," Ike reassured Mitch. "Hey, we don't have to worry about that slob anymore."

"All right, I'll see you later at the Trestle," Mitch confirmed.

Maybe Ike wouldn't need to worry about the Rat anymore, but it sure sounded like Mitch should be worried.

When Mitch got to the course later that morning, John Getz pulled him aside to talk about Ray Munger getting fired.

He didn't have much to say but he took the time to remind Mitch of the club's biggest event coming up.

"We've got the big invitational tournament coming up, and I can't afford to have Ray's bullshit around here anymore. I gave him every chance in the world to straighten up."

"Everybody's glad he's out of here," Mitch admitted.

John changed the subject.

"So, how are you liking high school football so far?"

"It's going well. I think we're going to be pretty good this year."

"That's great! I wondered: Could you give me some of your time to help us get ready for this tournament? You know it's the big one."

"Sure." Mitch nodded. "I can't be here during the day, but I can come up here after practice as much as possible this week."

"Great! We've got a lot to do around here, so any help you can give me is greatly appreciated—and you will be well compensated, of course." Mitch smiled and nodded in agreement.

By the time Mitch left the course after two loops, he was absolutely gassed. Two loops in the late summer heat was all it took to take him down, apparently, and it was supposed to be hot just the same all week, football practice notwithstanding. With the two-a-day football practices all week in this heat, Mitch just knew it was going to be rough.

He made his way up the path to the Trestle and, as expected, no one was around this time of day. He walked down the trail that runs along the fence near the tracks. It didn't take much to find Ike's new spot. Ike was comfortable, sitting back having a smoke, drinking a beer, and hanging out with old Buster, the wood tick magnet of a dog.

Ike looked up.

"You look thirsty, Mitch, want a beer?"

"Does the Pope shit in the woods? Of course I want beer."

Ike reached into a Styrofoam cooler and pulled out an ice cold can of Hamm's beer. He handed it to Mitch, along with a church key. Mitch cracked open that beer and guzzled half of it before he even sat down.

"Ike, where'd you get the beer? You didn't take it from the golf course, did you?"

"Hell no," Ike said. "I have a source. Don't worry about it. Did you hear anymore about Ray the Rat?"

"Yeah, though there wasn't much more to add. I talked to John about it, and I heard more than once today that Ray's going to be looking for me. I sure hope Manny and Zitz are around when he finds me."

Ike nodded, and then patted the ground beside him.

"Mitch, sit down. We're up here to celebrate."

"What are we celebrating?"

"Well, celebrating might not be the right word for it, but I gotta tell you some stuff and then maybe you can tell me if we're celebrating or not," Ike confessed.

Mitch sat down and got ready for what he was sure was something horrible.

Ike began.

"Last night, I had a minor run-in with my dad."

Mitch cringed.

"What the hell does a 'minor run-in' look like at your house?"

"When I got home last night, my mom and the kids were already back from your house, and I was fully expecting rage from my dad, but he was more like a zombie in his chair. My sister Sarah was napping on the couch, keeping him company. He asked me where I had been and I told him I was hanging out with Buster. Clutching his Bible, he asked me straight whether I had been down at your house. I told him no and then asked him where my mom was. 'Doing laundry,' was his answer.

"Then he changed the subject and started pumping me about getting all my paper routes back. He told me we were all going to Temple tomorrow, and when my mom came up from the basement, he looked at her and muttered 'Everybody and their smart mouths better straighten up. I'm going to go to bed, I'm tired.'

"After my dad went upstairs, my mom went to the back door and asked me to come outside. We went over and sat on the old bench by the bunker next to the garage. In a nutshell, she said that she loved me and my siblings very, very much, and my dad stopping his medication was the last straw.

"My mom told me once before what was wrong with my dad, but I couldn't remember, so I asked her again what was wrong with him. This time I remembered to write it down because I wanted to look it up myself. She said my dad was diagnosed as a 'paranoid schizophrenic.'"

"That sounds really bad. What does it mean?"

"It means he thinks everybody and everything is out to get him," Ike said. "And that his mind is really screwed up."

"Is he dangerous?" Mitch asked.

"My mom thinks so. She thought with all the therapy, medication, and shock therapy she might be able to hang in there, but she doesn't want to live like this anymore, not knowing which version of Leon Tiller she has to deal with. She said it's only a matter of time before the violence starts again, so she's going to leave him anyway, medication or not."

"Holy crap, Ike, did you say shock therapy?" Mitch was incredulous.

"Yup. My mom thinks that was the only thing that did him any good."

"Did you say your mom is going to leave your dad? Wow, a divorce. I don't know anybody's parents who are divorced. Where are you guys going to go? Do you have to move?"

"I don't know, Mitch. I don't know what's going to happen, but she said she can't take the chance of all of us being around him anymore. She's seen both versions of Leon Tiller—on the medication and off the medication—and she hates both of them. It's done. It's just a matter of when."

Mitch had not been expecting this level of news.

"When my dad came home, I figured he'd been arrested, put in a hospital, and that was it. But it turns out it's a lot more complicated. My dad was charged with a number of crimes. His lawyer got the charges reduced, and right now he's on some sort of house arrest. They've given him probation, which means he has to check in with someone on a regular basis, and then we've had a couple of visits from this man. I guess he's a probation officer. So, my dad can't leave the house unless it's for work, only now he's not working. This is on top of the doctors he has to see all the time. We've got big changes coming, Mitch."

At that moment, a deafening roar rose from the south. You might think a fast freight train was approaching, but nope. There were about a dozen bikers on their Harley's coming up the path. As they passed over the Trestle, Ike had a big smile on his face.

"I bet some of those guys are the same bikers that have been riding around our houses lately," Mitch observed.

"I'll bet you're right," Ike said with a laugh.

After the bikers rode down the path on the other side, Ike continued.

"I think the only thing holding my dad together right now is my sister Sarah," Ike said. "Even though she doesn't talk, he seems to be much calmer with her around, and I think it's been good for her too. The bad news is she's going off to school down in Faribault soon."

"What's that all about?"

"It's another special school where she can get the help she needs with her speech. She's going to be sent down there, and she's going to live down there too. She got some sort of special grant that's going to pay for it all."

"That's a huge change, Ike. How do you think she feels about it?"

"Sarah is tougher than all of us. I know she'll miss us, especially Jacob and Ruthy, but my mom has taken her down for visits and I guess she loves it. My mom will take her down and move her in over Labor Day weekend, so my mom's not going to do anything until after that."

"When is she going to tell Sarah and the other kids?"

"My mom said Sarah already figured it out," Ike replied. "Tough and smart, that's my sister, Sarah. I think that's why she stays so close to my dad. She knows it's going to be rough. The other kids, I don't know. But, there's more."

"More?!"

"This next bit might actually blow your mind," Ike said.

Mitch shifted in his seat, mentally preparing himself.

"OK, are you ready?" Ike was antsy. "After sitting there on that bench with my mom for a few minutes, not saying anything, I told her there was something I needed to ask her. When I looked at her, I could tell she already knew what I was going to say."

"What did you ask her, Ike?"

He paused for a minute, summoning the right words.

"I asked her if it was true that Leon Tiller wasn't my real father," Ike confessed. "When she started to cry, I knew."

"Wait, what do you mean? What are you saying?"

"I'm saying, Mitch, that Leon Tiller is not my father. And he's not my brother Aaron's father, either. He's just father to the other kids in the family."

Now Mitch was shocked.

"I can tell by the look on your face that you need another beer."

"Boy, you ain't shitting, Ike."

"Help yourself, my man. My beer's good for now."

Ike had more.

"My mom told me how that had happened. Without getting into too much detail, she said she and Leon had split up a few times many years ago after he hurt her, and in those times, she'd had a couple of 'indiscretions' with an old friend down on Payne Ave. She said to me, bawling her eyes out, that 'all these years, Leon took out my weakness on you boys and I stood by and did nothing. That's my greatest sin. That's why I'm going to burn in hell.'"

"And, in case you're wondering, Mitch, she revealed that my real father has been dead for years."

"I don't know what to say, Ike," Mitch said quietly. "I mean, this is a lot. Can I ask you a couple questions?"

Ike nodded.

"You know Leon's not your dad, but does Leon know he's not your dad?"

"That's a good question. And yeah, he knows. I guess he's always known."

"OK, so what made you ask her that in the first place? I mean, how did you figure it out?"

"Let's just say that I've suspected he wasn't my dad for a long time, but someone else confirmed it—and don't bother asking me who because I'm not going to tell you."

"Oh, hell no, that's fine. I understand."

They both sipped at their beers for a few minutes, digesting it all. It didn't really feel like celebrating, though, so Mitch had to ask.

"Ike, are we at the celebrating part yet? It's a little hard to tell."

"Like I said, Mitch, celebrating might not be the right word. Maybe relief? Yeah, I guess relief, because I'll tell you this much: I'm not going back to delivering newspapers, he's not going to make me quit working up at the golf course, and I'm not going to live in fear anymore. I'll never ever let him hurt me or my mom ever again. Needless to say, I didn't go to Temple this morning." There was a new resolve in Ike's voice and manner, and Mitch did feel happy for the guy in some way.

"So, he knows about you working at the golf course now?"

"No, but I'm not going to hide it either," Ike confirmed. "Anyways, I thought this was all worth having a couple of beers over. In fact, I'm going to have another cold one right now. Where's that damn church key?"

Mitch tossed Ike the can opener.

"As exciting as this is, I gotta finish my beer and shove off, pal. I have football practice tomorrow and I'm dead on my feet."

"Are you guys in full pads yet?" Ike asked.

"Yeah, for a couple weeks now."

"OK, me and the old Buster dog are going to hang around here a little longer. Hopefully Leon's in bed when I get home."

Mitch stood to leave, but Ike delayed him.

"Hey, doesn't the state fair start soon?"

"Yup, next Thursday."

"Well, when are we going?"

"Right now, it probably looks like that Sunday. I have to work at the course for the tournament on Friday and Saturday."

"What about football practice on Friday?"

"We have a scrimmage Thursday night, so no practice Friday."

Ike nodded.

"Perfect. Next Sunday it is."

"Are you sure your dad won't care?" Mitch asked.

"I'm sure I don't give a shit. I'm going to the fair," he said.

"Well then, maybe we can get a bunch of us to go on Sunday."

Ike beamed.

"Yeah, that would be a blast. Redeem the experience at the county fair."

"Cool. I'll make some calls and see what everybody wants to do. We have to take the 14-B bus and then transfer downtown to Saint Paul to get to the fairgrounds."

"Hell, I don't care how we get there, I'm going to my first-ever Minnesota State Fair!"

"Shoot, I'm glad you said something about the fair," Mitch said. "I have to get a hold of Maggie to find out when she's going to be around."

"So how's that going anyway?"

"Who knows," Mitch said vaguely. "I don't see her enough to really give a shit anymore. I'll call you tomorrow."

CHAPTER 33

THE HILLCREST INVITATIONAL

While Mitch and the rest of the guys were at football practice every day that week, Ike and EZ were working up at the golf course, getting the place ready for the tournament—stuff like getting the driving range ready and manicuring the tee boxes. John Getz hired the landscape outfit down on Maryland Avenue to get the place shipshape, and man oh man did they ever. The 150 feet of hedges that lined both sides of the driveway leading up to the clubhouse were squared off to perfection. They brought in two dump trucks of mulch to freshen up the landscaped areas around the bungalows and pool. The flower gardens on the property looked like something you would see at the Masters or U.S. Open. The place truly looked fabulous for the big tournament, and the course itself was in pristine condition. The first thing you'd see driving up to the country club was a banner of the main sponsor of the golf tournament: Grand Rickhouse Bourbon, the Getz brothers' newest venture into the whiskey business.

The next thing you'd see was the star of the show, right in the middle of the flower garden in front of the clubhouse: a bright red 1969 Oldsmobile Cutlass 442 Convertible, similar to the one Mr. Dawson had bought and returned last fall. But this one had the low-profile black hood scoops, and instead of a white interior, this car had a black interior. Mitch didn't think it could be possible, but this car was even sexier than the other one. It had a sticker price of over $5,500. This Cutlass also had the W/30 package, including the high-performance rocket 455 V8 engine and the rally wheels. It was on display as the prize for the hole-in-one competition for the golf tournament. During the tournament itself, the car would be parked over at the tee box for hole number nine. The ninth hole at Hillcrest is a 155 par 3. They have a nice car out there every year for the tournament, but nobody's ever won it. Mitch would make it a point to tell his dad all about the car once he got home that day.

EZ got dragged inside for a couple of days to be first assistant to the High Priestess of all vanity, the Grand Empress herself: Sylvia Getz, Sid's well-kept dragonlady wife. Every year, Sylvia would impose herself into the invitational tournament and try to be relevant. Sylvia was a tanned, disorganized disaster with a big rack. She would bark out nonsensical orders and keep everybody on edge.

Sylvia didn't have the first clue on how to put on an event. Still, Sid would indulge her and give her the title of "Hospitality Director." Sylvia would breeze in early every day and make a complete mess out of everything.

EZ was her gopher, as in, "OK Eric, go for my cigarettes." "Eric, go for my Manhattan," or "Eric, go for my sandwich." In the end, EZ still managed to get a lot of work done. He got all the name tags put together and hung all the placards and banners for the sponsors. EZ was surprisingly good at administration, not so much physical labor—"administration" being code for not doing real work, but still, his efforts weren't lost on Sid and John. EZ kept Sylvia out of everybody's hair for a couple days, and for that alone, EZ made more money than all of us.

Sylvia wasn't completely useless, though. She was at her best when she was working the guests. Whether it was at the bar, in the ballroom, or on the sprawling patio by the pool, Sylvia knew how to turn heads. She made everybody feel important, and she added an air of sophistication to the weekend. Like Sid would occasionally confess: "Sylvia always looks good, keeps the dogs fed, and can suck start a farm tractor."

Mitch found himself wishing that Hillcrest Country Club would run a big-shot tournament every weekend. He'd be rolling in dough. That weekend alone, he made three times more money at the golf course than he did the entire rest of the summer. He put in a lot of hours, but the work wasn't very hard. Plus, everybody tipped well. All the guys got two new Hillcrest golf shirts and had to wear tan slacks. No shorts, no jeans—except for the girls. Gloria, Izzy, and the rest of the girls wore the shortest of short shorts.

Every day after work, Gloria and her shorty-short shorts jumped into a Mustang convertible with a guy she'd started dating, Toby Schmedlap. Toby was the son of Irving Schmedlap, the patriarch of one of the wealthiest families at the country club. They owned a produce company and must have been selling a lot of bananas because everyone in the family drove a brand-new car every year. That year, Toby was a senior at Highland Park High School and often bragged about going to Arizona State next year. Of the millions of guys Gloria has to choose from, she chose this jerk. Mitch had to caddy for the asshole last month; the smug prick treats everybody like shit because his family has money. The only friend he ever had at the golf course? Ray the Rat, which tells you everything you need to know about Toby Schmedlap. The fact that he managed to convince Gloria to date him was just one more reason to hate him.

Despite their long tenure at the course, Mitch and the others didn't do one bit of caddying for the tourney because the tournament players brought their own pro caddies for that. Most of the time, Manny, Zitz, and EZ were humping golf bags from limos to the clubhouse and then from the clubhouse to the tee box. Mitch did the shuttling back and forth to the driving range, which is where he made most of his money. Every time he dropped a golfer off at the driving range, they gave him a few bucks, sometimes a five—one guy even gave him a ten spot. And every time he took a golfer back to the clubhouse, Mitch would get a few more bucks. These tips were on top of the envelope full of cash each of the guys received from Sid Getz. The rest of the time, they took turns hauling trash, stocking the bar, and even helping out in the kitchen, which meant doing dishes for a couple hours. Doing dishes sucked just as much at the golf course as it did at the VFW volunteer events.

Ike worked all week leading up to the tournament, too. He was lucky because he didn't have to suffer any of Sylvia's bullshit, being stationed outside every day. But then, Ike's luck ran flat out.

Friday morning, Mary Tiller was sitting at the heavy oak kitchen table. Just as Ike was heading out the kitchen door to go up to work at the course for the tournament, he gave his mom a kiss on the cheek and noticed her skin was damp. She'd been crying. She and Leon must've been fighting.

"What's going on, Mom?" Ike quietly asked.

Then Leon yelled to him from the living room.

"Isaac, get in here."

Ike stood, glanced back at his mom, and walked to the living room, saying nothing.

"Where do you think you're going?" Leon demanded.

Silence.

"I asked you a question, boy. Where are you going?"

"I got stuff to do," Ike replied before turning on his heel and walking away.

"Get back here!" Leon yelled.

Ike stopped and turned around, but stayed where he'd stopped.

"Here." Leon held out a piece of paper.

"What's that?" Ike asked.

"You're going to start delivering newspapers again," Leon said. "I made a couple of phone calls and got you some paper routes. This tells you the addresses. You pick up your papers at Curve Street and Cottage Avenue. You'll do one route in the morning and one in the afternoon."

Being a paperboy seemed like a lifetime ago to Ike, and it was the last thing he was going to do. Leon was determined to do everything he could to set things back to the way they were before he went away. Mary entered the living room, dish towel in hand, and stood by Ike, visibly upset.

"No way, not a chance," Ike stated. "I'm not delivering newspapers again."

Moving toward Ike, Leon glared.

"Oh, yes you are."

"No, I'm not."

"Yes, you are." Leon was standing within arm's reach now. "You're going to start delivering newspapers for this family Monday morning, you hear me, boy?" He jammed his finger into Ike's chest to emphasize how serious he was. "You and your mother and your smart mouths are going to straighten up and straighten up right now." He paused. "You skipped Temple last week, but you'll never skip it again. You hear me? I won't let Satan sink his claws into this family. We're going to a new temple now, and we're going to attend as a family, and by God, you're going to start delivering newspapers next week, and that's final."

Ike had known this moment was coming, and he was more than prepared to stand up to Leon, knowing that it might boil down to more violence. Ike had plenty to say.

He pushed Leon's finger away from his chest. Defiantly, and perhaps foolishly, Ike took the paper from Leon's other hand and crumpled it, dropping it to the floor when he couldn't crumple it any more.

"I told you, I'm never, ever going to deliver your fucking newspapers again."

Leon the asshole, meet the new Ike Tiller. Ike knew there was no going back from this, and his mom knew it too. Everything was going to come out at that moment. Leon was shocked. For a moment, it looked like he was going to hit Ike, but then he shifted gears and fumed.

"How dare you use that filthy, foul language in my house. You're no better than your worthless brother. In fact, you're worse because he never dared use language like that in front of me."

Ike knew Leon was insinuating that he'd picked up such filth from his friends, 'that Dawson kid' and the others.

"I'm sure you and all your little friends are hanging out at that dreadful bridge over by 3M like your brother did with the rest of the despicable sinners. Well, you listen, and you listen well. As of right this minute, you are not allowed to have anything to do with that Dawson kid or any of those other boys, you hear me? They are nothing but vile sinners that want to take you to hell with them."

"Mitch Dawson, Eric Golyn, and Manny Klaus are my friends," Ike defended. "I'm not going to stop seeing my friends. In fact, we're going to the state fair on Sunday."

Dumbfounded, Leon rejected the idea.

"You're not going to any state fair. What have I always told you about those things? There's nothing but evil at those fairs. Besides, where are you going to get the money?"

"That's the other good thing about all my friends; I work with them every day." Ike smiled, knowing exactly where this was headed.

"Work with them?" Leon smirked. "Where do you work?"

"You haven't figured it out by now?"

"Figured out what?" Leon demanded.

Then Ike delivered the bomb.

"I work up at Hillcrest Country Club, for the Getz brothers. I've been working there for months."

Ka-Frickin-BOOM.

Leon stood as though thunderstruck, then turned and made his way back to his chair, slumped down, and shook his head.

"It's a lie," he muttered. "You wouldn't dare. You wouldn't betray me like that."

Ike gazed at Leon.

"I'm not lying," Ike said.

"Please tell me that you don't work for those Jews." Leon said it so quietly Ike almost didn't hear him. Then the screaming. "NOT THE JEWS!" He paused to catch his breath. "It's a lie, I know you're lying, Isaac. Your mother would've told me." He glared at Mary Tiller. "Wouldn't you?" he said, directing his question at his wife.

"It's the truth," Ike reassured him. "John and Sid Getz have been great. I love working there. See, John and Sid don't beat me or constantly say horrible things to me, and they don't make me feel worthless like you do."

Ike summoned the rest of his courage.

"You know when you threw me out on Christmas Eve? Do you remember that night? I sure do; I broke into one of their bungalows at the golf course to stay warm for the night. When the Getz brothers found out, they showed me kindness, not hate and not violence. They heard about this nightmare we've all been living in with you. Like my friends and people from all over this neighborhood, the Getz brothers helped me, Mom, and the other kids, and they supported us when you were gone."

Ike continued, changing his angle.

"And, by the way, why were you gone? Why?" The question hung in the air. "You were gone because you beat me and you beat mom, so they locked you up in a fucking mental hospital, that's why. The people in the neighborhood brought us food, the Getz brothers gave us clothes because all you gave us was hate. They didn't care you were the bastard that burned that swastika into the green on number 9. Yeah, I know about that. The Getz brothers helped us anyway."

Leon's breathing was heavy and he had a glazed look on his face. Then something shifted; his eyes began darting around the room, trying to sense if all of this was real or not. His paranoia was on full display.

"First, your detestable brother and now you," Leon said in low tones, menacing. "You're Satan spawn. You *and* the Jews. I should have burned their Jew club to the ground."

Nothing could be worse for Leon than someone in his family being involved with the Getz brothers. Yes, even a kid working part time for tips. This wasn't some evil empire that Ike had become a part of, but that's not the way Leon saw things. To Leon, this betrayal was rivaled only by Ike's brother Aaron joining the Navy and Leon himself being thrown out of his Jehovah's Witness temple. This was Leon Tiller's hell on Earth.

Ike looked at his mother and defended his choice.

"He was going to find out sooner or later. We should tell him now."

"Now's definitely not the time, Ike," Mary warned. "It'll only make matters worse. Don't say another word. Just leave and go on up to the golf course."

Leon had been sitting there in his chair, his mind awash with the news of this latest perceived treachery against him. He luckily hadn't heard a word that Ike and Mary were saying until the words "golf course" came up. Leon stood up suddenly and threatened Mary and Ike.

"I want you two out of my sight, you hear me? You get out of my sight right now before I—" he stopped. "I'll tell you this right now, Isaac. If you so much as dare to set one foot on that course—so help me God, cops or no cops, I don't care anymore—if you set one foot on that course, I swear I'll come up there and drag you off by the throat. And I dare anyone to try and stop me."

Ike and Mary turned and went through the kitchen to the back door.

"Isaac, we'll tell him the other thing soon," Mary promised. "But now is not the time. And please, don't go up to the golf course. He's serious. Don't go up there."

Ike deflated a little bit.

"What are you going to do, Mom?"

"This might be a good time to go up and call on Penny Dawson," she said. "I know she's home. I spoke to her yesterday. I'll grab the kids and go over there and hopefully your dad will cool down, but we both have to get out of here now. I'm going to go upstairs and get the kids."

Ike nodded. He then called Buster and out the door they went.

This interaction had gone long past the point where Leon Tiller would normally have gotten violent. If this were a year ago, simply saying, "No, I'm not going to deliver newspapers" would've been all the provocation Leon needed to unleash his fury on Ike. Leon had been threatening since he got home, but he had yet to get violent. Even still, there was something foreboding and sinister at play now, more than before.

The guys didn't see Ike for a couple of days, not until they went to the state fair on Sunday. Mary and the rest of the kids had sought sanctuary at the Dawson house, so they knew something had happened. It was the first time Mary had actually taken up the Dawon's offer, even though it'd been talked about and offered to Ike many times.

When Mrs. Tiller showed up at the Dawson's house with Ruthy, Jacob, and Sarah in tow, she was quite a sight. It took a little while, but Mrs. Dawson was able to calm Mary Tiller down and reassure her that she and the kids were in a safe place.

"Mary, your timing is actually perfect," Mrs. Dawson said in her calmest voice.

"How so, Penny?"

"Well, the kids and I, along with Nancy and Joy Golyn, were getting ready to go off for an adventure. How about you and your kids come with us?"

"Sure, Penny, that'd be great. It'll take our minds off everything. What did you have in mind?"

"I'm packing a big picnic lunch and we're taking all the kids over to the beach at Tanner's Lake off of Century Avenue."

"Penny, that sounds wonderful, but we don't have any stuff for the beach and I don't want to go back up to the house and deal with Leon."

Mom reassured her.

"Mary, my dear, I've got you covered."

Casey had some old trunks Jacob could wear, and Mrs. Dawson found one of Stephi's suits for Ruthy. Sarah didn't need anything, as she was just happy to go to the beach. She only wanted to wade in the water, anyway. Mrs. Dawson outfitted Mary Tiller in one of her spare bathing suits, which, according to Casey, was a little snug on Mary in the upper torso region.

And so, Mrs. Dawson took the big picnic lunch, a big jug of Kool-Aid, as many beach towels as she could find, and a bottle of Coppertone, loaded it all into the Olds Vista Cruiser wagon with all nine of them, and the Tanner's Lake adventure was on.

It doesn't take much to imagine how much fun the kids had on that perfect August day. With temps in the 80s and a slight breeze, it was in all regards the perfect day. Tanner's Lake Beach also had a playground with swings and monkey bars. Goofy Casey brought his flippers and goggles. The younger kids were learning how to hold their noses and dunk their heads under water. They even learned how to float. The moms left the miseries of Leon alone for the day.

While enjoying their picnic lunch, the moms decided their next adventure would be to take all the kids to the state fair over Labor Day weekend. Mary Tiller mentioned then that she had to take Sarah down to school in Faribault, so they were out for that one. Mom and Mrs. Golyn said they would be happy to take Jacob and Ruthy with them anyway. After further discussion, they thought the state fair might be a little bit much with all the kids, so they decided then and there to go to Como Park Zoo instead, which was near the state fairgrounds.

With everybody gone, Leon Tiller could be alone with his thoughts and the beginnings of some strange new behavior. His paranoia had gripped him by the throat; Leon had never felt so isolated in his life and in his mind. He felt the whole world piling up against him, but most recently the Getz brothers with their personal attack by employing Ike. After everything that had happened, Leon should have immediately sought his doctor's help to find a way to cope with it all, but instead, Leon kept his own counsel because, when you're paranoid, you don't trust anyone.

Over the next week, Leon began taking off in his old Dodge station wagon. He'd drive around the neighborhood, up by the golf course, and then he would drive off, come home for a few hours, and do it all again. A couple of times, he tried to chase down the Harley riders that rode through the neighborhood. All of these actions violated his probation, as he wasn't supposed to leave the house; even his attendance at the temple was not permitted. He doesn't speak a word to anybody in the house when he is at home. He wasn't handling his new reality very well, and little did he know, another big change was on the horizon: Sarah would be moving down to her new school in Faribault, Minnesota.

CHAPTER 34

MINNESOTA STATE FAIR

As Mitch was getting ready to head out to the state fair, he noticed a pickup truck in the driveway, which was pretty strange for 9 a.m. on a Sunday morning. When he walked out on his way to EZ's place, his dad was standing next to the garage talking to a couple of fellas Mitch didn't recognize.

"Where are you heading? Up to the golf course?" he asked.

"No, we're going to the state fair today."

Mr. Dawson smiled.

"Oh yeah, that's right! Have fun! Oh, hey, Mitch, before you go, let me introduce you to these guys."

He walked closer to his dad and the two other guys.

"These are Ralph Flint and his son Joe." Mr. Dawson pointed to each respectively. "They're here to help us build a new garage."

Mitch looked puzzled.

"We are?"

"Yup," his dad confirmed. "We're just trying to figure out how big it should be. Ralph seems to think that you can never build a garage too big. What do you think Mitch?"

"I agree with Mr. Flint; always go bigger."

"I think it's time your mom gets her own car, and we can't fit two in here as it is."

Two cars? Mitch thought. Nobody has two cars. That would be kind of nice, actually.

"That's really cool, Dad," Mitch said. "I gotta go meet EZ."

Mitch said his goodbyes and headed to EZ's house.

They had a big crew heading to the fair that day. When Mitch got to EZ's house, Izzy was already there getting prepped for the day with Gloria. EZ's girlfriend, Linda, was going with them too.

When Gloria came upstairs from her bedroom, she looked absolutely dazzling. She made a point of walking over and presenting herself to me, as if to indicate, "Here's your chance, idiot, don't screw it up." The encounter at Casey's birthday had developed into a sort of inside joke, and I tried not to laugh.

"Wow, Gloria, you look great," Mitch said. "Did you do something different with your hair... again?" Wink, Wink.

Gloria, with a big smile, almost purred.

"Why, yes, Mitchy-poo, I did, in fact, do something with my hair. Thank you for noticing." She then leaned over to him. "See, that wasn't so damn difficult, was it?" she whispered. "By the way, you're looking pretty good today yourself."

Huh, that was a surprise to Mitch. Gloria had never said anything about him, one way or the other. Then she punched him in the arm. Gloria had already been to the fair. She'd made an appearance on opening night with the rest of the winter carnival royalty, but this time she was going to have fun.

Izzy made her way up from downstairs.

"Are we ready to go?" she asked.

"Yup!" EZ yelled. "We're all set. Let's fly."

When they got outside, Mitch noticed Gloria hadn't followed them out.

"Do we have to wait for Glo?" he asked.

"No, she's not coming with us," Izzy said. "She's going to the fair with her new boyfriend, Toby."

Mitch couldn't help but feel a little let down. He'd wanted the whole group to be at the fair at least one time, but perhaps the old saying is true: You can't always get what you want.

Zitz and Manny were already at the bus stop, along with some other kids from the neighborhood. The only one missing was Ike. As much as Mitch knew Ike wanted to go to the state fair, it sounded like things were really bad at his house again. The bus arrived only a few minutes later, and everyone filed in, moving to the back. Then, sure enough, there was Ike. He boarded the bus, a little out of breath, and plopped down in front of Mitch. To everyone's surprise, Izzy plopped down next to Ike.

"Are you going to ride some of the midway rides with me today, Ike?" Izzy asked.

Ike appeared to be a little confused by the question.

"What?"

Izzy slowed it way down.

"Now Ike, pay attention." Her tone had become sarcastic and playful. "Are you, Ike, going to ride some of the midway rides with me, Isabelle, today?"

Ike grinned, realizing what she was asking.

"Sure, if you want to."

"Good, because there's lots more rides at the state fair than the county fair, and they're a lot cooler too."

By all appearances, Izzy and Ike seemed to have made a thrill ride connection. Of course, Mitch had to stick his nose in.

"Remember, Izz, he's never been to the fair before, so he has a lot of ground to cover."

"No problem, Doc. We've got all day, right Ike?"

Ike nodded.

"Hey, did you have any trouble getting out of the house this morning?" Mitch asked, thinking about the uptick in Leon's weird behavior.

"No, I just had to wait for Leon to leave." Ike shrugged. "Oh, Mitch, here's a juicy detail: He found out I work at the golf course the other day."

"Holy shit, Ike, what happened?"

"He tried to force me to take paper routes again, but I told him I wouldn't do it. Then I told him I've been working at the golf course. I thought he was going to explode. He hates the Getz brothers, and he said some really terrible things about you guys. He doesn't want me to see you guys anymore, so I told him to go to hell."

He continued.

"My mom's getting real worried again because there's a couple of other things Leon's going to find out about that's going to make things much worse, like that my mom is divorcing him. I have no idea what's going to happen, but it won't be good.

"You said there were a couple of things... what else is happening?"

He noticed that everyone was listening at that point, so he backed off the conversation.

"I'll tell you later."

Mitch nodded.

"Hey Mitch, do you know where a place called 'Young America' is at the fair?"

Mitch was a little surprised by the question. How would Ike know about such a specific spot, having never been to the fair?

"Yeah, it's kinda back behind the Midway. Why?"

"Somebody told me to go there to listen to the music."

"I've never been in there myself," Mitch confessed. "My mom and dad have never let me go in there because they thought I was too young. They have bands playing there, and there's a lot of cool displays. It's kind of a hippie hang out."

Ike laughed.

"That makes sense. Are we going there today?"

"Hell yeah!" It's one of my goals to go hang out there and listen to the bands."

Twelve of them went to the fair that day, including Mario DiMucci, his sister Gina, and three of her friends. They had to transfer buses in downtown Saint Paul, which was inconvenient, but they knew it would all be worth it. The moment they had been waiting for all summer had finally arrived. If the day went the way it should, Mitch would get to see his gal Maggie, he'd stuff himself full of food, ride the Midway, watch some bands at the Young America Center, and go to the stock car races that evening. Mitch had a pocket full of cash that predicted he'd have a lot of fun that day. No football, no work. A perfect day ahead.

The 14-B bus pulled out on time and got only a couple blocks down Curve Street before it pulled over to make its first stop and ruin his perfect day. Ray the Rat and three of his buddies were waiting for the bus. Mitch knew two of Ray's buddies—Bill Robillard and Victor Snyder—but he'd only ever seen the other guy. Robillard acts like he's tough and Snyder was nothing special, and they're all only a year older than the guys.

They walked onto the bus, looked around, and saw everyone sitting at the back. The Rat looked right at Mitch and Ike and glowered.

"I hope you fags have fun at the fair today."

Mitch knew the Rat was coming for him, but he was praying that it wouldn't be that day. Everything had to be perfect.

As the bus went down Maryland Avenue, it stopped to pick up more people on their way to the fair. Right when the bus got to Johnson Parkway, a car came screaming past, its driver honking the horn aggressively. The whole crew got up to look outside: Lo and behold, it was Toby Schmedlap in his Mustang convertible, taking Gloria to the fair. The day so far was not what Mitch had hoped, and it was only just beginning.

When the bus made a stop at Payne Avenue and Bush Street, there was Mario, his sister Gina, and Gina's three friends. Mario and the rest of them made their way back toward us, and it was then that Mitch started to get real fired up for the fair again. He recognized a couple of the girls who had boarded the bus with Mario and Gina—they were the ones who'd stolen the boys' hats down at Phalen Playground during the hockey tournament last winter, the ones who had invited them to the dance at Arlington Playground.

The 14-B pulled up to 7th Street and Wabasha Street in downtown Saint Paul. When they got off the bus, the driver handed them their transfers. All they had to do was cross the street and catch the Como/Styker bus that goes to the fairgrounds, and they'd arrived just in time to make their connection.

Mitch and his crew were all in the back of the bus again, but as Gina, Izzy, and the other girls were passing by Ray and his buddies, the pricks blocked the girls' way down the aisle and made a bunch of nasty comments to them. One of Gina's friends is a bigger girl, and those guys said some real mean shit to her. All the girls were furious by the time the bus driver yelled at Ray's crew to cut it out.

Ike was one of the last ones on the bus, and as he made his way down the aisle, the Rat tripped him. Ike fell flat on his face, and the clowns with Ray thought it was hilarious.

"Hey, asshole, leave him alone," EZ yelled at Ray.

Ike got up, didn't say a word, and came back to sit with the rest of the crew. The Rat and Bill Robillard got out of their seats and walked back to us. Ray looked at me, a real nasty sneer on his face.

"What did you say, Dawson? Did you say something? Why don't you say it to my face?"

"He didn't say anything, asshole, I did," EZ growled.

"Oh no, no, it was Dawson," Ray said. "The backstabbing little kiss ass." He loomed over Mitch, making himself as threatening as possible. He grabbed Mitch's shirt.

"How about I teach you to keep your big mouth shut right now?"

Manny stood up and pushed Ray back, forcing him to let go of Mitch's shirt.

"That's OK, all right Manny, don't get excited," Ray grumbled, backing off. "Dawson, I'm gonna catch you one of these days real soon and pay you back for fucking me over at the golf course. Yup, real soon, Dawson." Ray and Robillard went back to their seats and got atta boys from the other two.

Manny, EZ, and Zitz were filling Mario in on the Rat situation. Mitch asked Ike if he was OK, to which he just nodded.

Mitch had a sick feeling in the pit of his stomach. He'd waited all summer for the fair, and now he didn't even want to go.

After a few minutes, Mario tapped him on the shoulder.

"Mitch, is all this crap true?"

"What crap?"

"That guy up there is some big tough bully."

"Yeah," Mitch said. "He used to work at the golf course and he's pissed at me because he got fired."

"What about those other guys?" Mario asked.

"They're just neighborhood assholes. They follow Ray's lead."

"So, the big jerk and these other clowns waltz in here, trip Ike, say shit to my sister and the other girls, and try to scare everybody?"

"Yeah, I guess so."

"OK, that's all I needed," Mario said. "I fucking hate bullies."

"Me too, Mario."

And that's when it hit him. Mario had just spelled it out in a way Mitch hadn't thought about before: "try to scare everybody." Dealing with a bully wasn't just about getting beat up or taking some knocks once in a while; it was all about fear. They want you to live in it. Fear that you can't walk home a certain way or that you can't be someplace when they're around. It's about keeping people scared. Mitch knew his dad would rather see his son get the shit kicked out of him than get pushed around by a bully.

Mario got out of his seat to go and confront Ray and his cronies, but Mitch stood up in front of him to stop him.

"Paisano, let me handle this."

"Are you sure, Doc?"

"Yeah, it's time. I'll talk to these assholes… just make sure they can see you, Manny, and Zitz the whole time."

"Okay, Doc, we've got your back." Mario sat back down in his seat.

Mitch had no clue what he was going to do or say, but the time had come to address the situation. Hell, what's the worst that could happen? A beating? That was going to happen anyway—so at least he'd be ready for it in this situation.

Mitch wobbled his way up the aisle to the Rat and his posse, and when he got to their row, he clung to the overhead bar and stood quietly, just looking at them.

"What are you looking at?" Bill Robillard asked.

"Not much," Mitch said. "I'm here to talk to all you tough guys who trip people on buses and talk nasty shit to girls they don't know," Mitch declared.

Their crew didn't say anything, but the snickers were plentiful.

"Ray, you blame me for losing your job, right?" Mitch singled out the ringleader.

"You're damn right I do, and I'm gonna beat your ass because of it," Ray snarled.

"OK, tough guy," Mitch said with a nod. "I bet these guys are tough guys too." He waved his hand, indicating the other three. "We're all going to find out all about the tough guys today. Ray, when we get off this bus, it's you and me, asshole. We're going to go at it today because I'm done waiting for you to decide when you're going to 'beat my ass.' We have about five minutes left on this bus; when we get off, things are going down. You act like some big tough guy, so I'm telling you this right now, so help me God, if I'm going down, you're coming with me. You think you're going to push me around? You better think again. I'm so sick and tired of your shit. I don't give a goddamn anymore, you fucking clown. I'll take a beating, sure, but if you think you're getting out of this without a scratch, you're dead wrong. I fucking promise you that." Mitch emphasized his words with the deepest glare he could muster.

"As for the rest of you, let's recap a few things: You guys said some nasty things to those girls back there and upset them pretty frickin bad. It was you, Robillard, wasn't it? You think you're a real tough guy too, huh? Well, we're going to see just how tough you are, Robillard, because today you'll get to meet Golden Gloves Champion Mario DiMucci. You see Mario right there?"

They looked over to see Mario and his menacing glare.

"Ever heard of him? Mario is the toughest son of a bitch on the lower East Side. He's going to introduce himself to you when we get off the bus because one of those girls you said some shit to is his sister, Gina. That's Gina right over there."

Bill Robillard started to look real uneasy.

"Snyder, you were saying some shit to the girls too, to Isabelle Petri and the rest of them. You guys made one girl cry, and the morning has barely started. Well, guess who Isabelle is going out with? It's somebody you know, Snyder. Yeah, you know him from the playground, that's him right there. See Zack Deitz? Zack is Isabelle's boyfriend." That was bullshit, but they didn't need to know that. Snyder knew he was in real trouble; Mitch could see it on his face.

"Zack happens to be the toughest SOB from the upper East Side and still remains undefeated," Mitch explained. This info was met with a blank stare from Snyder. "Fellas, Zack and Mario are the two toughest guys I know. Hell, they're two of the toughest guys at Johnson High School and they don't even go there yet. They're going to rip your fucking heads off."

Mitch then turned his gaze to the last guy.

"I don't even know this asshole, but hey, pal, I hope you're feeling strong today, because you're left with my clean-up hitter, heavyweight wrestling champion, Manfred Klaus. If you don't know Manny Klaus, he's that big 235-pound blond gorilla sitting right there. When he delivers his first punch, you'll think somebody threw a car battery at your head. And it just gets worse from there. So, buckle up, jerk off."

By the end of Mitch's tirade, everyone on the bus was watching him rip into those assholes. It must have been a sight. And the oddest thing of all was that when Mitch looked at Ray again, he seemed smaller somehow. He was trying to keep his cool, sitting there with his arms crossed high on his chest.

"Now you, you rat prick. Have you ever been in a real fight before or do you just pick on little kids and act tough? I'm going to come after you for every little kid you've bullied, every caddy you pushed around, everybody you made to feel scared. They're all coming for you today."

The Rat looked visibly shook but threw his threats out all the same.

"Oh yeah, Dawson? We'll see about that. We'll be ready."

Mitch could feel the heat creeping up his face. No doubt, it was beet red already. Mitch had never felt so enraged in his life, and he had little doubt as to how deranged he must have looked.

"You tough guys have anything else to say? Anything?" Mitch paused and watched them shift under all the attention. "No, nothing?" They were dead silent.

"All of you guys said some bad stuff to the wrong girls today, and Ray here tripped our friend, Ike. So, here's something for you other three to remember. Today, each one of you is going to get the beating of your life. That's how you'll always remember the Minnesota State Fair. You guys are going to get off this bus and get the living shit kicked out of you. I'll get my own beating, sure, but you three don't stand a fucking chance." Mitch maintained eye contact with the crew while pointing at Ray. "You came all the way to the state fair to get your brains beat in all for this fucking loser sitting right here. Think about that. You've got about three minutes. I'll see you girls later."

Mitch walked back to the group and sat down.

"I just got us all in a fight with those guys when we get to the fair," he admitted. "We'll see what happens." This was met with nods of approval from Zitz, Mario, and Manny.

They were only a mile away from the fairgrounds, so they didn't have a lot of time to think about what was about to happen. But just before they got to the fairgrounds, traffic ground to a complete stop, and they could hear a commotion up ahead. When the bus began to creep forward again, it wasn't long before they passed the problem: anti-war protesters were lined up and down Snelling Avenue in front of the fairgrounds, protesting the Vietnam War. It looked mostly like hippies. Ike had his head stuck out the window like a puppy to take it all in.

When the bus finally pulled up to the fairgrounds, there were three buses already at the bus stop unloading dozens and dozens of fairgoers. Finally, they all unloaded after what seemed like an excruciatingly long wait. There must have been more than a hundred people milling around and getting in line at the gate. Everybody in the main group gathered by the fence.

Mitch didn't know what was going to happen with the Rat. He didn't know if they were going to do something right there or if they'd go someplace else to have a brawl. It didn't matter either way, though, because Mitch was ready.

The four guys planning to be involved in the brawl looked around, but nobody could see Ray—or his cronies—anywhere. Maybe they'd pushed forward to get in line for the fair already; They'd seen them all get off the bus together. They were ahead of Mitch's crew.

Just as the bus was pulling away, Ike pointed at it and yelled.

"Look, look you guys."

Mitch looked up at the bus and couldn't believe his eyes. They all began to laugh their asses off; EZ was actually on the ground he was laughing so hard. Mario was pumping his fist in the air, and Manny was nodding, as though he could've predicted the turn of events. It looked like Ray the Rat and all his tough guy pals got off the bus, turned around in the madness of the crowd, and then got right back on the bus. They rode away to safety down Snelling Avenue. Mitch, all the guys and all the girls waved and hooted.

CHAPTER 35

IKE TILLER, MIDWAY THRILLER

Once everyone got inside the fair, they tried to get themselves organized. There was no way twelve people all wanted to do the same things at the same time; everybody had a different agenda, so the crew needed to split up in groups that had similar priorities. Mitch made it clear right from the beginning that his first order of business was to track down Maggie to find out when they could hang out later. This was something he wanted to do alone. Izzy decided that everybody would meet at the entrance to the midway in an hour and they'd take it from there. As everybody else took off in different directions, Mitch headed to Maggie's French fry stand. It was barely 10 a.m., but the fair was already getting really crowded. It was hot and humid, and there was a chance of some thunderstorms later.

Mitch could smell the French fry stand before he saw it. It was right in front of the grandstand, next to the pizza place. It wasn't busy yet, and the first person Mitch saw was Renée from school, Maggie's cousin.

As soon as Renée saw Mitch coming up to the stand, she came out from behind the counter and gave him a hug.

"Hey, Renée. Is Maggie around?"

"That's what I've got to tell you Mitch: Maggie's not here."

"Is she working later today?"

"No, Mitch," Renée said, a hint of something in her voice.

Mitch couldn't figure it out. Had something happened?

"Maggie's back home in Virginia."

"Really? She didn't call or anything."

"I knew she wouldn't," Renée said under her breath. "See, Mitch, Friday night, Maggie went on break with a bunch of friends of hers that were here from the Iron Range around 6 o'clock. But she never came back to work that night."

"I still don't understand."

"Mitch, Maggie went and got high and drunk with a bunch of her friends. She got fired from this French fry stand, and her dad drove down from Virginia to pick up her and Della yesterday. Maggie got in a lot of trouble. She didn't call and tell you because one of the friends she got drunk with was her new boyfriend. She was going to break it off with you this weekend."

Boy, did Mitch feel like a frickin idiot. Yet he felt relieved too.

"I'm sorry, Mitch, but I have to get back to work," Renée said. "I'm sorry I had to be the one to break it to you. How about some French fries and a Coke on the house?"

"Hell yeah, Renée, I'm starved."

"One large fry and a Coke, coming right up."

After eating the best French fries he'd ever had in his life, Mitch decided to grab a slice of pizza, which also happened to be one of the best he'd ever had in his life. There was something about the Minnesota State Fair that made everything taste better. Even better, Mitch still had corn dogs, mini donuts, and the five-cent bottomless milk later today.

As Mitch sat there finishing his pizza, it all began to sink in. The girlfriend he thought he'd had this whole time turned out to be a phantom girlfriend—or really none at all. His feeling like an idiot morphed into a feeling of anger; specifically, anger at Maggie for not telling him herself. He felt like she'd played him like a fool. But he was also angry at himself for believing that this relationship could possibly work with two hundred miles between them. Ah, the slippery slope of inexperience and young love.

Before he knew it, it was 11 a.m., so he walked over to the entrance of the midway. There were twelve of them heading into the midway, which meant nobody would be without a ride pal. Once everyone had reconvened, EZ pulled Mitch aside and asked him if he'd seen Maggie. After he told EZ what had happened, EZ patted Mitch's shoulder.

"That's rough, Doc, but if it makes you feel any better, the girls that came with Gina were asking about you. They remember you from the hockey tournament at Phalen Playground—and one of them had your Hayden Heights hat."

Mitch smiled at EZ.

"Yeah, that does make me feel a little better."

Maybe today won't be a total loss, Mitch thought.

Over the next three hours, all the kids had a blast. They went on all the rides, some of them multiple times. There were a bunch of new rides this year that they all had to try, too. Mitch and the guys took turns going on rides with different girls, but there were two couples that went on every ride together: EZ and Linda and Izzy and Ike. Nobody knew Izzy was such a thrill seeker; Ike discovered that day that he was too.

There were lots of new arcade games, too, and of course they all made the classic state fair mistake of trying to win a bunch of stuffed animals and other crappy prizes. The real problem with these games wasn't losing; after all, these games were designed to make the player lose, so it's kind of the expectation. The real problem is that if you do win, you're awarded a four-foot-tall stuffed donkey that you have to drag around with you all frickin' day. But, you know, it's all about impressing the girls, so that's what they did. Ike didn't win anything, so Mitch gave his donkey to Izzy. Let those two drag it around all day.

After getting off the double Ferris wheel for the second time, Ike and his co-pilot Izzy came back toward the group.

"Is that the Young America place right back there?" he asked, pointing.

"Yeah, that's it right up there."

"Remember, we have to go there today," he said.

"Ike, believe me, that's one of my main goals today. It's open right now, but the music doesn't start for a while."

They decided there were some more traditional things at the state fair that Ike should experience, one of which was the Sky Ride. The Sky Ride wasn't a thriller, but riders could see a lot of stuff all over the fair. It takes you up on cable cars from the midway and delivers you all the way up to where the Space Tower is on the other side of the fairgrounds. The boys figured that once they were on that end of the fair, they might as well go up in the Space Tower too.

When Mitch mentioned to the group that Ike wanted to go on the Sky Ride, everybody agreed. So, sure enough, the twelve of them paired off and got on six different cable cars that stretched across the fairgrounds. They only got one-way tickets because they were planning to get off and check out the Space Tower, and after that, they'd take Ike on a few runs down the Giant Slide, another state fair tradition.

While they were waiting in line to get tickets for the Space Tower, Mitch noticed Manny staring straight up in the sky at the rotating ride.

"What do you think?" he asked Manny.

"How high does this thing go?"

Mitch pointed to the ride info sign.

"It says right here that it goes up about three hundred feet."

Manny shook his head.

"I'll be waiting for you guys right over there, then."

"You're kidding," Mitch teased him.

"That Sky Ride over here was bad enough; there's no way I'm doing this too."

At that, Manny walked over by a hot dog stand to wait for his friends.

"Manfred, where are you going, man?" Mario asked after him.

"I'll tell you where I'm not going," he said, pointing at the Space Tower. "I'm not going up in that thing."

"Oh, thank God." Mario sounded relieved. "I thought I was the only one."

So, Mario joined Manny for some well-deserved, stay-on-solid-ground foot-long hot dogs.

When everyone got to the very top of the Space Tower, they could see everything for miles, including some really nasty weather heading their way. By the looks of the clouds, the state fairgrounds and everyone in them were going to get hammered later.

After the Space Tower, the group started to splinter off, which was to be expected. Zitz and one of Gina's friends, Kelly, seemed to be getting cozy, so Mitch knew he was going to be a lost cause for the rest of the day. Originally, Mitch thought he'd be the one taking Ike all around the state fair, but it was Izzy doing all the work. She'd made up her mind to be Ike's personal fairground guide for the day. She led Mitch, Ike, and Manny through the sheep and cow barns—and the horse stables too. Mitch thought it was actually pretty cool because she showed them lots of stuff they normally wouldn't have spent time on, like looking at all the fish in the pond by the Department of Natural Resources building and seeing all the 4-H displays.

Izzy gave Ike a comprehensive state fair experience, which helped because he was game for absolutely everything, including several turns on the bumper cars.

As 3 p.m. rolled around, everyone started to head over to the Young America Center. The music was about to start. The Young America Center was considered the state fair's "teen center," so unsurprisingly, the closer you got, the more pot you could smell. The place was pretty cool but a little bit scary at the same time owing to the rough characters wandering around. Mitch's group had just about the youngest people in the whole place, and some of the roughest characters were the people working, a lot of those long-haired biker types.

Young America was a much bigger deal than Mitch had thought. Its description as 'a teen center' had him expecting to see bands like what he normally saw at school or the playground, but boy was he wrong. There was a huge stage, and the first band to play was called Crow. They were a big deal locally, which Mitch and the group were going to find out.

Mitch, Ike, Manny, and Izzy got to the Center early enough to find seats against the back wall to watch the music. Once they'd claimed their seats, Mitch had to get rid of the copious amounts of milk he'd just consumed for a nickel. When he got back from the can, Manny and Izzy went and did the same. Mitch noticed Ike was not with the group, so he scanned the crowd and spotted Ike walking toward the stage. He struck up a conversation with the guys who were setting up for the first band.

What the hell is Ike doing? Mitch thought.

After a few minutes, Ike walked back over to their seats with one of the rough characters. This guy had tattoos up and down his arms, a red beard, and a ponytail that reached the middle of his back. This was one scary-looking hombre.

When Ike and his strange friend reached Mitch, Mitch could see clearly the huge smile Ike had. He put his hand on the strange guy's shoulder and introduced him.

"Mitch, this is my brother Aaron."

Mitch could've died. In one million years, he wouldn't have ever guessed that that's what today was all about. This whole day was oriented around Ike's connection with his brother Aaron.

"You look a little surprised, Mitch," Ike observed.

"I just don't know what to say."

Aaron stepped forward and shook Mitch's hand.

"I remember when you were little, and I've seen you around the neighborhood lately, too," Aaron said.

Then it hit him: the bikers cruising through the neighborhood.

"Aaron, have you and your friends been cruising around our neighborhood on those Harleys?" Mitch asked.

"Yeah, me and my boys started driving through, hoping to see Ike and let him know I was back in town."

"Does your Harley have cool flames on the gas tank?"

"Yup, that's me."

Ike broke in.

"Aaron's been back in town for a couple of months. My mom and I are the only ones who know so far, so I'm asking you to please not say anything. A lot of big stuff is going to happen pretty soon." Ike looked Mitch right in the eye, and Mitch knew exactly what he was talking about. "Aaron is helping us out with some stuff that our family has to take care of, but we can't let anybody know, especially Leon. I told Aaron that you can be trusted."

"I know you and your family have been good to Ike and the rest of the family, Mitch," Aaron said. "I'm very happy to know that he has so many good friends now. Life at our house has never been easy, but hopefully here soon things will change. Right, Ike?" He ruffled his brother's hair. "But, until that time comes, please keep my presence quiet. It's been great to meet you, Mitch, but I've got to get back to work. I'm working every day here, setting up and tearing down for the bands. It works out great: I protest the war outside the fair for about an hour every day and then come to work."

Ike looked like he was on cloud nine.

"Oh, and by the way, you two listen up very carefully: Do not take anything from anybody in here," Aaron cautioned. "When I say anything, I mean it. Don't smoke anything, don't drink anything, don't eat anything. There's some bad stuff floating around in here. A kid was hauled off to the hospital yesterday. You guys read me loud and clear?"

Ike and Mitch nodded their understanding.

"Now then, you guys have fun, and Ike, I'll talk to you later."

Aaron headed back to work, and both boys watched him go. You could've knocked Mitch over with a feather, honestly, but suddenly even more things were starting to make sense.

They sat back down, Ike still with a big smile on his face. Mitch couldn't help but shake his head in disbelief.

"Ike, holy shit, this is huge."

"I know. The main thing is to make sure Leon doesn't find out—but I had to tell someone. It's been hard for my mom to keep this from Sarah and the other kids too. Jacob and Ruthy were pretty young when Aaron went away, and they've heard nothing but bad stuff about him since he's been gone."

Mitch found out that Aaron was responsible for pointing Mrs. Tiller to the school for Sarah down in Faribault. He had a friend who'd lost his hearing over in Vietnam, and his friend said that the school in Faribault was the best in the country for the hearing impaired, and it's all paid for through scholarships.

"Mitch, my Mom has filed for divorce with the county, and she's seeing about getting Leon removed from the house. Aaron's been helping with that, too. When my mom and Leon actually separate, they'll have to get him out of the house, which won't be easy. Aaron himself has been living in a few different places since he got back, and he just gave me the phone number for the next place that he's going to move to. He says it's near White Bear Avenue, close to our house."

After talking to Ike for a while about these revelations, Manny and Izzy both finally made it back from the bathroom and a quick lap around the Center in time for the music to start. At that point, Young America was filled to the brim. Mitch glanced around at the crowd, and he spotted some other members of their big group who had filtered in: EZ and his girl Linda, and in another spot was Gina, two of her friends, and someone else—Gloria. While pleasantly surprised, Mitch knew it wasn't a good sign. Curiously, there was no boyfriend in sight, and she did not look happy. The look on Gloria's face was similar to the one she wore when she beat the snot out of Snag and Crime Scene.

Izzy jumped up and got the attention of Gina and the other girls and waved them over. Once they maneuvered their way over, Gina pointed at Gloria.

"I found this one loitering over by the Penny Arcade."

Izzy lost no time.

"What happened, Gloria? Where's the new boyfriend?"

Gloria turned and looked right at Mitch.

"I don't want to talk about it," she grumbled.

Mitch hadn't said one word about the situation, yet somehow she felt it necessary that he hear what she had to say. Mitch looked away, up toward the band, and then looked back toward Gloria—and she was still looking at him. Damn, if only that damn band would start already.

CHAPTER 36

CROW

It only took hearing two songs from the band Crow for Mitch to fall in love. They were his new favorite band in the whole world. If the Center had had a roof, they would've blown it off. There was a horn section and everything. Crow was a band that you might see on TV, they were so good. Mitch wouldn't have been able to tell anyone the name of a single song they played, but each song was better than the one before. He hadn't given them much thought before, but Mitch realized that night that he loved horns.

And he wasn't alone. The crowd went crazy for this band. They weren't slotted to play at the fair again this year, but if the other bands were anything like Crow, Mitch might consider returning next weekend for the show. Hell, he'd have come back every night if it wasn't for football.

During the show, dark clouds crept in, piling thicker and thicker until, by the time the band was done, the sky had become black. Aaron Tiller and the rest of the crew worked frantically to tear down the band equipment, and the crowd worked frantically to get the hell out of the Young America Center and seek shelter before the rain came down.

Taking charge, Izzy told everybody to meet over at the grandstand, which made sense because the place was huge and there'd be a lot of cool stuff in there to look at while everyone waited out the storm. As soon as they were able to start moving with the crowd toward the exit, Gloria walked up to Mitch and grabbed his hand without saying a word. Of course, this was about the impending storm. However, as they were walking, she let go of his hand and adjusted her grip so that their fingers were interlocking. That felt different; it felt like a connection with more connection. They walked like that all the way to the grandstand, the wind picking up as they crossed the pavement and the rain starting soon after.

Just about everybody from Young America had the same idea to migrate over to the grandstand and wait out the storm. The grandstand had two floors of displays and food, and later that day, they had stockcar races on the schedule.

Judging from what they'd seen up in the Space Tower, the storm was going to be a doozie. Mitch was glad there was a place to go, as he was sure Gloria was going to start to fall apart once the storm really got going. Gloria pulled Mitch through the crowd to a set of stairs leading up to the second floor.

"Come on, let's head up here," she urged.

A few rumbles of thunder bowled over the sky.

On the second floor, Gloria pointed to a bunch of old displays that had been pushed back into a corner.

"Look, over there. Let's go sit down."

It was kind of a secluded spot—secluded enough that they probably weren't supposed to be back there. After sitting with her for a few minutes, Mitch blurted about the Maggie situation.

"Maggie and I broke up."

Gloria looked at him.

"Yeah, I know," she said.

"But this just happened today," he said, confused. "How the hell would you know that already?"

"Oh shit, I thought it was over a long time ago."

"Well, you're right, I guess. It did end a long time ago... but it's officially over today."

The storm was picking up. Thunder and lightning boomed and flashed outside with increased frequency. Mitch noticed Gloria was in a really dark mood, so he squeezed her hand and reassured her.

"Well, at least we're not in one of those big metal buildings where the sheep and pigs are. The thunder would be unbearable—"

"It's not that Mitch," she cut in. "You're here, so I know I'm okay."

She paused and explained.

"I came to the fair today with Toby Schmedlap."

"Yeah, I saw. Where is old Toby?"

"Probably home by now," she grumbled.

Mitch sat in silence, waiting for her to continue.

"Mitch, I was hoping it would be different this time, but it's the same old thing with every guy I go out with. It always ends the same way. I don't know what's wrong with me."

Mitch nodded.

"I'm not going to see him anymore," Gloria stated. "Not Toby or any of his other snobby friends."

"Snobby friends?"

"Yeah, the friends he goes to school with. We met his buddies and their bitchy girlfriends today." She sighed. "Right from the beginning, I knew the girls hated me. There were three other couples, and within the first five minutes, one of the other guys started flirting with me. His girlfriend got mad, obviously, and ran off. He ran off after her, begged forgiveness, and brought her back."

"The snootiest bitch of them all was this girl from Durham Hall High School named Meredith. The other girls hung on every word she said, and early on, she started peppering me with little questions like I was five years old. Like, 'Have you decided on a trade school for after graduation? We're all attending Saint Cates' and 'The girls and I went Europe on spring break. Have you been?' She and the other girls were getting a big kick out of their little inside jokes at my expense."

"After a while, Toby started bragging to the others that I, his 'girlfriend Gloria,' was the 'Winter Carnival Queen of the Snow Flakes.' Meredith said she was really surprised, and I snapped. She said she was surprised that they would choose somebody from 'Uh, where are you from?' I told her Hayden Heights, up by Hillcrest on the East Side. Chuckling, she rolled her eyes and said, 'Well, wherever that is, they usually don't go for you East Side types,' meaning middle class neighborhoods aren't worthy, which is bullshit. East Side girls win all the time, but they didn't care. The other girls in this group, Bethany and Kara, thought she was hilarious."

"Mitch, I wanted to slap the piss out of those three girls, and it took everything I had to hold back. I was furious because I've been down this road so many times with other jealous girls. Then Meredith implied that the judges have some sort of quota and so have to choose someone from the East Side to prevent the appearances of favoritism. Old Bethany and Kara thought that this was hilarious too, but that was it for me. I said, 'Obviously, one of the things you must think about us "East Side types" is that we're too dumb to know when we're being insulted.' That stopped Meredith in her tracks and everybody else in the group, too. Apparently, queen bitchface Meredith doesn't get a lot of pushback in her little world. I stood right in front of that scrawny hag and dug in. 'You say they usually don't go for us East Side types? You mean the smart and pretty girls with big boobs? I'm sure you're right. They're always on the hunt for those plain, flat-chested homely girls with bad complexions like you and these other mutts from Summit Avenue.' That did it. The girls stormed off and their boyfriends went with them. This left me with that turd Toby, who is about as interesting as lint."

Mitch couldn't help but laugh at the way Gloria was telling the story. Despite the humor, though, it was in that moment that Mitch realized it was the first time he'd heard Gloria describe herself as how and what she really was: smart and pretty with big boobs. He'd never heard her refer to herself in any kind of flattering way, ever.

"This happens all the time, Mitch. Some girls hate me because of the way I look, and I'm so sick and tired of feeling bad about it. I know who and what I am, so from now on, if somebody doesn't like it, they can go to hell."

She hadn't flinched once during the raging thunderstorm outside.

To take Gloria's mind off her problems, Mitch told her about the bus ride over and his showdown with Ray the Rat, how he and the boys were going to handle business right there.

"Who else was with Ray, and please tell me that someone beat Ray's brains in?"

Mitch told her the rest of the story. She especially liked the part where the bullies rode the bus back down Snelling Avenue like pussies.

"You know, Mitch, you're the leader of all those guys," Gloria noted. "Everybody knows it at the golf course, and your buddies know it too, whether they admit it or not. Maybe that's why I'm always finding you. It all comes back to you, Mitchy-poo."

Gloria surprised Mitch with that last bit.

"So, what happened to Toby?" Mitch deflected.

"Oh yeah, that." She rolled her eyes. "After the rest of them disappeared, Toby and I walked around while I tried to pretend to have a good time. Toby suggested we take a ride on the Ye Old Mill ride, so I agreed. But, right after we got into the boat, and as soon as it got dark, he started grabbing at my bra. And other things. I almost threw him in the water. I was so pissed, Mitch. When we got out of Ye Old Mill, I told him I was done with him and walked away. He whimpered that he was sorry and apologized for about three blocks. In the end, when I didn't give in, he called me a bitch and a tease."

"I'm telling you, Mitch, it never fails. There are three types of guys in my world and that asshole Toby fits perfectly into one of them."

"What do you mean there are three types of guys?"

"Well, maybe there are more, but I've only encountered three. The first type are the guys who are usually my age or younger. They're scared to death of me and won't ask me out on dates, they always feel fidgety around me and can't bring themselves to even talk to me. The second type are the older guys who want to put me on a pedestal."

"How would they put you on a pedestal?"

"It's an expression, really. They hold me up like some delicate flower and treat me like I'm some untouchable princess. They never say what they really mean because they think if they say the wrong thing, I won't like them. They fawn all over me and say what they think are nice and complimentary things, but I can't ever really get to know these guys because they act so phony. The third group is like Toby. They're always older guys that want to take me around and show me off like a trophy. Like I'm some kind of prize, and because they're older, they think they can treat me like shit and get away with whatever they want."

I laughed, amused mostly because I'd had no idea.

"Gloria, I didn't know things were so complicated for you."

"But the girls make it even more complicated," she remarked.

"Ok, you've lost me again."

"Well, girls are funny," Gloria started. "I've got a lot of girlfriends, but there's always a lot of backbiting and jealousy. Then you become the Winter Carnival Queen of the Frickin' Snowflakes and some of them flat out turn on you. I lost some friends when that happened. They say really nice things to your face, then go and tear you to bits behind your back. Izzy is an example of the best kind of friend because she doesn't treat me any different compared to before."

Mitch could tell Gloria had more to get off her chest, so he just kept nodding her on.

"I actually did make a new friend after the Winter Carnival stuff last winter. Julia Glenstad was a senior last year and was crowned last year's homecoming queen at Johnson. She's just stunning, and every guy in school had a crush on her—and I think some of the girls did too. But becoming homecoming queen cost her friends. They hated the fact that she'd won."

"About a week after I won the Queen of Snow Flakes title at the Saint Paul auditorium, I was sitting by myself at lunch and Julia came and sat with me. She was so beautiful and so nice. She congratulated me on winning, and I could tell she was genuinely happy for me. Then she told me something that has stuck with me: People hate your success. She encouraged me not to be surprised when I lose friends as I go through life and become more successful."

"Damn, Gloria, I hope to hell that's not true."

"I said the same thing. But Julia insisted that not only is it true, but she also said people are their happiest when you fail."

"This Julia really knows how to build a person up, doesn't she?" Mitch joked.

Gloria punched his shoulder playfully and chuckled.

"Julia goes to college at Gustavus Adolphus and still calls me once in a while. She's my hero."

"Well, Gloria, it's a complicated world you live in."

"Tell me about it."

They sat in silence for a little while, both mulling over their experiences that day. Maybe confronting his arch nemesis, Ray the Rat, coupled with breaking up with Maggie gave Mitch a needed shot of confidence because he was about to say things to Gloria that he'd never dared say to anyone before.

"It's funny, but I can see myself in all three categories."

Gloria raised an eyebrow at him.

"Well, first of all, I get the scared to death part. I can understand why guys are scared of you. I've known you forever and you *still* scare me sometimes."

"Why?" It was a simple demand, but heavy.

"Don't make me say it," he begged. "Don't make this harder for me than it is."

"Mitch, c'mon, say it!"

He sighed and looked down at his feet.

"It's because you're so pretty, Gloria. In my eyes, you're the prettiest girl there is, and it's damn intimidating." He moved on quickly. "Secondly, I get the pedestal part. I get that a lot. I've felt that way about you my whole life."

"Well, you don't gush all over me and say sappy stuff."

"I know, but it's because I have nothing to lose. I don't have you, so I can't lose you." Mitch shrugged. "But I understand the worship."

"Okay, and what about category three?"

"Now, if you were my girl, the first thing I would do is show you off like some kind of trophy," he said, stretching his hands behind his head in a self-satisfied kind of way. "Then I'd pull at your bra and try to do... other stuff. And I'd treat you like shit." Mitch laughed at his own joke, and Gloria looked at him and shook her head in mock disgust.

"Mitch, you couldn't have flunked this test harder if you'd studied for a month." She folded her arms around herself. "I don't think you're giving me the truth, Mitch. I think you're full of shit."

"All right, smart ass, then tell me about me," he argued. "What do you think about me?"

"Mitchell, I've had a category for you as far back as I can remember, and you're the only one in it." After a long pause, she continued. "I want every guy to treat me the way you treat me, I want people to look at me the way you look at me, I want them to see me the way you see me. What does that tell you?"

"I haven't got a clue."

In his head, he'd always felt like a complete clown around girls, especially Gloria. She must see something in him that he couldn't.

"I told you before, Mitch, you're always the one in charge, and I love that. I love your take-charge confidence. I think all girls love that, actually. My brother and the rest of them wait for you to decide on everything, and I think you must realize it... somehow, the responsibility just comes to you, and you're not an asshole about it. You're a lot more mature than the rest of them. But, here's the part that kills me, Mitch." She took a deep breath. "I'm going to say this, and you can believe it or not, but you're exactly the kind of guy I want."

In his mind, all he heard was "the *kind* of guy I want." Oh my God, did that hurt. Yeah, Mitch believed it and he hated it.

She sat quietly, waiting for her words to sink in a bit, but Mitch got up and walked away.

"Where are you going, Mitch? It's still raining!"

"Talk about flunking a test, Gloria, you just bombed."

"Maggie broke up with me today and now I have to listen to this shit? If you see the rest of the guys, tell them I went home."

Mitch walked down and out of the grandstand, down the big ramp in the pouring rain. His hair was plastered to his head, water dripped from the edge of his nose, but he hardly noticed.

"Mitchell, you come back here right now!" Gloria yelled at him from the entrance of the grandstand. Then, of course, right on cue, a huge clap of thunder bowled across the sky. She yelled again.

"Mitchell!"

He stopped at the shrill note in her voice. Then, he turned, ran back up the ramp and back into the grandstand.

"I can't believe you'd leave me here," Gloria said.

"And I can't believe you'd put me through this shit," he retorted.

"What do you mean?"

"We should've never talked about any of this stuff. I could've gone the rest of my life being okay with you holding my hand once in a while, or you hugging me once in a while and being your thunderstorm security blanket. I could've been fine with all that, but the last thing I wanted to know is that I'm the *kind* of guy you want but not *the* guy you want. It sucks, you know, being the chump that holds a place while you wait for a better version of me."

"Oh my God, Mitch, I'm sorry," Gloria said. "I'm so sorry I said it like that! That's not what I meant *at all*. I was trying to say that you're the perfect guy for me, and I think about you a lot. Mitch, I'm an idiot, I did this all wrong." She rubbed her temples with the heels of her hands. "Listen to me carefully now—" she trailed off, but she was obviously searching for the right words.

"Mitchell, the only person I want to impress when I get dolled up is you. You. I find myself hanging on every word you say because you always seem to say the right thing. You're so damn cute I can't stand it." She sucked in a deep breath. "But here's the problem. You're a year younger than me."

"Seven months," he muttered back.

"Fine, seven months, yes. But you're still a grade younger, you're my brother's best friend, we live next door to each other, and we see each other almost every single day. Plus, this stuff never, ever works out. Even if we got together, this is high school, and I see it every day: people who are madly in love on Monday hate each other's guts by Friday. It doesn't work and it doesn't last except for maybe one couple out of a hundred. I can't risk that with you, Mitchell. You have to believe me; you mean too much to me. I couldn't bear to ever lose one of my best friends, and if we get together, it just about guarantees the loss."

It was the second time that day you could've knocked Mitch over with a feather.

"We'd get together, break up, and then guess what? We'd still have to live next door to each other and see each other every day."

After standing there for a few seconds, water puddling around his shoes, Mitch nodded.

"I know you're right, Gloria. It would ruin everything." He wiped some of the water from his face. "But it's just so hard to accept it because it's all in the future. We're here right now. And, let me tell you my problem." Mitch was about to say something out loud that he'd never admitted to anyone. "I measure every girl I meet against you, and none of them ever compare. I can't wait to see you every day. There's always been something about you, Gloria. I think about the night you were crowned Queen of the Snow Shoes or whatever—there were a thousand people in the auditorium that night, but the only one I saw was you. You were just head and shoulders above every girl in the place and everybody knew it. That's the way you are, and it crushes me still that I can never be in your league."

By this time, Gloria was fighting tears.

"Mitch, you feel that way because I'm all you've ever known. Pretty soon, you're going to feel completely different about all of this. In a little over a week, you're going to meet over a thousand new girls at Johnson and forget all about me. Just imagine that, Mitch, a thousand girls and you'll have your pick of any of them."

"Why do you say that?" he pressed, not sure what she meant.

"Because the word is out about you, Mitchy-poo. I get asked about you all the time because I live next door to you."

That sounded strange. People asked about *him?*

"Mitchell, you don't realize it yet, but the girls will line up for you because they'll see what I see: that you have it all."

I don't have it all, he thought to himself. *I don't have shit, Gloria's just being nice.* Nobody's going to be lined up for old Doc Dawson. But, if she cared enough about him to bullshit him like this, that's saying something.

"Now, before you go to school and meet a thousand new girls and completely forget about me, there's something I've been dying to do."

His breath caught in his throat. Did she—

"And Mitchell, this goes against everything we just talked about, but I don't care." Gloria leaned in right then and kissed him; kissed him on the mouth and kissed him deeper and longer than he'd ever been kissed before. He thought he was dreaming. They hurried back to their corner and kissed some more until the rain stopped. At that point, Mitch had no concept of time. He was completely under her spell.

The conversation and make-out sessions seemed to have helped get some stuff out of their systems; Mitch felt lighter than he had in a long time. But they weren't quite done yet.

"Mitchy-poo," she declared. "We've got to take a ride in Ye Old Mill before they close for the night.

"OK," he agreed. "If that's what you want. Or we could stay right here?"

"No, no, it's nice and dark in the Mill. Besides, the race cars sound a lot like thunder."

The races had commenced, and the atmosphere *had* become more chaotic. Mitch caved.

"Okay, let's go. But are you sure you want to go on a ride that reeks like my old basement?"

"Believe me, Mitchy-poo, you won't be sorry."

On the walk over, Gloria stopped in the bathroom and Mitch stopped for some mini donuts. Mitch bought their tickets for the ride and handed them to the ride guy once Gloria had rejoined him. Glo and Mitch climbed in the boat.

"Are you ready for your first lesson?" she asked in a low voice.

"Lesson?" Mitch gulped.

She laughed.

"Yeah, lesson number one on 'What to do with a girl.' I can see it in your eyes you're not ready for this, so hold on."

And by God, Gloria was right. Mitch was not ready for that, and he was not sorry they took a ride in Ye Old Mill. The moment it got dark in there, the lesson began. Gloria kissed Mitch again and insisted that he slide straight into second base. To his great surprise and delight, the confusing armor that usually guards second base was gone. She must've put it in her purse.

Mitch never could have imagined in his whole life how wonderful and very big second base could be. Lesson learned.

They talked about it all later on the bus ride home, and they both understood that that evening's entanglements didn't mean they were getting together. It was clear neither of them were ready for that level of commitment. Maybe someday.

Gloria grinned at Mitch, the background moving behind her through the bus window.

"Mitchell, you've been my best guy friend, and today, you got better."

Something changed that day. Mitch no longer needed to elevate Gloria on a pedestal; her position after that evening was better than a pedestal, actually, because she was down on Earth with Mitch. Of course, he'd always be terrified and madly in love with her; there was no getting past that. But Mitch was pretty sure he could live with that.

CHAPTER 37

BAD PLAN, WORSE TIMING

The following week, the double practices became single practices each day. Two-a-day practices are done for the year. The football season would start next week and so did school. The good news for Mitch was that he was voted JV team captain, along with Mario. When he got home from practice on Thursday, Ike was just coming up the street toward the Dawson house on his way to the course to get paid, and Mitch figured he'd go with them.

"What'd you think of your very first Minnesota State Fair?"

"Mitch, it was awesome," he exclaimed. "I can't believe how big it is and how much cool stuff there is to do. I'm thinking about going back this weekend, maybe Sunday again."

"Nice! I want to go back and see more bands, and you can see your brother Aaron again."

Ike agreed.

"By the way, where did you disappear during the thunderstorm?" Ike asked.

"I hung out with Gloria. We caught the last bus home."

Ike nodded.

"Yeah, we all split off eventually. I ended up with Manny, Mario, and Izzy. What a blast."

They walked on for a few minutes, enjoying the slightly cooling weather.

"Things are about to explode at my house," Ike lamented. "My mom told Leon this week that she wants a divorce. Leon laughed in her face and called her a whore. He said she was a weak sinner and that she doesn't have any guts. Then he started spewing all of his psycho Bible bullshit at her. He's been terrifying. They've been fighting all week about Sarah going down to the special school in Faribault, too, but Mom is not backing down. Sarah is packed and ready to go. She can't wait."

"How are your other siblings doing?"

"Jacob and Ruthy are okay. They had a lot of fun at the beach with your family last weekend, I can tell you that."

"I heard they're all going to the zoo this weekend."

Ike nodded.

"My mom went up to Shoppers' City the other day and met Aaron to figure out a plan to deal with Leon and this divorce. It turns out that Leon can't be removed from the house, and he doesn't have to leave if he doesn't want to."

"I don't understand any of this, Ike," Mitch shook his head. "What's going to happen?"

"It's going to be bad, whatever happens. Leon will get served papers for the divorce this Saturday afternoon after my mom gets back from dropping off Sarah in Faribault."

"What do you mean 'served'?" Mitch asked.

"My mom said she can't give Leon the papers herself, and he can't get them in the mail. Someone else has to physically hand him the papers. I guess Mom will be home between 2:00 and 2:30, and the guy is coming at 3:00 with the papers. Mom will call Aaron when she gets home. He'll come to the house to support her. My mom said I shouldn't be there, but I know I need to be. I'll work at the course that day, but I'll head home after. The timing is good for Jacob and Ruthy's sake, since they'll be with your family at the zoo."

Saturday morning, as Mary Tiller was getting Sarah, Ruthy, and Jacob in the car, Ike made sure that Buster had food and water for the day. He chained up old Buster by his dog house and went off to work at the course. Mitch was already there to do a couple loops for more fair money. The plan was for Mary to drop the two young ones at the Dawson's house for the zoo adventure, after which Mary would go down to Sarah's new school in Faribault. Meanwhile, Leon paced the backyard, stewing over the fact that Sarah was being shipped off to school and the other two were going to the zoo.

Leon once terrorized the lives of everyone around him because he was overbearing and cruel. As he paced, the reality began to settle on him: he'd lost everything since he got out of the hospital, including his job. He'd lost battles he never used to lose—like Ike working at the golf course for the Getz brothers and hanging out with the rest of the neighborhood kids. He'd lost the battle, with Sarah being shipped off to a school out of town. Even something as innocent as his children going to the zoo without his go-ahead was a loss in Leon's eyes. But his greatest loss was Mary. He'd lost the wife he used to be able to control in every respect—from who she could talk to, to where she could go. He could not control Mary anymore. Leon had lost everything he thought made him a man, and what made it worse was that he had nothing more to lose.

It was with this sense of deep, crippling loss and utter failure that Leon opened the divorce papers, three hours ahead of schedule and just about the time Mary was saying her tearful goodbyes to Sarah at her new school in Faribault. The papers that were supposed to be delivered at 3 p.m. were instead delivered at noon, throwing a wrench in the carefully timed plan. This gave Leon plenty of time to think—to think about what he was going to do to Mary for her betrayal. Never once did the thought cross his mind that he was at fault for the failure of his own life.

When Mary got home just before 2 p.m., Leon was sitting calmly in his chair. Mary got out of her car and knew she was in for a battle, but she had no idea that Leon already knew everything until it was too late.

When Leon saw Mary, his rage was immeasurable. Holding the divorce papers in front of her face, Leon was nearly foaming at the mouth.

"You miserable whore!" he screamed.

Mary was scared to death. She ran to the backyard, Leon followed. He kept coming toward her, and she kept backing away, and backing away. She tried to go back in the house, but Leon blocked her path.

Leon was yelling at Mary, and Mary was screaming back at Leon.

"I can't take this shit anymore," she screamed. "I can't take you anymore. This has to end."

"And end it shall," he professed. "I told you; I'd never divorce you."

"I hate your fucking guts," Mary screamed. "You're a sick bastard, and you have to move out, you have to go."

Leon laughed at this.

"You whore, you think I'm leaving my own house so that some Payne Avenue trash like you can live here? You're pathetic."

"I'm going to call the sheriff, and if the sheriff comes, they're going to lock you back up again, Leon," Mary warned. "The cops, the sheriff, everybody knows about you, Leon. If you lay one finger on me, they're going to lock you up again down at that mental hospital. They should have never let you out in the first place."

Ike could hear the yelling before he got to the house. He quickened his step, and once he was at the front door of the house, he could hear Buster barking like crazy and other commotion in the backyard. Has something gone wrong? This was all supposed to happen according to a plan, which included Aaron being there for support.

Ike's heart was racing as he moved through the house into the kitchen. Where was Aaron? Every second felt like a million minutes, and the pressure began to build. Ike didn't know what else to do, so he picked up the phone and called his brother at the number he'd given him.

An unfamiliar woman's voice picked up.

"Hello?"

"Is Aaron there?"

"Hold on, please."

Mary threatening the mental hospital was the tipping point for Leon. He wasn't going back to that mental hospital in Saint Peter, and he knew his life here with his family was over. Leon had nothing left to lose, which made him the most dangerous he'd ever been because he simply didn't care anymore. Leon caught Mary over by the garage and punched her repeatedly until her body went limp.

"This is Aaron."

When Ike told Aaron what was going on, Aaron asked where the other kids were.

"Not here."

Ike looked out the back door and saw his mom, unconscious and bleeding on the ground in front of the garage. "Oh, God, Aaron, Mom's not moving. Leon's picking her up."

"Ike, hang up the phone and call the cops now, hear me? Hang up the phone and call the cops. I'll be right there."

There wasn't enough time to call the cops. As Ike hung up the phone, Leon came into the house, dragging Mary. Ike ran out the front door and went down the street a few houses down, waiting for Aaron. About a minute later, Aaron came roaring up Wyoming Avenue on his Harley. When he pulled up in front of the house, Ike was waiting for him.

"Did you call the cops?" Aaron asked him as he jumped off his bike.

"I couldn't. Leon came inside too fast. And he was dragging Mom." Ike could feel his resolve beginning to break.

"Does Leon have a gun? Did you see any guns?"

"No, I didn't see any guns. I think the cops got them all out of the house when they arrested him last winter."

"Let's hope so," Aaron said with some trepidation. "Okay, you stay out here, Ike, I'm going in. I've got to see Mom."

When Aaron went through the front door, he could see his mom laying across the kitchen floor. When he approached her, he saw Leon about to go down the basement steps. Leon turned toward Aaron, the two facing each other for the first time in years. Leon was startled, but not badly enough to say nothing.

"It's Aaron, the Demon himself." Leon shook his head. "This is all your doing, isn't it? You came to infect this family again with your evil." With that glazed-over look on his face, Leon tried to sort out all the pieces to this puzzle. "It's all starting to make sense now, I can see it. Of course. I can see what you've done. You came back here with your evil to set your mother against me and destroy this family once and for all. The only good thing I had left in this whole world was your sister Sarah, and now your mother has sent her away from me. The betrayal is complete."

"There's no betrayal here, Leon, you're sick," Aaron contested. "It's all in your head. You are a sick man and you need to get help."

Leon raised his clenched fists and lifted his face to the kitchen ceiling, his eyes rolling back in his head.

"Behold the Antichrist," Leon shouted. "He brings with him the smell of sulfur and burning flesh."

Now kneeling over the beaten and bloodied Mary Tiller, Aaron's body shook with rage.

"Oh my God. Mom is really hurt bad. Leon, you sick fuck. She needs a hospital."

"The suffering of this whore and adulteress will be over soon, as it will for you and the other unholy bastard," Leon declared, pointing at Ike who was now standing outside the back door. "Your foul brother, the one who consorts with those Jew bastards up the street. Today, you all perish, for I am the Deliverer, and you, Aaron; you are the Antichrist."

"And you're insane," Aaron snapped back.

"I am the Deliverer by God's hand. I am the rock and fortress and the horn of salvation and I will dispatch you all to the eternal damnation and darkness of hell you deserve. The world must be cleansed of you and your kind. It is God's will—"

"Leon, you twisted fucking maniac!" Aaron yelled. "You are Satan himself!"

Aaron readied himself for Leon's all too familiar attack, knowing things would be different this time. Aaron wasn't the skinny kid who left home years ago; he was a full-grown, battle-hardened Navy veteran. But Leon ran down the basement steps instead of attacking, which meant only one thing: He must have a gun stashed.

Ike rushed into the kitchen and knelt next to his mom, and Aaron slammed the basement door shut.

"You know that door doesn't have a lock, right?" Ike said, frantically. They could hear Leon screaming more biblical shit from the basement.

"Come here, grab the table with me. Hurry up, grab the table," Aaron said. "We'll shove the table in front of the door." The two of them pushed the heavy oak table in front of the basement door, hoping that it might hold long enough to buy them some time.

Aaron called the police while bracing himself against the table and the basement door. He told them about Leon's attack on their mother and requested an ambulance. He said that their mom was unconscious and bleeding, and he said Leon was in the basement and threatening to kill them all. The police told Aaron to get everybody out of the house.

"My mom's unconscious," he implored.

"Okay, get everybody else out of the house, and whatever you do, do not try to move your mother, no matter what. We're going to get there as quickly as we can, but you all need to get out of the house now!"

"I'm going to take Ike someplace safe," Aaron said as he hung up the phone.

Leon started hitting the basement door—hard. Was he using a shovel or a club? It sounded like Leon might come through that door any second. After a few seconds of silence, Aaron and Ike looked at each other, then a deafening BANG, BANG. Two gunshots came through the basement door. They ducked and crawled away from the table.

"Come on, let's go, we gotta get out of here," Aaron commanded.

Ike was frozen in his tracks.

"Ike, we have to go now before he gets out of the basement," Aaron screamed.

"We can't leave Mom!" Ike wailed.

"Ike, listen to me! We have to go and we have to go now. I don't want to leave Mom, but we can't move her either," Aaron pleaded with his shocked brother. "If Leon gets out of the basement, he's going to kill all of us. The cops and ambulance are on their way. We have to hope that they get here before he gets out of that basement. Either way, we've got to go now."

Ike had barely relented when Aaron grabbed his arm and half-dragged him out of the house. Aaron kickstarted his Harley and yelled to Ike.

"Come on, brother, let's ride."

Ike jumped on the back of the motorcycle, clinging to his brother, and the two of them tore down Wyoming Avenue away from their house, their mother, and the psychotic Leon Tiller.

As they crossed Curve Street, they could hear sirens approaching the old house. They knew the cops were on their way.

CHAPTER 38

THE BRIDGE TROLLS

Within minutes, Ike and Aaron were riding around Lake Phalen. Aaron pulled into the parking lot by the pavilion and switched off the Harley. Ike climbed off and went to sit in the grass

"What do we do now?" Ike asked.

"Hopefully by now the cops are there with an ambulance for mom," Aaron replied. "But if Leon gets out of that basement before the cops get there, he'll come looking for us, so I think we should split up."

"Where were you when I called you?" Ike asked.

"I've been staying at the house of a Navy buddy. He's a guy I went to school with. He's overseas right now, and I'm staying with his mom and dad, right behind the 88 Cent store."

"I swear you got up to the house in a minute," Ike observed.

Aaron nodded.

"Now, let's figure out where you should go," Aaron pressed. "It can't be your friends' houses or anywhere obvious. You don't want to get your friends mixed up in this stuff. The man's insane and he meant what he said. He wants us all dead."

"Let's just go to the police," Ike suggested.

Aaron hesitated.

"We can't go to the police—or, at least, I can't go to the police."

"Why not?"

"Because I'm wanted by the police," Aaron admitted.

"Ah, for fuck's sake, what did you do?"

"Shush, there's no time to explain right now. Where's a good place for you to go?"

"Take me over to Blessed Sacrament Catholic Church on White Bear Avenue."

Aaron looked puzzled.

"Why BS?" Aaron asked.

"Because I know the priest from last Christmas when Leon kicked me out. He helped me."

"Okay, if you're sure, then Blessed Sacrament it is," Aaron agreed. "When was the last time you ate?" Ike looked at him blankly.

"I can't even remember."

"OK, we're going to roll into McDonald's by the Phalen Shopping Center first and get you something to eat."

After stopping for hamburgers, the two rode up Maryland Avenue on their way to Blessed Sacrament. Just as they turned south on White Bear Avenue, more Saint Paul police cars went screaming past them, heading north, leaving little doubt that this was about Leon Tiller. When they arrived at Blessed Sacrament Church, Aaron pulled around to the back door, closest to the office of Father O'Dea, as Ike directed.

The pair climbed off the Harley and went to seek out the good father. It didn't take long; they found the priest sitting at his desk. Father O'Dea looked up at them and seemed puzzled at the sight of them for a moment.

"Isaac Tiller, what brings you here, son, and who might this be?" Father O'Dea asked, standing up to greet them. The looks of desperation on Ike's and Aaron's faces told the priest everything he needed to know.

"Father, my name is Aaron Tiller. I'm Ike's brother. May we come in?"

"By all means," agreed the priest. "What's going on?"

"A whole pile of trouble, Father," Aaron admitted. "I'm afraid some really bad things happened and we need Ike to stay here for a while."

"Trouble, is it?" asked the priest. "Is it your father?"

"Yes, in a manner of speaking. He's the man we grew up thinking was our father, but he is not our real father."

After a pause, Father O'Dea nodded.

"I think I understand."

"Now, here we are again for the same reason, but this time, Leon said he was going to kill us. He even shot a gun at us through the basement door."

"Oh, my heavens," said the good father.

"What's important now is that Ike is safe and... I think you should call the police to let them know that Ike is here with you."

Aaron then described to the priest all the events of the last few hours at their house, and the priest promised them that they would be safe there.

Father O'Dea began dialing the police.

"Father, I have to go," Aaron waved.

"Go? Wait a minute young man, where do you think you're going?"

"Father, please believe me, I have to leave. I got Ike here, that was the goal."

"Hold on now, just a second."

The police picked up and Father O'Dea directed his attention to the call. "Lieutenant Hallinan, please."

Aaron turned to Ike and looked at him with eyes of reassurance.

"Listen, pal. You're fed, you're safe, you're in a Catholic church, for Christ's sake. You're going to be fine. Hopefully Mom will be fine too, and let's hope the police got to Leon before he did any more harm."

Ike started to unravel. The sum total of the reality of this crisis began to show on Ike's face. It was amazing he held up this well for this long.

"This is a lot for a kid to deal with," Aaron acknowledged. "And pal, you're doing great. Once this all blows over, we're going to have to figure out what to do about you, Mom, and the rest of the kids because life with Leon Tiller is over. For good."

A few minutes later, Father O'Dea hung up the phone.

"I spoke to a lieutenant friend of mine and he said that Ike should stay here for now, until they get this all figured out. They'll come by later and get him when it's clear. He also said your mother is on her way to Saint John's Hospital, and that they don't know the whereabouts of Leon Tiller, but they're looking for him right now."

"Thank you, Father." You could tell Aaron was relieved.

"Aaron, my son, I offer you the same protection as Isaac. The Church of the Blessed Sacrament can be your sanctuary too."

"Believe me, Father, I appreciate the offer, but I happen to have a little bit of trouble with the police regarding some anti-war protests I've been involved in. Please, it's better this way. Until I can get some things sorted out, I have to go."

At that, Aaron turned around and left.

Now that Ike was safe, Aaron had to figure out what to do with himself. He knew that if Leon found him, he'd kill him straight out. There would be no talk, no reasoning, nothing. Ike might be spared, but Aaron was definitely going to die at the hands of Leon Tiller. Aaron checked his gas tank; it was near empty. Thankfully, Aaron's own personal sanctuary was just a few blocks away from Blessed Sacrament. He thought that what once offered him solace would also offer safety and friendship until the cops caught up with Leon. So, Aaron went to the Trestle.

The Trestle truly was a simple bridge, a relic on the far end of the East Side of Saint Paul. It was a pivotal piece of the fabric of the lives of the kids in the neighborhood. There was good, there was bad, there was fun, and sometimes desperation at the Trestle—it was just a matter of what you were looking for.

Every neighborhood has a place where kids gather. Sometimes it's an empty lot, dead end street, down by a lake, or a place called Witches' Woods. There were spots like this all over Saint Paul, and probably in every neighborhood of every city. But the Trestle was theirs. There was nothing more iconic than the Trestle.

There were at least twenty people hanging out at the Trestle when he arrived. Those who came to the Trestle that evening had come for the usual: hanging out, having a good time with a few beers, smoking a couple of joints—the perfect recipe for a post–Labor Day party. The people who had gathered at the Trestle had no idea that they would witness something that evening that would change their lives forever.

And there was Leon Tiller, stopped at the bottom of the path that leads up to the Trestle from the north, two hundred yards away from the span. Leon Tiller had begun a personal, sick, demented, religious revenge crusade—he must rid the world of Satan's Spawn. Somehow, even in the thick veil of his manic rantings, he knew where Aaron would go.

Aaron thought he'd have had more time, but the final confrontation wouldn't wait. Aaron didn't have the time to try to figure out how Leon found him so fast. The time was now. The cops must've figured it out too because you could hear sirens and see red flashing lights coming from both directions. There on the Trestle, Aaron would make his stand.

Just fifteen years ago, streetcar tracks were still planted on the very path Leon was creeping up. Those streetcars carried people over the Trestle to and from work every day or maybe downtown Saint Paul to go shopping. That day, a very different story was being told.

Aaron had been shot before and had survived Vietnam. He'd survived the horrors of war and now lives with the degradation and stigma of being a veteran of the most unpopular war in this country's history. While the veterans of other wars were heralded as heroes, the guys who came home from Vietnam were considered villains. These young men came back from Vietnam only to face a lifetime of emotional and mental anguish. Aaron was certainly among that number.

The people on the Trestle panicked as the cops approached. They didn't understand that the cops were coming for Leon.

When the madman approached, Aaron yelled at everybody to get off the bridge to the other side. Everyone complied, leaving Aaron alone in the middle of the bridge span, sitting on his Harley defiantly.

The enraged Leon Tiller slowly crept up that dirt path from Maryland Avenue to the south, stalking Aaron in his old Dodge station wagon. Steering wheel in one hand, a loaded pistol in the other—both covered in Mary Tiller's blood. There was no doubt, Leon Tiller was coming to kill Aaron.

A fast freight came rumbling through on the tracks below as Leon crept toward the bridge. With about one hundred and fifty feet to go, he couldn't believe what he saw. There was Aaron in the middle of the Trestle, sitting on his Harley, chugging a beer, and smoking a joint as plain as day, as if to bait Leon. Aaron dropped the beer can and reached into his saddlebag, but not for another beer. He pulled out a 9 mm pistol of his own. But this wasn't going to be a gun battle, as Aaron soon found out.

Leon dropped the pistol and grabbed the steering wheel of that old Dodge wagon, tightening his bloodied grip. The madman didn't know anything about the Trestle or its history. To Leon Tiller, it was just an evil place where Aaron and the other sinners gathered to do the Devil's bidding.

Aaron could see Leon peering over the steering wheel on his slow approach. What Leon Tiller saw was Aaron defiantly sitting in the middle of the Trestle, drawing down on him with his pistol. He saw Aaron, the soon-to-be-dead "Unholy Bastard," the blood of another man. Leon saw Aaron as the principal actor in the failure of his own life.

Leon Tiller also saw a half-dozen cops coming up behind him, the lights flashing as some navigated the path.

Leon Tiller floored it with murderous intent, blind rage in charge now. He was going to run down Aaron and not waste a bullet. Leon saw Aaron, Leon saw the cops. What Leon didn't see were the two four-foot-tall rusty steel I-beams set four feet apart that guard the Trestle. Kicking up a big dust cloud on that dirt path, Leon sped toward Aaron and hit the pair of rusty old beams at full speed. Everyone present watched the crash unfold in slow-motion horror.

Leon Tiller rammed those beams so hard that his old Dodge got wedged between them and nearly flipped over, never reaching Aaron. The rear end stuck nearly straight up in the air before it came crashing down, and the car's engine burst through those beams while the rest of the car landed in a twisted, mangled mess jammed in between them.

Aaron and the others stood for a moment in utter shock, then he and some of the guys ran across the bridge to try to get Leon out of the car. These were all the same people Leon Tiller despised and thought were in league with the devil, but at the end of the day, they were just simple kids, drinking beer and looking for a good time.

After professional and wayside help arrived, the rescue crew realized there was no way to get him out. The screams of the onlookers were deafening. Some people were hysterical; they didn't know what to do, even though they felt driven to do something. The sound of Leon hitting those steel beams could be heard for a mile. The cops rushed up the path and yelled for everybody to stay back, the car might explode.

It didn't matter; Leon Tiller was dead on impact.

His head got smashed coming through the windshield of that old Dodge station wagon. He never had a chance against those steel beams. Aaron Tiller and the Trestle both came out unscathed. The steel beams saw to that.

Firetrucks and ambulances made their way up to the bridge from both directions. The fire department had to cut the car up in pieces to free Leon's body. Somehow, the car didn't explode.

Leon Tiller joined Hack Helvik and Dennis Pinder in the Trestle's hall of infamy.

CHAPTER 39

GROUP PHOTO

Leon Tiller's funeral was set to take place Tuesday at Blessed Sacrament Catholic Church. Father O'Dea agreed to perform the Mass of Christian Burial, and at the request of Mary Tiller, an ordained minister from the Jehovah's Witness temple would deliver a brief sermon on the resurrection. The wake would be held at the funeral home on White Bear Avenue on Monday. Because of his Army service, he would be buried in peace at Fort Snelling National Cemetery. Finally, gone were his torments and demons.

It should come as no surprise that nobody was too broken up about the demise of Leon Tiller, but that didn't stop the steady stream of neighborhood moms and other sympathizers from visiting the Tiller house with all kinds of hotdish and other food in support of the family. Mrs. Dawson and Mrs. Finch had been at the Tiller house almost every day since Leon died. According to Mrs. Dawson, the one person taking his death hard was Ike's sister, Sarah; she was inconsolable.

Aaron Tiller had been at their house all week, too, and Ike said that they were trying to get Aaron's legal issues straightened out and that the plan was for Aaron to move back in for a while to help out.

Mitch tried on his suit for the funeral, but it was so small it was almost comical. He traipsed into the kitchen to tell his mom that they'd have to figure something else out for the funeral because there was no way he was going to wear such an ill-fitting suit out in public.

"Look at you, Mitch," she said. "You must have grown a foot in the last year! Let me see what I can do."

He wiggled out of his suit and jumped in the shower to get ready for work.

The first week at Johnson High School was a blur. The place was enormous compared with Hazel Park—there were well over two thousand students in three grades. Gloria was right; there were a thousand new girls to meet. Things were different this year for Mitch and his best pals. He only got to see them at lunch because they all had different class schedules. Mitch's favorite class was A-choir; he was one of only a few sophomore guys in the class. All the girls in the class are juniors and seniors because the sophomore girls had their own glee club class. There were some major babes in A-choir, topmost among them being Gloria and Isabelle.

Thanks to someone getting their hand inside Mitch's face mask during a fumble scrum at last night's football game, the bridge of his nose got split—not enough for stitches but enough to make both of his eyes turn a little black and blue. His team dominated Monroe, 28-0; the defense scored, Mitch caught a touchdown pass, Zitz ran one in, and Mario ran a punt back for a touchdown. Mitch put a butterfly bandage on the bridge of his nose and headed to the golf course to get a few hours of work in. As he got to the screen door, he saw Ike standing there, ready to go to work with Mitch. It would be Ike's first time back to the course since Leon Tiller died.

Mitch and Ike had pool detail that day. They hadn't been at the golf course to work for more than half an hour when Mr. Dawson walked up to the clubhouse. He went inside, presumably to talk to John and Sid, and not five minutes later, he came out by the pool and waved and shouted at Ike and Mitch.

"Come on, let's go."

Mitch had no clue what he wanted, but he started walking toward his dad, who shouted again.

"Both of you! Let's go."

Ike and Mitch caught up to Mr. Dawson and followed him to the parking lot.

"It sounds like somebody outgrew his good suit," he teased.

Mitch laughed.

"Yeah, that's now Casey's good suit."

"It's about time you got some new duds, anyway. Ike, you're getting a new suit today too."

Ike stared blankly at Mr. Dawson.

"I don't understand."

"Mitch's mom talked to your mom this morning, and she conveyed that you don't have a suit to wear for the funeral. I just spoke with John Getz, and he declared that he'd buy you a new suit for your dad's funeral. You gotta look sharp, boy."

Mitch looked around the parking lot.

"Where's the car, Dad?"

Mr. Dawson lit up like a tree at Christmas.

"We're going in that," he said, pointing to the red Cutlass convertible from the tournament. No one had won it, and it hadn't been returned to the Olds dealer yet. "I told Sid I'd drive it back to the dealer. Luckily, the place where we're going for your new suits is right across the street on University Avenue." Mitch knew the place he had in mind; it was a men's clothing store that also sold uniforms to local cops.

"Now, boys, I have an appointment set up at this place with my old pal Seymour just for you both. He's going to measure you guys up and get your suits put together. And here's the deal. We can't be at this all day. I have to make a run down to

Rochester later this afternoon, so you guys just do what he says and we will get it all put together and be on our way."

"Do you have to go down there for work?" Mitch asked.

"Not exactly, but it is important." Mr. Dawson dropped the top on that convertible beauty and they climbed in.

My God, what a machine, Mitch thought.

Mr. Dawson stepped on it a couple of times and Mitch could've sworn the front wheels were about ready to lift off the ground. His dad was wearing his sunglasses and a grin from ear to ear.

Once they pulled into the Olds dealership and parked, Mr. Dawson was in no hurry to get out of his seat.

"There's something else we ought to discuss, Ike," he said. "The day of the funeral for your dad is going to be a long one. Traditionally, Catholic funerals are extra long, but if you ask me why I wouldn't be able to tell you. It's been decided that there is going to be a luncheon after the burial at Fort Snelling, and the luncheon is going to be held right there at Hillcrest Country Club. A Sid Getz idea!"

Sitting in the backseat of the Cutlass, Ike looked really confused.

"Mr. Dawson, why are they doing all this? First the suit and now this deal at the club? I know for a fact that Leon hated those guys, and I'm sure they weren't big fans of his either."

"All I can tell you Ike—and Mitchell, you listen to this too—is that life is for the living. This part isn't about your dad; may he rest in peace. It's about your family now. You, your mom, your brothers and sisters. The brothers understand what your family has been going through, and they want to help out. They're going to take care of everything. Sid called your mom from the clubhouse to ask her if that was OK, and she said that it would be great. Now, I'm releasing you two to pick out new suits. The suit store is across the street. Go ahead and walk over there and ask for Seymour, he's expecting you. I have to go into the dealership, so I'll be over in a few minutes."

Considering he was about to drop off their transportation, Mitch thought it imperative to figure out how they were going to get home.

Mr. Dawson smirked.

"Don't worry, I've got it covered."

The boys got out of the car, walked across the street, and wandered into the shop to look at suits with Seymour. Mitch picked out a blue one and so did Ike, but they weren't good enough, so they had to choose differently. In the end, Mitch picked out a gray one. After about half an hour, Mr. Dawson came into the store. Mitch showed him his suit, and he was really happy with the choice. Mitch tried it on and it fit perfectly.

When Ike went into the dressing room to try his suit on, Mitch poked at his dad.

"So, are you going to be late for a plate of spaghetti at Pasquale's?" Mitch asked, fully aware of how much of a smart ass he was acting with such a comment.

Mr. Dawson smiled.

"I was going to tell you about this one of these days, but you look so grown up in that suit that I'll tell you now."

Mitch felt a little flutter of nervousness.

"You know that shopping center where Pasquale's is?"

Mitch nodded.

"Well, believe it or not, I own it," he said.

Mitch was stunned.

"What?"

"It's true! The Getz brothers and I own that shopping center where Pasquale's is. They took me on as a partner in that shopping center about ten years ago, and now we have a chance to expand and buy some other properties around it," he explained.

Mitch didn't know what to say; all he knew was that his dad had some duplex deals with the Getz brothers—but nothing like a whole shopping center.

"This is important stuff, Mitch," Mr. Dawson went on. "You know these guys are big-time operators. I'm lucky they gave me the opportunity to be in business with them in the first place. I do this for our family, Mitch—for our future and your future because you're going to go to college someday and the world is an expensive place."

"Is that why we always go down there once a year to have spaghetti?"

"Yup," he confessed. "And believe me, Pasquale's is good, but that's not why we go. I go down there because I like to check on the shopping center from time to time, and spaghetti is just a good excuse. I have other investments with the brothers, and in the near future, we're looking at lakefront property up near Webster, Wisconsin, around Devil's Lake and Yellow Lake. This could be big Mitch, maybe as big as a resort."

Mitch had always had great respect for his dad: he was a hard worker and he deserved it. You could count on his no-bull-shit attitude, but somehow, that day Mitch's respect grew. With the exception of Ike, Mitch was sure most of his friends felt the same way about their dads. Knowing how incredibly successful the Getz brothers were, Mitch wasn't surprised he felt the way he felt, knowing that the brothers trust his dad enough to do business with him. That's saying something.

Ike and Mitch got fully outfitted. Not only did they get suits but they also got a new shirt and tie each. Next stop was Thom McAn up by Shoppers' City on the way home for new shoes. Like his old man had said: "You gotta look sharp."

After Mr. Dawson settled up with Seymour for the new clothes, they all walked outside.

"Now, how are we getting to McAn's?" Mitch asked. "Last I checked, you dropped our ride off at the dealership."

Mr. Dawson laughed.

"What's so funny?"

"We're going home the same way we got here, Mitch; I just bought the red Cutlass convertible."

"WHAT?!!" Mitch yelled, shocked.

"No shit, that's awesome," Ike said.

"Mitchell, as soon as you told me about that car, I took Casey and we went to see it at the golf course. I decided right then to buy it. Of course, I didn't tell that to your brother. We kept it at the golf course so it didn't get bought out from under me. Mitchell, this is one of the cars they produced as the Indianapolis 500 Pace Car for next year. It has every possible option and a special design package. There's not another red Cutlass like it in the country. I didn't buy it to drive it every day, either. This is an investment-grade automobile, which is why I'm building the new garage, which, by the way, will be heated and two stalls wide and two stalls deep."

"Does Mom know?" Mitch asked. "I can remember what she'd said about the last Cutlass you bought."

"Of course she knows; your mom's getting a new Olds Delta 88 later this week."

Mitch couldn't think of anyone who deserved a new car more than his dad and mom. It sounded like his dad's investments were already paying off.

When the Dawsons got to the funeral home, they had a hard time finding a place to park. Mitch was surprised to see so many people there—there were way more than he thought would show up. Once inside, the first thing Mitch did was look around for Ike. He wanted to see him and his new suit, but Ike was nowhere to be found. In fact, after further investigation, Mitch didn't see anybody from Ike's family at all. Confused, he asked his dad about it.

"Where the heck do you think Ike and his family are?"

His dad took a second and looked around the room.

"They're probably all together in another room," he said. "They should be out pretty soon, and I'd guess that they will all approach the casket together as a family before the service. I'll bet a lot of these folks are from the Jehovah's Witness temple, here to pay their respects to Mr. Tiller."

Right behind the Dawsons was the Klaus family. EZ, Gloria, Joy, and their parents were already there, and so was Izzy, Reno, and Mr. and Mrs. Petri. They were all sitting near the front of the room, but it was so packed that the Dawsons had to resort to seats in the back.

Just like his dad said, after a few minutes, Ike and his whole family, accompanied by Father O'Dea, came into the big room and together they walked over to the casket—all except Ike's sister Sarah. She took a few steps toward the casket but then would not budge. She broke down, wailing and shedding giant tears. Her mother and Father O'Dea tried to console her and urge her to come up to the casket, but the more they tried, the worse it got. She was about to collapse when a tall woman in a blue dress walked up to Sarah and grabbed her, hugged her, and just held her there to comfort her.

They held each other, rocked back and forth, and cried like no one else was in the room. That's when Mitch got a closer look—and he couldn't believe his eyes. He'd barely recognized her, but that tall woman in a blue dress was Charlotte Finch herself. Charlotte had been the one to run up and pull poor Sarah into a hug and wouldn't let her go. Then Beverly Finch walked over to the two of them, also nearly unrecognizable. Somehow over the summer, the two girls really cleaned up well. Bev gave Sarah some tissues, and Sarah hugged her too.

Beverly put her arm around Sarah's shoulder and Charlotte put her arm around Sarah's waist, and they walked that way up to Leon's casket.

They did a good job on old Leon considering how banged up he got after hitting those steel beams at the Trestle. Sarah broke down again once she looked inside the casket at her father, but Bev and Char were there for her, like pillars. Everybody in the whole funeral home was a bit misty eyed.

After the service was over, Mitch walked out of the main room into the big lobby area. People were still coming in for the visitation, and even more people were milling around and visiting. It didn't seem like a wake; it felt more like a social event. Mitch eventually caught up with Manny, EZ, and Zitz, and still more came through the door. They found Ike over in the lounge area where they had some sofas and chairs. He was holding up just fine.

Within a couple of minutes, Gloria, Izzy, and Reno came over to join them. The girls delivered their hugs to Ike and then he thanked everyone for coming. Mitch stood up to give his chair to Gloria.

"Go ahead, sit down," he told her, motioning toward the seat. Instead of sitting, she took a step back and looked at Mitch up and down. She smiled and leaned over to straighten his tie.

"You know something, Mitchell? You could cut glass in that suit," she informed him. "I mean, my God, and with that bandage across your nose and half of a black eye, you're just taking my breath away." Mitch could feel himself turning beat red.

But then Gloria chose to stand next to him instead of sitting. She took his arm and they calmly stood there just like that. No one seemed to notice or care that they were standing arm in arm. Gloria was not Mitch's girlfriend, but she was more than just a friend. While she had been right about Mitch meeting a thousand new girls in high school, she was wrong about the part where he'd forget all about her. It simply was not possible.

After the crew stood around for a while, Charlotte and Bev Finch were spotted coming down the hallway toward them. They both looked so different. Mitch could feel Gloria's hold on his arm start to tighten. She cleared her throat and looked at Mitch; it actually looked like she was about to cry. She cleared her throat again and sighed.

"OK, I have to do this."

Gloria broke away from the crew and hurried toward Charlotte Finch. Gloria didn't say a word, looked Char in the eyes, and then hugged her. You could tell Gloria was beginning to sob. Charlotte broke down too. Beverly, well, Bev was Bev, just kinda looking on.

After holding each other there for a bit, they took a half step back from each other and were crying and laughing a little bit at the same time. Gloria took a tissue and began to dry her eyes. Then she reached over and dabbed Charlotte's tears too. It was right then and there that something happened. In an instant, it didn't feel like they were just a random collection of neighborhood kids anymore. Everything had changed. They were only teenagers, but with all the guys in suits and ties and all the girls dressed up, it was evident that they'd chosen to lay their differences aside and come together to support one of their friends during a terrible time. They were expected to act like adults, which they did with flying colors. But what really drove the feeling home for Mitch was Gloria and Charlotte. There was no more hate left in the room among them. It was time for all of them to grow up.

Bev gave Gloria a big hug too, and after they all had their moment together and did their best to compose themselves, Gloria and Charlotte walked over to the rest of the crew, hand in hand.

"Charlotte, show them, show everybody," Gloria encouraged.

Charlotte proudly revealed a big, beautiful smile. All of her teeth had been fixed, so now she had a straight and bright white smile. This was no longer Snag, the she-ape. She now looked like a fully grown adult woman at a fancy social function. It was as though her awkwardness had melted away. She looked mature and confident, and she was even wearing earrings and had had her hair done. The same could be said for her sister, Beverly. Statuesque, really.

To everyone's surprise, EZ stood up in front of Char and boldly asked if he could see her new teeth. You could feel the mood get a little snug, but Charlotte smiled coyly.

"Wow, you look great," EZ declared. "What do you say, Charlotte, you got a hug for me too?"

Char rolled her eyes.

"Alright, you little shit, come here."

Everyone busted out laughing as the two embraced. As all this was happening, Gloria moved back next to Mitch, still a little bit teary-eyed, and grabbed his arm again.

"Char, where the heck have you guys been all summer?" Zitz asked.

Char and Bev explained that they'd both got jobs at the Ramsey County nursing home up by Aldrich Arena. Bev works in the kitchen and Char works with the nursing staff attending to the old folks. Char wears a nurse's uniform and everything. They're both taking driver's ed and are working up enough money between them to buy a car. You could see Manny cringe at the idea of those two behind the wheel of a car. Now that the summer was over, they'd be working up at the nursing home nights and weekends.

"How do you like working up there?" Reno asked.

"I like it juth fine, but Charlotte loves it," Bev replied. "She got a thupid boyfwend who works there."

Gloria cheered.

"Way to go, Char! What's his name?"

"His name is Roman." Char blushed. "He goes to Hill and he lives off of Highway 212 in Lake Elmo."

Mr. Finch walked over to the group, marveling at how they cleaned up.

"Boy, oh boy do you kids look great! Look at you, all dressed up. Can all of you stay right here? I'll be right back." Within a couple minutes, Mr. Finch came back with his Pentax camera to get a group photo.

"OK, gals on the couch and guys in back," he instructed.

After a few seconds of shuffling the lineup, Gloria, Isabelle, Charlotte, and Beverly were perched on the couch, and Mitch, Ike, Zitz, Reno, Manny, and EZ were in the back—ten altogether. What a crew! As Mr. Finch finished setting up his tripod, Mitch noticed that some of the parents had begun to gather. By the time he was done with the photos, they were all asking for copies of the pictures.

After the photo shoot, they all broke off into self-contained conversations, the topics of which included the first week of high school and the first football game of the season. Mitch saw his dad chatting it up with John and Sid Getz by the front door, maybe cooking up some new real estate deal. Mrs. Dawson was sitting on a sofa with Ike's mom, flanked closely by Sarah Tiller and Barb Finch. Stephi, Joy, and Casey were clowning around with Ruthy and Jacob Tiller. Manny's mom and dad were chatting it up with Izzy's mom and dad and EZ's parents.

In a flash, Mitch had another realization. He looked around at all his friends, family, neighbors—with Gloria on his arm—and he realized that his whole life was right there in front of him. Right there in the lobby of a funeral home in the far northeast corner of the East Side of Saint Paul, where streetcars used to run across the Trestle, where kids adventured into Witches' Woods, where there was both a shopping center and golf course named Hillcrest, where kids were left to make decisions, good or bad, because their parents weren't hovering over them twenty-four hours a day. Mitch would treasure that moment of realization for the rest of his life.

A few moments later, Mario DiMucci arrived. Mitch was sort of surprised to see him, but maybe it wasn't so strange. Mario had taken a real shine to Ike when they had played knee hockey down in Rochester and when they'd all gone to the state fair too.

When he moved to go talk to Mario, he noticed that Gloria was still holding onto his arm, and then she was walking with him. Mitch stopped for a second.

"If I live to be a hundred, I'll never figure you out," he said. "What are we doing?"

"You mean this?" She grabbed his hand and squeezed his arm tighter.

"How about you just relax and not ask so damn many questions. I can't explain it myself, it just feels right."

She looked Mitch dead in the eye.

"I'm serious, Mitchell, when I say I'm holding on to the sharpest guy in the place and I don't care who knows it."

Her words made Mitch feel like he was ten feet tall. His chest swelled in pride and the smile on his face would not be easy to get rid of. And then, pretending to be all serious but having a rough go of it, Mitch patted her hands.

"All right, Toots, listen up. We're going to go talk to my Paisano Mario, so just try to stand there quietly and look pretty. Can you manage that?"

Gloria looked taken aback, and Mitch did his very best not to crack up at her reaction. Now it was her turn to figure me out for a change.

"See, because I don't like women who are too yappy," Mitch offered.

She looked at Mitch, let go of his arm, grit her teeth, and punched him in the arm—then proceeded to punch him in the arm again. Mitch smiled, pulled her in, and kissed her on the cheek. She kissed him back and whispered.

"OK, Mitchy-poo, yappy? I'll give you yappy. Maybe later tonight, I'll take you up to the Trestle for another lesson and absolutely kick your ass."

And that's all Mitch wanted to hear. She was tough, she was gorgeous, she was Gloria, Queen of his Snow Dreams. Mitch Dawson was terrified and madly in love.

ABOUT THE AUTHOR

JAMES (JIM) A ENGEN

For more than eighty-five years, four generations of Jim's mother's family lived on the corner of Payne Avenue and Bush Avenue on the East Side of Saint Paul, near Hamm's Brewery, where his dad worked. In the early 1960s, Jim's parents moved the family from Payne Avenue to the Hillcrest neighborhood of Saint Paul, a few blocks east of White Bear Avenue and not far from The Trestle. Jim, his older brother, and his sister graduated from Johnson High School in the 1970s, where Jim participated in both sports and music.

During his early career in the radio business, Jim started his family. He raised his four children—Andrea, Brandon, Jacquelyn, and Katelyn—in the North St. Paul/Oakdale area while working a variety of other jobs and staying involved in local youth hockey. He now owns a real estate appraisal company serving Minnesota and Wisconsin.

Always known as a bit of a storyteller, Jim enjoys spending time with his grandchildren as well as playing music, camping, fishing, and golfing. He's still in touch with many friends from his East Side childhood, who—along with his brother, sister, and cousins—were the inspiration for telling this story.